T0365930

BLIND JUSTICE

MARK ANTHONY TAYLOR

authorHOUSE®

AuthorHouse™
1663 Liberty Drive
Bloomington, IN 47403
www.authorhouse.com
Phone: 1 (800) 839-8640

Published by AuthorHouse 02/24/2016

ISBN: 978-1-5049-8080-7 (sc)
ISBN: 978-1-5049-8073-9 (e)

Contents

To my wife, Megan. "Stop talking about writing a book, and do it already!"

Prologue

Gary, Indiana— 1980

"Tell me what we're doing here." The officer leaned against the passenger door of the squad car, face smashed against his hand. He was clean shaven with a square jaw, mid-20's, with close cropped hair. He looked bored and annoyed.

The officer at the wheel took a large wad of tobacco and tucked it between his bottom lip and teeth with a slurp. The older man had a few more wrinkles around the eyes, but his face was softer, cherub-like. "We're keeping an eye on the streets because there have been a lot of complaints about this block of town."

The younger officer rolled his eyes. "What are you, 32, McMann?" His southern accent emphasized the "2."

"35."

"So you've been on patrol for what, 13 years now?"

"That's right."

"That's freaking depressing."

Officer McMann sighed. "What is it with you, Denton? You wake up on the wrong side of the bed today? I happen to be very thankful for my job. I protect and serve our citizens every single day."

Officer Denton laughed. "Good speech, man. Do you rehearse that in front of the mirror each morning?" McMann didn't reply. He was watching the people on the sidewalk, but his eyes never strayed too far from the convenient store across the street. "Is your wife proud of you?" Denton asked with a sour smile. The words came out in a sneer.

McMann didn't look at Denton. "No."

"Sounds like a fun marriage."

McMann remained silent.

"So when did it end?"

"When it did."

Denton laughed again. "See, that's my point."

"What's your point, Denton? I wasn't aware there was any point to your hollow chatter."

"Man, I haven't been on the force one year, and it's apparent we're the butt of a very unfunny joke."

McMann sighed and scanned the rearview mirror. Some teenagers were laughing and pushing each other at the corner of the street. He tried to ignore the comments from his partner. He told himself not to take the bait.

"And you just take it. Sit there and act like nothing's wrong. We're taking a rigged test. Can't help but fail."

McMann's knee ached from sitting in the car so long. He finally broke. "What is the joke, Denton?" he asked, throwing his hands up in defeat. "What is it?"

Denton sat up and became very still. He stared out the windshield. "Over there, we had everything. You name it, we had it. Blank check. Flame throwers, M-16's with M203 attachments, M60's, light, heavy, specialized, you name it.

We had it. Only problem was," he turned toward McMann, "we couldn't find the freakin' Gooks!" He laughed. "Special forces with special training and special equipment, and we're crawling in holes and tunnels on our hands and knees. We're getting eaten by ticks as big as your thumb, and we see a lot of jungle. I killed Gooks, but it's like trying to kill ants in the grass. But over here," he gestured outside the squad car, "they're out in the open. Homicides, up. Drug running, up. We've got Chicago gangs doing work here in Gary. And they're out in the freaking open—broad daylight. We know who they are, and where they are, and we can't do a damn thing about it. If you do arrest someone, good luck getting a conviction. If they're sentenced, they'll be on the street again in a year. And if you run into the true scum, we have these. Peashooters. Against full auto and shotguns. What the hell is this supposed to do against those? It's rigged, McMann. We'll never come out on top. We can't."

McMann pushed up on his hat and scratched at his forehead. He thought for a moment and then added, "Guess we'll never be out of work then, huh?"

Denton dismissed the coy response with frustration and sank down into his seat, closing his eyes. McMann began to say something when a brick slammed into the back window, shattering it. He looked at the brick lying in their back seat, and then opened his door to confront what must have been the hooligans on the corner. He felt a hand grab his wrist violently from inside the car. Denton pulled back as hard as he could, causing McMann to lose his balance and fall to the pavement outside the car. The rapid cracks of gunfire pelted the door, bullets missing McMann's head by inches. Denton was already leaning over the center console, firing his pistol through the windowless door, while McMann scrambled back inside the vehicle. Two of the teenagers had stayed behind the vehicle, using the brick as a distraction. The other three teenagers were crouched behind cars on the other side of the street firing a pistol, a shotgun, and an Uzi.

"Where the hell did they get that?" screamed McMann.

Denton rapidly replaced the empty chambers in the revolver, snapped it shut, and fired off more rounds. McMann, practically lying underneath Denton, fumbled with the radio and managed to call for backup amidst the blasts from the revolver in his ear and the shards of glass littering the car's interior. Denton cursed, and McMann saw the red splatter on his partner's shoulder. McMann worked his way to the passenger side, firing out of open area where the windshield used to be. He felt a sharp pain in his calf. He twisted around to see the two teenagers standing ten feet from him holding pistols in their hands. Their eyes narrowed as they aimed their weapons. Denton appeared, fired twice, dropping the assailants.

McMann tried to shake his head clear, get some sort of picture of what was taking place. He looked back at the two boys--no they were men he told himself--but they weren't moving. They had shot him in his calf. The pain returned with the acknowledgement. They would have killed him. Denton saved him. Denton had already been hit, too. McMann thought he remembered it being in the shoulder. Denton cried out again, this time clutching his stomach. His revolver clicked empty.

McMann stood up, aiming over the car roof. The bottle was green, semi-transparent. The flaming cloth sticking out about 4 inches from the mouth of the bottle. It arced through the air, landing on the hood. The impact of the bottle shattering sent gasoline pouring over the entire hood and in through the open windshield, igniting the car in flames. McMann didn't hesitate. He reached in the car and dragged Denton out by his left arm. Denton's whole right arm and torso was engulfed in flames. McMann ripped off his uniform and smothered the flames with the shirt.

He heard the teens yelling as they kept firing. McMann grabbed his gun, while still trying to pat his partner down and stop the bleeding from multiple wounds. Denton gasped and labored to inhale. McMann began to pray and prepare for his final stand when the cars and sirens screamed around the corner. The teens fired off a couple more shots and took off running. McMann heard two cars race by, he assumed they were in pursuit, while others stopped in front of his shredded squad car. He looked back at the teens, lying in crimson pools on the sidewalk, and then back down as Denton's hand squeezed his arm, chest rising and falling in shallow tremors. *We're taking a rigged test. Can't help but fail.*

Chapter 1

Avon, Indiana— Present Day

The humidity was almost unbearable. Condensation formed on the inside of the gas station's windows. The asphalt in the parking lot melted into distorted waves, and Marla was fading into a heat induced coma. How long had she been working her shift? It seemed like forever. She almost dreaded looking at the clock hanging above the restroom doors. She knew that time crawled during the summer hours, and the sun was only just beginning to make its way toward the horizon. One hour and twenty five minutes. She swore under her breath. She still had six hours to go. Six hours of sticky, hot, miserable work. More than once, Marla had thought about putting her head underneath the ICEE machine.

The bell on the door let her know that someone had come in, but Marla didn't look up from her cell phone. Eric had finally broken up with Amber, and he already had a picture of himself with Laura. Marla didn't care; Eric was hot, and all she had to do was get him to notice her. A shadow fell over the counter and her phone. Marla rolled her eyes in annoyance. She kept her head down.

"Excuse me."

Marla almost dropped her phone. It wasn't because she was ashamed of being caught looking at her phone on the job. It wasn't because Marla really cared about helping the needy customer who came into her convenience store. It was the voice itself. If the owner of it looked half as good as his voice sounded she decided she would run away with him right there and then. Marla slowly looked up from her enthralling mobile device.

Standing before Marla was a character out of a comic book. A black, bullet-proof vest over a white t-shirt covered the broad shoulders and massive arms of the customer who had stirred her out of her stupor. His eyes were covered by dark Aviators. Her eyes widened as they came to rest on the two, custom-built pistols resting in holsters in the front of the vest.

The man must have observed this because he slowly pulled at a chain around his neck until a badge emerged from underneath the bulletproof vest.

"It's alright, miss," he assured her, as he removed his Aviators. "I'm one of the good guys."

Marla nodded in agreement, captive under the customer's spell. She found herself staring in disbelief at the man before her. His eyes were beautiful, dark and mysterious. She wondered what mysteries they held. She attempted to reply to his comment, but the words stuck in her throat. She imagined his jawline had been chiseled out of solid granite, and black, afternoon stubble covered his face. A toothpick protruded from his beautiful mouth. Dark brows created a brooding figure leaning over the counter, and jet black, tousled hair completed the immaculate portrait. Marla guessed the man was 6'4" or 6'5." The temperature felt like it had risen about ten degrees. She checked discreetly for pit stains. The thought horrified her. She was safe.

Slowly, his grim mouth shifted to a disarming smile. "I didn't mean to disturb you."

There it was again! The voice of an angel. A baritone, stubble-faced, coal-eyed angel. "You're not bothering me," Marla managed. "I'm happy to help. Is there anything I can do for you? Anything?"

If the man noticed her innuendo, he ignored it with a straight face. Instead he asked pleasantly, "Is the coffee fresh?"

"It's gotta be 95 out," Marla replied without thinking.

"I always have coffee. Black. Straight up. I have to be ready for anything, at any time."

Once again, Marla nodded, unaware of the movement. "Yes, you do." She caught herself and added, "I'm sorry. I'll make a new pot right away."

"Fully caffeinated, please. None of that decaf crap. It could be a long day. Don't mean to be any trouble, miss."

"It's no trouble!" Marla called over her shoulder as she practically jogged to the coffee pots. She worked frantically, pressuring herself to brew the best pot of coffee she ever had in her life. She glanced over her shoulder at the addonnis-of-a-man leaning on her counter, chewing that toothpick of his. He was incredible looking, but he was no pretty boy. Biceps and triceps, and what other muscles are found in an arm, made the t-shirt the man wore seem tiny. Was he a cop? No, he must have been higher than that. FBI maybe.

The thought made Marla stop what she was doing, her thoughts leaving the convenience store and looking to the future. To think, an FBI hunk asking her to make a fresh pot of coffee. Her friends would never believe her. Of course it was only because they would be jealous. She thought of herself as very lucky. The FBI guy moved to an aisle and began looking at cigars. Marla shook her head back to reality and continued working.

"I'm almost done," she called out as she pressed the button for the hot water.

"It's alright. I'm going to use the can while I wait."

"Okay," she said brightly. "It's right over there." Marla pointed to the brightly painted "Restroom" sign. "My name's Marla, by the way."

"I appreciate the help, Marla." The lawman disappeared through the doorway as Marla stood up and carefully pushed her hair behind her ear. She then straightened her gas station polo and took a deep breath. She was going to have to be on her game if she was going to impress someone from the FBI. Their kids would be named Chet and Willow. He'd make a great father, and she would be a very helpful wife. When he got done using the restroom she would make him see that his life was empty without her. What good is upholding the law if you don't have a woman by your side while you're doing it?

The doorbell chimed during Marla's sudden flood of optimistic dreams. Her hope of two hunks in one hour was quickly dashed, however, with the appearance of the new customer. Brooding, but not in a attractive way, the man's face was set in a heavy scowl. He wore a hoody despite the blistering temperatures, and he kept both hands in the front pocket. Marla didn't like the look of the new customer at all. Even in the shadow of the hoody, a long scar crossed the right side of his face. His appearance, his demeanor—it all screamed trouble.

"Let me know if I can help you with anything," Marla feebly managed.

The man continued to look around, Marla wasn't sure what for, and then he looked directly at her. She swallowed hard and wished that the FBI guy was out here right now.

"Where's your bubble gum?" The man slowly growled.

"It's up here at the counter." Marla tried to keep her cool, but she could feel that something was off about this guy. She slowly circled behind the counter, keeping an eye on the creep the whole time. He glanced around the store one more time and then walked up to the counter.

"Which one would you like to buy?" Marla stammered. The man smelled of heavy amounts of weed and body odor. It was no wonder he did, wearing a hoody and heavy pants like that.

"This one." Keeping one hand in the front pocket of the hoody, he placed a packet of Big League Chew, grape, on the counter. "It's sweet, but the flavor lasts a long time." Marla merely nodded. "You look kinda sweet too," he crooned. His smile revealed a surprisingly straight smile with a few gold teeth.

Marla didn't know what to say; she just wanted the man out of her store. Where was that guy? Was he constipated? What was taking him so long?

Tiny drops of water spotted the cracked mirror in the restroom as the lawman ran wet hands through his hair.

The cool water was refreshing as it soaked his scalp and ran down the back of his neck.

"Comeon, baby. Wanna be my Big League Chew?" The man sneered from underneath the hood and leaned in closer on the counter. Sweat dripped down his face.

"Please. Just take your gum and go away," Marla pleaded.

"I'm going to need you to empty that register."

"No, please. I can't. My boss will kill me!"

"You don't seem to understand," the man said as he pulled a gun out of the hoodie pocket. "*I'll* kill you if you don't do what I say."

Chapter 2

The lawman flicked his old toothpick into the trash and removed a plastic container. He flipped open the cap with his thumb and deftly removed a fresh toothpick, placing it in its rightful resting spot between his back molars.

"But how will you get the money out if I'm dead?" Marla asked the man in the hoody who was robbing her right after the man of her dreams had come into her life. Alanis Morissette had been right.

The man squinted hard at Marla. "I'll just take the register then."

"But they're not easy to get open. Someone stole a register from a gas station on Raceway road a couple weeks back, and they found the register in a dumpster behind Chick-Fila. It wasn't open."

The man began to lose patience and pointed the gun at Marla's face. "I can get a stupid register open. It's not a damn safe! Now give me the money!"

"I can only open it if there's a purchase," Marla reasoned.

"I said I wanted to buy this Big League Chew. Doesn't that count as a purchase?"

Marla thought about it. He did have a point. And she didn't want to die. "Yeah, I guess it is. But we really don't have much money in here anyway."

The man in the hoody kept the gun on Marla and hung his head wearily. "I just want the money. Give me the money, and I'll be on my way."

The lawman put on his aviators and stood staring at the mirror. He clenched the toothpick between his teeth, muscles flexing in his jaw. Outside the bathroom, the lawman could hear a man screaming—screaming at the girl who had just brewed him a fresh cup of coffee. He removed his pistol from his vest, pulled back the slide to reveal a shell in the chamber. He checked the other pistol and grinned. "It's a great day for Justice," he said as he reholstered both weapons and pushed through the bathroom door.

Marla poured the cash tray into a plastic sack.

"And the Benjamins underneath the tray! Make sure to double sack that," the man said, pointing to the plastic bag with the gun.

Marla rolled her eyes. Where *was* he? She reluctantly took the 100's under the tray and placed them in the bag. She knew she should have put them in the safe when she had the chance.

Just then the man in the hoody caught movement in his peripheral and spun to his right with his gun outstretched. His mouth opened slightly as he registered what stood before him. The movement was made by a hulking figure, gigantic arms glistening in the humid air, Aviators creating a half-mask of mystery, bullet-proof vest wrapped around the chest with dual holsters containing handguns with custom grips, and a toothpick tucked firmly to the side of his mouth.

"Looks like we both had the same idea," the lawman said coolly. "How 'bout you move that gun off me, and we get back to the business at hand?"

The man in the hoody stood puzzled. "You're here to rob this place?"

"No, professor. I always dress like this. I was just checking out the back to see where the safe was." The lawman folded his arms across his chest. "Looks like you're handling things out front."

The creep kept his gun trained on the new guy. "I'm doing this myself. I don't work with partners. Get your own store."

The lawman considered this. "I'd rather not," he frowned. "You see, I kinda like *this* one."

"I just want the money, but I'll kill you if you get in my way."

The lawman smiled in amusement. "You're going to kill me? With what? That pea shooter? Do you know what I'm wearing?"

The creep stood still, breathing hard. He glanced at Marla, and then back at the lawman.

Marla watched the standoff, not sure what the lawman was doing. She trusted him though. How could she not? His confidence became her confidence.

"Hey! I'm talking to you, creep," the lawmen said with menace, arms still crossed. "Do you know what I'm wearing?"

"A bulletproof vest. Do you think I'm retarded?"

"All the evidence points to yes; I do think you're retarded."

"Differently abled. Use people-first language," Marla interjected. Both men looked at her. She shrugged. "What? You're not supposed to say retarded. It's a derogatory term."

"I'm trying to be derogatory." The creep quickly swung the gun back to the lawman. He stared at his reflection in the man's glasses. The lawman continued speaking. "This is a level 3A tactical vest made to withstand a .45 caliber round from five feet. You're holding a piece-of-crap 9mm and standing eleven feet from me. I'd ask you to do the math, but you're robbing a gas station at 10 in the morning." He paused. The thief didn't breath. The lawman slowly smiled as he watched the uncertainty on the man's face. "Now me, on the other hand, I'm carrying two, Kimber Custom II Model 1911 .45's with double-stacked mags containing 13 nasty hollowpoints just dying to mushroom in some tough guy's sternum."

The creep swallowed as his eyes widened. "I'll sh-shoot you in the head then."

"That makes sense," the lawman said slowly, nodding. "Except for the fact that your hand is visibly shaking, and I'm beginning to worry that I'm about to witness a grown man piss himself, and poor Marla here is going to have a mess to clean up."

Marla didn't hold her laugh in.

"Shut up, man!" the creep pleaded. He began to look around wildly. He kept the gun on the lawman and pointed to the bag in Marla's hand. "Give it to me! Hurry up!" Marla began to reach over the counter.

"Don't do it, Marla," the lawman said with arms still crossed. "This is my territory."

"Who the hell are you?" the creep asked motioning with his gun.

"I'm Detective Justice of the Avon PD, and you're under arrest."

"A detective!" Marla exclaimed.

"Justice?" the creep repeated.

"I thought you were FBI or something," Marla mused.

"No, too highbrow. You don't get to bloody up the criminals every day in that business."

"Justice? Really?" The creep raised his eyebrows in disbelief.

"Yeah, Detective Blake Justice. You got a problem with that?"

"I mean, detective is really nice too. I bet you're unbelievable," Marla continued.

"When there's only one, you better be good."

"Justice? Detective Justice is really your name?

"Yes."

"I've heard them talk about Detective Justice, but I thought it was just a nickname, some dumb name for a pig. That's ridiculous!"

"The only thing ridiculous is you thinking that you're going to get out of here without a neck brace on. So why don't you put the gun down like a good little pussy cat."

"Go to hell." The creep lunged over and grabbed the double-bagged money from the register, but Justice moved with lightning reflexes, drawing both .45's before Marla could even let go of the sack.

"Freeze!" Detective Justice stood with legs shoulder width apart, both Kimbers held straight out in front of him and aimed at the perp's head. "You think about moving, and I won't hesitate to blow your head off." Marla kept a tight grip on the bag of money.

"OK, OK. You got me. Easy. Do you want me to keep holding on to the money, or can I let it go?"

With a fierce look in his dark eyes, Justice replied, "Let go of the bag slowly. Face the ICEE machine, and put the gun on the ground."

"You have no idea what you're doing."

"Don't look at me! Stay facing the ICEE machine."

"You don't have a clue, muscle man."

"Clue? I don't play board games. Unless it's Operation, and I always leave the bullets in." Justice slowly stepped toward the creep, .45's up high, like two birds of prey ready for the kill. Without thinking, Marla placed both hands up to her mouth in awe. She was holding her breath. Moving efficiently, Justice holstered his left Kimber and removed handcuffs from his vest.

A car skidded to a stop outside the convenience store, and Justice glanced over. Police. Two officers jumped out of the squad car with hands on their holsters. The distraction was only a second, but the creep grabbed his gun and jumped behind the counter, pulling Marla to the floor. The two officers burst through the entrance with their weapons drawn.

Justice groaned. "You've got to be kidding me."

One officer—a lean, dark skinned man—took up position behind a magazine rack, while the other officer—a stocky man with red head—quickly moved down an outside aisle.

"Freeze!" the thin cop screamed.

"He was already frozen, Philips, before you and Opie over there came in and mucked things up!"

"I resent that name!" came a reply from the back of the convenience store.

"Heard you needed backup, Detective," stated Officer Carl Philips, his gun raised in thin hands.

"From who? I didn't call it in."

"Looks like someone called it in for you, Justice," came another shout from the back.

"I feel so much better knowing you two morons are here, Furman," Justice shouted back.

The creep popped up from behind the counter, using Marla as a shield and jamming the gun into her temple. His hood had fallen off his head revealing red matted hair and a scar that looked like it had been drawn pink with a crayon in the uncoordinated hands of a toddler.

"Hey, he kind of looks like you, Furman—only he looks less like he would die after running a hundred meters."

"Is that some sort of fat joke?" Furman remained hidden still.

Justice wondered what he could be doing. "Just an observation, Furman."

"He thinks you all look alike," laughed Philips.

Justice threw his hands up. "Woah. I was not going there. Gingers are precious."

"Shut up, Urkel," came Furman's response.

"That's racist," Justice said.

"How?"

Mark Anthony Taylor

"I'm just saying."

The thief's eyes darted back and forth between the hulking detective and frail looking cop. "I'll blow her head off. I swear I'll do it."

Philips turned and re-sighted his weapon. A crash of cans came from Furman's direction in the back of the store. The creep repositioned himself toward the sound.

"Amateurs," Justice sighed. "Hey, numbnuts! You're not going to blow her head off. You're a low-level, bottom feeding, gutless, lackey. So go ahead and put down the gun before I put one between your eyes."

"What are you doing?" Marla cried out.

"Shut the hell up," shouted Furman, who was peering out from the end of the far aisle. "We've got this, Detective."

"I had everything under control before you jokers arrived. Now go home before you get us all killed." Justice slowly returned the handcuffs to their designated pocket on the vest and brought his left hand up to the grip.

"We're just here to help, detective," the Philips said as the creep began to slide out from behind the counter, muzzle buried in Marla's hair and an arm around her neck. Marla's face was contorted in fear.

"You! Back up! Hulk! You better put that gun down before I blow her brains out."

"Keep talking," Justice muttered to himself as the creep's head inched closer to the Kimber's sight. But just as the the sights neatly framed the round head of the perp, the Philips shifted his position, obscuring the figures of Marla and the creep. Justice's index finger relaxed, and he pulled his weapon back in defeat.

The creep was backing out of the store, telling the cops to stay where they were, not to follow him. The gun was still buried in Marla's hair. She was trying in vain not to cry. She wasn't cut out for this. A business student trying to pay her own way through college wasn't supposed to be used for collateral! It wasn't fair. Maybe a high school drop-out. Maybe the over-zealous parent screaming at the ref in his child's little-league game, but not her. She was supposed to catch a break. Of course, getting to watch Detective Justice in action might warrant getting taken hostage once a week. This thought helped her fight back her tears, and then she was roughly shoved to the ground.

The creep bolted toward a white hatchback parked next to the ice freezer. He threw the double-sacked cash in the front seat and slammed the car into reverse. The sedan slammed into a car at the pump, knocking the owner onto the ground and dislodging the pump from its foundation. Gas immediately began to pour out onto the concrete.

Both cops sprinted toward the door. Officer Furman bent over to see if Marla was OK. When he saw that she was, he slid across the hood of the squad car, his red hair catching the wind, while Philips hit the lights and took off after the thief. Justice holstered his weapon and walked over to Marla. He extended his hand and helped her to her feet. His hand engulfed hers, and her heart began to race. It was as if the fear and stress from the whole ordeal washed away in the detective's hands.

"You'll be alright. I can tell you're tough. You handled that situation pretty well." Justice gave Marla a smile, adjusted his Aviators and stepped into the blistering heat of the sun.

Marla ran to the door and called out to him. "Wait!" Justice stopped and then looked back. "I wanted to say thank you. You saved my life."

"Miss, I'm just doing my job. But if you want to keep your life, and save some others while you're at it, get these people out of here. That's gas pouring out, and this place could blow any second."

Marla stood only for a second before she sprang into action. People left their vehicles or drove away from the gasoline geyser as Marla shouted for people to clear the area.

Justice ignored the commotion, walking steadily until he came to a stop in front of four wheels of pure, potent power. The matte black finish dulled the reflection of the glaring sun on the body of the custom Dodge Challenger SRT-8, while the tinted windows showed a mirror image of the detective. A quick examination revealed a smudge above the front tire well. A moistened thumb removed the stain completely.

Once inside, Justice sank into the black leather seats and closed his eyes. With the door closed, the sounds of traffic and screams of pedestrians faded away. The officers' squad car had already disappeared. Justice opened his eyes and took a deep breath. The 7.2 liter V8 engine protruded through the hood like the nostrils of some wicked dragon—valve covers deep red as if hinting of internal fire and destruction. Sometimes he felt bad for the criminals. After all, 650 horses and 600 pounds of torque didn't give them much of a fighting chance.

The engine roared to life. Justice put the Challenger into reverse and backed into the street. Gasoline continued to flow from the pump, but it seemed like Marla had gotten everyone to safety. The gas dammed up against the curb and then poured over the edge into the street. The two cops had probably called all of it in, but Justice didn't rely on the competence of others when law and order was on the line. It was just one of the things that made him who he was in the department. If it had just been him and the creep, there wouldn't have been any need for the call, but the busted gas pump alone called for emergency personnel. "We've got gas pouring out of a dislodged pump on the corner of Reagan Parkway and 36."

"Copy that."

Justice reluctantly provided the rest of the information. "Oh, and a perp in a high speed pursuit heading east on Rockville just past Eden. White hatchback. Crap car. Probably redlines at 3000 rpm. I doubt we'll need back up, but you know, just in case."

Justice bit down on his toothpick and adjusted the rearview mirror. Fingers were relaxed, palm pressing into the steering wheel. He revved the engine twice, and the Challenger shook. He popped the clutch, and the tires sent plumes of smoke into the air. Flames shot out of the quad exhaust, igniting the gasoline snaking into the street. The flame rushed backward, up and over the curb, seeking out the source of the gasoline river. Gas spraying off the spinning tires ignited into a miniature Fourth of July display, sending bits of flaming magma into the air. The tires finally caught, and the 605 horses leapt forward in unbridled power. The flames rushed up and into the gaping wound in the pump, igniting every ounce of the fuel. A terrific concussion shook the convenience store with the explosion. The Challenger sped away from the giant fireball rising up into the hot, blue sky. "Their prices weren't that good anyway."

Chapter 3

The Challenger whipped past cars, Justice skillfully maneuvering the beast through the traffic. The dashboard siren whined with red flashing lights, but they were hard to pick up as the Challenger shot past them as if they were standing still. Justice shifted again and darted through cross traffic at a busy intersection. The mph rose steadily and neared triple digits. For an amateur, speeds this high would have meant certain disaster; but for Justice, this was speed brought focus. It was the sweet spot. High speed had always been in his blood. His dad had helped him build his first go-kart when he was only 8 years old—one year before his father was killed. He hadn't slowed down since.

Up ahead, he began to make out the lights of the squad car and just ahead of that was the white hatchback. What a sorry excuse for a car. Justice grinned. "I gave you the head start, and this is all you did with it. That's just sad." Even at 100 miles per hour, the Challenger didn't shake in the slightest, and it easily accelerated when Justice called for more from the vehicle. He got on the radio once agin when he began to get close to the squad car and the hatchback. "This is Detective Justice requesting room for a pit. Let the big boys have some room please."

"That's a negative. It's too crowded. Plus we have this, hot shot."

"Like you did back in the convenience store. We're in good hands then. He pulled a gun on the girl and on me, so move aside."

"That's a negative, Justice."

Justice switched off the radio. "I tried to play nice and share with others, and this is how they repay me." The hatchback narrowly missed a car turning into a gas station and swerved into oncoming traffic sending cars scattering like roaches with a light on them. The cop car slammed on its brakes, and the Justice whipped the wheel to the left and downshifted, blowing past the cop car. The Challenger pulled alongside the hatchback, and Justice rolled down the passenger side window. The scar-faced man looked over, his face contorted in a weird mix of craze and fear. Justice winked. The perp tried to slam the Challenger, but Justice hit the brakes and watched the hatchback swerve and then almost spin out with an overcorrection.

The two officers had caught up once more and pulled up on the right side of the hatchback. Justice pressed down on the accelerator and moved up on the left side of the perp's car. He was sandwiched; he had no place to go. Justice switched on his intercom and looked over at the perp. "You've got nowhere to run. We can do this the easy way or the hard way. Personally, I prefer the hard way, but you might want to take the first option." The perp responded by pulling up his pistol, opening fire on the Challenger, striking the passenger side door, and ripping into the leather seat. "You did not just do that," Justice said softly.

The three cars came to an intersection and the perp whipped to his right, grinding into the side of the cop car, forcing it to turn right or smash into the back of a mini-van with a "Baby on Board" sign hanging from the rear window. Justice followed the turn going around the van on the other side. He didn't see any baby inside the van. "That's typical."

The three cars returned to their side-by-side formation at the completion of the turn, and Justice decided it was time to end the deadly chase. Pulling a gun on an innocent girl just trying to brew some coffee at a gas station was one thing; driving recklessly and almost killing innocent bystanders was another; but Justice couldn't tolerate bullet holes in his leather upholstery. And that baby thing made him mad too. Who would throw a "Baby Aboard" sign in their back window when there was no baby aboard? Plus, what was the point of the sign? Would it stop another car from hitting that car? Did the driver of the vehicle assume other drivers were out to hit them, so they needed to put up a baby warning? It just didn't make sense.

Up ahead the road narrowed as it passed through a tunnel under railroad tracks. Justice saw his chance to end the chase. One tap to the rear end of the perp's car and he would lose control and inevitably end up smashed into the wall. Justice didn't lose sleep over criminals' complaints of broken noses, whiplash, or split lips after they encountered the detective. Justice had one job, and that was to stop bad guys from doing bad things. Sometimes that meant playing a little rougher than other times.

The three cars were side by side, the perp's in the middle, and the 4 lane road would be down to 2 lanes shortly. Justice was waiting for the perfect moment to execute his pit maneuver, but before he could, the squad car swung out wide.

"Oh, this should be good," Justice muttered. "Don't you guys ever learn?" he shouted in the squad car's direction. The police car strayed onto the shoulder, kicking up dirt and then cut back hard to the left, attempting to smash the hatchback. But the hatchback accelerated, narrowly escaping the collision. Instead the cruiser found the rear quarter panel of the Challenger, sending Justice into a spin.

The hatchback zipped through the narrow underpass, while the squad car skidded into the opposite lane. Its tires finally caught just before it smashed into the bridge. The back end of the vehicle lifted off the ground, the force of the impact shattering all glass and mangling the front of the vehicle. Justice fought his own vehicle's momentum, correcting the spin into a simple 180, and shifted into reverse. Looking in his rearview mirror, he straightened the car out and pressed down on the accelerator. The Challenger scraped the side of the underpass as it shot through.

"Damn it!" the scarred man said slamming his fist against the steering wheel. "Doesn't this guy give up?"

Justice looked back at the underpass he had just come through. Two police cars followed through while another one stopped to tend to Furman and Philips. "Oh no you don't. This was my perp all along, and I'm not sharing today. This chase just needed was a little reversal of fortune." Justice rolled down his window, drew his Kimber and began firing at the hatchback with his left hand. He wasn't accustomed to shooting over his shoulder, aiming with a rearview mirror, but he welcomed the challenge.

The passenger tail light of the hatchback shattered and another bullet passed through the rear window causing the man with the scar to curse and involuntarily duck. The third bullet caught a tire. The man felt the car yank to the right as it rocketed toward a raised sidewalk lining the road. The chassis hit the embankment at an angle, launching it into a series of violent rolls.

Justice spun the steering wheel clockwise, whipped the car around, and skidded to a stop next to the overturned hatchback. Smoke billowed from engine, hood dangling like the broken jaw of a beaten fighter. Justice approached the vehicle cautiously, gun drawn, as the two other cop cars arrived at the scene.

The driver's door creaked open and the man with the scar half crawled, half fell out onto the grass. Some people had started coming out of the nearby houses, hands over their mouths. Some had their phones out to record the ordeal for the latest viral sensation. The thief looked up at the advancing detective with fierce eyes. Justice had to give it to him, he wasn't a wuss. A feeble hand, trembling, attempted to lift a pistol toward the detective, but Justice closed the distance and kicked the gun out of the perp's hand. The small audience of curious neighbors didn't react, but waited for the next move.

Justice holstered his weapon and lifted the man to his feet. The scar was an ugly one. Justice stifled a cough at the smell of alcohol and B.O. "You should have just stayed down," Justice said with disdain and head butted the man right in the nose. He dropped as if dead. "Cuff this scum."

"Hey, he wasn't doing anything," a man called out. "I've got you on video!"

"That was excessive force."

"He's just doing his job!"

Justice turned to the spectators; they immediately became silent. "This is what happens when you break the law," Justice barked, motioning to the groaning criminal being dragged to a squad car by two officers. "Justice might just break your nose. Thanks for your support."

Chapter 4

"Hey, nice work today, Detective." A thin, pale police officer with thinning hair stood beaming. He had the look of a puppy dog begging for scraps at the feet of its owner.

"Thanks, officer Mike. Just doing my job. Nothing special."

"Nothing special? You saved who knows how many people, and that driving? I heard you took him out going backwards."

Justice took off his Aviators and looked directly in Officer Cruise's pallid eyes. "First, the young lady working at the gas station saved those lives, and she makes a mean cup of coffee. You should go there sometime. It's worth the stop. Second, you think I wanted this? I had to go with my gut, reaction, and instinct. If you think too much, if you plan your moves, you might as well hang up your badge. This creep tried to run; someone had to trip him up."

"I'll say you tripped him up. He looks like he went through hell."

"Maybe that's where he deserves to be. Hey, where are Furman and Philips?"

"You mean the cops who crashed?"

"Those would be the ones. They almost botched the whole thing up. I want to talk to them."

"Can't. At least not yet. They were taken to the hospital to get checked out."

"They OK?"

"Should be."

"Good, I want them nice and healthy when I kick the crap out of them."

Cruise stood close to Justice, hoping that by close proximity he might absorb some of the demeanor, the confidence, the skill that Detective Justice exuded. Justice was a legend in the Avon Police Department, and Cruise hoped everyday he could be half the cop Justice was.

A tune cut into the conversation. "Is that 'Gypsies, Tramps, and Thieves?'" Cruise asked, puzzled, and looking for the source of the music.

"Oh, that's me," Justice replied, pulling out his cell phone. "It's my mother. Don't ask." Justice moved away from the commotion of the crime scene. "Hi, mom."

"I'm kind of busy, mom. Can it wait?...Someone's stalking you?...Mom, I've got some work to take care of here, and then I was going back to my apartment....Mom-what man?...How do you know?...OK, mom. OK. I'll be right over."

"Everything OK, detective? I heard some of the call." A female voice interrupted Justice's thoughts.

"No, it's OK, officer." Justice turned toward a petite, attractive officer with short, platinum blond hair. He had seen her around the precinct. Jane Grant. Grant was indeed small, but she held her own on the beat. In the spring, she apprehended a drunk urinating on a car in the mall's parking lot. He must have been at least 6'3," maybe even 6'4." Not being content with urination in public, he took a swing at Grant when she tried to arrest him, and ended up face down on the asphalt with a broken arm and bloody face. The man was too embarrassed to even press charges, despite the advice from his lawyer.

"Need us to send someone over there? I think Nicks and Davis are over by Orchard Hill."

"I appreciate it, officer, but it's probably nothing."

"Call me, Jane, Detective Justice." Grant smiled and flipped her hair. She wasn't quite sure why she flipped her hair, or why she was asking him to call her Jane. She was a professional. It wasn't looks or sexuality that got her a job as a cop—it was her skill and competence. Yet around Detective Justice, Grant felt more like a woman than any other time she could remember. And it wasn't just his looks that were attractive. It was his supreme control of any situation. Even though she had never been afforded the luxury of personally working with Detective Justice (a pity), his reputation was incredible; some stories almost seemed too far-fetched to be believable—legendary. He was the precinct's standard in more ways than one.

"I can't call you Jane until we're off the clock, and unfortunately that hasn't happened yet," Justice said with a twinkle in his eye. "Besides, an officer as good as yourself should demand to be addressed by your surname." He whispered, "First names are for the amateurs. Hey, Mike. Get this to the precinct, will you? Thanks."

Grant laughed and returned to the wreck.

"What do you want me to do about him, sir?" Michael Dupé cradled the phone against his shoulder while checking the temperature of the formula that had just come out of the microwave.

A low and menacing voice, like the quiet growl of a confident and dangerous dog replied, "You will wait."

"He's good. He's very good."

"I'm quite aware of Detective Justice's skill and aptitude."

"Yes, I know you are sir. But he could be a problem."

"And what would you propose we do about the detective?"

"Well-" the clear voice hesitated. "I'm not sure."

"Yes, you do," came the flat reply.

"No, sir. I don't. It's just-- he'll figure this all out. He's too good not to."

"That's the point, isn't it?" Though the voice softened, relaxed, the tension remained.

"What if he doesn't like it?"

"That's why I'm bringing you in, Dupé. I trust you'll be able to handle him. The bump from your measly salary isn't going to waste? I didn't bring in the wrong person, did I?"

"No, absolutely not, sir. I'll figure something out." Dupé paused. "The added money is much appreciated."

"I'm glad to hear that, son. With Justice with us, the filthy drug war would soon be over. It would be peace and prosperity the entire community could take pride in."

Dupé used a towel thrown over his shoulder to wipe some spittle from the infant's mouth. He readjusted the phone so that it lined up with his mouth. "Why not just do it the old-fashioned way?"

The voice on the other end sounded worn out. The man rasped, "I've done it that way. The longer you're around, you'll see it doesn't work. Results come through action. It doesn't matter how you feel about it; that's just how it is."

"But you think Justice would join us that easily?"

"Of course I don't think it would be that easy." The menacing tone returned. "Justice is complicated. You'll see that soon enough. He sees the world in black and white. You'll have to show him that white isn't always white, and black isn't always black."

"Which one are we, sir?"

"These things always have a way of sorting themselves out. You'll come to find out that there is only an illusion of black and white. It's an ancient and trite way of viewing the world. Sometimes you have to paint the way you see fit. The bad guys often look like good guys, and the bad guy might turn out to be the hero."

"So what if Justice doesn't join us?"

"That would be a problem I hope we don't have to address."

"So what happens if Detective Justice doesn't understand what we're doing?"

"Sometimes the law can become murky; a man's moral compass becomes screwed up. They can't see the bigger picture. They don't understand that sometimes doing the best thing might not seem like the right thing. They might find, God forbid, our little operation inexcusable, reprehensible. In that case, there is always need for a fall guy."

"Like Tango and Cash?"

"What?"

"Tango and Cash. They couldn't kill Tango and Cash because they would be martyrs, so they had to smear their names."

"No one is killing Detective Justice," the man on the other end of the phone line growled.

"Of course not. I didn't mean that, sir. Just that if Detective Justice doesn't join us, it would be better for his reputation to be ruined like in Tango and Cash."

"This is not like Tango and Cash."

"Well pretty much, except we're not bad guys. We're not the bad guys, are we, sir?"

"No, we're not the bad guys. I'm hoping it doesn't come to anything nearly as drastic as any of that, and certainly nothing as drastic as Tango and-"

"Cash, sir."

"Cash. You will make sure that Justice becomes aware of the operation on our terms; the revelation must be logical and the only possibility. Which it is. Don't think I haven't weighed the consequences or that I do this lightly."

"I don't, sir."

"Good. You will start tomorrow." And with that, the line went dead. Michael Dupé bounced his infant daughter in his left arm, watching her gulp down the meal with drooping eyelids.

Chapter 5

Despite the air conditioning blasting through the vents of the black Challenger, Justice's shirt underneath the flak jacket was damp from sweat, and beads of perspiration clung to Justice's eyebrows, nose, and upper-lip. The humidity had not let up in the late afternoon, and it seemed to be more intense than ever. It was the humidity, and not the recent events, that caused the perspiration to form. Rarely did Justice sweat while engaging violators of the law. People usually sweat when uncomfortable or anxious. Justice was sweating because it was July.

The Challenger purred, came to a full rest at a stop sign, and then turned right onto Green Street. Justice's mom lived in a small ranch home in an older neighborhood behind the movie theater. She moved there recently to be closer to Blake, but her old residence was also just too much house for one person. She loved her new home; it was quaint, and she was able to see her son more often than before (even if she did have to insist on his visits). Things had changed so much since Blake's father had been killed.

Justice turned on to his mother's street and began scanning the properties for any sign of a "prowler." Across the street from his mother's house sat a very used, blue sedan. Inside was a male teenager. Justice parked behind the car and got out. The youth was looking at his phone when Justice tapped on the window with his badge. The kid started and dropped his phone. He started to pick it up, thought better of it, and struggled to roll down the window.

"Excuse me, I'm Detective Justice. You must be Mark." Justice stared at a tanned kid with shaggy blond hair that was swept over to one side of his forehead.

"Um, yes sir," Mark managed without his voice cracking.

"Is this your vehicle?"

"Yeah. I mean no. It's my dad's."

Justice had both hands on the windowsill, his massive frame casting a shadow on the young man. His eyes flitted from seat to dashboard, from center console to back seats. "The good news is, I believe you, Mark."

"There's bad news?" Mark's eyes were wide, and his Adam's apple bobbed once more.

"I'm afraid there is, son. You started dating the young lady across the street from a wild, unpredictable, and extremely paranoid woman."

Mark looked puzzled.

"My mom," Justice laughed, and extended his hand. "Blake Justice. Good to meet you, Mark."

Mark forced himself to exhale and laugh at the same time. He shook Justice's hand. "So you're a cop then? I mean, *police officer?*"

"Detective actually."

"So how did you know my name was Mark? You're really good."

"Well, I *am* that good, but like I said: you're dating Jenny, who happens to live across the street from my mom, Wanda. Her life consists of snooping, gossip, paranoia—the usual. I've heard your name before. I was just guessing it was you when I saw you outside the Stevenson's house. Sorry to make you so nervous. I was just messing with you."

"No, no. It's OK. I was really nervous even before you showed up."

"Why's that? You casing my mom's house?"

"What? Casing her house?"

"Were you scoping out my mom's house so you could rob her?"

"What? No, sir. I wasn't!"

"Mark, lighten up! It's a joke. Why are you so nervous?"

Mark inhaled slowly. "Well for one, I just had a huge police—detective—who's wearing a bulletproof vest tap on my window. But that's not the reason. I'm taking out Jenny Stevenson! We're not even dating. I mean, this is a date, but we're not boyfriend or girlfriend or anything. I mean, she's Jenny Stevenson!"

"So, is she like, off limits or something? I mean, she does know that she's going on a date with you tonight, right?"

"Of course she does. I just didn't want to be late." Mark looked at the clock on the center display. I still have 27 minutes 'till I'm supposed to pick her up." He put his head back on the seat and looked up at the ceiling.

"Wait, so how long have you been outside her house waiting?"

"Probably a half hour, sir. Am I a stalker? Go ahead, tell me."

"No, it's not that." Justice smiled and looked over his shoulder at his mom's house. All the blinds were shut. He turned back to Mark and shook his head. "My mom told me a man had been outside her house all day…or 45 minutes. So you're not planning to rob my mom or kidnap her?"

Mark laughed. This time it wasn't forced. "No, sir. I'm not trying to rob your mom or kidnap her."

"Promise?"

"I promise."

Justice blew out an obscene amount of air and wiped his forehead. "That makes me feel so much better. My mom will be disappointed though, when she finds out that her house is not the center of all things diabolical and treacherous."

"Well, I'm glad I'm not getting arrested, but at least then I would have had an excuse to back out of this date."

Kneeling down so that his head was a little bit below Mark's, Justice said, "Mark, just be yourself. Go out. Have fun. And just relax! How old are you?"

"Almost 17."

Justice made a sour face. "Don't do that. Either you're 17 or you're not."

"Well, I'm going to be 17."

"So you're not 17 yet?"

"No."

"Then just say 16. There's nothing wrong with being where you're at."

"Easy for you to say. You're not going on a date with Jenny Stevenson."

"Fair. Just say 16, OK?"

"Not that I don't appreciate you talking to me, but aren't you supposed to be doing some detecting or something?"

"I'm a detective. I'm on my own clock. And I was checking out a suspicious person in the neighborhood."

"Right, I forgot."

Justice smiled. "I promise you, tonight will not be the best night, or the worst night, of your life. Just go have a good time."

"I feel like I'm talking to my dad," Mark mused. "But thanks, Detective."

"It's Blake, and I'm sure dads would say some wise stuff like that, huh? Alright, I have to get inside before my mom calls a SWAT team over here. If she sees me talking to you, she'll end up thinking I've started to work with the bad guys! Good luck tonight, and good to meet you, Mark."

"Thanks, Detective Justice. I need it!"

Justice turned and headed towards his mom's house. When he tried to enter, he found the door locked.

"Mom, it's me. Blake. Come on and open up!" Justice shouted leaning against the door frame. After a little while, he heard a few clicks and the door opened.

Wanda Justice was thin, with silver hair falling down her back in a ponytail. Her eyes were the same color; it was apparent where Justice's coal-grey eyes came from. She looked older than her age of 61, wrinkles formed around her eyes, edges of the mouth were pinched. One hand was on her hip, and the other held a cigarette. "Well?" she said with a smoker's rasp, standing in the doorway and motioning to Mark sitting in his car.

"Well what, mom?" Justice asked with a sigh. "Can I come in?"

"Well, are you going to arrest him?"

"He said that he'll wait until you're asleep to kill you so you don't feel a thing," Justice said in a flat tone.

"I'm not joking, Blake. Are you just going to let him watch me all day and not do anything about it?"

"Mom, it's the kid who likes Jenny across the street. I'm surprised you weren't able to figure that out with your gossip file."

"I don't like it. He's acting very suspicious. He looks nervous, like he's up to something."

"He is nervous; he's taking a pretty girl out for the first time."

"Why don't you take any pretty girls out, Blake?"

"Mom, I didn't really come over here to discuss my love life. I'm too busy with work, anyway. You know, that thing I was doing when you called me."

"Oh hush, what would be more important than checking on your mother when she has a stalker outside her house?"

"His name is Mark. Captain's got me on a string of small time robberies. Nothing big, but they seem to be related somehow."

"Of course they are. Probably shadow government work."

Blake rolled his eyes. "Or then again maybe they're just some old fashion robberies. I was in the convenience store today that got robbed."

"You didn't hurt him too bad, did you, son?" Wanda had a pained look.

"No, mom. He got off easy. May have broken his nose though when I head-butted him after I flipped his car." Justice shook his head. "It's the darndest thing. When you shoot out a tire, it's a lot harder to control the vehicle. Weird."

"OK, shut up and get in here. I'm air conditioning the whole neighborhood, and I'm missing my show." She held the door open for Justice and closed it behind him.

"You have anything to eat in here? I'm starving." Justice patted his vest covering his stomach.

A contestant on the TV spun a giant wheel, while the other contestants stood clapping. The host pointed to a large puzzle with missing letters that was bookended by two attractive female assistants. *The category is "Two Times the Fun."*

"I don't know what's in there. Might be something for a sandwich." Wanda motioned blindly as she sat down in front of the TV. "I was going to go to the store today, but that guy was out there. Would have mugged me and stolen my car."

Justice opened the fridge and bent down for a better look. It *was* sparse. He found some lettuce, ham, and mustard for a sandwich. He also found a beer before shutting the door. "Mark would probably be more afraid of you than the other way around."

The audience clapped for a correct letter on TV. "I watched a fascinating documentary on ancient aliens and the cover ups by our government. It's amazing what they did."

Justice spread the mustard onto the bread. "And what did they do, mom?"

"There are these ruins in Russia with these massive stones. Only the cuts in the stones are so perfect that you can't even fit a piece of paper into the cracks. And there are other designs cut into the stones that couldn't have been made by hand tools. Only, these ruins are from thousands of years ago before there ever were power tools!"

Carefully, Justice placed the mustard covered slice of bread on top of the ham and lettuce. A sandwich should be even, precise. "So they think what?" Blake asked as he eyed his sandwich ravenously.

"Aliens, Blake! Aliens did it."

Blake garbled something from the kitchen.

"What?" Wanda called as the beautiful woman turned a few blocks into letters on the TV.

"I said," as Blake swallowed, "So aliens are the only possible explanation?"

"Well, yeah. What else would it be?"

"Mom, why would aliens come to earth to play with Legos? If you were some high intelligent being that roamed the universe, why would you come to earth to stack stones?"

"Why not? Don't you think aliens would want to have fun? But the aliens are here; the government just keeps everything hush-hush."

Justice wiped his face with a napkin, walked into the living room, and sat down in a recliner. "What are they being hush-hush about?"

"I think it's 'Grassy Knoll.'"

"Mom, there are three blanks there. The category is 'Two Times the Fun!' The puzzle is not about Kennedy."

"Well, it might be. The government is trying to cover up the fact that aliens are not only a part of this earth's past, but they're also a part of its present."

"What present?" Blake asked with eyes half closed.

"Well, aliens took Jimmy Hoffa for one. That's why you can't find him. It's the only theory that makes sense. They were trying to start a colony in New Mexico."

"Mhmm."

"It's true. Just wait and see. And then I'll be the one telling you I told you so."

Justice took a swig of beer. He closed his eyes once more.

"Mom, I miss dad." Wanda stared at the TV. "I wish he was around still."

"I do too, Blake," his mom said in a matter-of-fact tone. The man on the TV clapped his hands as a contestant jumped up and down. Apparently they had won something. Mother and son sat, one watching the TV, the other with eyes closed. No words were necessary. Finally Justice stood up, put his dishes in his sink, and walked out the door.

Chapter 6

The final camera crew had left five minutes ago, and Marla leaned back in the white plastic chair on her porch. The glow of fame still shown on her face as the sun sank down. Some neighbors were outside still—a few mowing the yard, but mostly drinking beers while leaning against bumpers and hoods. Grass pushed up through cracks in the crumbling street. She used to rollerblade down this street. At least now she would have an excuse if she suddenly lost her balance and fell face first on the pavement. The street used to be smooth, more families in the houses. Things always seemed to break down. What was it? Entropy?

Lenny wasn't big time back then. She had seen lots of drug deals— some she had been aware of, some she hadn't. It had never really bothered her. It was just a part of growing up. Her mom simply told her to be careful and keep her eyes open. She had kept her eyes open, and they saw a way out: school. She had loved school; her teachers, the new ways to solve problems, the challenges, the creativity. High school eventually ended, but she didn't want to be done. Marla wasn't ready for it to be over. But she also knew her mom didn't have the money to send her to school. The motivation of getting off this street and away from a bratty brother back home were enough motivation however, and Marla enrolled at IUPUI after a hefty school loan and a summer spent working at Gas 24. She had kept the job during her freshman year and finished with a 3.6 her first year. Summer meant more work and more classes, though she had gotten to see friends from high school who had returned home from their respective schools.

Marla's glow faded. Her gas station didn't just blow up; her job did too. She had to have a job. She sighed as a breeze stirred up the stew of stagnant air on the front porch. A metallic green sedan with tinted windows rolled past her house. She watched it continue all the way to the dead end in front of Lenny's hideout. It wasn't a hideout, but Marla had always thought of it as Scary Lenny's Hideout when he kicked his mom out and used it as his weed selling headquarters. Now there was a 10-foot chain link fence around the perimeter of the lot, with a gate patrolled by two hooligans. The green sedan stopped in front of the gate, waited until it opened, and then proceeded to the back of the house.

A tiny beep interrupted Marla's gawking, and she worked to remove her cell from her jean shorts pocket.

Shane: Tyler said he's up for it
Marla: K, I am too. Not like I have anything else to do.
Shane: no more gas stations to blow up?! jk
Marla: screw you. No, but I need a job though. Seriously
Shane: I know I'm just playin with you. Where do you want to eat?
Marla: No bonfire?

Shane: too dry. Smokey says no. Plus, I don't want to get shot

Marla: Shut up you wuss. We've always done in those woods. Lenny's not roasting marshmallows. They don't go out there. Your going to throw ten years out because of a drug house.

Shane: I'm just sayin. Too dry anyway

Marla: So let's hit up the Archer building sometime

Shane: We were almost caught last time

Marla: Comeon! These summer classes are gonna make me throw a brick through my own house window. we haven't gone there since this past winter. I need to smash some windows

Shane: Fine we'll do it let me know when

Marla: Soon gtg See ya tomorrow after classes

Shane: Where are we eating?

Marla: Wherever is fine. I'll text Nicole. Cya

Shane: Cool cya

Marla yawned and went inside. Tomorrow was unfortunately just another day. Detective Blake Justice hadn't swept her away from this dying street, her sophomore year of college, or her mundane existence. She was still just Marla White: unemployed gas station hero. Maybe there would be a demand for those.

Justice put the Challenger in park outside of his apartment building. It wasn't a slum, but Justice had never seen a Beemer in the parking lot. Several children were skipping rope in the waning twilight. With no school and longer days, their laughter could be heard well into the evening. Justice smiled as he watched innocence in its prime. A meaningless activity and yet it was the freedom of the play that made Justice fight harder. In a world where a pusher wouldn't think twice before offering a kid a dime-bag, or young lady could find herself being used as some play thing, Justice had to focus on what he stood for: hope of a better world, freedom from fear, innocence and justice.

A mother called out through an open door. One of the little girls with dark hair scampered off. Justice looked over at the rips from bullets in the upholstery in his passenger seat. Ballistics wouldn't need the slugs; they wouldn't tell him anything he didn't know already. But the guy with the scar certainly would.

"Hi, Detective!" a little girl yelled.

"Hi, Camiya," Justice replied with a smile. He stretched while the kids surrounded him.

"You have to arrest Danny!" one little boy shouted as he tugged on Justice's pants.

"Oh, and why's that?" Justice asked. He looked at Danny who had his head down.

"He threw rocks at DeMarcus," another girl offered.

"Is that true, Danny?" Justice asked in a serious tone, bending down toward Danny.

Danny nodded his head slowly, and then looked up with an earnest look in his eyes. "But he made fun of me. He called me an-" Danny leaned closer and whispered, "A hole."

Justice frowned. "What have I told you kids about that kind of language? That's the kind of language people use who end up in jail. Do you want to end up in jail?" The kids all shook their heads vigorously. "Good! Now go play and be good." Justice slapped Danny on the shoulder and headed up stairs to the second floor apartments.

Justice unlocked the deadbolt of 23 B and poked his head inside the door. "Honey? Honey, I'm home. Where's my baby?"

Immediately he heard a rapid clicking of nails on the tile floor, and a beautiful red haired creature came prancing into the entryway. "There's my girl!" Justice exclaimed as he bent down and scooped up the red, long-haired dachshund spinning in playful circles before him. "What have you been up to, Honey?" Justice asked, while holding his head back to avoid the tender licks on his mouth. Honey didn't pay attention to the question and continued to lick anywhere she could reach.

"I missed you too, girl. I missed you too. Ok, that's enough. Daddy's tired from knocking the bad guys around all day. He needs to rest." Honey squirmed to escape Justice's arms holding her down. Justice walked into the kitchen and grabbed a beer from a barren fridge. It must have run in the family.

The apartment was equally bare—no pictures on the walls, no decorative touches to soften the apartment. The original plastic blinds hung in not so parallel lines, and a single chair sat at the wooden kitchen table. Justice lived with the essentials—none of the frills that softened a man. If Justice existed for upholding the law, his apartment existed to shelter Justice. No more. No less.

Sitting in the one chair at the kitchen table, Justice removed his Kimber's from his vest and placed them on the table. Honey placed her front paws on the chair, nose in the air, sniffing.

"I love the smell too, Honey," Justice grinned. Honey barked in agreement. He lifted her up onto the table. With the skill of a surgeon, Justice's fingers worked quickly and efficiently as he broke each gun down, cleaning each piece as if his life depended on it. In many ways, it did. He tested the sightlines, the trigger weight, slide friction. He took a swig of beer and continued. Like best friends who finish each other's sentences, Justice knew just how each mechanical piece of the guns should function. He knew it could be the difference between taking down the bad guys, and taking two to the chest.

He placed the empty beer bottle in a paper bag full of bottles by the fridge and opened a cabinet door. He paused for a second and then pulled a bottle of Old Scout from the shelf and set it down on the table next to Honey whose head rested on her paws. He poured two fingers for himself, neat, poured half the contents of the glass into a gaping mouth, and then set the glass down.

Justice closed his eyes, swirling the bourbon around his mouth, swallowing a little to let the warmth seep into his core. The man with the scar. He had seen him before. There had been a few other robberies recently. Pedestrian in nature. Was there something behind it? Simple theft? As of now, the robberies had added up to about $12,000. Not necessarily massive hauls. He'd talk to Maya tomorrow, find out if she had heard anything. He downed the rest of the bourbon in the glass and placed it on the table. Honey licked his hand, and he stood up.

Justice's vest was propped up on a metal folding chair next to the bed. His Kimbers were loaded and within reach.

It was a habit that came like breathing. Honey nudged her way under the covers and settled in at his side.

Before he turned off the lamp next to his bed, he looked down at the picture frame on his end table. A handsome man with a close-cropped hair cut, and thick brown mustache stood smiling next to a shorter, blond woman holding a small child in her arms. She looked down fondly at the wide-eyed child. One of the man's hands was around the woman's waste, and the other one rested on the stock of a police issued revolver. The black of night deepened as Justice's window went dark.

Chapter 7

Inside the headquarters of the Avon Police Department, Detective Blake Justice leaned back in his chair, taking a break from his report on the gas station incident from the previous day. He clasped his flak jacket with both hands and bit down on the toothpick, grinding the saliva soaked wood into a soft pulp. Justice drew out the embossed plastic container and removed a fresh toothpick. A trashcan sat next to a desk across the aisle. Justice rotated and flicked the old toothpick toward the trashcan. A thin blond man in a white dress shirt and blue silk tie stopped in the aisle, blocking Justice's shot.

"Seriously?" He turned and looked at Justice. His indignant attitude softened somewhat at the sight of the behemoth leaning back in the chair.

"Seriously, what?" Justice asked.

"Did you just flick a toothpick at me?" The man appeared to be contemplating defending his honor versus walking away with full use of his limbs.

Justice leaned forward and pointed past the man at the trashcan. "I was trying to throw my toothpick away, and you caused me to litter. I don't like littering. It's against the law."

The man looked confused. "You flicked a toothpick at me."

"I don't know who you are. I was trying to throw my toothpick away, and you prevented me from doing so. So if you'll kindly pick the toothpick up and throw it away, we'll just forget this ever happened."

"Who the hell is this guy?" the man inquired out loud. A few of the officers and law personnel smiled.

Justice kicked his boots onto the desk and folded his hands behind his head. "I'm Detective Blake Justice."

The man in the tie frowned. "You're Justice? The hero cop, huh? Is blowing up gas stations your motif, Detective Justice?"

"You mean my MO?"

"What?"

"You said motif. You meant MO. Modus Operandi. Latin for "method of operation." I'm trying to help you out. I'd hate for you to make your second mistake in two minutes."

"You're a real smart-ass, you know that? M. O." The man said each letter slowly and articulately. "Is blowing up gas stations your MO?"

"No, but stopping armed robbery is. The fire and gasoline blew up the gas station, not me. A girl working at the gas station saved everyone's lives, and I caught the bad guy. But I am glad my reputation precedes me because I have absolutely no idea who you are."

The man smirked. "You will soon enough." And he walked away.

Justice watched the man walk away and laughed to himself. "Everyone thinks they're the biggest and the baddest." He eased out of his chair, tossed the old toothpick in the trash, and headed towards the holding cells and interrogation room in the back of the building. Avon wasn't a major city, but Justice appreciated that headquarters had pretty much everything he needed within walking distance.

"Hey, Decker. I need to have a little TLC with Scarface. Daryl Starkman."

The dark haired officer swiveled slowly and glanced over Justice. Beady eyes, like some sort of rodent, Justice thought to himself.

"Really, Justice? Coffee? Every time?"

Justice held up the mug and smiled. "Really, Decker? You mention my coffee? Every time?" Decker feigned interest in something on the desk.

"Helps calm them down. Makes them feel as if someone cares about them."

"They're scum."

"Well, I can hardly argue with you there." Justice didn't like have something in common with Decker.

"Well, you can drink the coffee yourself."

"What are you talking about?"

"He made bail this morning."

"Who did?"

"Scarface."

"I've got a file on him as thick as your head."

"Someday you're not going to be wearing that vest of yours…"

"Decker, I hope that day comes. I really do. Who got him out?

"How the hell should I know? Some hot shot lawyer? Some relative with a small fortune? I got the call; he was released this morning."

Justice slammed his hand down on the desk.

"Easy, gorilla. You break it, you buy it."

"The guy pulls an armed robbery and a high speed chase, and he just walks?"

"Yeah, welcome to the real world, Captain America."

"The Cap OK'd it?"

"Of course. You think I'm just letting criminals walk in and out of here, Justice?"

Justice raised his eyebrows.

"Well, I'm not. I take some pride in my work, OK?"

"Yeah, yeah. Exemplary Officer Decker."

"Of course. Just trying to be like Saint Justice."

"Have a wonderful day, Decker," Justice called out as he walked away.

"Don't get shot," Decker yelled back.

Justice arrived at the Captain's office, giving an obligatory knock as he burst through the door. Captain Frank McMann looked up from a mess of papers on his desk, eyeing Justice through bristled eyebrows. "Nice of you to knock. What is it I can do for you, Detective?" The slow drawl matched the large mass of a man settled deep into the leather chair. He hardly opened his mouth when speaking, perhaps in order to prevent his large jowls from shifting too much. Silver hair lay flat on the passive, bulldog face, but his eyes shone bright above the sags of flesh; they were full of fire.

"Captain, you just let the guy go?" Justice demanded.

"That is correct, Detective, I did. As the acting Captain here," his voice grew more stern, "and I am the Captain of this department, that would fall under my responsibility. The paper work was in order, and word came in from some higher ups. I follow the orders." His eyes narrowed. "Doesn't mean I agree with it, Detective."

Justice ran a hand through his jet-black hair and bit hard into his toothpick. "Sir, I hope that this is just some bums trying to get some cash, but they might be related. This guy, Daryl Starkman, I was *in* the gas station he was hitting. He could be the key to whatever this is."

The captain folded his hands on his stomach and looked intently at Justice. "And what, might I ask, do you think *is* going on?"

"Sir, I don't know exactly, just a feeling, which is why I needed to talk to Scarface in there. I think I've seen him before."

"And when was that?"

"I think he might have ties to Lenny."

"So you think Lenny is orchestrating these robberies?"

Justice, hands on his hips, stared out the window. "I'm not saying that."

"This would be pretty elaborate for Lenny, don't you think?" McMann asked leaning farther back into his chair.

Justice looked back at the captain. "Yeah, I do, but even drug dealers want to expand their territories, diversify their services. Heck, I don't know. But these don't add up. If this guy with the scar is working for Lenny, then why is he knocking off convenient stores. Shouldn't he be outside with his dime-bags? And he robbed, what, a few hundred dollars at most?"

"Look into it," McMann replied. "Maybe you could even go talk to our old pal Lenny." The captain smiled. "Let him know that we're not going to tolerate new ventures or unrestricted play. He knows the rules."

Justice gritted his teeth, and scowled, hands gripping the collar of his flak-jacket.

"Listen, detective. You know the end goal. I don't like it any more than you do. But with Lenny on a leash, he keeps the truly bad guys at bay."

"It sounds like cutting deals with criminals."

"There are far worse things than scratching a pothead's back."

"There are worse things than a faulty transmission, but that doesn't mean it still doesn't make me weep like a baby."

McMann began to speak, then frowned. "Right, Justice. Anyway, I think this would be the perfect opportunity to introduce you to your partner."

Justice visibly started. "My what?! Cap, I work alone. You know that."

"Not anymore you don't. And if there truly is something big going on, you could use the help."

"I work alone, Captain."

"This is not a discussion, Justice." McMann pressed the intercom button. "Send him in."

"You!" Justice said with eyes wide.

In walked the man who blocked Justice's toothpick from reaching the trashcan.

"Good to meet you, Detective Justice," the man grinned as he stuck out his hand.

Justice shook the hand with a set face, staring directly into the man's eyes and squeezing harder than necessary.

The man winced. "Wow, that's a heck of a grip you have there, partner."

"You're not my partner," Justice said slowly.

"Yes, he is," McMann said, paying more attention to the papers on his desk than the obvious tension exuded by Justice. "It seems you two have met, so that's good. Detective Dupé here, will assist you in the investigation, and you will show him how it's done." McMann looked up. "That means you will have to play nice, Detective."

Justice never took his eyes off the new detective. "He was referring to me, Doop. The only Detective in the room."

"It's pronounced Doo-pay," replied Dupé with a smile. "Like the French."

"Are you French?"

"German."

"Listen, I don't like you. Let's get that out in the open right now. If we're going to be working together, it's important we have an open line of communication."

McMann smirked. "I said to play nice, Detective."

"OK, Doop it is," Justice said, pronouncing the name quickly and crisply, leaving off the French accent. He looked the Detective up and down with disdain, noting his small, wiry frame. "Yeah, I'll play nice. Good luck keeping up." And with that, Justice walked out the door, leaving Detective Dupé scrambling to keep up.

Chapter 8

"This is yours?" Dupé exclaimed with awe as the two approached the black Challenger parked at the curb. Justice removed his Kimber Custom II's from his vest while Dupé slowly circled the car, crouching to feel the full effect of the vehicle before him.

Justice checked his sights and slides and re-holstered his weapon. "What's the matter? Haven't you ever seen a car before?"

"A car?" Dupé managed to reply. "Not like this, I haven't."

Justice unlocked the car. "Well at least you can appreciate a masterpiece. So it looks like I just removed 'worthless' from my long list of adjectives for you. Come on. The bad guys aren't going to cancel their activities just because you've never seen a real car before."

Dupé examined the interior of the Challenger with the same admiration and awe as the exterior. His hand explored the different materials and amenities. "This sure beats Alonzo's car."

"Whose?"

"Detective Alonzo Harris. Denzel? *Training Day*?"

Justice pulled some papers out of a file, not paying attention.

"Anyway, they get to his car and it's pimped out like this. Well, not quite like *this*. This is amazing." Again the words fell on deaf ears. Dupé's eyes were wide, and he whispered an oath of awe.

"Watch your mouth, detective. This is holy ground," Justice snapped. "She doesn't do well in the presence of vulgarity."

"She's beautiful."

"Of course she is, and she's got power," Justice added. Dupé raised his eyebrows. "7.2 liter V-8 for starters. 650 horses. Some people have jazz; her throttle helps me relax. Listen." Justice pressed the ignition button and the engine roared into life.

Dupé swore once more.

"Watch your mouth, Detective!"

"Sorry, man- detective. Didn't mean any offense. Wow, you really are Denzel. Except, like, the exact opposite in terms of swearing. And skin color."

"I'm not a movie star. I'm a detective, and I have a job to do. *We* have a job to do."

"So this is my *training day?*"

Justice focused his full attention on Dupé. "Get this straight. I'm only going to say this one time. There is no training day. There is no training. It is my understanding that you are a detective, not some trainee. I don't train. I don't hold hands so that you can get your bearings. I don't have time to wipe your nose and butt. I stop bad guys, and they meet justice. I need someone I can trust—someone I know has my back."

Dupé smiled. "You *are* Denzel."

Eyes locked, Justice removed a fresh toothpick from his case. "Can I trust you, Doop?"

"Yes," Dupé nodded solemnly. "And it's pronounced Dupé."

"Right, you're German. I forgot. And another thing, get a bigger vocabulary. Swearing shows ignorance."

Dupé rolled his eyes. "I'll try and remember that. How in the world did you end up with a car like this?"

"I bought it, genius."

"How? You're telling me they're paying you this much? How good are you?"

"Good enough. Plus, it's necessary equipment."

"How the hell is this necessary equipment?"

"I use it to fight the bad guys. Think of it as transportation for justice."

Dupé frowned. "Transportation for justice? What does that mean?"

"Justice will be driving 650 black horses when he comes."

Dupé stared in silence at the hulking man at the wheel, his mind reeling. Who was this guy? What was his story? Was he being serious? If he was half as good as any of the anecdotes he had heard in the academy, he was excited and also a little nervous. Stories of criminals brought to their knees with a garden hose or the shootout at the bowling alley. This whole situation was completely new to him. "So where to first?" Dupé finally decided to ask.

"I've got to run an errand, and then I have someone I need to talk to about the robberies." The Charger merged into traffic with a low growl. "Let's take some justice to the streets."

The Challenger came to a stop between the two yellow lines in front of grey propane tanks for sale. Detective Dupé looked at them and swallowed. "You're not planning to do anything heroic today, are you?"

Justice followed Dupé's eyes and smiled. "You never know what might happen. You want anything?"

"No, thanks, I'm still full from some biscuits and gravy. My girl sure can whip up some mean biscuits and gravy. You got a girl, Detective?"

Justice turned back, bending down to look in the open car door. "A redhead." Justice grabbed a Marsh Supermarket paper bag from the door panel and then shut it. Dupé watched Justice stop to look around and then enter the convenience store. Condensation smeared the windows. It must have been nearing 100 degrees outside. Unconsciously, Dupé turned up the AC. He half-heartedly thumbed through the folders on the center console and then leaned back in the chair, pulling his sunglasses off the top of his head and down into place. Not a cloud in the sky.

It had been about five minutes, and Dupé was considering going in and letting Justice know that he had reconsidered the offer and did, in fact, want something. But then he thought better of the idea. Justice didn't seem like the kind of guy to offer something twice. There definitely was a presence about the guy; Dupé had to give him that. Cocky or not, it was hard not to buy into Justice's aura. Sure, he had heard all the stories, but close, physical proximity was a whole different experience. The sunglasses, the toothpick, the bulletproof vest—they all shouted, "I'm a badass!" Either this guy was the biggest fraud ever to walk the streets, or he was the real deal, and therefore had to be respected and feared. Besides, you couldn't fake 6'5" and 260.

Movement near the side of the gas station coaxed Dupé out of his stupor. A woman, slender with long, blond hair frizzed by the humidity, hugged the wall with small, uncertain steps. Her clothes announced a party, but it was only 10am. Or perhaps it was *already* 10am for her. To the common passer-by, she may have looked overdressed, or simply frustrated by what the humidity had done to her clothes, make up, and hair. But to a detective with 10 years on the streets, or to a trick, this woman might as well have had a sign around her neck that read, "Prostitute."

Perhaps if Detective Dupé were still on foot patrol, he would have taken some action; Prostitution was illegal in Avon, after all. However, he wasn't a common cop. He was a detective, and he hadn't actually seen any soliciting going on, had he? Let the rookies take care of it. It was best for a detective not to get mixed up in these things. Besides, Justice's reputation preceded him. Though he could be a loose cannon at times, he played by the book. If this truly was an issue that should be taken care of, Justice would handle it— maybe even make an example out of her for the rest of the prostitutes in Avon. He wondered what Justice would say when he saw her.

A moment later, Justice stepped outside, coffee in one hand and the paper bag in the other. Without hesitation, he turned to his left and walked deliberately up to the woman. This is it, Dupé thought. Justice is about to do something drastic. And he did. Justice touched the woman's arm and handed her the paper bag. They exchanged some words and she smiled. Then he as deliberately as he had approached the woman, he returned to the car.

Dupé was silent as Justice pulled out onto the street. What had he just seen? Justice shifted and passed a minivan.

Dispatch reported a 314, and Justice smiled. "Wanna check it out?" Justice asked.

Dupé moved his hand across his chin. "What was that back there?"

"Probably some old senile guy. Real saggy," and Justice laughed.

"I'm serious. What happened back there?"

Justice stopped smiling and glanced over at Detective Dupé.

"Oh come on. So you owed her for a little poke. No big deal, right?"

"Is that what you do, Detective Dupé? Flash your badge, flash your junk, while your wife's making you biscuits and gravy back home?"

"What? No, man! No way."

"You cheat on your wife, Dupé?"

"No, man, I'm faithful!"

"Because a man who would cheat on his wife might find it easy to turn his back on his partner. Can't be trusted as a husband, why would I trust you as a partner?"

"It's not like that, detective. If that's your thing, that's your thing. No big deal. I just wanted to know what I saw."

"I have nothing to say to you, detective. You're in my car, on my time, on my case."

"Fine, whatever. Just thought I should have the right to know."

"You have the right to know when to shut your mouth and look straight ahead."

Beautiful brick buildings were replaced by faded signs and cracked concrete. Potted flowers morphed into weeds protruding from parking lots. People with blank expressions sat on crates or on peeling benches outside of dying stores, staring as the Challenger rolled past.

"What's our business on the Southside?" Dupé asked, looking out the window at the new scenery. "We have a lead?"

"No, we don't. Which is why we're here."

Dupé thought it best not to ask any more questions and resigned himself to wait for whatever Justice would do next. They left the Challenger in a parking lot that was more gravel than pavement and walked toward a row of apartments that couldn't decide whether it wanted to collapse or be condemned. Justice seemed to know where he was going. Was he ever unsure? Would you know it if he was? Two men of the law—one slender with professional shirt and tie, while a flak jacket increased the size of the other, already hulking frame. Dupé looked like he might pick a lock while Justice would kick the door down. While he never longed for violence on any job, Dupé tried to suppress his desire to see the renowned Justice in CQC, hand-to-hand. It would be quite the spectacle.

The heat had been unbearable outside, and Dupé found the inside of the building to be suffocating. Even Justice seemed affected by the onslaught. A lone fan struggled in vain to circulate the heavy heat, and the light penetrated halfway down the hallway before giving up. Paint peeled off the walls—probably lead.

Justice walked with measured steps. His head faced forward, but his eyes never lingered on one spot too long. He knew this building, but even familiar environments could change at a moment's notice. "Keep your eyes open, detective," Justice said softly.

They mounted the stairs at the end of the hallway. An old man sat propped against the corner of the landing. His eyes were closed and in the dim lighting it was hard to see any movement of the chest.

"Is he dead?" Dupé almost whispered.

"He might be. But that's not our concern right now," Justice replied.

About halfway down the hall, Justice stopped and surveyed his surroundings. After observing both directions in the hallway, he approached a door, knocked twice, and then twice more. He stepped back hands folded in front of him. Dupé assumed a similar stance slightly behind him.

They barely heard the turn of the dead bolt over the noise of old AC units and other machinery that may have been installed half a century earlier. The door opened a crack, two chains and their locks preventing it from opening farther. A young female face peered through. "You're going to knock on my door in broad daylight?"

"I can kick it down if you prefer."

"That sounds about right. Harassment and vandalism. Right up Detective Justice's macho alley."

"You know her?" Dupé asked.

"Who's the rocket scientist?" the girl asked, still from behind the door, eye peering out.

"Don't mind him."

"I do mind him. I don't know him. So I mind him."

"He's alright. He's with me."

"Right." She imitated a male's deep voice, "I can't tell a lie. Listen, Detective, I know you're about this whole truth and justice thing, but the word of a cop ain't worth nothing here. So you can save it."

Justice moved closer to the door. "I'm getting impatient out here."

"Geesh, I was just joking around. Can't take a joke. Fine." The door closed, followed by the sounds of chains, and finally the door opened. A dark haired, dark eyed girl of about 20 stood in the doorway with arms crossed. "He stays."

"I don't think so," Dupé protested.

"You stay," Justice repeated.

"I'm not some dog, and just who the hell is this chick? She can't talk to a detective like that."

"Well, I did, and this meeting will be over if he keeps talking." She looked at Justice, waiting for a response.

Justice turned and moved close to Dupé. "She doesn't know you. Shoot, I don't know you. She knows everything going down on the streets. If there are connections between these robberies, she'll know about it. So unless you feel like making calls on cats stuck in trees, stay out here and keep your mouth shut. Do something useful and keep a look out or something."

Dupé fought the urge to respond, staring directly at Justice. The door shut, locked, and Dupé was left alone in the hallway oven, sweat trickling into his eyes.

The apartment was similar to Justice's own. Justice had never been to Maya's apartment before, but he had nothing more to go on than a hunch, and he needed ears on the streets. Maya was the best, and she was a good person and had proved herself invaluable in the past.

"You losing your touch? You've never come here before," Maya asked Justice as she poured some orange juice. She didn't offer any to Justice.

"I was involved in a robbery and assault at a gas station."

"Wow, that's pretty hardcore, even for you," Maya responded with a smirk.

"I was not committing the robbery. I was preventing it. I caught the perp, but he got out immediately. But there have been other minor thefts recently: restaurants, gas stations, movie theaters. Something doesn't feel right."

"Aside from the fact that people still refuse to abide by your perfect law, what makes these strange? Some people want to knock over a convenient store, and this somehow peaks your interest? I kind of pictured you giving petty theft the finger. More of the triple-homicide-we-kidnapped-the-mayor's-daughter kind of Detective."

Justice ignored Maya's comments. "Do you have anything or not? You owe me, remember?"

Maya took a swig of orange juice and brushed a piece of hair out of her eyes. "I could have done that by myself. I didn't need your help, muscles."

"Right."

"Snow," she said flatly.

"What?"

"Cocaine. You know, a narcotic."

Justice straightened up. "Yes, I'm aware of cocaine and its classification. What about it?"

"It's on the streets right now."

"You're sure about this?"

"Yeah, I've got a kilo in my drawer." Justice's eyes squinted and his jaw tensed. Maya threw her hands up. "It's a joke, detective! I'm not sampling the stuff, but yes, I'm sure. Hell, I live on the streets, don't I? What self-respecting street urchin can't identify coke when she sees it? And from what I can tell, it's only the beginning."

"When was the first time you saw it?"

"Eh, probably a couple of months ago. Kind of caught me by surprise. I mean, unless Lenny has decided to go to harder merchandise, you don't sell on his turf. But I'm seeing more and more. And people are whispering."

"About what?" Justice thought he was doing a poor job concealing his curiosity and excitement. Scumbags pushing hard drugs didn't get the detective excited, but the possibility of taking down something big did cause his pulse to increase. And it was also possible that his hunch may have been correct. It usually was, but he also usually had more to go on than what he did.

"Oh, just potheads talking to each other. With the new stuff on the streets all kinds of rumors are starting. Some say Lenny is branching out, looking to take over central Indiana. Some say that the cops are putting it out as a set up. Some say that some ghost is organizing a takeover of Lenny's territory."

"And what do you think?"

"I don't think anything. I just keep my head down and try to make a living like anyone else. I don't like any of the options. All of them mean bad news for someone like me. I like things I can control. Change is bad. Big is bad. No thank you."

Justice stood for a second, processing.

"Well, Detective? Did I earn it?"

"I suppose so," Justice said slowly. "It's more than I had before." He unsnapped a pocket on his flak jacket and pulled out some beef jerky. "Don't eat it all at once now. I don't want you to get a stomach ache."

"Thanks, dad," Maya groaned.

"What are you? Some sort of lab rat working for cheese?"

"What. Beef jerky is delicious. I don't need anything from you. But you need to leave, now. Detectives in my apartment doesn't help the image, so if you would kindly get the hell out, Detective Justice."

"If you find anything else out, Maya, I need to know. Right now, none or all of those rumors might be true."

Dupé snapped to attention as Justice stepped into the hallway, the sounds of locks behind him bidding him farewell. Justice moved quickly. "Come on."

Dupé had to half jog to catch up. The beautiful kiss of fresh air and a breeze greeted the two detectives as they left the dying apartment. Both stood still, pausing to enjoy the blue sky. "So who was that? What did she say?"

"I don't kiss and tell, detective. She talks to me, and it only stays that way because I respect a lady's privacy."

"Fine, whatever."

"Now as to what she told me—I think something's going on. She said someone is distributing coke. Started showing up a few months ago."

"So now what?"

"It's time to find out if papa goose is laying golden eggs."

"I'm not even going to ask."

"You coming?" Justice called back as he got into the Challenger.

"Hold on a sec, got to make a call."

"Well, hurry up. The train's leaving the station."

Dupé walked to the corner of the parking lot and dialed.

"Well?" came the low growl.

"We're at some old apartment building on the Southside. Justice just got done talking to some street informant chick." Dupé looked over to the tinted windows of the Challenger. He couldn't tell if Justice was watching him.

"What's her name?"

"He wouldn't tell me."

"So what *did* he tell you?"

"He seems to think something big is happening. She says that coke's showing up on the streets."

"That's what I was afraid of."

"So what's happening? Do you know?"

"No, not yet. But from my sources, we need to be ready. I don't do this lightly. You know that right?"

"Of course." Dupé pushed his hand through his blond tufts and began pacing.

"Keep digging. Justice will need proof before he sees what we already see."

"I will. But I'm not really sure what I'm going to be able to do, sir. I wouldn't exactly call us chummy."

"Relax," came the soothing reply. "You'll win him over. I know it. That's why I chose you. We need Justice with us."

"You said he might not join us."

"Let's worry about that *if* the time comes, Detective Dupé. Keep working on him, and keep me informed. Goodbye." The line was silent.

Dupé breathed in deeply and walked toward the car.

"You seemed awfully involved in that conversation, detective," Justice said, focusing on a toothpick in its container.

"The wife. She gets so worried sometimes. Gotta check in every once in a while."

"Perhaps," Justice said placing the new toothpick between his teeth, "the streets aren't the place for a family man such as yourself. Wouldn't want call the wife someday to report you killed in the line of duty. Those conversations are so awkward."

Dupé forced a laugh. "You done many of those?"

"Enough," replied Justice with a yawn. "Tell your wife 'hi' for me the next time you talk to her, will ya?"

"Sure," Dupé measured. "So where to now?"

"Time to see if the golden goose likes cocaine."

"What?" asked Dupé, confused.

Justice glanced indifferently in both directions of the street before ripping the Challenger out of the parking lot and throwing Dupé against the window at the first turn.

Chapter 9

The manager peered down over his glasses, boring a hole into the paper in his hands. Marla swallowed. "Is there something wrong?"

"Ut-shshshshsh," the man blew through his strawberry mustache, hand raised and eyes never leaving the application.

Marla involuntarily clasped her hands in front of her and straightened her shoulders. For heaven's sakes. Couldn't she just say that she was like, the hero of convenient stores? That she saved the day? That while that hunky Detective Justice was off running down the creepy scar faced dude, that she, Marla White, had single handedly cleared the danger zone? That when the explosion had ripped through the gas station, there had been zero civilian casualties?

The strawberry mustache twitched as the manager silently read Marla's work history and references. He stopped suddenly and looked up at Marla over his glasses. "This one," came the sharp, nasal voice. "It says you worked at Gas 24 until, yesterday. What happened?" The tone was accusatory.

"Nothing," came Marla's immediate defense, before she realized what she was saying.

Then came the recognition. "Wait a second," the manager muttered, memory working furiously to recall where he had seen this girl before. "Gas 24 was the one that blew up yesterday. You blew up Gas 24?"

"No!" Marla pleaded. "That wasn't me. I was robbed, and the guy who robbed us did it. I had to get everyone to safety. There was nothing I could do."

"Do you make a habit of blowing up your places of employment, Miss White?"

"No, never. That's the first time it's ever happened. I mean, I didn't blow it up. It just happened. I didn't want it to. I worked there."

The manager's eyes had narrowed and he stood erect, slightly taller than Marla's 5'4" frame. "I'm not in the business of hiring employees who are likely to blow up my building, Miss White. Thank you for applying, but I'm not sure I'd be able to use you. Best of luck out there, Miss White." The manager gave a half smile, and began working on merchandise order sheets at the register.

Marla frowned, hands still folded in front of her. She was the gas station hero. This wasn't supposed to be happening to her. *God, I'm going to college. I don't swear, much. I saved a bunch of people yesterday. This isn't supposed to be happening to me. Maybe those damn parents screaming at their kids at little league practice, but not me. And not damn. Darn.*

Marla turned, but hesitated. Then she turned and walked up to the register where the manager was once again studying a piece of paper in front of him. She stood tall, chin raised slightly. The strawberry mustache remained twitching at the figures in front of it. Marla cleared her throat. "Excuse me."

The eyes rose over the top of the wire frames in annoyance.

"I have two years' experience working in a convenience store. I know the in's and out's of everything here. I'm punctual. I'm polite. I actually give a damn about the bathrooms. *Sorry, God. Bad day.* That guy had to pull a gun on me, and I still wasn't going to just give him the cash. Maybe that was stupid of me because, hey, it's just a register at a gas station. Who gives a crap? Why lose your life over it? But maybe I think that working a job is important. Maybe I take pride in my work. Maybe I needed that job. Maybe I take my job a little too seriously. And if that makes me unfit to work here, then, fine." Marla's chest moved up and down with heavy breathing and her eyebrows had jutted out over her face. She could feel the heat in her face despite the ice-cold air inside the gas station.

The manager stood up and smiled once more. But this smile was genuine and warm. "I didn't want a celebrity. I wanted a good worker. I'm glad I'm getting one. You start tomorrow. Be here at 7am."

Marla's face struggled to react in time to match her emotions. It twisted through confusion, satisfaction, and then thankfulness. "Thank you, sir."

"The name's Steve, Miss White. See you tomorrow."

Marla walked out of the gas station into blinding sunlight, heels barely touching the ground. Marla smiled at the large marquee: *Let Us Give You Gas.* A blue SUV pulled up to a spot in front of the propane tanks, and a beautiful blond, severely made-up, approached the driver's side window as it rolled down. Her smile was professional.

Gross. I can't believe that's even real. What a skank.

"What are you looking at?" A man's head had moved to see around the blond, eyes burning.

Marla realized she had stopped and was staring rather conspicuously. She felt a strange confliction of embarrassment and indignation and didn't know what to do with either one. So she turned, walked to her car, and got in. She would work as hard as she could, so she never had to do that. No. She would never do that.

Chapter 10

The Challenger turned onto a dead end street, pocked with broken pavement and weeds, and lined by overgrown yards. Some of the heads turned at the sound of the gargling engine as it passed by slowly, but most were too preoccupied in booze or conversation. They had seen a thousand tricked-out cars. One more wasn't worth the effort.

"Why aren't these people at work?"

"Do you really care to know about their lives," Justice asked, "or are you rhetorically making me aware of your disapproval through the device of a stupid question?"

Dupé glanced sideways at Justice. "I was, uh, just asking a question. Just curious."

Justice navigated through chunks of pavement and massive pot-holes until he reached the end of the street which dead-ended in front of a tall chain-fence surrounding a blue, one-story ranch. The paint was pealing on the white shutters. Obviously the priorities of the owner lay in places other than upkeep.

Two tough looking guys with sunglasses stood by a gate. Sweat dripped down their faces and darkened their light gray t-shirts. There were no trees in the front of the property, or any other shelter to take refuge from the baking sun. While this meant discomfort for anyone unlucky enough to be on guard duty, the result was a completely impeded view of the only road leading to the house. The two men had been watching the matte black Challenger from the moment it had turned down their street.

Dupé didn't see any guns, but he knew the two men must be packing. Justice eased the car to a stop and rolled down the window. A large man with short stubble and curly brown hair on a deeply tanned head approached the car with confidence.

"You must be lost, man. There's nothing back here. You need to turn around and get lost."

Justice smiled back. "My friend and I were just in the neighborhood, and we were looking for some sort of weed distribution headquarters or something. Do you know where that might be?"

The curly man pulled a gun from the back of his pants.

"Woah," Justice said with hands up. "Where did you have that thing?"

The man held the gun up as he got closer to the car. "I don't know what you think you've heard, smart guy. But unless you want your head-" He stopped short when he realized Justice was wearing a flak jacket and had two pistols in holsters. "Who the hell are you!" he screamed. The other guard immediately sprang into action and positioned himself on the passenger side with his pistol trained on the window. Dupé felt one of his hands go to his gun by habit. Justice sighed. The guy on the other side of the car was screaming too.

"Are you being serious right now?" Justice groaned loudly.

"I will waste you!" screamed the curly man.

Drawn by the yelling, and maybe cameras, several guys came sprinting out of the house, all with guns. Most of them held pistols, but two of them had shotguns.

"Lenny is going to be pissed," Justice said calmly, staring straight at the thug with curly brown hair. "New guy," Justice said to Dupé, motioning to the man in his window.

One of the guys who had come out of the house started shouting too. The guy with curly locks turned back to the house, and then back to Justice. He hesitated. Then he shouted, "Are you sure?" The head of the crew who had just come out of the house motioned with his hand emphatically. The curly man lowered his gun and relaxed. "Hey, cool it, Nos." The man on Dupé's side lowered his pistol and relaxed as well.

"Nos?" Dupé made a face.

"Smart choice," Justice said. "You should probably let us through now."

The man scowled.

Dupé's man stuffed his pistol in the back of his pants once more and brought out a key to unlock the chain around the gate. Both men pushed open the large gate and the Challenger pulled through and stopped in front of the group of guys who still stood outside the front porch.

"Now what?" Dupé asked.

"Now we ask the goose about the golden eggs," Justice said with a wink, and got out of the car. Dupé rolled his eyes and opened his door.

"Damn," said a guy with dreadlocks, eyes wide and focused on the hulking figure with the bulletproof vest.

"I don't get anything?" Dupé said, sounding disappointed.

"A cap in your ass, pig," replied a goon with a goatee and one of the shotguns.

"Woah, easy there, hoss," Justice said. "No need to get worked up quite yet.

"How'd they know we were detectives?" Dupé asked.

A small, darker guy laughed. "Some of these fools don't know, but you can hear Detective Justice here, and that car of his, from miles away. Plus," and he pointed at Dupé, "you've got pig written all over *you*."

"You better watch your words." Dupé's words fell flat.

"I'm flattered that I make such an impression," Justice said. "I'm only around here, what, every other day. I've probably arrested a few of you several times."

A heavily muscled man with hair shaved to the scalp pointed a pistol at Justice. "Let's just kill 'em."

Again Dupé fingered his holster nervously. The rest of the men focused on Justice to see how he would respond. They clearly weren't worried with numbers in their favor.

Justice just smiled. "Hey, man. Your safety's on. Nah, I'm just messin' with you. Did you see that? They all thought you actually had your safety on."

The muscle shifted nervously, though still trying to show the necessary bravado. Was it for the detective, or did they feel they needed to prove it to themselves, to each other. This was their turf, yet they didn't have the power to do what they wanted to do—to do what they should do. It was sickening to watch a pig walk in like he owned the place. And that big mouth!

The same guy stepped in front of Justice and Dupé. Justice stopped, hands on his vest and feet shoulder width apart, looking the man over who had just blocked his path. Tattoos, muscular, white wife-beater, generic 9mm semi, bald head— a generic grunt in the drug trade.

"What kind of gun is that?" Justice asked as if looking at moldy piece of bread.

"Hey, guys. Looks like this cop don't know what a piece is." The goons grunted their approval of the quip, and the bald man smiled at his own humor.

"Oh, I'm sorry. I said, 'gun.' What kind of *piece* is that?"

The bald man's smile faded. "This," he said, holding the gun so Justice could see its profile, "is a 9-millimeter semi-automatic. Pop the clip in, and bang, bang, bang!" His hand tilted the gun at an angle and took imaginary shots. "And look, the safety's off…officer."

Justice stood facing the man, all the while keeping the other thugs in his peripheral. Dupé stood behind him, rigid. "It's Detective. You must be new here, so I'll cut you some slack. I'm here to talk to Lenny."

"Man, what's to keep me from dropping you and your partner right here? There's 8 of us and 2 of you. And that pretty face of yours don't have no protection. It'd be quite a mess."

Justice spit his toothpick on the ground and smirked. "Listen, Cueball, my mom's retired or whatever. She sits at home watching daytime television. I try and be a good son and see her, but I'm a busy guy. All she does is stare at that television and spy on her neighbors. Personally, I think she needs a cat or a dog or something. But she's got so much to *say*. So when I go over there, all she does is talk and talk. I can never get a word in. It's very frustrating. Because I think *I* have important things to say and talk about too." He paused, still staring the muscled man in the eyes. His eyes showed confusion and uncertainty. He unknowingly glanced to either side of him as if to say, "What the hell is this?"

"And right now, all these good things I have to say, all my ideas, all my magnificent orations are being wasted on a vomit-inducing, balding, puffed up, flea-infested dog like yourself. I didn't come here to talk to you. Now go tell Lenny he has a visitor."

Dupé was ready to draw his weapon any second. The situation seemed as unpredictable as any he had been in, but Justice just stood there, hands loosely gripping either side of his vest. The balls on this detective! The bald goon looked simultaneously shocked and offended at Justice's words and looked to his fellow muscle for indications at what he should do.

They in-turn shifted their weight, 8 small brains working overtime, weighing their options. They knew that to sit there and do nothing after the challenge and insult would mean the power rested in the detectives' hands, but they also knew they didn't have the authority to make a call to off a detective on their front porch. The cicadas surged into a deafening crescendo, and the stifling breeze died. Dupé dry-swallowed. The dark bristle of Justice's jaw line straightened into a sharp edge, his weight forward on the balls of his feet. Someone dribbled a basketball a world away.

The front door opened. And as if the door uncorked the bottled air around them, a breeze started up once more, cooling the skin and the attitudes of the men outside.

A man in crisp blue jeans, white tennis shoes, a pale green polo, and frosted tips walked out of the front door, flanked by a man with wild red hair and a bright pink scar. The man with frosted tips looked to be in his late 20's or early 30's, and he walked with a measured confidence and air of authority. A shiny holster poked out the front waistband of his jeans. He appeared to be in a good mood. Daryl Starkman was not.

"Don't want to shoot your children off," Justice said motioning to the gun. "Those things can just go off sometimes."

"Ah, so good to see you, Detective Justice," the man smiled, ignoring the remark.

"Equally delighted, Lenny," Justice replied. "And you," Justice said pointing to the scar, "must be Daryl."

Lenny glanced to the man with the scar, and then back to Justice. He quickly regained his composure. "So you two know each other, huh?"

"Oh sure, this joker put some unwanted holes in my car's interior. He'll pay for that."

Daryl glared at Justice. Lenny glared at Daryl. "My, my. Getting around?" Lenny's eyes didn't match his smile.

Daryl didn't look at Lenny. He stared at Justice, mouth quivering—uncertain.

"Does his scar glow when cops are around?" Justice asked.

"You probably mean, 'does his scar hurt?'" Dupé clarified.

"What do you mean?"

"Harry Potter's scar hurt him. The sword from *Lord of the Rings* glowed when the orcs were around," Dupé reasoned.

"You're right. I always get them mixed up," Justice said.

Daryl and the other thugs listened, not sure what to do. Lenny refocused the conversation. "So Tony's been getting into trouble, huh?" Again, the question was directed at both Justice and Daryl, but he only looked at Justice.

"Tony? Is that what you call him? Daryl Starkman is what I called him when I was writing up reports after chasing his butt down and wrecking his car, after he held up a gas station and had the barrel of a gun stuck in some poor girl's face."

Lenny threw his head back and laughed, but it was strained. "Wow, you *have* been busy, Tony."

"What's with Tony?"

Dupé leaned toward Justice. "Scarface?"

Justice shrugged. "Whatever. Yeah, I've got a whole theory on it. Want to hear it?"

Lenny finally stepped to where he could see both Justice and Daryl. "I would love to, Detective Justice. Tell me your theory about my boy Tony."

"Oh, it's not just Tony. I think it's something bigger. Now, we know Avon's no Carmel." Everyone chuckled in agreement. "But let's be honest; it's too hot for crime right now. Look at fatso here," Justice said pointing to a round henchman. Lenny held up his hand, and the man relaxed. "He's sweating like the scarecrow on the Fourth of July. You go dormant, comatose when the heat turns up. And here we're getting all kinds of hits. There's been a pretty big spike of small-time theft and burglary. Local businesses, restaurants, you name it. Not bank robberies. Nothing Hollywood. But enough that it makes you scratch at your flak jacket that's chafing your armpits and ask yourself, what if? What if there's something bigger behind it all? What if it's not just coincidence? What if they all mean something? And what if Daryl, i.e. you, is a part of it?"

Daryl shifted his weight. Lenny stuck out his lip in consideration, looking around at his guys. "Not bad. It's a little hot, and some mom-and-pops have gotten hit, so there must be some big conspiracy. Makes sense to me. What about you guys?"

The goons snickered. Daryl managed a smile.

"Well, believe me, if there's something going on, you'll be the first person I tell, detective. But, there is no *it*. I think you're getting a little loopy in the heat. I love chatting with pigs, but we've got some business to get back to. So unless you've got something official signed by a judge saying you can stand in my front yard, I'm going to kindly ask you to get the hell off my property." Lenny held out his hands to the gate and smiled.

"Well, like I said, Lenny. It's just a theory," Justice said and he turned and walked toward the Challenger. Dupé stood half a moment longer and then followed him.

As Justice opened the door to his car, he turned and yelled to Lenny who was just about to walk inside the house. "Oh, one more question. You wouldn't happen to know anything about some coke that's circulating on the streets, would you?"

"If there is, I'm just as outraged as you are, Detective." And he went inside with Daryl following closely behind.

Chapter 11

"So what was that back there?" Dupé asked with disgust as moved down. "Do you usually just go stream of consciousness with perps and criminals? Just run your brainstorms by them. Whip out your journal and have them proof-read it for you?"

"I was getting information." Justice downshifted with a slight flick of the wrist. The Challenger merged into traffic with little effort.

"What information? Did you think they would actually tell you what they knew about some sort of big operation? Geesh."

"Yes."

"Yes, what?"

"Yes, I thought they would tell me, and yes, they did."

"Really? What did they tell you? I heard you tell them plenty, but I didn't hear them offer us one helpful tip."

"That's because you were listening when you should have been watching. Lenny's not behind any operation, but Daryl definitely knows something about it."

"And how do you know that? They never said anything like that."

Justice shook his head and sighed. "This is the stuff I was talking about. McMann must really have it in for me."

"Comeon, you act like you're all superior, but all you do is talk in cryptic code. If they told you all of that, how do you know?"

Justice talked in a quiet, measured voice. "It is a theory, and it's not much different than how Lenny put it. It *was* a theory. I really didn't have much more than a hunch and a series of curious robberies. But when I *neurotically* spilled my guts to them, Lenny had no clue what I was talking about. And he had no idea that Daryl had robbed that gas station. And what's more. He was ticked." Dupé frowned and was about to interject, but Justice continued. "He laughed and acted like what I was saying was amusing, but he never once looked at Daryl. He never defended him, and his eyes were always searching. They weren't knowing eyes; they were inquisitive and calculating eyes. Lenny's not some mafia lord, but he keeps a tight ship. He likes to know what his guys are doing 24/7, and his reactions of surprise were real enough. His voice was strained and his cool air was an act. He honestly didn't know what Daryl had been doing, and he didn't like that. And did you see Daryl?"

Dupé sat silently; he knew the question was rhetorical and he didn't have a response anyway.

"One time in third grade, my friend and I were riding bikes around town during the summer. We had nothing better to do so we decided to ride up to the Pepsi Coliseum. Well there was an old gas station on the way that had closed down years ago. The parking lot was all busted up, and a small brick wall that ran along the street was crumbling. I was bored, so I got off my bike and grabbed a brick. Tammy got off her bike and grabbed a brick too. There were no cars, nobody watching, so we started smashing windows. That's one of the best feelings in the world: smashing glass. Glass giving way and just shattering. We knocked every last piece of glass out of those windows that day." Justice looked both ways at a stop sign and turned left.

"Eventually the sun started to go down so we headed home. Tammy lived just down the street from me, so she came by my house first before she went home. I was on a high. Throwing bricks through those old windows made me feel kind of good, but also kind of lawless, if you know what I mean. When your dad's a cop, things tend to be pretty strict around home."

"I didn't know your dad is a cop," Dupé said too enthusiastically.

"Yeah, he was. Anyway, like I said, it felt good break those windows. But they were all broken anyway. I wanted to break something new—something whole. So I grabbed one of the rocks lining my mom's flowerbed and threw it through our garage window. I thought Tammy was going to cry. Throwing bricks at an abandoned building was one thing; I hadn't really considered the consequences of breaking the windows in our own garage.

"Tammy rode away fast, and what I had just done started to sink in. I didn't eat that night. I don't think I looked at my parents once during dinner. I was just praying they never went outside again. I thought maybe they would both get sick and have to stay inside for the next week. I didn't sleep. My mind alternated between exploring different ways my parents would kill me and wild explanations for the broken window in the garage.

"Early the next morning, I snuck outside to get my bike. Tammy and I had already agreed the day before to go riding early. She rode up to the end of the driveway, and I thought I had escaped, when I heard the sound of my father's voice like a death omen or something. He called both of us over to him. He asked us what we knew about the broken window. I was just about to launch into a story when Tammy opened her mouth. She told him everything. Everything!" Justice pulled into the station, and put the Challenger in park. An eclectic mix of uniformed and shabby-dressed people filed in and out of the front doors.

Dupé sat waiting. Justice flipped through a file. "And?" Dupé finally asked.

"And, what?" Justice said without looking up.

"And what the heck does that story have to do with Lenny and Daryl giving us information?" Dupé demanded.

Justice stopped, and looked at Dupé. "The moment Tammy opened her mouth, I knew she was going to rat me out. She may have been mischievous, but her conscience always got the best of her. I might have been home free, but now here she was telling my dad, the cop, that we had been busting out windows at a gas station and threw a rock through our garage window. I knew I was busted. I could have killed her. The way Daryl was looking at me when I was sharing my *theory* with Lenny? That was the exact look I was giving Tammy as she ratted me out to my dad. I told Lenny something he didn't know, and something Daryl didn't want him to know. Now we just have to start pushing where it hurts." Justice winked and started in on the folder once more.

Honey nudged Justice impatiently. He obliged by lifting the covers, allowing the Dachshund to crawl beneath them and curl up next to Justice's legs. Another robbery. He had caught the guy, but Daryl Starkman had immediately made bail. From the outside. No interrogation. Nothing. And it didn't seem like Lenny was behind it. They were becoming more frequent now, but they were small. No bank robberies or armored trucks. Nothing flashy. Maybe that would draw more attention, more effort from the law. And then Maya said that coke was supposedly showing up on the streets now. Were they connected? Of course they had to substantiate that the drug was actually on the streets. Rumors. Rumors of rumors. Justice took a sip of the usual night cap, Old Scout Whiskey, turned off his lamp, and closed his eyes. Honey's warmth had begun to make his leg sweat, so he hung his other off the bed to find some balance in temperature. Balance. Lenny and the law. Allow length in the chain. Give and take. Had Lenny begun to take too much? Justice drifted off to the sounds of the night.

Chapter 12

The night had been a good one. Because the dining room consisted of two small tables with four chairs total, Julia Netz had very little cleanup work to do in the front of the family-owned diner. Only occasionally would someone stop and eat inside during their lunch break, but the majority of customers ordered to go. It was an unspoken rule with regulars that the diner operated in such a way. Mrs. Netz had officially retired from teaching three years ago, and opening a restaurant had always been a dream of hers. She thought of it as a scary, yet exciting, adventure. Her building in the strip mall on Rockville road wasn't spacious by any stretch of the imagination, but the dollar amount on the lease was the perfect fit.

Because she didn't serve breakfast, she stayed open later than most of the stores in shopping center, and her diner was popular with the younger crowd and anyone looking for good home cooking after hours. She wiped her face on her sleeve and began to put the last items in the industrial dishwasher. It had been her present to herself on the two-year anniversary of the diner first opening; it had been worth every penny. The air conditioner hummed as if starting its cycle, but never seemed to come on. She was just about to write down a note about calling the building owner the next day, when she heard the bell ring out front. She rolled her eyes, but she did note that it was officially eight minutes until closing time. Probably a few teenagers joy riding during the last few summer days.

A trip out to the counter revealed that it was not the teenagers she had assumed, and instead two men wearing windbreakers with their hoods up were standing just inside the door. One of the men was taller and well built. He didn't seem to be paying much attention to anything inside the diner, but he kept surveying the parking lot out the all-glass storefront. His smaller companion approached the counter. She noted a jagged scar on his face despite the shadow from his hood.

It was at times like these that Mrs. Netz wished she had a silent alarm button or something that could instantly trigger police action. There were always risks owning a store, and from time to time she would get the customers she liked to call "the crazies". She hoped these two didn't fall into that category.

"What can I get started for you?" Mrs. Netz asked Daryl Starkman. "I'll admit, I don't think I could fix everything on the menu this late in the evening; we close in five minutes, but I'll get you what I can."

Daryl didn't look up at her. Instead he placed a one hundred dollar bill on the counter, and said "I need you to break this for me."

Mrs. Netz swallowed. She doubted very much that this gentleman had virtuous intentions, and the scar on his face seemed to intensify all the initial misgivings she already had. She knew she shouldn't stereotype, but she trusted her gut, and her gut said this guy was trouble. She smiled as pleasantly as she could and said, "Oh dear. I'm sorry, but all the money is in the safe all ready, and it's time locked until tomorrow morning when the bank truck comes. I'm sorry."

Daryl was clearly tired of the act and pulled his gun out, sticking it in the face of Mrs. Netz. "Give me all the money you have!"

Mrs. Netz trembled with equal parts fear and anger. "How dare you," she managed. "Preying on decent folks in the community who are just trying to get by!"

"Listen Aunt Bee, this is for your own good. Now give me the money!"

"For my own good? How do you figure that?"

"Come on, Daryl. Hurry up!" Nos pleaded, peering into the darkness outside. "What's taking so long?"

"We don't use names, you idiot. Shut up. The money, lady!" Mrs. Netz didn't want to give in to thugs like this, but she also wanted to live. She could think of very little worth losing your life over, and cash was not one of them. She opened the register, and emptied its contents into the bag Daryl held out.

"Please, go. Get out of my restaurant."

"Thank you very much. Have a good evening."

"Come on, man. Let's go!" The two men ran out of the restaurant leaving Mrs. Netz trying to slow her breathing and heart rate. As soon as she was sure the men were gone, she dialed 911 as quickly as she could.

The black and white squad car pulled up about five minutes later with its lights flashing but no siren. The two officers left the lights on as they got out of the car. The thin, dark skinned officer came in, while the stockier man shown his flashlight around outside.

"Thank you for coming," Mrs. Netz said in relief.

"Not at all, ma'am. My name is Officer Phillips, and my partner is officer Furman. May I have your name?"

"Mrs. Netz. Julia Netz. I can give you a description of the men; they stole the money from the cash register. I should have put it in the safe before I closed. I got busy, and then they came in. I know better; I just didn't do it tonight." Mrs. Netz wrung her hands, looking around at nothing in particular.

Officer Phillips held up a hand while he brought out a pad and pen. "Now, now. You did nothing wrong. They're the animals. Just tell me what you remember."

The stocky, red-haired officer name Furman came in. "Nothing out there. Quiet and hot as hell. What'd they get?" Furman asked, slouching down in one of the four chairs.

"Mrs. Netz was just getting to that," Phillips said soothingly.

"Well, I tried to do totals before you got here. I, I must have kept the money in a lot longer than I thought today. I had 832 dollars and thirty one cents." Mrs. Netz looked defeated.

"Now don't you worry, ma'am. We'll get whoever did this, and we'll try and get your money back." Phillips gave a reassuring smile. He was such a nice policeman, Mrs. Netz thought. He understood how upsetting this must be, and he was being as gentle as he could be.

"Thank you. Thank you so much, Officer Phillips. Like I said, there were two men. And they were wearing light weight jackets, or windbreakers. One was blue, and the other one was red. The jackets I mean. One of the man, the blue one, he was big. Bigger than you," Mrs. Netz said, motioning to Officer Furman. "Not fat, like muscular. A big guy." Furman frowned. "He was the lookout for them. He kept looking outside. The other guy, the red guy, he stuck a gun in my face. It was awful."

"I can't imagine, Mrs. Netz."

"He had red hair, like him," she said, again pointing at Officer Furman. "And an awful scar. You could tell he was evil. Not all scars mean someone's evil, but it was almost like the devil's stamp of approval for this man."

"Stamp of approval," Phillips said as he wrote on the pad. "And he had a scar?"

"Yessir."

"All right, well we'll get on this right away," Phillips said smiling.

"Wait a second. Don't you need more information?"

"This is just preliminary, ma'am," Phillips said in an assuring tone. "We'll call you for more information later." Furman smiled from his seat.

"Well, OK," Mrs. Netz said, unsure of what else she was expecting.

"Have a good night, ma'am, and keep the door locked after we go," Phillips said.

"Stay safe," said Furman. Phillips smiled as he looked down at the grocery list on his pad of paper. He shut the pad and followed his partner out to the car. "Is it enough?" Furman asked as they slid into the cruiser.

"Not yet, but it will add up," Phillips said calmly as he switched off the lights and backed out of the parking spot.

"Those two are idiots. Lucky that hag didn't have a shotgun and blow them both away."

"Why do you think they were picked? After all, the devil has approved them," Phillips said with a hexing motion of his hand and both men laughed.

"So, how is it that we do all the dirty work, and we get ten percent?" Nos asked, leaning against the white hatchback with arms folded in front of him. Daryl Starkman was dividing the money into separate bags in the deserted parking lot behind the Pottery Barn.

"Well you're sure not getting ten percent to think or ask questions," said Starkman, not looking up from his work.

"Seriously. This is bull. None of this makes sense."

Starkman put the bags in the trunk and finally focused his attention on his partner. "You need to stop asking so many questions. You do the work; you get paid. It's that simple. You don't need to know why we're doing what we're doing. You don't need to know who we're doing it for. Now get in the car so Lenny won't start asking the same dumb questions you are."

Chapter 13

The black challenger eased into the parking lot of Maple Grove Elementary School, whose mascot was a creepy leaf with oversized hands (much like the Hamburger Helper guy) and a permanent grin that looked as natural and charming as the Joker. Every time Justice entered the doors of the school, he recalled his days in elementary school—fond memories of recess and punching Eric in the nose because he put a frog down the back of Lauren's shirt. And there was the time he caught Ellen cheating off of his spelling quiz, so he spelled "chest," c-h-e-a-t. Needless to say this raised some suspicions from the teacher, and Justice was able to prove she had been cheating with skillful presentation of the evidence.

And then there had been Tammy Shaw. Tammy Shaw moved to Avon in the second grade. Every boy in his class had fallen in love immediately. But Justice felt that this was simply because she was newest girl, the newest novelty. Justice too, had been smitten with her dark, curly hair that cascaded over her shoulders and her large brown eyes. But most of all, Tammy had been fun. She would play kickball during recess and argue whether Billy Graham or Gorilla Monsoon was better in the ring when they should have been learning their times tables. They both agreed that Gorilla Monsoon had the better name. Justice just thought the name was fantastic, while Tammy simply turned her nose up at the thought of a wrestler sharing a name with the world-renowned evangelist.

It seemed Tammy's family had always gone to church. Justice recalled attending Mass a few times with his mother, but the idea of doing calisthenics in the pews while someone spoke or sang for an hour and a half didn't really appeal to him. And the only snack at the end was a stale cracker and little cup of disgusting wine. Justice didn't understand what Tammy or her family saw in it. Of course, Justice didn't understand a lot of things about Tammy. Even in second grade, she didn't seem phased by anything kids thought or said about her. Justice admired that.

And though there were times when they lost touch over the years, Tammy was one of the few people Justice ever felt truly knew him. She had been there when his mom stared blankly and told him in a small and eerie voice that his dad had been killed in the line of duty. She had been there when he graduated the academy. And now she served as a steady dose of reality in a world grown cold in the grip of injustice.

The elementary school was a haven, an escape from the dangers of the real world. Stresses of finger-painting replaced those of hardened criminals skirting tough sentences because of a loophole in evidence presentation. Miniature chairs, low drinking fountains, and color-coded room doors made one feel as if they had stepped out of a black and white house into the wonderful world of Oz.

So while Justice pounded the pavement, Tammy read stories of talking bears and magical beanstalks. Yet Tammy was as grounded as they came. She was grounded enough for both of them.

Justice pushed through the large glass doors plastered with posters of upcoming events and other various announcements. A sweet-faced secretary looked up from her typing and flushed. Justice couldn't recall her name.

"If you could please sign in, Detective Justice." He looked down at the half-filled sheet of names and times. "I know it's a hassle," the secretary said in a low voice, as if sharing an understood frustration.

Justice merely flashed a smile and took the pen. "Not at all. We have rules for a reason."

The secretary nodded and quickly added her thorough agreement. "Oh I know, but some people think the world revolves around them. Can't stop to bother with necessary procedures. Don't worry, Detective. I don't let things slide when it comes to the children's safety."

Justice finished signing and glanced at the nameplate on the desk. "I know I can count on you, Miss Lawson."

"Oh, please. Just Anne."

"Is Tammy free, Anne?"

She looked disappointed, but she recovered. "Yes, I think she has a free period right now."

"Thank you," replied Justice, and he walked toward the hallway.

Justice eased the library door shut behind him and glanced around the room, finally spying Tammy shelving colorful books. "Excuse me, miss. Do you mind if I check you out?"

The beautiful brunette continued shelving the stack of books, her back to Justice. She moved as if unaware of his words.

"Really?" Justice sighed.

Tammy finally stopped and turned around. "Really, what? Please tell me that line doesn't actually work. You've had much better ones than that." Her head tilted in a disapproving manner.

"Oh come on. That was pretty decent."

"For a pig."

"Well?"

"So it fits then," Tammy said laughing.

"I see what you did there," Justice nodded approvingly.

"But seriously, you're going to have to work on better lines if you ever expect to pick up some classy woman in a bar some day. I don't know that elementary school libraries are ideal."

"OK. Fair enough." Justice scratched his stubble. "What about this? Are you an overdue library book?"

"Geesh, Blake. It's a good thing you have some muscles or you would be in serious trouble."

"Just answer the question," Justice insisted with a twinkle in his eye.

"No, Blake," Tammy replied, rolling her eyes. "I don't have 'fine' written all over me."

"Dang it. You've heard that one?"

"I'm an elementary librarian, yes. And I've also progressed past middle school humor. So yes, I've heard that one before. You could always go with something like, 'I know you shouldn't judge a book by a cover, but if I judged you by yours, then you'd be a beautiful classic.' Something like that."

"Eh, I'll keep that one in mind. How's the day going?" He picked up a green picture book and flipped through it with little conviction.

"Richard Scary. Good stuff."

"What?" Justice asked, and then noticed the book. "Oh, right. You've mentioned him before."

"Who doesn't like Goldbug?" Tammy scoffed.

"Oh of course. A classic. Although I do like a book without many words. I think I could tackle this one without too much trouble."

"It's going fine."

"What?" Justice asked again, brow furrowed.

"You are out of it, huh?"

"Sorry."

"Last period, Eric decided that every time I said the word 'class,' he should yell the word 'fart.'"

Justice laughed. "I admire a kid who has goals and sticks to his convictions."

Tammy smirked. "I'm glad you approve of 2nd grade fart jokes. Only the finest protecting us on the streets."

"Well, I should probably arrest him, then, for extremely inappropriate behavior. Maybe I could sprinkle some crack on him and get him placed in solitary like the animal he is." Justice shook his head solemnly and growled, "Filthy second graders."

"So what has you so preoccupied today? Big case?"

"Actually, no." Justice adjusted his Kimber in its holster. "Well, I'm not sure. I don't know." He shifted his weight between legs.

"You don't know? Usually you have some sort of gut feeling. So what is it? Can you tell me?"

Justice scratched at his stubble and sat down at one of the round reading tables. His knees practically came up to his chest. "Yeah, it's not really anything right now," came the muffled reply through large hands covering the face. He leaned back; the tiny blue chair threatened to buckle under the massive frame.

"All legs on the ground, please," Tammy said casually, looking through another pile of mismatched books.

Justice frowned at the back of Tammy's head, started to say something, and then leaned the chair back onto all four legs. "There's been a string of petty thefts all around—convenience stores, gas stations, restaurants."

"The guy you grabbed?"

"Yeah. And there's also word on the street that someone's pushing coke. Weed is pretty expected. We scratch backs. Our back is scratched. I hate it, but it keeps the hard stuff out. But now the white stuff is supposedly out there."

"And you think the robberies and the coke are related."

"Yeah." Justice sighed. "I don't know why. I just do. Something feels off. The guy I grabbed yesterday—he was out today. Out on bail, just like that. And his boss doesn't seem to be too happy about his extracurriculars. I mean genuinely upset. I know the two are connected. But I have absolutely nothing to link them yet."

"They're still not taking hunches as probable cause in court?"

"They should; a detective lives on hunches. The intuition, that's what makes or breaks someone on the streets."

"So what would that mean if they were connected?"

"I'm not sure. I feel as if all the puzzle pieces are there, but they just don't fit together."

"Just a couple more periods to go, and then it's the weekend. Thank you, Lord."

Justice rolled his eyes. "It must be nice having weekends, woman."

Tammy turned and flashed dazzling white teeth. "Oh it is. Do you have to work Sunday too?"

"Not scheduled to. And it's not like there's anything really happening in this case anyway. It will be there Monday."

Tammy moved over to her desk. "I have a class in 5 minutes. Wanna help me read *Berenstein Bears Go to The Zoo*?"

"Maybe if it was *The Berenstein Bears Learn to Field Dress a Kimber 1911*, I might be interested."

"Well how about church on Sunday then?"

Justice narrowed his eyes and ground his toothpick. "You're a viper. You know that right?"

"Oh come on. It wouldn't hurt you. When was the last time I asked?" She smiled. "You're not afraid are you?"

Justice was silent, staring intently at Tammy.

"You know this matters to me."

"I know it does, Tammy. Of course I know." He shook his head. He hesitated for a moment before his response. "What could it hurt? Sure, I'll see you on Sunday."

"Seriously?"

"Well, you've been asking me almost a decade now. It's the least I can do."

"Thank you, Blake. Now you better get out of here before the kids come in."

"Hey, I love kids."

"I meant for them. I don't want to deal with crying first graders. Get out of my library."

Honey pulled and tugged at the covers, fluffing them into the perfect nest. Justice placed his flak jacket on the folding chair next to his bed, and pulled the blind back. Clouds laced over the moon, obscuring the bright white orb. Honey peered up at him, small head between her paws.

"What? Don't look at me like that. OK, OK. I'm coming."

The moment he sat on the edge of the bed, she rolled onto her side, arching her back to extend her barrel chest, making it easier to rub. Justice absently reached back with his left hand to oblige her as he took a sip from the glass of whiskey on his nightstand with his other hand. What was it about this case that had him bothered? It was just some robberies. Some bad getaway driving. Rumors of coke on the street. Why did they have to be connected at all? Detective work wasn't Hollywood nonsense. Honey licked his hand, and Justice downed the remnants of whiskey. As he turned out the light, memories of his dad began to play in his mind.

Chapter 14

Crowds of people, looking like walking flowers in their multi-colored clothing, streamed toward the massive church building. The black Charger prowled the large parking lot, idling impatiently as families crossed the lot from their cars to the building. Ladies fanned themselves and men pulled at their collars. The lucky children laughed and ran in shorts and short-sleeved shirts. Justice pulled to the back of the parking lot and backed into a spot just in case things got hairy and he would need to be mobile. He wasn't sure how bad the sermon would be.

Somehow the modern looking architecture and casual dress of the people filing into the building caused a mild uneasiness that Justice was unaccustomed to. Churches were large, gothic structures made of stone, concrete, or brick, and they amplified cheerful sounds into sterile echoes. But lancet arches and flying buttresses were nowhere to be seen in this church building. Of course it had to be like this: the very things Justice thought he wished to leave behind from his Catholic upbringing were the very traditions and devices he clung to for comfort and normalcy. Somehow this modern church building lacked the concrete presence. It lacked the presence, and the concrete.

Father William, with his nasally, vaudevillian voice would half speak, half sing the liturgy while the congregation, or the audience (Justice never knew what he was supposed to be), repeated their proper lines. He supposed most people saw the services as additional security blankets in times of trouble and strife. Justice had attended because he had to; it was understood in the same way that it was understood that talking back would earn raised red stripes from a belt and time spent inside on a beautiful summer day. Justice's father insisted on it. He never understood why.

And then came the call and an empty place setting. Saturday evening no longer required attending mandatory Mass. After all, it had been his father who had insisted that the family attend in the first place, and he couldn't very well gather in God's house out of obedience when he was dead.

Justice realized his fist had been clenched and slowly relaxed it. If God wouldn't uphold justice, Blake would. His father's killer had never been found. Never brought to justice. There was right and wrong; that's it. Those who break the laws of the land had to pay. Those who had been wronged needed an advocate. Justice had vowed to do just that. How hard could it be? Help those who need it, and take down the bad guys.

A petite woman absently opened the door with a smile, looked up at the behemoth walking in the front door of her church in a flak jacket and pistols in holsters, visibly shrunk back. Then she noticed the badge hanging from the chain around the neck of the visitor, hesitated, and finally watched as Justice walked past her with a nod of greeting. She noticed her mouth was slightly open and she had let the door fall shut in the face of a young couple and their two small children. She quickly gathered herself and opened the door with an apology.

The twenty or so people in the foyer of the church parted, Justice playing the part of Moses. Justice walked slowly, thumbs tucked in the armpits of the vest, oblivious to the attention he had gained. There was no statue of Mary or holy water basin to be seen. In fact, in Justice's opinion, it looked like an oversized waiting room at the doctor's office. Fake plants. Plush chairs. A coffee station. All that was missing was the children's toy with hollow shapes that you push along intertwining metal pipes.

Justice was brought out of his daydream by a sheepish looking man wearing an earpiece and a laminated tag on the front of his vest that read: "Security."

The man hesitated. Justice looked down at him. The man's Adam's apple bobbed up and down. "Sir, c-can I help you?"

Justice noticed that most of the people in the church's lobby were watching them. He reached to pull his badge out from beneath his vest but found that it was on its chain, hanging in plain view. "I'm a detective. Don't you see the badge?" Justice held it between his thumb and pointer so the small man could get a better look. Several people returned to their conversations, satisfied by what they had witnessed.

"I know, sir. I know. It's just, some of the little old ladies. You know." The man's face was an odd mix of pain and hope.

"No, I don't know," Justice answered flatly. "What about the little old ladies?"

The man glanced over his shoulder, searching for help. Three other men wearing the same earpiece and plastic tag distracted themselves with the coffee maker. This was not going how the man had hoped. "The-They were worried about your guns," the man said pointing to the two spotless Kimbers.

"These two little ladies," Justice said while pointing to his pistols, "will keep the little old ladies safe. I'm on your side. What do you plan to do if some crazy person comes in here shooting up the place?"

The security volunteer held his hands up to pacify whatever he thought could possibly develop. "We don't want anyone shooting up anybody anywhere," he said in agreement. A short, doughy man in his late 50's, also wearing his official security badge, joined his much-relieved companion in front of Justice. The first man acknowledged the new guy with poorly disguised relief. "Hey, Alan."

"Hey there. What's going on here?"

Justice stood, staring at both men with a blank expression on his face. Getting no response, the doughy man turned to his companion for an update.

"I was just explaining to the detective here, that some of our, uh, congregation is concerned about his firearms in the church."

The doughy man nodded in thoughtful agreement. "Ah, yes. Some people can be a little bit jumpy about that I suppose. Why don't you leave the guns in the car, detective? I don't think we'll be needing them in here."

"You *hope* we won't need them in here," Justice retorted.

"Well, yes," the pudgy man nervously laughed. Justice's blank face remained staring at the two men. They glanced at each other and then back at the cartoonishly muscular man in front of them who looked like he and Rambo had a date with Death in Vietnam after the service. "I, uh, well." The two men cleared their throats at the same time. The first man patted his partner on the back and smiled. "We're glad you joined us this morning, detective. We're always glad to have visitors."

Justice inhaled deeply as he moved to the double doors in front of the sanctuary. Once, when he was just starting out on the beat, he and his partner caught a kid breaking into a Radio Shack. Justice's partner had been reading the kid his rights when his two friends snuck up and cracked his partner's head with the butt of a revolver and then pointed the barrel straight between Justice's eyes. He remembered the embarrassment of letting two low-life's get the drop on him. And he remembered the perspiration spontaneously forming all over his body as he stared into the yawning darkness of a revolver's barrel in his face while a crackhead's trembling finger played with the trigger. As the synapses fired uncontrollably in that moment of life and death, thousands of memories vying simultaneously for prime focus, Justice had momentarily felt completely helpless and out of control. That is, until he slowed down his breathing, oblivious to muffled roar of the shouting perp, watched for the split-second shift of the perp's eyes. That split-second allowed him to bob his head and ram his arm upwards, causing the firearm to discharge harmlessly into the ceiling. The small-time thieves and assailants panicked, and Justice quickly took charge of the situation with some well-placed punches and a Taser. He had never fired his weapon, though some annoying lawyers were upset about cuts and bruises around the mouths and eyes of their clients.

An usher handed Justice a church bulletin as he entered the large sanctuary divided into sections by neatly angled pews. Justice felt as if he were reliving that night in Radio Shack – the adrenaline rush and complete lack of control – once more as he scanned the royal purple pews, analyzing the room for the most discreet seating area. He was thankful he had entered in the back of the sanctuary. A few people had noticed him and not-so-gently elbowed their companion beside them, but for the most part, he had entered this hallowed ground unobserved.

This was not his element, and he became painfully more aware of it every minute. He couldn't legally shoot or arrest the pastor, or even the security detail, and he somehow felt that even his wits and intelligence couldn't save him in this place. He absently touched his brow; it was moist. He took one more deep breath. And then he saw Tammy. Her legs were crossed elegantly in a floral patterned skirt that fell over her legs as if she were somehow draped in a meadow of wildflowers. She was intently reading her bulletin, oblivious to the chatting going on around her. An older lady touched her on her shoulder, and she jumped up with a smile to embrace the woman.

Justice smiled and then, catching himself, moved quickly to the rear of the sanctuary on the opposite side of Tammy. He wasn't quite sure why he had done it. After all, she had invited him. Wouldn't she want to see him? Didn't he want to see her? He would see her after the service he justified to himself. Besides, she seemed to be in her element, and he didn't want to take that from her.

"So in the grandest of ironies, the young Amalekite dies for the lie he thought would gain him power, or at the very least, riches." Here, Father Henshaw's pleasant face transformed into angles of serious earnestness. "This was David's enemy," he reasoned. "Surely the man would gain some favor in the eyes of the new king by killing his predecessor, Saul, his greatest adversary. This was the man who had hunted David down after David had loyally, and selflessly, served him for a number of years. David had only made Saul look good, and to repay him, Saul hunted him down again and again.

"And now this Amalekite was giving David the good news that his most dangerous enemy had finally been vanquished and that he himself had killed him! What in the world is David's problem? Isn't this a good thing?"

Despite himself, Justice found himself paying attention to the sermon. He shifted his weight away from the edge of the pew and settled back into a more relaxed, indifferent posture. He glanced around him. It seemed no one had noticed him do this. He tilted his head back slightly and was just able to make out Tammy's face across the sanctuary framed by several heads in-between the two of them. She was listening intently to Darren Henshaw—a slender, middle-aged man with smooth, dark skin and jet-black hair, cut close to his scalp with perfectly landscaped edges and a goatee to match. Justice touched the black waves on top of his head. To each his own.

The man had a practiced tone and measured cadence that drew Justice back in to the sermon. "Most men would have rejoiced over the death of the man trying to kill them. But notice the response of Saul's armor-bearer when Saul asked him to take his life. He was terrified. He knew what a serious thing Saul was asking of him. David knew what a serious thing it was that the Amalekite said he had done." Father Henshaw scanned the crowd. Justice found himself looking around, much like a child would try to avoid eye contact when the teacher was calling for volunteers. "Was Saul a good man? The evidence would say no. But the armor-bearer and David recognized that Saul's kingship came from God, and it was not their call to end that reign. The blood of the innocent could never be repaid by the blood of the guilty. This is why the innocent laid down his life for the guilty.

"David recognized the God's love and forgiveness in Psalm 103, when he said, 'He does not treat us as our sins deserve or repay us according to our iniquities.'"

Justice frowned at this last part. David not killing the Analbite, or whatever the heck he was, was confusing enough, but throw in the fact that God wasn't giving people what they deserved was a little too much. How could the God of the world not distribute justice? It didn't seem right. The soft lines in Justice's face quickly evaporated into a scowl. He glanced over at Tammy across the sanctuary. She was nodding intently as Father Henshaw finished with emphatic statements that at least half of the congregation seemed to acknowledge with murmured "amens," earnest looks, and slight nods of approval.

When the service had concluded, Justice cleared his throat, checked his watch and waited patiently for the congregation to clear out of the sanctuary. The majority of the people were gone within the first two minutes, most likely racing to their cars to be the first in line at the restaurant, but a few pockets remained with loud laughter, handshakes, and amicable smiles. Justice supposed that as long as Kool-Aid was nowhere to be seen, there were far worse places than churches to be dragged to. As the line of obligatory pastor/congregant handshakes dwindled down, Justice pulled his large frame up from his pew and headed toward the open doorway where Father Henshaw was stationed.

The shadow Justice cast on the remaining few waiting for handshakes sped the process up considerably and soon Justice stood in front of Father Henshaw. The slender man smiled revealing bright white teeth that gleamed next to his dark skin; he extended his hand. "You must be Detective Justice. Tammy has told me so much about you."

Justice's hand engulfed the smaller man's hand, but he was impressed with the grip nevertheless. He towered almost a full foot over the slender man, yet Justice was fully aware of the easy confidence standing in front of him. Unlike most of the people he had encountered that day, Father Henshaw seemed to be in no way intimidated by the 6'5" Justice decorated with 45.'s and a flak jacket. Justice smiled.

"Father Henshaw," Justice replied in acknowledgment.

"It's just pastor or Darren, please," the pastor laughed. "It's a little different than our Catholic brothers and sisters."

"I was raised catholic," Justice said a little sharper than he had intended.

"Excellent," Henshaw nodded.

"So I'm not going to hell?"

"Well, I can't make any promises, but you won't for that." Pastor Henshaw winked.

"I thought you guys were opposing religions or something like that."

"Denominations, and no, we're not opposed to each other. There are some differences in practices, but we worship the same God. Martin,Luther had a lot of problems with the Catholic church, and there *were* a lot of problems with the Catholic church, but there were actually a lot of Catholics willing to make reforms. Now here we Protestants are with our thousands of denominations." Pastor Henshaw laughed. "Don't get me going Detective. You're in my element and I could talk about this stuff all day."

"I know what you mean. When I'm squeezing off a couple hundred rounds, feeling the recoil kiss my palms, and I'm studying my hit patterns on targets—it gets the blood going! Or we could always talk about my supercharged Challenger in the parking lot."

"Perhaps my Civic will have to give you a run after church, when the lot's cleared out."

"I don't know if that would be legal, pastor. Wouldn't be good to be arresting the local pastor, would it?"

Pastor Henshaw nodded solemnly. "I appreciate you looking out for me, detective. It is so good to finally meet the man behind the stories."

Justice's eyebrows raised. "Stories?"

"Please, I'm standing in front of a man wearing body armor in church, and you're surprised I've heard stories?"

Justice laughed. "I guess I don't even notice it anymore."

"Tammy's told me so many good things about you."

"She better have; she dragged my butt here. I mean, invited me here." Justice cleared his throat, but the preacher merely waited for him to continue. "So she's pretty involved here, huh?"

"Oh yes, she's one of our most passionate and dedicated members."

"Pretty much a perfect little Christian, huh?" Justice didn't know why he was trying to irritate the pastor.

Several small boys ran between the two men, laughing and pushing each other. Pastor Henshaw snatched one of the boys by his collar. "Alden, where are you running so fast?"

"Sorry, Pastor Henshaw." He was missing a tooth.

"Slow down, son, or you're going to end up knocking out another tooth."

The boy's face lit up. "More money!" And he ran off.

"Well, that wasn't the right thing to say, was it?" Pastor Henshaw shook his head, chuckling. He took out a handkerchief and dabbed his forehead. "Sometimes I wonder if that AC's even working." Justice wasn't sure if the pastor was purposely ignoring his statement or whether he had even heard it. The pastor shook his head again and waved to a family as they went by. "Are you perfect, Detective Justice?" He turned back toward Justice.

"Of course not."

"And neither is Tammy. And neither am I. Not on our own at least. Do you know what makes someone perfect, Detective Justice?"

"I really don't know. Do you?"

"The forgiveness and grace of God through his Son Jesus."

Justice swallowed. The room was getting warm again. He was definitely not in his element. He was beginning to wonder how he was going to make a run for it when Tammy's beaming smile came bounding up.

"Mr. Detective, did you take a wrong turn somewhere?"

"Very funny; I'm here aren't I?"

"Why in the world didn't you tell me you were coming or sit with me?"

"Well, I didn't want to make a promise I might not be able to keep, and then you looked so into the church thing that I didn't want to take you out of it. Father- Pastor Henshaw gives an engaging message."

Tammy frowned. "Well that's dumb; next time come sit with me." She paused and smiled. "Thank you for coming, Blake."

Justice turned to Pastor Henshaw. "She's been asking me for literally a decade." Pastor Henshaw just nodded, as if Justice were the hundredth person that day with the similar story.

Tammy looked at her cell. "Listen, Blake. Some of us are meeting at O'Charley's, just past Reagan. You could come?"

"No thanks. We can go get some White Castle some time. A Snack Attack box. 30 sliders. Just you and me."

"Or I could just puke in a bag and save my money. I'll talk to you later. Thank you for the sermon, Pastor D." And she bounded off.

Chapter 15

The glass slammed down once more, empty of its contents. Its owner opened his eyes wide, straining. The act was more lifting his eyebrows than actually opening the moistened, bloodshot eyes. He tried to focus himself, intensifying his gaze.

"Come on, man. You're not crapping out after just a couple rounds are you?" The bright shock of red hair was pushed out of the crudely scarred face as Daryl coughed into his sleeve. The dimly lit dining room of the Boatyard Café was completely empty. Chairs were still stacked on tables from cleaning the night before. Customers wouldn't be showing up for another two hours. Daryl wiped his sweaty face with the bottle of Jack Daniels and poured another shot. He hoped he would be long gone by the time customers would be arriving. But Nos could hold his liquor. Daryl had to give him that. He took another drink of water from the glass underneath the bar.

"Hey, man. You guys almost done? I've got to get this place ready to open and the employees are going to start showing up soon." A portly man with graying sideburns and untrimmed stubble came out from the back wiping down a pint glass.

Daryl squinted and looked at the massive hand with balloon like fingers. He looked back at the shot glass Nos had just picked up off the counter. Daryl made a face as he wondered how clean the glasses here really were. "Yeah, yeah. We're almost gone. Thanks. Nos and I just have some more celebrating to do."

"You sure are celebrating pretty early. You guys need me to call you a cab?"

This guy could be so annoying. Daryl shook his head and held up a hand. "No, thanks. We're good, Ray. Might try a little boating before we head out."

Nos looked disgusted. "Boating? You said we were going to have the day of our lives. So far all you've done is give me cheap whiskey, and now you're going to take me boating? Is this eHarmony? Did you get me chocolates?"

"OK, smartass. I told you. When this deal goes down. We're going to be pissing Jack Daniels and drinking stuff fit for kings."

"What kind of deal you got going down?" Ray asked.

"Nothing. Ray. Just some Lenny stuff."

"Why would we be pissing Jack Daniels? Wouldn't that hurt? Gah, that would hurt!"

"Finish your shot; let me pour you another."

"Hey," Nos said excitedly. "We could bottle that crap and sell it again! You know, like purify it and stuff. Like Tom Cruise in *Castaway*. Seriously."

"Tom Hanks. Anything I'd be interested in, Daryl?"

"No. It's boring stuff. You're missing the point, Nos. We'll have so much money, Jack Daniels will be like drinking our own piss."

"I feel like that's kind of the appeal now, though. Know what I mean, Tony?"

"I have other stuff on the shelves, but I can't just let you have the bottle. I'd be losing too much money if I did that. Nos, how many have you had?"

"5?"

"Not enough," Daryl said, glancing over at Nos. "Nos, how you feeling, buddy?"

"I feel great, Tony. But seriously, are we going boating. That sounds a little gay, doesn't it?"

"We're going out on a boat, not getting married. Have you ever been on a boat?"

"Why does it have to be gay, Nos? Comeon, man."

"No, I meant like actually gay. Like it's two guys on a date in a boat."

"OK, if you meant it like that."

"Nos, just take this bottle, and let's get going." Daryl looked at the clock and then back at Nos, whose cheeks had started to redden, but seemed to be doing quite well other than that. "We need to get drunk. I'll pay for it, Ray. What's good?"

Ray motioned to the shelf behind him. "I'll give you that Johnny Walker for 60. That's a great deal, and it'll do the trick all right."

"Fine. I'll take two," said Daryl, pulling a few bills off a rubber-banded roll. "We don't need glasses, we'll just drink 'em straight. Thanks. OK, buddy, let's get outa ol' Ray's hair. Thanks, Ray."

"OK. Here, give me one of those." Nos reached out clumsily.

Ray nodded. "Good to see you, Daryl. Tell Lenny to come in and see me soon."

"You got it, buddy. We'll see ya."

Darren Henshaw smiled. Justice thought he must always be smiling. Probably a requirement for a pastor. Can you read a Bible? Do you like to smile? You're in.

"OK, I can handle it. What did you have a problem with?" Pastor Henshaw asked.

"Why would David kill the Amalekite?"

"Well, I admit, that's something I find a little hard to stomach as well. Though David may have killed the man, we see a different way to handle someone in sin in the New Testament."

"No, I'm fine with killing him. I mean, David's the king. His word was basically law, right? Sometimes people need to die. But why the Amalekite?"

"Why? Because he killed Saul? And Saul was bad?"

"Yeah, I mean, if I can remember what you were saying, Saul was trying to kill David. Weren't they enemies? David worked his butt off for Saul, and Saul repays him by trying to kill him. Wouldn't David be thrilled by the news that his adversary, that piece of crap, was dead?"

"You would think so. So why would he be upset?"

"I don't know! That's why I'm asking you, pastor! You've got one of the worst people, and someone kills him, your enemy. You'd thank him.

"What for?"

"What do you mean, *what for*? Because you had a scumbag trying to kill you and this guy killed him for you. You'd give him a reward or something."

"That's certainly what the Amalekite thought, right? If I say that I got rid of David's enemy, maybe he'll reward me when he's king. But what if David didn't want Saul dead? And then this guy comes up and tells you that he killed the king, your best friend's dad, the king anointed and chosen by God."

"When you put it like that, maybe it's different. But the king got what he deserved. He was a scumbag that was trying to murder his loyal servant. It would have been the just thing to do. That's what our law system is based on. Right and wrong. You do something wrong and there is a punishment. Everyone knows about it. Black and white. Impartial." Justice realized his face felt hot and he had folded his arms across his broad chest (a defensive body posture). He took a deep breath and tried to relax. Pastor Darren didn't seem bothered by the large detective's tense disposition. He didn't interrupt. He waited his turn. Justice had to hand it to the guy. But what good would preaching and reading the Bible do in the real world?

Daryl realized he was going to have to cool it or he was going to end up drunk, and that would do him no good. Nos had already clambered into the small outboard and was working on the seal of the new bottle. A large sheet of gray covered the sky, effectively blotting out the morning sun, but the temperature remained sweltering. And even though the rain had yet to fall, the humidity continued to rise and both men were sweating within minutes of walking outside. The Eagle Creek Reservoir provided water for several towns outside of Indianapolis as well as creating a habitat for diverse wildlife. Because of this, only small motor fishing boats were allowed on the water. The surface danced in dark ribbons as gusts of wind moved across the surface. Daryl didn't see any fisherman at the moment; it was too hot for fishing, but he knew he would have to be careful.

"Hey, Nos. Go ahead and fire her up, OK?" Daryl grabbed a fishing pole leaning against the railing.

"Yeah, sure. Why are we going out again, Tony? We're fishing? Come on." Nos looked like a bouncer at a prestigious nightclub, but he had an intellect that failed to project more than 10 minutes into the future. Daryl hoped he wouldn't be projecting anything at this point. It was going to be hard enough to do it cleanly if Nos was slobbering drunk, let alone if he was stone sober and suspected something was up. "This seems kind of fishy, doesn't it?" Nos's hard eyes rested on Daryl. Daryl stopped untying the boat, stopped breathing. "Get it? Fishy?" Nos laughed and took a long swig of the Johnny Walker.

Daryl visibly exhaled. "Good one, Nos. Such a comedian." He finished untying the small craft, pushed off the dock, and managed to step into the boat.

"So lady justice is blind, huh?"

"Absolutely. You're innocent until proven guilty, but the law exists for those who are proven guilty. That's why I get up every day— to protect the innocent and punish the guilty."

"And we thank you for that." Darren raised his eyebrows and said, "Let me ask you something, detective. Do you consider yourself innocent?"

Justice smirked despite himself. "You mean, like, am I without sin? Well, we already established I'm not perfect."

"So then, who is innocent, detective? Who is guilty?" The pastor's face remained passive.

Justice swallowed as he thought of Elizabeth standing on the corner of the gas station. He thought of the night he had found a small woman beaten by a pimp adorned with ornate rings on his fingers. A woman whose right eye was swollen shut, whose cheek was bleeding from a gash where a large ruby had torn through her skin. The pimp did community service, said it was self-defense. And Elizabeth had landed in jail, unable to post bail. She didn't call a lawyer. She called another hooker to take care of her baby girl. Justice swallowed again. Far from innocent, yet his heart had broken when he read her her rights. She had been guilty of a state crime. And yet no part of him felt vindicated as she was driven away in the back of squad car, hands cuffed behind her back looking like a whipped animal. Blood, mascara, and heavy tears converging at the mouth of a dark river on her face. He still wondered sometimes why he was helping her out. She was part of the decaying society. Yet all he saw was a broken girl, a desperate mother.

Justice's eyes focused on the pastor still standing before him. He cleared his throat twice and rediscovered his control and authority. "We're not talking about taking cookies from a cookie jar, pastor. We're talking about murderers, rapists, drug dealers, pedophiles. Yes, I think they're guilty, bad, wicked, whatever you want to call them. Children, single moms, the guy at the grocery store—I call them innocent."

"And I don't think I would disagree with you there, detective Justice. Nor do I think God would either. But do you really seek blind justice?

"Of course I do. Don't you?"

"No, I don't. And I don't think you really do either. I don't think anyone really wants that. Blind justice fails to observe God's image in each created person. Blind justice gives no second chances. Blind justice rules on behavior, on what someone does. It says what you do defines who you are. It creates a standard that no one can live up to." Pastor Henshaw stopped, eyes staring at Justice with a mixture of despair and fire.

Justice didn't really want to ask, but he decided to take the bait. "As opposed to…?" He paused, waiting for the pastor to continue.

The fishing skiff made only a slight wake in the already choppy water. Daryl operated the outboard, and though he had done it before he couldn't help but make a lazy zig-zag across the reservoir as he attempted to guide the vessel toward a small inlet obscured by trees. Daryl made slow progress across the dark water as Nos continued to make steady progress with the liquid in his bottle. His face became more flushed, covered in perspiration, and his movements less sure. Daryl smiled. Perhaps it would still go as planned. He swallowed and touched at his shirt where the 9mm's barrel pressed warm into his hip bone. Despite Nos's deteriorating state and the July temperature, Daryl noticed his hand was cold and shaking. He pressed it between his knees and held it there.

They found their way into the small cove. Several turtles scrambled off a log jutting out of the water, and the sound of cicadas grew into a shrill chorus. "Tony, you going to join me or am I drinking by myself today?" Nos held up the second unopened bottle of whiskey, condensation beading on the glass.

"Just got to drop anchor and the fun can begin," Daryl said slowly, concentrating as he navigated his way between two logs below the surface of the water. This would be perfect. Out of the way. Plenty of junk in the water to hide a body.

"I'm still not sure what it is we're doing, man. I don't even like fishing. Aren't there any strip clubs open or something? You could have at least brought out the other guys."

Daryl wiped the sweat out of his eyes and blinked several times. His breaths came shallow and fast. He played out the scenario in his head, trying to visualize each possibility. Despite his run-ins with the law, he didn't relish the thought of killing a man, let alone one of his own crew. But he knew that Nos had brought it on himself. It was the reason Daryl didn't ask the questions he was dying to. Nos continued to drink and waved the other bottle in front of Daryl. Daryl smiled and leaned over to pick up a rag from beneath his bench. Then he took the bottle with the cloth, broke the seal, and took a swig. "Woo, that's good stuff. Drink up." He began to wipe the bottle down with the rag. "Too much condensation, and plus I don't really know how clean Ray keeps the place," he answered in response to Nos's inquisitive look. The answer seemed to be acceptable. He downed the remaining contents of his bottle and closed his eyes, beaming.

"So what's so much better than justice?" Justice queried.

"Grace. The second chance. The gift that Jesus gave us on the cross. The viewpoint that takes into account our common denominator in our Father. That no matter how bad someone may appear or act, they are never beyond God's restoration to who they were intended to be. I thank God every day that I'm not judged for what I've done or will do, but rather, I am judged by the perfection of Jesus Christ."

Justice looked down and shook his head. "I don't know about that. That sounds wonderful in here, pastor, but that's just not how it works in the real world. I don't really see an image of God in the people I deal with every day, and if that was his image, I'm not sure I want much to do with that kind of God. I prefer justice to grace. It's easy to preach grace in here, but try telling that to the guy who just assaulted an elderly woman in her home and starts popping off shots at you when you pull him over for a broken tail light."

"I can't imagine what that's like."

"No you can't. I appreciate you talking to me, Pastor Darren. And like I said, Tammy speaks the world of you. I'm glad she's got her religion."

"And it was equally good to see you in this place, detective," Pastor Darren added extending his hand. "You ask good questions. Don't stop doing that. I wish more of our members would ask questions like that. I hope to see you soon."

Justice shook the hand with extra vigor and said, "No promises, pastor." He smiled. "No promises."

Daryl eased his body weight forward, gripping the bottle by the neck through his cloth. Nos's eyes were still closed, face flushed in a smile, and his head bobbed slightly back and forth. Daryl steadied himself with his left hand, squatting in front of Nos, bottle in front of him. Suddenly Nos let forth a howl. "Don't cry for me, Argentina! I seemed that I hardly knew you!" There was a semblance of a melody, but the words seemed more like an utterance of pain, like someone trying to perform a recital while passing a kidney stone.

Daryl dropped the bottle in surprise and cursed under his breath. He exhaled when he saw the bottle was undamaged. He had his gun, but he preferred not to use it for this endeavor, and his original plan might keep the authorities guessing for a while. Besides, the sportsmanship of offing a drunk guy with a 9mm was minimal at best. Nos had opened his eyes at the sound of the bottle hitting the aluminum hull of the boat, and he worked to keep them that way.

After quickly opening the undamaged bottle, Daryl forced it into Nos' half-open mouth. "Down the hatch, Nos. Come on, don't crap out on me yet." Nos swallowed twice and then spit up the contents, wiping his mouth with the back of his hand. Daryl watched Nos double over and seized his chance. He quickly screwed the lid back on the bottle, raised it high, and brought it down hard, smashing Nos on the back of his head. He made an "ooph" sound and collapsed on the side of the fishing boat. Daryl knew he had to move fast. He poured the contents of the bottle over Nos's head until it was only a quarter full, and then he screwed the lid back on. Then he began to remove the man's shoes. He placed the pair on the bench next to him and struggled to remove Nos's shirt. Finally, that too sat next to the shoes on the bench.

Daryl stripped down to his boxers and hopped out of the boat. The water almost came up to his shoulders. It was actually quite refreshing. If he hadn't been trying to stage a suicide, he wouldn't have minded cooling off in the water for a while. But his mind turned to leeches and snakes and snapping turtles. He decided to focus on the suicide and cool off later. Nos was a huge man; Daryl was not, but at least Nos had helped by falling partially onto the side of the small boat. After a couple of minutes of floundering around, almost tipping the boat over, and scraping up his legs on the sticks in the water, Daryl managed to pull Nos into the water.

Then he jumped on top of Nos, forcing him under the dark water and grey skies. Daryl praised his own intelligence and pulled a log over the back of Nos. In his inebriated state, it wouldn't take long now. Still, Daryl acknowledged it had to be an awful way to go. Perhaps he should have just shot him. But it was too late for that now. And there were still leeches.

Justice slid the Aviators out of his vest pocket. Habit trumped the cloudy day. A finely carved toothpick soon found its familiar resting place between the molars, and Justice stepped out into the oven. He could have used some time at the gun range, but there were also far worse ways to start off a Sunday. Besides, he saw how much it had meant to Tammy to see him at church. He smiled. Who knew? Perhaps he really was just overthinking the robberies. Maybe they were just robberies. But they could wait until tomorrow.

Justice slid his hand over the finely crafted curves of his black beauty. The Challenger had waited patiently. He remembered the bullet holes in the upholstery and vowed to break some minor appendages the next time he ran across the man with the scar. The Challenger could handle almost anything, but he would talk to Torque about the possibility of bulletproof glass. It would add some weight, but she needed new suspension anyway. Justice slid into the car. Most of the church goers had left for lunch; the parking lot was practically empty.

The parking lot only had a few cars in it by the time Daryl maneuvered the craft up to the dock. The final aspects had only taken a short time after the disposing of the body. Daryl was quite pleased with himself. Confidence and perspiration oozed from his person as he sauntered up the dock. He patted his white hatch back and threw open the door. The hatchback pulled out onto the winding road near the restaurant and disappeared around the curve.

Justice eased the clutch and pulled out of the parking spot. Despite the few cars in the lot, he resisted the urge to redline the Challenger. Law and order always prevailed over non-emergency speed. Fazoli's was only five minutes away, and Wanda never tired of their lasagna. Justice, on the other hand, practically turned into Pavlov's dog over their breadsticks. In another 20 minutes he would be enjoying a cold beer with his feet propped up, engaged in deep conversation with his mother about which host he preferred for *The Price is Right*.

A black and white pulled out of an access road entrance and accelerated to the speed limit. The white hatch back was a small dot in the distance.

"He was alone," noted Carl Phillips. He took a sip of coffee as he punched keys on the onboard computer.

"You surprised?" asked Ed Furman. He pushed a hand through his bright red hair, and eased his portly frame back into the driver's seat of the police cruiser.

"Well, considering he's still driving that hunk of scrap metal that Justice pretty much totaled when he broke his nose. Yeah, I guess I am surprised."

Ed laughed. "Even good ol' Daryl Starkman is of some use. Call it in and let him know it's done. We can find the body tomorrow."

Carl sat quietly.

"What's wrong?"

"Don't you think it's weird letting this happen?"

"If you think I'm going to lose sleep over someone like Nos getting killed, you can forget about it."

"I don't mean that," Carl said slowly. "I mean, how in the world does sitting idle for something like this play into gun caches and some mystery dude?"

"That's not something I'm worrying about either," Ed said flatly. "I'm going to follow orders and watch these fools off themselves."

"How long do you think it takes Justice to figure out Daryl did it?"

"Not long; that's kind of the idea. We need him on our side, but frankly I wouldn't mind him getting caught in a nasty turf war."

"I don't know, something tells me that guy *can't* get caught. He does the catching. The question is: who is he going to catch?"

Chapter 16

Marla put the last of the styrofoam cups under the counter, placed a loose strand of hair behind her ear, and stood up with a groan. She stretched her back and yawned. Sunday's were usually slow, but today couldn't go by any slower. Besides a usual influx of weird church people at about 12:30, the day had consisted of single motorists here and there.

A chill ran down her spine and she involuntarily rubbed her arms riddled with goosebumps. Why bother with refrigeration when you're going to keep the temperature inside at, like, 40? She would have to remember to bring a jacket next time she worked. Classes all day tomorrow. Tuesday probably, but she wasn't sure. Still it sure beat the heck out of working outside all day. She thought of workers laying tar on roofs and almost felt physically ill. Poor guys. She had no idea how they did it. But, she reasoned, it did help them keep in shape and she had nothing bad to say about that.

The day was overcast, grey, dreary. The light outside looked filtered and reminded her of old black and white movies. What a boring world it must have been to live in. No color. She laughed. Her brother had once asked

Mark Anthony Taylor

why there was no color in the world back then. What had she said? Something about a cave, an evil prince, and a courageous frog that freed rainbow man from his cell deep beneath the earth. That why there's no color in caves, and it's all outside. He had bought it too. Little moron.

Some of the movies even looked like the filtered grey outside during their night scenes. A little too bright. Still better than that blue filter crap that the color pictures tried to make look like night. She rolled her eyes. Then her eyes hardened and remained fixed outside. She noticed her forehead was scrunching up along with her eyes, like she had just tasted something sour. She wanted to call the cops or something. It seemed like she was always outside. Of course, Marla thought, that was better than her with some guy. Marla shuddered. Selling yourself like that. Marla pulled her cell phone out of her pocket, still watching outside. She stood like that for a moment and then put the phone back in her pocket. It didn't seem right. Almost like betraying the female code.

Elizabeth Turner's feet were sweating badly. That wasn't good if the trick liked feet. She pulled at her skirt. It felt like every stitch and seem was clawing at her; every inch of fabric and material stuck and pulled on her damp skin. Elizabeth's long, blond hair stuck to the back of her neck. She pulled the hair back letting the hair flow between her fingers and outstretched thumbs. She practiced her smile and immediately thought of Molly Grace posing in front of the mirror—high heels, a string of fake pearls, lipstick crudely applied by small cherub hands. She was going to be a model like mommy when she grew up. She would pick up Molly Grace each day from *La Petite*, and she would immediately ask a thousand questions about mommy's day. That was Molly Grace. She wanted to know about her mother's day. While most children would direct all attention to their self, Molly Grace wanted to know the details of everyone else's day. Elizabeth smiled—this time genuine.

A familiar growl of an engine brought an even wider grin, and she turned to watch the beautiful supercharged Challenger of Detective Justice pull into a spot. No squeak, just the low rumblings as the beast's fire was put on momentary hold. The dark boots hit the pavement, and Justice stood up with two bags, one plastic and one paper, in his hands. He held them up above the roof of the car and gave a slight smile.

Marla moved to gain a better vantage point. She felt her heart pounding. Her hands involuntarily started straightening all items of clothing and hair. This Sunday wasn't going to be so bad after all. What was the detective doing? Was he talking to that- slut?

Justice closed the door and strolled over to Elizabeth. "You hungry?"

She gave him a suspicious look and smiled. "Depends. Cop donuts?"

"I would never. How about some authentic Italian fast-food? I was about to head over to my mother's and I thought, gee, I wonder if Elizabeth would like a couple slices of pepperoni pizza and some bottomless breadsticks." Justice looked in the plastic bag. "Well, three."

Elizabeth nodded. "I'll take it," she said as Justice handed her the Fazoli's bag. "Detective, what is that?" Elizabeth motioned to the Marsh paper bag still in Justice's hands. "You just gave me some." She frowned. "Listen, I know you don't think of me as some charity case, but I'm not the only one. I'm OK. Really."

Marla watched the exchange, mouth slightly open. He knew her? It certainly seemed like he did. Of course the guy solicited prostitutes, right? I mean, he was too good to be true. Quit daydreaming and get a grip on reality. You live on a street with a drug lord after all. Why should the rest of the world be any different? She watched as he held out a brown paper bag. Was he picking her up right now? Sick. To think that she had fawned over him so much. She should have spit in his coffee. He was no different than anyone else. Why couldn't he be ugly, though? Like some big gash on his face or a lazy eye or a smushed up face or something. Why did he have to be perfectly sexy? He could at least *look* creepy. That would make it easier to hate the guy.

Justice looked down and shook his head. "Elizabeth. You know I don't think of you as some charity case. I know there are others. But I met you. You have a daughter and you're out here, doing this."

Elizabeth's eyes flashed. "I'm not a victim."

"I'm not saying you are. But your circumstances are- tough. Mine are-." Justice hesitated. "You are doing everything you can for your daughter. Don't you want to be around for her more?"

"Of course I do. What mother wouldn't?"

"Then take this. Spend more time with your daughter. Hug her tight. My dad wasn't always around. My mom raised me. I saw what he did to you that night. I'm not asking you to accept charity. But I will do anything it takes to make sure that never happens to you again. If this keeps you at home with your daughter, then I'll keep doing it. But I'm not going to make you take anything you don't want to."

Elizabeth studied Justice's face, the contours, lines, the eyes. "Damnit." Elizabeth pressed her index finger into the corner of her eye and pressed in. "You're going to make my mascara run!" She was laughing as she blinked rapidly, willing the tears to stay put. "You're a good man, Detective Justice."

"That's what I keep telling them. Come on, I was just bringing you some greasy pizza, and now you're crying. That wasn't part of the plan. Go inside, clean yourself up, and cool off will you?"

Elizabeth looked around. "I shouldn't."

"Or what? I'll pay you for your time. Don't want you getting in trouble."

"You're ridiculous. Thank you."

Justice held the door for Elizabeth, who couldn't help but close her eyes and smile as she felt the refreshing wave of cool air wash over her. Justice looked up and grinned when he saw Marla. Marla was scowling. She waited until Elizabeth had gone in the ladies' room before hissing at Justice. "I thought you were different!"

"Woah, woah." Justice's voice dropped to just above a whisper as well, but the authoritative tone checked Marla's attitude immediately. She tried to keep scowling but between his gravelly voice and a whiff of his intoxicating musk of sweat and Brut, it was hard to think straight. "I don't know what it is that's going on in your pretty little head right now, but whatever you think you know, stop it right now." Marla wasn't sure what was going on in her head either. "There's a woman in there; her name is Elizabeth. And she's a very special woman. A special woman to me." Justice's full 6'5" frame leaned toward the counter and towered over an ever-shrinking Marla.

"I just thought," Marla began.

"You thought Elizabeth was trash? Some slut. You thought that I was some sleazy cop getting my jollies on? Perception is reality, huh? Let's get some things straight, Marla."

"You remembered?" She was blushing.

"Of course I remember. I'm a detective. That's what we do. Now, let's get some things straight."

"So you're not hooking up with hookers then?" Justice stared down at Marla. She was beaming now. "I'm so glad. I can't believe I thought you were. That was stupid of me." Justice cleared his throat. "Sorry. You were saying."

"One, Elizabeth is not trash. Guys who take advantage of her are trash. She's a mom doing what she has to take care of her baby. Two, she can have whatever she wants in here. Just charge me later."

"I can't really do that. I don't own this place. I don't even know if we do that. You're thinking of a bar."

"How old are you?"

"20. Oh come on. You going to arrest me? Plus it's called TV and movies?" Justice was caught mid-thought, mouth half open. "So I can't do some tab or anything…but she can have ice water whenever she wants."

Justice thought it over. "Deal. And three, I'm glad you're working here, Marla."

Marla wasn't sure if her face could get any warmer. She wished the AC was turned up more than it already was.

Funny how things are so relative. She wished she was 15 years older. "You are?" she murmured.

"Of course." Justice smiled. "I thought we made a heck of a team back there, Marla. No casualties and everyone OK, which is not something I can always say. Glad to have you here keeping an eye on things for me. Glad you got another job too."

"Yeah." She should have said something better, but she was happy just to be seeing the detective's face once more. The thought of little detectives running around outside a house in a perfectly manicured lawn with a white picket fence jumped into her head once more. Don't be stupid, Marla. You have to graduate first. And maybe it would be a wrought iron gate.

"Alright, well I've got some lasagna getting cold in the car, and my mom could be calling 911 on the neighbor's cat any minute now. I'll see you later."

"Absolutely, detective." Justice pushed through the door with an air reminiscent of James Dean or David Duchovny. Marla took long, deep breaths and willed her heart to slow down. She heard the familiar squeal of the bathroom door opening and then closing. She looked at the pretty, solemn, face framed by dirty blond hair. The blue dress was fancy, sequined, but looked as if it had been worn about 20 times too many. Elizabeth. She kept her head down, "looking" through her bags. She stuffed the Marsh paper sack deep in her purse, and took out a slice of pizza. She was about to push open the front door when Marla said, "Wait." Elizabeth stopped but didn't turn around. "I just wanted to say, uh, I mean-." The moment hung heavy like the moisture in the air accumulating on the inside of the window panes. "You can come in here whenever you want, you know to cool off, or to get some ice water or whatever."

Elizabeth turned to look at Marla. Her lips flattened out and she nodded. Then she moved out the door. Marla swallowed. She felt a bizarre mix of emotions she had never known before. She could be out there right now. She was sure she wouldn't have been the first girl from her street to have ended up in that situation. Hell, Leonard had turned into a drug lord and he lived at the end of her street. Emotions of disgust and anger seemed to dissipate, replaced with sadness and fear. A navy blue Impala pulled up to the curve. Elizabeth picked up her large tote, presumably with both the bags in it. Or maybe she had eaten the rest of the pizza by now. She walked up to the passenger window and leaned over, forearms resting on the car door. It looked just like a movie. Elizabeth looked like she was talking with the parents of a friend— chummy but a little fake enthusiasm. Marla could make out two figures in the front seats, but a reflection of the gas station and clouds allowed her to only see silhouettes. After about a minute, Elizabeth moved to the back door, opened it, and awkwardly slid in with her tote. Then the blue Impala backed out of the spot, pulled on to the street and was gone. Marla pulled out a piece of gum and chewed it vigorously.

Justice had spent the afternoon on his mother's couch, drifting in and out of consciousness while a narrator explained the process of making thumb tacks and the different uses of plastics. At some point he remembered his mother screaming at a contestant on a game show with shopping carts or something or other. Toward the end of the visit she had casually mentioned that she was being kept under surveillance. Justice had murmured that Mark was just the neighbors' daughter's boyfriend, or love interest, or whatever. Of course she had said she wasn't talking about Mark. This was different. Justice had asked if it was the aliens building pyramids at the end of the street. "Only if they drive black SUV's," she had replied. He smiled before replying, "The CIA must be giving the aliens the hookup now."

He was back at his apartment by early evening. He gave Honey some of the leftover lasagna and heated up some fettuccini alfredo for dinner. He always made it a habit to order enough for two meals. Honey practically inhaled her portion, then sat expectantly at Justice's feet while he slurped up his fettuccini. A practically inaudible whine came from deep within her barrel chest. Justice pushed the chair back from the table and held the plate down for the small wiener dog. With tail happily wagging, she proceeded to finish up the remnants of food, and then lick the plate completely clean. Not one speck of food remained when she was finished.

Justice moved onto the old green sofa in the living area. Justice couldn't remember when he had bought it, but it seemed to get more comfortable over time, even with its worn out springs. Of course he knew just how to position his body so as to maximize his comfort. He supposed most people wouldn't find it particularly comfortable. But he wasn't most people.

He pulled a wide cedar box from underneath his couch and closely examined its contents before pulling out a Julieta cigar imported from Spain. He lifted it to his nostrils as if

Mark Anthony Taylor

smelling a delicate flower handed to him by a wide-eyed child. He could almost picture the narrow cobblestone streets of Cordoba, winding this way and that until any out-of-towner was lost. Then he took out his toothpick, flicked it into the trash can, and stuck the Julieta in his mouth and began chewing on the end of it.

An etched glass of Old Scout Bourbon sat untouched as Justice closed his eyes, still chewing on the end of his cigar. Finally, he picked up the glass, took a gulp, and swirled it around in his mouth. Then he lit the Julieta and slowly inhaled, finally releasing the smoke out through his nose. He closed his eyes once more. Honey had crawled up into his lap and laid her head on his knee. Her eyes were closed as well. Justice let the day's events play through his mind; it had been a good day. He finished his glass of bourbon, savored the cigar a while longer, and finally crawled into his bed to close his eyes.

Chapter 17

Elizabeth's eyes hurt. Her feet hurt. She watched her daughter Molly Grace sleeping unaware, through the blur of tears and a swollen right eye. She sat like this for what seemed like an hour, the room split diagonally by the abrasive orange glare of a street light pouring through the blinds. Elizabeth willed herself to get up from the chair next to the bed and close the blinds all the way. The pain in her stomach hit her suddenly. She added that to the pain of her eye and her feet.

The pain in her stomach could be easily explained. She hadn't eaten in hours. Elizabeth had gotten into the blue Impala, throwing her tote with the money in the Marsh bag and the pizza into the back seat before she herself slid in. The guy in the passenger seat turned around and smiled at her. He looked to be about 40 years old. Plain, but decently attractive, dark stubble. Curly hair that just came over the ears. Large nose. She had guessed him to be about 6'2" or 6'3". His companion didn't turn around, but he seemed to be a bit smaller in stature. His side profile was clean shaven. Short, gelled hair (dark as well.) He looked to be in his mid-30's. The passenger had talked incessantly during the drive. Elizabeth didn't mind. The silent, brooding ones made the time as joyless as possible while the talkative ones at least helped the time go by more quickly. This one had talked about *The Eagles* non-stop, about their different albums, about how their sound was the most pure with Meisner but Frey pushed him out. Elizabeth decided there were worse topics to discuss.

About 20 minutes into the trip, the driver told the passenger to shut up already. He seemed agitated. The passenger looked back at Elizabeth, making a face and rolling his eyes. He told the driver to relax and chill. The driver muttered something back, but Elizabeth couldn't make out what he said. He never took his eyes off the road, and his hands were tense on the steering wheel. He hadn't even looked back at her in the rear view mirror. Occasionally he would wipe his forehead even though the AC was blasting throughout the vehicle. Elizabeth was grateful for this. The passenger seemed much more at ease, even kicking a booted foot up on the dashboard. The driver had growled at the passenger for doing this. The man took his foot down.

Finally, they turned into a parking lot of a rundown strip mall. A few cars were scattered randomly in the spaces. The younger man continued driving around to back of the businesses. Elizabeth hoped to heaven that they owned one of the businesses. She hated work in the car. The driver put the car in park and got out quickly and opened the rear passenger door.

"Get out," he said quickly.

"You're so grouchy," Elizabeth had said with a wink, trying to keep things light. As it was, she wasn't sure what she was going to have to do with these two.

"Dude, ease up, Dan. You're kind of being a jerk to the lady here," the passenger said, getting out of the car. He was, in fact, a large 6'3" with massive hands and shoulders.

"Shut up!" Dan had fired back, standing up straight to look over the car at his companion. Elizabeth got out of the car. She started to lean back in to grab her belongings but Dan had already removed them and shut the door behind them. "I've got them," he said without smiling.

"Thank you," Elizabeth said, smiling.

"OK, see we're all friends now." The passenger was leaning up against the car, completely loose and unbothered by his friend. "Now let's have some fun, shall we?" Elizabeth didn't like his grin. His eyes had changed from before. They were colder, more focused.

Dan said quietly, "Let's go."

"Woah, we picked her up, didn't we? It would be rude not utilize her skills and abilities, would it not?" Elizabeth tried to remain calm, thinking through what was unfolding before her.

"We have what we came for. Now let's go." The voice was calm. Firm, but gentle, as if scolding a snarling dog you knew could rip you apart if it so desired. "Come on."

Elizabeth had assumed at this point that the two men planned to rob her; it had happened before. What else they planned to do, she wasn't sure. They had taken her tote, the money, the pizza.

A car alarm brought Elizabeth back to her daughter's room. She hadn't eaten much of a breakfast—just some yogurt. Her stomach hurt, so she left Molly Grace's room and walked down the short hallway of the apartment to kitchen. She opened the cupboard, assessed its few contents quickly and pulled out a packet of instant oatmeal. She poured the contents into a green ceramic bowl with a chip in it, added water, and stuck it in the microwave. It probably wasn't microwave safe, but she didn't care. She opened her mouth wide and grimaced, gently touching at her right eye and cheek. The reason for that pain was also easy to explain.

The passenger's eyes had fixed on Elizabeth. "We haven't even asked what the lady wants. What about it, missy? Do you want to play some?"

Elizabeth's lips were dry. She licked them. "I think," she said, trying to manage the tremor in her voice, "that you two need to agree on what you want. It only makes sense."

Dan began walking around the rear of the car. "This was your idea. We've done it. I don't want to be involved any more than we already are."

"Danny, Danny, Danny."

"Shut up!"

The passenger finally took his eyes off Elizabeth, and turned to Dan. "Oh, shut the hell up. Who the hell cares if I use your name? Quit trying to play it so safe. I wonder how many opportunities have passed you by because you'll only do the bare minimum."

"We don't even know who this guy is. Or what he wants."

"We know what he wants, and we got it." The passenger turned back to Elizabeth, and sneered. "And I know what I want. The only question is: will I get it?"

"Let's go."

Elizabeth cursed herself for not keeping her belongings on her lap. It had just been so hot when she got in the car.

She also cursed herself for not keeping an extra can of mace in her dress.

"Eh, what the hell. Probably crawling with diseases anyway." Dan had gotten back into the car. Without Dan behind her, she gave the passenger her full, undivided attention. "Isn't that right, sweetcheeks? You got all kinds of diseases?" He stood tall and moved forward a step so that he was towering over her.

"I'm full of diseases," she said slowly and then swung her foot as hard as she could toward the passenger's groin. A massive hand swooped down faster and grabbed the ankle as it moved toward the groin. The passenger caught her ankle in a painful grip. He threw her leg down with his left hand and brought the back of his right hand squarely across Elizabeth's face, sending her sprawling onto the pavement and seeing yellows, blacks, and tiny stars dancing in her head. She couldn't feel the right side of her face, but her left side burned and her ears were ringing. A few tears rolled down her cheeks. She rolled over onto her stomach, chin resting on the uneven pavement. It was warm despite the cloudy day. She checked her face for blood, touching her mouth and cheek, but she didn't feel any. Like a vibrating gong becoming still, her vision began to return and she saw the Impala pull away and turn right behind the side of the buildings. She had tried to see the license plate, but the scene kept shifting on her.

Elizabeth blew on her spoon before eating the cinnamon oatmeal. It burned the roof of her mouth. She stretched her feet out under the weathered kitchen table. They still ached. There was also a simple explanation for this pain. After she was able to stand up in the parking lot and not fall over, she made her way around the buildings and to the street. She recognized the intersection and hung her head. She couldn't rely on finding a taxi, and no Samaritan would pick up a hooker to give her a lift home, let alone one whose eye was swollen shut and had cuts on her knees. She took off her heels and began to walk. She had stumbled into her apartment four hours later. Leeta had gotten ice for her face; her daughter was already in bed. When Leeta finally conceded and left, Elizabeth sat down and cried, silently at first, and then uninhibited. She wasn't quite sure why she did. It wasn't the first time she had been hit. She had just cried.

Elizabeth put the bowl in the sink, walked to her bedroom next to her daughter's and crawled onto the bed. 5 minutes later, Elizabeth Shaw was fast asleep.

Chapter 18

The first fingers of pale light were just starting to creep through the blinds of the apartment when Justice's cell rang. He put down his cup of coffee and checked the incoming number. "Dupé."

"Justice, sorry it's so early."

"I've been up. I'm listening," Justice replied while maneuvering the phone as he slid the flak jacket over his head.

"We've got a floater. Or a sinker. Well he's floating now. Well, technically he's probably been pulled out by local PD by now. But he had been sunk. I'm not sure how you classify a dead guy in that kind of situation. Not sure if it's what happened first or how you found him. Anyway, we need to get down to the reservoir. I'll pick you up in 5."

"What are you driving?"

"Black unmarked Impala." Dupé paused, then added, "SS."

"We'll take mine. I'll pick you up in 5," and Justice hung up. His Kimbers had already completed the morning ritual of cleaning and sighting, and Honey, after licking away all evidence in her bowl, had found her spot on the blanket on the end of the couch. 5 minutes later, Dupé heard the roar of 650 horses coming up the street and stepped outside to wait on the Challenger.

The ten-minute car ride took them north toward the Eagle Creek reservoir and park. Dupé explained that the cops who called in had said it looked like a fishing accident, but they thought it would be prudent to call in Dupé and Justice, just in case.

"Who found him?" Justice accelerated out of the apex of the turn and took the hard curve at

50.

Dupé braced himself before answering. "I think it was Philips and Fur- something."

"Furman. The same jackasses who botched the fugitive apprehension at the gas station and can't drive. I'm surprised they even had the sense to call us in. Ten bucks it's not an accident. Those guys aren't good for anything but parking tickets and traffic duty. Make me ashamed to wear the badge."

"They can't be that bad." Dupé had regained his balance as the Challenger roared and

dropped to third gear.

"When you think of pigs, the cops that earn no respect but demand all of it, those are the two finest examples of how to build rifts in the community. I'd love to see some citizen lodge a complaint about those two. They day they make detective is the day I retire. That's not a department I want to work for."

"So you don't really have an opinion one way or the other then, huh?"

"I pray one of them throws a punch at me some day." Justice clenched his jaw and gripped the steering wheel tight. Dupé raised his eyebrows and smiled.

They pulled into the parking lot of The Boatyard Café and parked near several other cruisers. Dupé explained they would have to take a boat to the crime scene seeing as it would be quite a hike to get to him by land. Furman and Philips were leaning against the gate to the pier. "He's all yours, Rambo," Furman said as Justice and Dupé approached. "Course, he's probably lucky he drowned. If you tried taking him in quietly, he'd probably end up shot 6 times and decapitated."

"And if you two idiots tried taking him quietly, you'd probably end up handcuffed together in the trunk of your squad car as he went joyriding around the city," Justice replied without looking at either of them. Then he turned to face them. "You found the body?"

"That's right, detective," Philips responded coolly. "Sometimes just plain old police officers can stumble on to cases."

"Why aren't you there, now?" Dupé asked.

"Looks like Rambo has a Padawan, Furman. And he speaks."

"I can do a lot more than talk, you disrespectful prick," Dupé shot back.

The corners of Justice's mouth rose slightly in a smile. "Guess my partner didn't take too kindly to that description."

"We were just joking around," Furman said in a honey-sweet tone.

"It's a Jedi student, Justice," Dupé pointed out.

"You really need to get out more, man," Justice replied. "How did you find a wife?"

"My wife is incredible, thank you," Dupé shot back.

"That's my point, what is she doing with you?"

"Hey, look," Philips said, nudging Furman. "It's Lucy and Ethel." Furman laughed.

Justice turned to the men with an incredulous look.

"Really?" Dupé looked at him questioningly.

"No, I got that one, Dupé. What? I've *seen* TV. Come on." He turned back toward the two officers smiling. "Some day you two pieces of crap are going to get scraped off of this department's boots. And I can't wait to be there when it happens."

Dupé watched as the two looked like they were about to say something back and then thought better of it. He followed Justice onto the pier shaking his head. "I'm beginning to see why you don't quite get along with those two. They're lovely."

Jane Grant looked up at the two approaching detectives and instinctively pushed her blond hair behind her ear. She felt the blood rushing to her face. She cleared her throat. "I'll take you out there. It's not too far." She nodded at Justice. "Detective."

"Officer Grant." Justice raised a hand in acknowledgment.

"There are two detectives. Just helping you with your plurals," Dupé said a little louder than necessary.

Grant led them to a green flat-bottom skiff with an outboard motor. The two detectives worked their way onto the rocking boat and Grant pushed off from the pier. "Ah, the Eagle Creek Reservoir," Dupé said looking out over the dark green water. The sun was momentarily hidden behind a massive, white cloud, and the relief, though momentary, was greatly appreciated by all three people in the skiff. "They started building it in 1965, and they completed it four years later." Grant and Justice looked at each other. Grant shrugged. Dupé continued, "It was intended to help control flooding from Eagle Creek, a tributary to the White River, but it eventually led to Eagle Creek Park being built as well as the developments surrounding it."

"What are you talking about?" Justice asked.

"Come on, Justice. This is pertinent information. Not a history buff?"

"It sounds like you're reading a Wikipedia page."

Dupé seemed unfazed. "They bought the land from Purdue. Did you know that, Justice?"

"No I can't say I did," Justice said.

"It's news to me," Grant added.

"Want to know how big it is?"

Justice sighed. "What's the point? You're just going to tell me anyway. It's big. I can see that."

"Over 1,300 acres of surface water. Pretty damn big."

"Watch your mouth, Dupé!"

"Geesh. Sorry, Justice. I forgot. Relax."

Grant just laughed and maneuvered the small craft into a small inlet where three other skiffs were on the bank and several officers were walking around. The cicadas' chorus was a shrill soundtrack to the beautiful scene of the reservoir and woods. Justice stood up and made an effort to balance his large frame in the tiny boat. "Don't mess up my crime scene!" Justice shouted at no one and everyone. They looked at the boat coming in stopped moving. Officer Cruise turned, annoyed, but his frown quickly changed when he saw Justice among the passengers. Once the boat was grounded, the two detectives and Grant jumped onto the shore. Dupé turned to say something, but Justice held up a hand, his brow furrowed, eyes dark and searching. He began to take in the scene in front of him. Like a clever archeologist, Justice began to skillfully remove everything in the scene that was of no importance, anything that would hinder him from seeing what truly mattered.

Chapter 19

They had been told that a fisherman saw something floating near the shore early that morning. Furman and Philips had apparently pulled the body up onto the shore, but then left it alone after that. The body was on its side. The officers had all stopped moving, as if by some general understanding that all should be quiet as Justice surveyed the area. Cruise had even shushed someone who coughed. Justice removed a pen from his vest and picked up an empty bottle of Johnny Walker. There was another one like it on the ground. He sniffed it and placed it back where he found it. "Dust these." An officer nodded. Justice knelt down in front of the soaked corpse. The skin had turned to a dull grey. The sun enflamed the entire inlet, erasing what little color was left in the body. He leaned forward and combed back some of the hair with the pen. There was a think black line of crusted blood juxtaposed to the colorless skin all around it. From his kneeling position, Justice turned to look at the shoreline. Some tall pussy willows lined one bank and a large log lay half submerged on the other bank. "One of Lenny's guys. Any ID on him?"

An older cop who looked like Mr. Clean walked up to Justice and the body. "There wasn't anything on him but a pocket knife and this slip of paper." The officer handed Justice a plastic bag with a sheet of yellow college rule paper inside. The paper was apparently still soggy as moisture clung to the inside of the bag. Though the water had smeared the black ink into indecipherable sections in some places, other words were still decipherable.

rick protor potent poort gosia??? p something who is he
where?? truck train airplanc
ukraine? eastern europe? russia romania

"Mean anything to you?" asked the officer.

Justice shook his head. Dupé knelt down next to Justice. "Hey, it's the meathead who almost blew my head off when we went to Lenny's. Good guy."

"I think they called him Nos," Justice agreed. He handed the bag with the note in it to Dupé. Dupé copied the note down in his notepad.

"My guess is that's not his Christian name," Dupé said dabbing at his forehead.

"I would agree."

"Any of that make sense to you?"

Justice spit on the ground and scowled.

"So Nos gets drunk while fishing, slips, hits his head, and drowns."

"Yep, looks like it."

"That's unfortunate."

"Yep."

Dupé turned and looked at a dark green fishing pole lying on the ground. "So that's what he was supposed to have been fishing with, huh?"

"Must have been."

"Think he was really that dumb?"

"I hope not. I want to give him the benefit of the doubt on this one. Maybe it got snagged on a branch or something."

Officer Cruise knelt beside Dupé. "So it was just an accident?"

Justice turned and looked at Cruise blankly. "Yep."

"Wow. And that's why I don't drink."

"You don't drink? At all?" Dupé asked incredulously.

"Don't want it to impair my judgment."

"No we don't," Justice agreed. The two detectives stood up and walked over to Grant.

"Kind of hard to fish without a hook or bait," she said.

"That's always been my experience," Justice said.

"And a blow to the head," she said, looking around.

"Nasty shoreline," replied Justice dryly.

"So this guy was one of Lenny's?" Grant asked.

"Yep."

"A bunch of fine upstanding individuals," Dupé said. "Such a shame to see one die in such an unfortunate accident. And I suppose there would be a number of fine upstanding individuals who would want to see him die in an unfortunate accident?"

"Probably a long list," Justice said staring out at the water. "I want you to start out with the guy who owns the restaurant by the docks. I doubt you'll get much out of him if it was Lenny related." Grant nodded. "They know each other," Justice continued, "but he could be helpful." He removed his aviators and wiped his forehead. The cicadas continued uninterrupted by the activity in the inlet.

"So who was the guy?" Grant asked.

"Named Nos. I've seen him with Lenny, talking. Grunt. Don't know how chummy they were," Justice said softly. "Could just be your normal gang on gang violence. Don't know. We'll wait for the autopsy. Come on. Let's go knock on some doors until they cave in."

Grant, Cruise, Dupé, and Justice headed back across the water to the parking lot of the Boatyard Café. Justice sat with his knees pulled up under his chin. The skiff was not built for four, let alone three and Justice. When the small crew was almost to shore, Justice's phone rang.

"Elizabeth. What's going on?...What happened?...Stay right there." Justice hung up. Dupé knew better than to ask what the phone call had been about. He would find out when Justice wanted him to, *if* Justice wanted him to. Despite the heat and humidity, Dupé's hair stood up on the back of his neck and a chill ran down his spine. Dupé had once responded to a call where a woman had been hit by her ex-husband when dropping off her son. The husband had been there when Dupé arrived, arm around his weeping wife. The husband and Justice both had the same looks in their eyes.

Chapter 20

A tan minivan honked its horn as the black Challenger roared past, crossing back over the double yellow line before a red Civic approaching from the opposite direction had to jam on its brakes. "Hey, man. I don't know what that phone call was about, but maybe we could at least switch on our siren or something."

Justice reached toward the dash and switched on the siren without taking his eyes off the road. He punched the clutch, upshifted, threw the wheel hard to the left, downshifted once more and flew past a Buick trying to pull to the side of the road. Dupé braced himself as he was pushed this way and that in his seat. "Damn," he whispered with a smile. Justice reached over without looking and smacked Dupé in his face. "What the hell?" Dupé exclaimed rubbing his cheek. Justice reached over again and this time Dupé blocked the blow. "OK, OK, man. I get it. Sorry. You're a psycho. You need help, Justice. Seriously." Dupé shook his head.

They pulled into the parking lot of an apartment complex about five minutes later. Justice parked the Challenger, turned off the engine, and took the keys out of the ignition. "I'll be right back. Stay here."

"Come on, man. Give me something. Is this something about the stiff back there? Or the robberies?"

"This is personal. Doesn't concern you."

"Well I'm here with you, so it kind of concerns me. Also, you're taking the keys while you're in there. That concerns me too. It's 100 degrees out there. At least let me listen to the radio."

Justice reached into the car, stuck the key in the ignition, cracked the windows, removed the keys from the ignition, and closed the door.

"Dick." Dupé sighed and watched Justice jog up the sidewalk and into the open staircase of building A. If he was half the athlete he looked, Dupé imagined that very few criminals ever escaped from Justice on foot. The guy was intense.

Dupé took out his cell phone and dialed.

The familiar growl greeted him on the other end. "Where are you."

"Outside some apartment building. On 10th Street just east of Raceway. By the Shell station."

"What are you doing there?"

"Not sure. He said it was personal."

"I want you guys to come in when you're finished there."

"Captain, it's not like he's really warmed up to me yet."

Dupé heard Captain McMann exhale slowly on the other end of the line. "Justice lives for, well, justice. He sees a wrong and he wants to right it. He's singular minded, a machine. He was born to uphold the law, and he's damn good at it too. He's what every police officer should aspire to be. He's fighting battles, but we're losing a war. We just need him to see the bigger picture, the greater overall good.

No, I'm not going to bring it up quite yet. I just want to get a report on the robberies."

Dupé watched a couple get in a car next to him and pull out. "Yeah, absolutely. And I'll keep working on him."

"You do that, detective. We need Justice." McMann hung up.

Dupé settled back in his seat. He knew he had to pull it off. Justice was necessary. In just the short time they had been partners, he had witnessed Justice's reputation in action; so far he was living up to the reputation.

Justice emerged from the stairwell. His gait was long, his steps determined. The entirety of Justice's 6'5" emanated power and destructive capability. The bulletproof vest almost seemed decorative at the moment, as if bullets would have bounced off of Justice anyway. Despite the Aviators, Dupé could see the deeply entrenched lines in Justice's forehead. He could only guess what had happened in the apartment that could affect Justice in such a way. Dupé hoped he was never on the receiving end of that look.

Justice got in the car, and sat silently, sunglasses masking the piercing eyes. He stared directly ahead. Dupé swallowed and waited. He finally spoke up. "How about some air, man?" he asked quietly. "I'm starting to chaff."

Justice turned the car on. The cool air blasted out of the vents. Both of his hands were on the steering wheel. "I'll freaking kill them."

"Who are you going to kill?"

Justice's voice was barely a whisper. "How do you hit a woman? How do you even-?" His voice faded out before the question could be asked.

"Who did you talk to?"

"My friend." Justice's voice was suddenly clear and cold. It made Dupé shudder.

"Her boyfriend? Husband? Do you know him?"

Justice shook his head. "She said two of them picked her up, took her to a parking lot, robbed her, hit her, and left her bleeding on the asphalt."

"Picked her up? She knew them?"

Justice pulled the Challenger out of the parking lot and onto the road. "No. She thought they were clients."

"The hooker? The one you're tapping from the gas station?"

Justice swerved the car onto the shoulder and slammed on the brakes. He reached over and grabbed Dupé by the collar. "Her name is Elizabeth," Justice said quietly through clenched teeth.

"OK, I'm sorry," Dupé managed to choke out. "We'll get the guys." Justice let go and returned to his side of the car. Dupé rubbed his neck. "Did she give you a description?"

"One guy was early 30's. White. Short, slender. Clean shaven, short dark hair. Gelled. The other guy was white and big— 6'3 maybe. Longer dark hair, curly. Big guy. He called the smaller guy Danny. She didn't get his name."

"Not much to go on."

"They drove a dark blue Impala. Early 2000's."

"Alright, that will help. Hey, turn around here. Captain wants us back at the precinct."

"The captain can wait. It's time to find out if the fox has been in the chicken coop."

"I'm not going to ask." Dupé rolled his eyes. "I'll just find out when we get there."

Chapter 21

The brakes of the black and white squeaked as the car rolled to a stop in front of the small office building of More 2 Store. Furman and Philips got out of the squad car and walked toward the office building. A ten-foot high chain link fence with double rolls of razor wire on the top extended from either side of the small structure to form a perimeter around the storage structures. 10 rows of long, orange-roofed storage units stretched to the back of the compound where a large gym sized storage area rose 4 stories for larger items that wouldn't fit in the small garages.

A mechanical chime announced their arrival, but the office was empty. The walls were a drab tan and had two boxed windows on either end. Three green filing cabinets stood in one corner and a basic wooden desk stood in the other. Papers were scattered all across it.

"Hell of an establishment," Furman said looking around.

Philips nodded in agreement. "Think he's out back?"

"I'm sure the doorbell is linked to the lot. If there's only one guy."

"So there's only one guy, one employee watching over all of this?"

Furman moved over to the desk and absently flipped through a stack of papers. "Only need one. People get a lock for their unit and a code for the gate. That's it. You don't even have to talk to them again until they want to close out their storage garage. Talk about easy money. Why don't we just buy one of these?"

"Hell of a lot easier, that's for sure." Philips leaned against the wall. "Can't be that good though. No AC?"

"Seems kind of boring though. Ours is a lot more fun," said Furman.

Philips nodded. "So there's just this one guy then?"

"Seems like it."

"And Cap says we can trust him."

"No, we can't trust him, but the Cap wants us to use him anyway. You're an idiot, Philips. Of course we can trust him. Leech, I think. Can't remember his first name."

"Listen, I'm just trying to cover my ass, and you should too."

"You worry too much. Just relax." Furman moved away from the desk and toward the front door.

Philips pointed behind the desk. "I'm thirsty. See if there's anything in there."

Furman squatted down and opened the mini-fridge. "Diet Coke and Miller Lite."

"It'll do," resigned Philips.

Furman took out two Diet Cokes and handed one to his partner. "OK, we'll come back later. I'm not waiting for this guy, and I don't feel like walking around outside trying to find him."

The two officers got in the squad car and pulled out of the small parking lot in front of the offices. Philips put on the left blinker, waited for a break in the traffic and pulled west onto Rockville road. Five seconds later, a black Tahoe with tinted windows pulled out from the Dollar General and merged into the westbound traffic.

Chapter 22

Marla heard the Challenger before she saw it. The familiar throaty rumble stirred something inside her that caused her to run to the window. She followed the car as it rolled slowly by and then ran to the door to see its eventual destination at the end of the street. Lenny must have been up to no-good again. There was no real news in that development.

Two goons at the gate also heard the familiar engine roar and immediately radioed their fellow thugs. The black dot grew until they could make out the silhouettes of Dupé and Justice through the windshield. The Challenger appeared to be driving through water as the heat danced in waves on the asphalt. Justice pulled up to the gate and rolled down his window. The same guy with curly hair approached the vehicle.

"I'm kind of getting tired of seeing you around here," he said as he stooped down to look at Justice and then Dupé.

"Believe me," said Justice, "I can think of a hundred other places I'd rather be right now."

"Where's your friend?" Dupé asked looking at the guy on his side. "What was it?"

"Nos, I think," Justice said. "Yeah, Nos." Lenny's guy clenched his jaw. "You should probably let us in now, princess." Justice picked at a molar with his toothpick. The guy finally backed up and opened the gate. Justice pulled into the lot and he and Dupé got out of the car. Three guys escorted them into the house.

"Thank God. I thought we were going to have to sweat out here again," Dupé said quietly, leaning in toward Justice. Justice said nothing and surveyed the front room. It was an unremarkable room in every sense of the word. Drab curtains, a worn brown sofa, old recliners, glass coffee table with gold trim, bare egg-shell walls.

"It's actually pretty clean," Justice remarked.

"We're not the pigs," a tall dark man with short dark hair replied.

Dupé laughed. "That was actually pretty good."

"Wait here," the tall man said. Justice sat down in one of the recliners. Dupé remained standing.

"Sit down, Dupé. Everything about you says cop."

"I *am* a cop, Justice," Dupé said. "And your bulletproof vest with pistols and a badge around your neck like some John McClane wannabe is so much more casual. Let me become less like a cop like you and find some full combat gear."

Justice leaned forward and felt under the recliner. He leaned back and looked behind the couch. The three guys that brought them in stood by the door, hands in front of them like poorly dressed bouncers. Justice looked over at them. "You guys are as bad as him. Sit down. Doesn't Lenny let you sit?"

One of the smaller guys with a neck tattoo spoke up. "We can do whatever we want. Lenny doesn't own us."

"So you're telling me you chose those outfits on your own?" Justice made a face at Dupé. "I would have stuck with the *Lenny dresses us* excuse." The three men glowered at Justice. "I feel like you're really living into the stereotypes most people have about you guys."

Just then Lenny walked into the living room. "You guys are going to have to start paying rent if you show up any more," he said casually. He looked at both men, mulling over what to do with them. "I don't like this habit you're getting into. It's not good for a guy like me to be seen in the company of such questionable characters as yourselves." Lenny adjusted his gold watch on his wrist and sat down. He motioned to the free recliner. "Please."

Dupé held up a hand. "No thanks. I'm good."

"No I insist," Lenny replied.

"Why is everyone so concerned that I'm standing?" Dupé said rolling his eyes.

"It makes me nervous. Please, sit."

"It makes him nervous, Dupé," Justice chided.

"Yes, Dupé." Lenny overemphasized the name.

"That's detective, you punk," Dupé shot back.

"It's Lenny," said Lenny.

"Girls, girls," Justice sighed. "Listen, Lenny, we didn't really come to chat. One of your guys, I believe he goes by the fantastic name Nos, tried to be a fish last night."

"I heard," said Lenny.

"Know anything about it?" Justice queried.

"No."

"Where were you yesterday?" Dupé asked.

"I was a lot of places. None of which concern you."

"Well they do concern us, if one of those places was Eagle Creek Reservoir while Nos was dying. So do you have anybody who could corroborate your alibis?" Justice asked.

"I didn't kill him," Lenny said quietly. His eyes shown bright and moved from Dupé to Justice. Justice shrugged. "Got any suspects?" Lenny asked.

"Looks like he was fishing and it got out of hand. Just an accident," Justice said.

"Sometimes accidents happen," Lenny said coolly.

"I bet they do in your line of work, don't they?" Dupé growled.

"My line of work is business, not killing, detective—Dupé."

"Business, my ass," Dupé snapped.

"Where's your associate, Daryl?" Justice asked.

Lenny raised his eyebrows in innocence. "Why would I tell a couple of pigs where Tony is?"

"Do you know where he's been?" asked Justice. "Because I believe you when you said you didn't know about the robberies. But Daryl sure did. And I want to believe you're not a murderer. But I don't know Daryl that well. Do you know where he is right now? Do you know what he's been busy doing lately? Can never trust a guy with a scar."

"Don't you question the loyalty of my guys. Don't you dare come in here and do that."

"I get it, you're a drugged up, whack job family. But you know I'm right." One of the henchman flinched aggressively. "I'm just sayin'."

"Daryl's nickname is Tony," added Dupé, as if he was simply trying to convince a logical man of something very reasonable. "What if it's not just a nickname? I mean, ol' Tony Scarface kills Frank Lopez in the movie. He was never content being under anybody. He was always gunning for number one. And that would be-." Dupé looked around, stupefied.

"Oh, that's you, Lenny," Justice helped out. "He would be coming after you." Both detectives' faces demonstrated their concern and sympathy in the troubling scenario.

"Screw you guys," Lenny answered, a little too forcefully. He tugged at his watch. "You don't know my guys. They answer to me and they respect me."

"Is that so?" asked Justice skeptically. "Is that right, guys?" Justice asked, turning to the men by the front door?" They sneered at him.

"Let us help you," reasoned Justice. "God knows I would love to throw you in the slammer, but unfortunately even the police department has bureaucratic nonsense."

"You mean they have a leash on their bitches," smiled Lenny. The goons nudged each other and sniggered.

Dupé was about to let a string of obscenities loose against Lenny and his drugged up failures, but the look in Justice's eyes told him not to. Justice leaned forward in the recliner. His voice was so low that Lenny involuntarily leaned forward to hear the words over the heat-induced drone of insects outside. "Someday, this dog is going to chew through his leash and you'll have nowhere to hide. Not that smart mouth of yours or your punks-for-hire will keep you from my wrath. Justice will rain down on you until your friends can't recognize your face, and they'll have to find your teeth first before they can try to identify you. Don't think for one second, Lenny, that your standing here right now is due in any part to my inability to act. Every morning

I get up just to put punks like you away. This is who I am. There is only justice. Believe me, you'll pay for everything you do, and if there's a god, I pray to him that it's me who gets to bring you down."

Justice stopped talking, face hardened into a terrifying mix of intimidation and glee. The insects continued, but inside the room was silent. Dupé looked at Lenny whose mouth was slightly agape. Lenny closed his mouth and licked his lips. Dupé saw his Adam's apple bob as he swallowed hard. His voice came out almost as softly as Justice's had, but it faltered where Justice's had remained clear and unwavering. "I, I started my own investigation. A couple of my guys reported, they reported coke on some streets that I, uh, have interest in. There are murmurs of a guy, some ghost. I don't' know. They just sound like bull. There's always some big fish, like some scary ghost story for, uh, people in my line of work. Someone said a name—Protoras or something like that. Foreign, Russian, or Eastern European sounding. I don't know. It sounds made up, but I've seen the coke." He was breathing hard when he finished speaking.

"Do you have the coke now?" Justice asked calmly.

"I got rid of it." Lenny looked away as he said it.

"Of course," Dupé said. Lenny shot him an icy look. His fists were clenched.

Justice hauled his large frame out of the recliner and stretched his back. "I'd be careful Lenny. Loose cannon running around, that Daryl Starkman. I'd find him. You might want to help us out. If you can't keep your turf safe, what use do we have for you?" Dupé started to follow Justice toward the door. Justice stopped and winked at Lenny. "The leash will come off eventually."

Chapter 23

Lenny watched the two detectives through the blinds of the large window in the front room. The Challenger started with a roar, backed up, and then rolled through the open gate. After the two guards had closed the gate and returned to their assigned positions, he stood tall and put his arms behind his head with fingers interlocked. He stood this way for maybe two minutes before turning to his men who remained in the front room with him. "One of you make yourself useful and get me a beer," he said suddenly. The tall dark man left the room and came back shortly with a can of beer.

"Do you think it's Tony, Lenny? Do you think he would do that?" asked the tall man.

"I don't know," mused Lenny. "But for Daryl's sake, I hope he wouldn't. Because if I get any whiff of you guys doing something like that, I'll make an exception and kill you myself."

The three men looked at each other and nodded in agreement. "You can count on us, boss," they affirmed.

Lenny cracked open the beer and took a long swig. He wiped his mouth and headed toward his bedroom in the back of the house. He walked through a dining area where two guys were placing money in duffle bags. They looked up and nodded as he walked through.

The two guards by the gate watched the black Challenger as it rolled past the gate and onto the neighborhood street. They had just closed the gate when the curly-haired guard's cell phone rang.

"Yeah?" he said taking the call. "Now?" His quiet question contained a mixture of anxiety and excitement. "Of course. Yeah. OK. I'll tell them. Yeah. OK." He hung up the phone without saying goodbye. The other guard looked at him expectantly. "We're just supposed to leave."

"That's it?"

"Yeah, text the others. I'll go get the keys."

"You're sure about this?"

"I'm not sure about anything, but I'm sure as hell not staying here to see what happens. Come on." The curly haired man swung the gate wide and trotted to the house, while his partner began furiously mashing the keys on his cell phone.

"That guy pisses me off. Explain why we can't take him down again?" Dupé's hands were balled into fists. He felt the nails press into his palms, and he relaxed his fingers.

"Rules of the game. Rules of a twisted game where we allow him to get our kids high, so that we can keep the *really* bad stuff off our streets. Only problem is, apparently that stuff is on our streets too now."

"Do you believe him?"

"I *believe* he knows as little about all this as we do. But I wouldn't trust him to make Easy Mac by recipe. He's a lazy piece of crap who wanted to make money as quickly as possible, as easily as possible. So he got into drugs. Expanding an operation into a full blown drug cartel isn't his idea of a good time, and frankly it's way out of his league."

"We have to find Daryl," Dupé mused. Justice didn't answer. "We need to head back to the station," Dupé continued, looking at Justice. "Cap's going to be wondering where we are."

"Captain McMann can wait a little while longer. It won't hurt him. I want to see if Maya knows anymore about this Proto guy or whoever he is." He pulled out his phone and hit a pre-set button.

Marla came to the window as the alluring sound of Justice's Challenger beckoned once more. She found herself smiling like a little school girl. She couldn't help it, she told herself. Justice was everything any girl dream up when it came to a heroic man who stood for the common people. His dark, tanned skin. The stubble of the man who didn't care about shaving as much as he cared about saving. His brooding, dark eyes. His jet black hair, equal parts disheveled and perfectly placed. She placed a hand on the back of her neck, watching the fading hero in his vehicle.

The Challenger had reached the end of her street and turned right, the rumble fading into the low murmur of the July ambiance. Marla was about to go back to her room to study, when she heard another vehicle coming down the street from the direction Detective Justice had just come. She turned and saw four cars driving bumper to bumper. She immediately recognized the cars as those of Lenny's crew. She had memorized their bright metallic paint schemes and chrome detailed exteriors over the years, at first watching their comings and goings with nervous curiosity and finally observing them with an almost dutiful reproach. She had always marveled at the gaudy decorations, most likely over-compensating for something. She smiled, remembering one of the low-riders leaking hydraulic fluid and dragging along the street like a dying animal. She had tears in her eyes when she was done laughing that day.

The four cars turned left at the end of the street. Marla lingered at the window. She wasn't sure why. No more than forty seconds later, two black Chevrolet Tahoes with tinted windows turned onto Marla's street from the same direction the four cars had turned. They maintained a steady, residential speed. The sky shown vibrant blue with full sunshine, yet a darkness seemed to follow in their wake.

Chapter 24

Tammy Shaw glanced down at her pocket as her phone started vibrating. A small, pale child read in a staccato cadence about the adventures of an anthropomorphic pork chop named Jimmy. Several kids were scattered around the library reading in small groups. When she saw the ID, she turned to the pale boy reading and said, "Very good! Keep reading, Shawn." Despite the school staff policy, she answered the call. "Blake, I'm in the middle of a class!"

"Yeah, but you picked up," Justice retorted with a grin. Dupé could hear a female voice on the other end of the line, but he couldn't make out what she was saying. He mouthed *who is it* to Justice, who ignored him. "Listen, I need you to check something out for me."

"What?"

"I need you to get any information you can on a guy named Protoros or Protar—something like that. It's eastern European or Russian or something."

"Seriously, Blake? Isn't this your job? Don't you have people for this?"

"I don't want *people*," Blake said slowly. "I want you."

"Ever heard of Google?"

"Please, Google is for amateurs. You're a professional."

"Of course I am, but flattery goes straight to my thighs. Fine, I'll do it. You sure have given me a lot of good information for me to find this guy."

Justice heard her saying something to someone he assumed was one of her kids. He paused and then said, "Hey, come on. You're telling me you don't like this kind of stuff?"

"Of course I do," she replied.

"It certainly beats that boring job of yours." He knew this would get her riled up. Even Dupé could make out the agitated response on the other end.

"I love my job, thank you very much. I wouldn't be doing it if I didn't." Several of the kids stopped reading and looked up at Tammy who was now pacing. When she saw the reaction, she quickly sat down and continued in an intense whisper. "Of course I love working my magic on a computer, but my heart is for children, and I believe God put me here for them."

Dupé watched Justice hold up a hand in mock defense. Justice looked over with wide eyes and a smile. "She just brought God into the conversation," he whispered to Dupé.

Dupé shook his head and laughed. He almost uttered the ironic "Jesus", but changed it into "geesh" for fear of getting backhanded by the lunatic at the wheel. He wasn't sure if it would have offended his partner. Though he was getting a better read than when he initially started, he still couldn't completely decipher Detective Blake Justice. He wondered if there was anyone who really could.

Tammy had stopped for a breath. Justice chuckled. "I'm just playing with you, Tammy. You're my Terri. I think you would be the best computer-coder-elementary-librarian-spy, so I'll just have to keep your skills sharp. God would want you stopping bad guys. Let me know when you get something."

"If I get something," she conceded.

"Of course you will," he replied smiling. Then his features became harsher, more severe. "Elizabeth, I need you to do me a favor."

"Did you just forget the last five minutes of conversation?"

"This is more important. It's about Elizabeth."

"OK," Tammy finally said.

"Listen, somebody roughed her up, stole the money I gave her. Just left her half-conscious in the middle of a parking lot-" He stopped, voice tense with rage. He continued in a more measured tone. "Can you stop by? Check in on her? See if she's OK, if she needs anything? I don't know, as a woman or something."

Tammy's hand was covering her open mouth. She uncovered her mouth and said, "Of course, Blake. I'll go right after school. Just text me her address. I'm so sorry."

"Thanks, Tammy. I owe you one."

"You owe me for the cryptic name hunt, Blake, but not for this. Of course I'll see if she's OK."

"Thanks." After saying goodbye, Justice hung up.

"So Tammy knows about, uh, Elizabeth?" Dupé asked with eyes wide.

"Why shouldn't she?" Justice asked with an edge.

"Oh, I don't know. Just trying to help my partner think straight."

"There's nothing to hide."

"If you say so. Wow. So where to now?"

"Off to see if the shrew has seen a snake," he said quietly.

"You mean, off to see Maya about this Proto guy," Dupé practically burst out. "Ooo, I'm Justice and I'm cryptic."

Justice slammed on the brakes, forcing a grunt out of Dupé as the seatbelt dug into his chest. "What was that for?" Dupé screamed.

Justice took a toothpick out of custom plastic case, placed it between his molars, and slowly accelerated back to the speed limit. "Who knows? I'm cryptic."

Chapter 25

Lenny relaxed as the cool leather enveloped him. The dark armchair was perfect. He knew it had been a good purchase. He smiled and opened the laptop. He knew good purchases; it's what had helped him climb the distribution ladder in Avon. And he was smart too. Maybe not for standardized tests and the lot, but he was savvy, sharp. He could read people. The laptop whirred to life. Daryl Starkman, Tony. The name slid into his mind, unsure of whether it should be a pleasant thought or not. He had known him for what, 8 years? They had been dealing near the middle school in the beginning. It wasn't as if they were friends (you couldn't be friends with a rival dealer), but they had never encroached on each other's turf or clients when they were starting out. He would often see him at the Taco Bell in the late afternoons, or if the weather was bad. 3 hard tacos, a cinnamon twist, and a large drink. Every time. Tony was predictable. He had a nose for the business, but he never could think outside of the joint. Lean on the kids he knew; get them to recruit for him. Good, safe plan. But he couldn't think very far ahead.

The detectives didn't know Daryl like he knew him. They were law. What could they know about anything in his outfit? He *was* smart, Lenny told himself. Win the game a little at a time. Don't just chuck it up there. A lot of the cops liked the grass; there would be no incentive for them to get rid of his operation. He gave them discounts and worked diligently against all competition. The cops kept out of his way for the most part. That fat idiot Captain McMann thought he controlled Lenny's operation. Of course he did. All lawmen were high and mighty, felt invincible. Lenny had never seen McMann touch the stuff himself, but everybody had their secrets. He was probably a flower child back then. Why wouldn't he take a hit? And the Captain was the type of bastard who would gladly watch someone else take the fall to keep his own hands clean. But what Captain McMann did privately was of little concern to Lenny. As long as the fat slob thought he had his hands around the distribution, Lenny could go about doing things the way he always had.

Keep the cocaine out, keep the distribution manageable. Don't get in over your head. He was smart. He was taking all their asses to the cleaners. He caressed the imitation leather under his hand. Don't forget your roots, he thought. Of course he liked nice things. He had to clean up this dump hell-hole his mom had left when he had thrown her lazy ass out. She would have kept him from achieving, he had always justified to himself. She was lazy, a moocher. He had practically taken care of her. Powdered donut. He took another swig from the Coors can.

Keep things simple. Nothing beat a nice deep dish and a cold beer. Lenny sipped at the can. Yeah, driving a Mercedes CLA coupe was nice, but he deserved *that* after all. Something had to set him apart. And set him apart, it did. He laughed when he thought of Tony's piece of crap car.

No, Daryl didn't seem the double crosser type. He wouldn't. He didn't have it in him. Too safe.

Lenny stood up and walked to the back window. The back yard was in heavy shade from large oak trees; it looked deceptively cool. Maybe this Protoros guy was just stupid talk. But the coke was real. He had seen it personally. One of his guys had confirmed it, and he had promptly had it all dumped down the toilet. The man who had confirmed it protested, but he quickly agreed after a broken nose and bloody mouth. He cringed. Memories flooded back to him. The stale cigarette air, fast food wrappers in the corner. His mother, eyes wide, unblinking. When he was little, he had asked if he could have the powdered donuts too. Crusted blood and coke under the nose. He closed his eyes hard and turned to the door.

"Blaze," he shouted. He wasn't going to just sit here as his territory was pulled out from underneath him. He wasn't a fan of violence, but sometimes it was a necessary business strategy. "Blaze," he shouted once more. He had already picked up his 9mm from the table next to his laptop and tucked it into the waist of his pants. He had gotten soft. It was time to go hard. What the hell was Blaze doing? He stopped and listened. He didn't hear anything. Even the cicadas had stopped. Lenny quickly removed his pistol from his waist, holding it down at his side. "Blaze," he called out once more. This time it was used as a sounding beacon, in hopes of getting a bearing on the situation.

The continued silence brought all of Lenny's senses to attention. He walked boldly into the room where Blaze and Moe had been counting the money. They weren't there; neither were the duffels of bills. He swore under his breath and gripped the stock tighter. He moved through the small hallway slowly, but deliberately. This was his house. He wasn't going to crawl. His neck tingled with adrenaline. Lenny moved into living room but stopped when he saw the open door. He picked up movement in his peripheral and swung his gun toward the corner of the room.

There, with his legs crossed and an easy air of confidence, sat a man overly dressed for the summer in black fatigues. His bald head was perfectly round and ended in an angular jaw. Silver stubble covered a weathered face. The man's eyes were crystal blue and untelling.

"Who the hell are you, old man? And where are my guys?" demanded Lenny, looking around. The man didn't seem bothered by the weapon in his face, and simply gestured toward the seat next to Lenny. Lenny didn't know if the guy was insane or just an arrogant prick. "You don't make the demands," he shouted in disbelief. "This is my playground. Tell me why I shouldn't blow your head off right here."

"You wouldn't want to do that," the man answered quietly.

The light bulb went off in Lenny's head. "Protoros!".

The man threw his head back and let out a genuine laugh. "Protoros. That's a new one." He shook his head smiling. Then his visage became grim once more. "Protagoras," he enunciated clearly. "It's Protagoras."

"You have the nerve to start dealing coke on my turf and then you come in my house? You've got some balls, man, but that was real stupid coming here."

As if they had somehow materialized out of thin air, Lenny was suddenly aware of several more men by the door. All of them wore black ski masks and the same combat fatigues. Lenny froze trying to process what was happening. All of them had pistols in leg holsters and carried fierce looking automatics. They stood perfectly still, silhouetted by the brilliant sunshine coming through the open door. In a fluid movement, one of them reached back with a foot and closed the door. The noise snapped Lenny to attention, and he turned away from the man in the chair, raising his 9mm to firing position. The silence ended in deafening staccato, dark silhouettes of the men simultaneously illuminated by multiple muzzles erupting in light.

Down at the end of the street, Marla sat up from staring at a paragraph on foreign financial policy. The sound of gunfire, most people on the street had heard it before, registered in the back of her mind. Once identified, however, the sound was gone as quickly as it had come. As was customary in similar situations, Marla quickly found Alex and Roberto and pulled them close behind their bunk bed. She imagined her neighbors were doing the same thing. Her mom wouldn't be home from work until later that evening. Alex and Roberto were silent, taking their cues from their older sister. Marla lay down on the ground, holding her brothers and praying. After what seemed like an hour, she wiped her face and sat up.

Chapter 26

Justice played through the actions of the past few weeks. Robberies of the local businesses. One of Lenny's crew murdered. Lenny's number two missing. Rumors of a crime lord. There had to be some connection, but he wasn't seeing it. Or maybe they were completely random. Life wasn't like the movies, but even the movies understood that most events weren't random. He needed to find Daryl "Tony" Starkman. His gut told him that all of this somehow revolved around him. He and Lenny seemed like the two most obvious suspects. And if this Proto guy was real, well, he needed more information then.

Dupé finally broke the silence. "Can I ask you a question?" he asked as he stared out the window.

"I don't know, can you?"

"Really?" Dupé asked, turning toward Justice. "We're in third grade now?" He paused as if trying to find the right words to say. "Do you ever get sick of any of this?"

Justice shifted and eased the powerful Challenger through the sharp curve in the road. "Naw, I love driving."

"I'm serious."

"So am I. If I wasn't a detective, I'd be racing somewhere. I love when the perps try and run."

"Do you ever feel like you're actually making a difference? Like you're actually making the community safer or if it's just some endless, repetitive task that will never see any progress?"

"Say all of that in the first place next time instead of a vague, leading question."

"Whatever. I've asked you now. Do you?"

"So do I feel like Sisyphus rolling a giant stone of justice up the mountain of crime just to watch it roll back down and have to start all over every time a new criminal pops up?"

"Sure. That was my question. Do you feel like that?"

Justice sat quietly for a moment. Then he answered, "The thought creeps into my mind sometimes. Pretty much anytime I see Lenny. He shouldn't be there, free like that. He should be behind bars. *That* makes me sick. But that's part of being a cop I guess."

"What if it wasn't?"

"What do you mean?"

"Well, can you imagine if we could just get all the criminals off the streets, no more criminals popping up behind them?"

"I suppose we can dream, huh? I know how I would handle the situation." Justice paused. "But then I had a preacher saying that a murderous king should be treated with honor. Changes the story. I'm glad he's not a cop." Justice laughed.

"Preacher?" Dupé asked incredulously.

"Ah, Tammy wanted me to go to church with her on Sunday. She's asked me since I can remember, so I figured I owed it to her."

"Boy she's got you whipped." Justice shot Dupé a look. "So how was that? You get saved? Find some Jesus?"

"They wanted me to leave my guns in my car."

"I thought they were all about Jesus and guns. Probably have paintings of Jesus and his AR-15."

"Well not this church. They acted like I was bringing a whole arsenal inside the sanctuary or something."

"Why the hell were you bringing your guns into church anyway? You didn't have your vest did you?"

Justice reached over and smacked Dupé in the mouth with the back of his hand.

"Gah, all right! Geesh." Dupé rubbed his mouth. "I get it. So you don't swear. Who doesn't swear but they've only been to church once? What do you have against a colorful vocabulary?"

"It shows a lack of intelligence to come up with alternative words."

"So you *did* bring your vest?"

"Of course I did. You never know when something's going to go down."

"Man, I don't get you. You don't need guns in a church, man. They might throw a Bible at you, but you have your vest for that. We need the guns out here. But all we get is these little pea shooters." Dupé took out his G25 .380 Auto. "Look at this. What am I supposed to do with this if the perp is going full auto?"

"Be a better shot. Fight smarter. It's not always the guy carrying the bigger gun who wins."

"Says the guy carrying two custom .45's. Right. All I'm saying is that we're supposed to protect our citizens and ourselves, but the armament they give us is a joke."

"Yeah, well, take it up with finances. Budget cuts aren't going to allow for all the stuff you're dreaming about."

"Maybe," said Dupé. "There's so much bureaucracy and red-tape bull crap. If they left law enforcement up to us and not some big wig politicians, we'd be fine. We wouldn't have to put up with trash like Lenny."

Justice drove in silence. He had thought about these things before, what things would be like if he was in charge. It was true that most police precincts were undermanned—

underpersonned (he had learned that "manned" was incorrect), and they were usually vastly underarmed. But perhaps it was good that not all cops had that much firepower. It could present the illusion of invulnerability or worse, corruption of power. Justice spoke. "Hopefully Avon will never see that day when we bring in bazookas and tanks. Yeah, it can be a cesspool, but there are criminals far worse than Lenny out there. It could always be worse." Dupé shrugged and settled in for the ride. Justice swallowed, remembering holding his mother's hand but not feeling her touch as uniformed officers knelt down to say that his daddy was a good man and Justice should be proud of him. It was odd, his entire life was devoted to this job, and yet he knew that he also wished it wasn't necessary. Maybe the preacher's dream world of forgiveness and pardon wasn't a bad alternative to the reality he faced every day. But until that day came, he would be on the streets dispensing justice.

The black Challenger crept along the curb, like a massive predator waiting for any suspicious movement in its peripheral. Justice and Dupé scanned the groups of shoppers. Colorful groups migrated between the stores in the outdoor mall. Couples sat on benches, and groups of adolescents bantered and played on the stone walls surrounding the fountains. Several sculptures stood like oversized kites made of multi-colored canvas and metal. A wide strip of grass and fountains separated the two streets that ran parallel with the stores. It was part Mayberry, part Consumer USA. Justice eased to a stop at a crosswalk as three girls, loaded down with bags, gave a sideways glance at the impressive car and then giggled amongst themselves. The Challenger could hardly be considered an undercover police vehicle considering its ostentatious presence the moment it pulled up. After the girls passed, the car growled into motion once more.

Dupé pointed. "Is that her?"

Justice followed the direction of the arm. A group of about five college-aged kids dressed in cargo shorts, skater shoes, ironic T-shirts, and an assortment of hair styles sat in a shaded alcove of one of the stores. "I think so."

Maya looked up as the Challenger pulled to the curb and came to a stop. She said something, and her four friends immediately got up and walked briskly in four different directions. Justice and Dupé walked up, watching the other individuals disappear around corners and into the crowds.

Dupé rolled up his sleeves and loosened his tie. It was unbelievable. They had only gotten out of the air-conditioned car a minute ago, and he could already feel the sweat beading up on his forehead and neck. "You've got some shy friends," Justice remarked.

Maya's eyes narrowed. "They don't feel like sharing their company with pigs. I don't blame them."

"Oh come on, we're not that bad, are we?" Justice asked, looking toward Dupé and then back to Maya.

"You guys buddies now? Isn't that cute."

"Yeah, we even have the same colored Trapper Keepers. We need information," Dupé said impatiently.

"Don't you always," Maya said scornfully. "And I don't talk to you. Detective Justice here may be your bosom buddy now, but I still don't know you."

"Oh come on," Dupé started, but Justice stopped him with a slight movement with his hand, as if to say, *not now*.

Justice waited until two guys passed them and entered an Old Navy. He spoke in a hushed voice, "One of your theories may have some validity to it."

"Oh, and which one is that, detective?"

"The ghost theory. The cocaine is showing up more, and there are others who have heard rumors of this new player in town."

Maya put her hands on her hips.

Justice undid the Velcro on one of the pockets on his vest and pulled out a packet of Bold Beef Jerky. He tossed it to Maya. Dupé looked questioningly at the jerky and then at Justice. "What is that?"

"Hey, my services aren't free," snapped Maya.

"You take beef jerky as currency?"

"Hell yeah, I do. This stuff is crazy good."

"How come you don't ever get me any beef jerky," asked Dupé.

"If you can tell me the things Maya does, maybe I'll think about it." Justice turned to Maya. "I have a partial name, but I need something more concrete. Protoras or Proto or something. People have to be talking."

Maya turned and motioned them to follow her. They walked around a corner and moved between two of the stores. It was cooler here. The way it was set up, the alley never received direct sunlight. Maya stopped by one of the store dumpsters. The two detectives waited for her to speak. After checking both entrances to the alley, Maya began in a hushed tone. "I don't have what you need. Just more rumors. But they're picking up. One pendejo was supposed to have been working with this new guy; he hasn't been seen in a couple of days. He's pretty regular. People were getting coke from areas he worked."

"Did he have a name?"

"Most everyone on the street goes by a nickname."

"It wasn't Nos, was it?"

"I think so," Maya said quietly. "It sounds right."

Justice and Dupé looked at each other. "Makes more sense now," Dupé said.

"What does?"

"Your, pendejo, Nos, he drowned fishing. Pretty crappy outdoorsman." Justice picked at his teeth.

Maya shook her head and looked over her shoulder in response. She began again. "I don't know if any of this crap about this ghost dude is true, but it's definitely making a buzz. Like I said, I don't like the spotlight; I lay low when I can. I want to know what I want to know, but I don't want to know anything about this ghost. Gets you into trouble." She was breathing hard. Justice had rarely seen her this anxious. She usually was cool in her arrogance. "But there's a guy who deals here, at the parking garage. He roughed my friend up a couple of weeks ago. I don't have any loyalties to him, and I want to see him off the streets." She emphasized the next sentence. "I don't exist!"

"I don't know who you are," Justice quietly assured her.

"I've seen him hand out coke," she said. "You hear things. Get him to talk. He goes by Noodles."

"Noodles?" said Dupé. "That's kind of racist."

"He's not Asian you dumbass. Now who's racist?"

"Thanks, Maya," Justice said. He and Dupé returned from the way they came. Maya walked in the other direction, exiting the shadow and emerging into blinding, blistering sunlight. She shielded her eyes and pulled out her phone. She moved through a group of people and walked past two guys with Old Navy bags. As she started talking on the phone, the two men stood up and began walking after her. One made a call as well. Both bags remained at the bench, stuffed with old towels.

Chapter 27

Justice and Dupé were both sweating profusely by the time they had walked to parking garage. It was a four level structure, purely functional in design. The busy mall meant that every single space on the bottom level was filled. The two detectives weren't sure where Noodles was supposed to sell from. They split up. The garage floors weren't large, four aisles. After searching the first level, they took the stairs and exited onto the second level. They scanned the garage. It was just as full as the first level. In one of the back corners, they made out the shape of a man leaning against a wall. A faint orange dot of a lit cigarette was just visible in his hand. He looked up as the door boomed shut, echoing through the concrete structure.

The two detectives began walking toward the direction of the individual in the corner. They could see that he was a big man wearing a wife beater that revealed large, undefined arms covered in tattoos. When they were about halfway to him, Justice asked loudly, "Are you Noodles?"

Immediately the man sprinted to a row of cars. "I guess that answers that question," remarked Dupé. The two detectives took off after the man, but he had disappeared a row of minivans. He moved surprisingly well for someone of his size and stature. The two detectives jogged to the end of the row, stooping as they ran to see between the cars. "Noodles, we are detectives with the Avon Police Department. We just want to ask you a few questions. No big deal," Justice announced, not truly believing that his announcement would make much of a difference. He had only encountered one person who had run initially give himself up when Justice called out to him. He had only been 16 and ran because he had cheated on a math test and assumed the detective was investigating. Justice didn't think this situation would turn out quite like that.

Justice motioned for Dupé to continue down the next aisle. They had just started to move once more when "Gypsies, Tramps, and Thieves" blared from Justice's pocket. Dupé looked back wild-eyed and mouthed some words Justice couldn't make out. He pulled out the phone. "Hi, mom. This is a bad time."

Noodles popped out from behind a green mini-van and opened fire on Justice, hitting him in the chest. The concussion from the gunfire was deafening in the concrete garage. Justice staggered and then dove behind a pickup.

"What's all that noise, Blake?" his mother asked in a disapproving tone. "I can hardly hear you."

"Justice! You alright?"

"What? It's a bad time, mom." He popped his head out from behind the truck holding one of his Kimbers in one hand, cell phone in the other. Dupé was crouched behind a vehicle on the other side of the aisle, several rows up. Dupé looked back and Justice gave him a thumbs up. He made out the large frame of Noodles perched behind the van about 12-15 cars away on Dupé's side.

"Blake, this is serious."

"Mom, there is a guy shooting at me. Can we talk later? I'll call you back."

"Well, why are you talking to me right now? Be careful, Blake."

"I will, mom. I promise." Noodles popped off two more shots, taking out a tire and hitting the bed of the pickup truck in front of Justice.

"The men are stalking me again, Blake. They've been at the end of the street watching me."

"It's probably just Mark who's dating Jenny across the street, mom," Justice said through gritted teeth. He dug the slug out of his vest just above his naval. He put it in his pocket.

"They're in a big black truck. You need to do something, Blake!"

"Mom, I love you. I'll call you later. It's probably just a neighbor. Goodbye." He hung up the phone. He leaned out far enough that he could see Dupé. Dupé noticed him.

"You done?" Dupé whispered in a hoarse voice.

"It was my mom," Justice mouthed in exaggerated facial expressions. "Sorry."

Noodles shot again, this time in Dupé's direction. "You're making this harder on yourself, Noodles!" Dupé shouted. Noodles didn't reply. Dupé knelt down and peered out past the wheel well. He could see the side of Noodle's back sticking out slightly beyond the wheel of the van. Dupé could hit him; he actually had a shot, but he was worried about killing him. They needed him alive. He looked back to Justice who was motioning that he wanted Dupé to flank Noodles. Just then Noodles took another shot and started running toward the exit door. Dupé popped up, gun drawn, but pulled it down again. He began to run, hugging the vehicles in case Noodles decided to turn and shoot some more.

Justice assessed the situation. Noodles was hurtling toward the only stairs in the garage, with Dupé cautiously running behind him. He drew his Kimber, fired twice into the concrete ceiling and took off at dead sprint toward the railing behind him. He vaulted it, throwing himself over the railing, plummeting toward the ground. He adjusted his body in mid-air so as to stay upright and hit the ground in a crouch, propelling his momentum forward into a somersault in order to minimize the impact on his ankles and knees. Immediately he popped up from the roll and began sprinting toward the stairs on the far end of the garage. People were taking cover all around him after hearing the gunshots, but his eyes were focused only on the Exit sign. Noodles had a good head start and moved well for a big guy, but at 6'5," Justice had a massive stride, and his years as a wide receiver in high school showed. His 240 pounds of muscle fed off of the exertion and kicked into overdrive. The cars were a blur now.

Noodles reached the door to the stairwell and turned to fire at Dupé who ducked behind the closest vehicle. When the gun clicked empty, Noodles threw open the door and leapt down the stairs, taking two at a time. He was beginning to wheeze now; the all-out sprint was taking an effect. But he was so close, if he could just get to where the people were, he would lose them for sure. This was his territory, after all.

Justice was closing fast on the Exit door. He frantically waved a couple away from the door, his legs pumping as oversized pistons. The door cracked open and Justice leapt toward it, one leg coiled.

Noodles had the door about halfway open when Justice's leg shot out with a massive boot slamming the steel door shut. Justice felt the impact on the other side and quickly drew his gun, pulling the door open. Noodles was on the ground, rolling to his side and reaching for his gun which must have been jarred loose on contact. Justice's boot stomped down hard on Noodle's wrist, pinning it to the ground and causing Noodles to cry out in pain. The massive detective leaned forward, placing more weight on Noodle's wrist and drew both .45's, pointing them at Noodle's face. "I said we needed to ask you a few questions."

When Dupé finally reached the bottom of the stairs, Noodles was handcuffed to the railing rubbing his wrist, his nose bleeding. Justice was standing in front of the closed door, thumbs tucked in his vest and feet shoulder width apart. Dupé stood there a moment, looking at the two men, trying to regain his breath. "You're fast," Dupé said breathing hard. "How did you get down here? There's only one staircase."

Justice looked calm and collected, like he had been standing in that exact position for the past ten minutes. "I made my own."

"You jumped off of the garage?" Dupé asked in wonder.

Even Noodles lifted his head at that. "Damn, man. You're crazy!"

Justice took one giant step over to Noodles and punched him squarely in the nose. "Don't swear. It's ignorant." Noodles howled and held his nose with both hands.

"Ah know mah rahts," Noodles sputtered through the blood and his hands. "Ah wahnt mah lawer or sumthin."

"We haven't caught you yet," Justice said coolly, stepping back to his position at the door.

"Wha?" murmured Noodles.

"You tried to kill us with no provocation, and now you're talking about your rights? Screw your rights, you fat piece of crap," growled Dupé.

"No one's seen us catch you," Justice continued. "You fired at us, then there was a chase, but I don't think we've apprehended you yet. Now we have some questions we need to ask you before we catch you. Now we could catch you with little incident, or there could be a big fist fight during the arrest where you take a few more punches to the face. That's all I'm saying."

Noodles looked up at Dupé. "Don't look at me," the sandy haired detective replied. "This isn't good cop, bad cop. I'd advise you to answer the questions."

"Ok, man. Ok."

"Dupé, search him." Noodles sat still, holding one hand over his nose, as Dupé patted him down and went through his pockets. Dupé took four bags out of one pocket and eight bags out of the other.

"Oh, my, detective," Dupé exaggerated. "What do we have here?"

"If I'm not mistaken, is that marijuana *and* cocaine, Noodles? I didn't even know you could get snow around here; at least not in July." Noodles sat quietly. "What did we say, Noodles?"

Noodles sat up, attentive. "Yes, yes, it's weed and coke."

"And what?" asked Dupé.

"And what, what?"

"Did you process this cocaine?"

"Hell no I didn't make it."

"So where did you get it?" asked Justice.

"I just got it."

"You just got it? That doesn't sound like you're cooperating," said Dupé.

"Alright, alright. There's a new guy. Lots of people are distributing now through him. He's got good caviar. The best."

Dupé tossed a bag to Justice, who pulled a knife from his vest, flipped it open and made a small puncture in the bag. He pressed his finger to the puncture so that a couple particles stuck to his finger. He touched his finger to his tongue, and his eyes dilated. "*That* is pure. So how is pure cocaine getting into Plainfield and Avon, Indiana, Noodles?"

"I don't know how it's shipped or made or anything like that. I just sell it."

"So you're just a dumb piece of crap who doesn't know anything?" asked Dupé. Noodles nodded.

"So the coke just materializes in your hand?" asked Justice. Noodles shook his head no. "I'm losing my patience Noodles. I don't have time for 20 questions."

Noodles tilted his head back to try and stop the bleeding. He looked as if he was about to cry. Finally he started in, "Every week, a car comes by. I toss 75% of what I make into an open window in the back."

"What do they look like?"

"It's tinted windows, man. They don't let me see their faces."

"What day and time do they come?"

"It's always different. It's never the same time or day. I just have to be ready."

"What happens if you're not?"

"I ain't letting that happen."

"So then what?"

"So I toss a stack in their window, they toss out the stuff, and they're gone. Except they're never gone."

"What makes you say that?"

"I can just tell. It's a feeling, like I'm always being watched or something."

"Who's the main guy?"

"Man, I've never seen the drop guy. How would I know the boss? He doesn't deal with me."

Justice rubbed at his dark stubble. "Detective Dupé, I keep hearing about this *new* guy in town. But I've never seen him. Have you?"

Dupé looked hard at Noodles. "No, I haven't, detective. This is the first time I've even seen the supposed cocaine."

"Same here," said Justice. "Noodles here doesn't see anyone or know anything, yet here he is, making it snow in July. I think we nailed the big dog, Dupé. Well done."

Noodles began to look back and forth in confusion. "Wait."

"Well done, yourself, Detective Justice. You were the one jumping off of buildings," replied Dupé.

"No, wait!" pleaded Noodles.

"All right. Call it in that we've nabbed our top suspect in the new cocaine ring, Dupé."

"Protagoras! Freidrick Protagoras. That's it. I remember. That's the name. But I've never met him, I swear. I never met none of 'em." Noodles was almost sniveling.

Justice knelt down to eye level with Noodles. "Protagoras." Noodles nodded solemnly. "How do you spell— never mind. Freidrick Protagoras?" Noodles nodded again in earnest. Dupé had his pen and pad out. Justice uncuffed Noodles from the railing, stood him up, and then handcuffed his hands behind his back. "We need to get him down to the station and then start putting all resources into finding out who the heck this Protagoras guy is."

The three men stepped out of the stairwell and into the parking garage. There were sirens in the distance. The remaining people in the area were watching the two detectives and the large, handcuffed man walking tightly in between them. Most were talking on their phones, snapping pictures, or recording the incident. They watched the two detectives holding onto the man's arms, which were handcuffed behind him. His nose was bleeding and he looked at the ground. The two detectives had their phones out in their free hands, the slender one dialing, and the massive one talking on his.

Noodle's head jerked back violently, pink mist in the air behind him. The man between the two cops went limp and the detectives ducked down, looking around frantically. The loud crack echoed off of several buildings in all different directions. The phone cameras, wild at first, then focusing back on the detectives, picked up the pool of crimson red blurred between rippling waves of heat coming off the sidewalk. The lawmen waved people back with demonstrative movements, but most people were behind whatever cover they could find, though they weren't quite sure of where the shot came from. Squad cars screeched to a stop soon after the gunshot with sirens blaring and officers scurrying out from their vehicles like roaches caught in a kitchen light.

"Where the hell did it come from?" Dupé was yelling, as both detectives dragged Noodle's body behind a car.

"Over there, from those buildings," Justice replied, cautiously pointing to some restaurants and hotels. "Officer! Get those people out of here, and start setting up a perimeter! I want half of you securing the mall area, and half of you searching those buildings over there. Report anything suspicious. Go!"

The young officer nodded and sprinted away, hunched over. Dupé and Justice waited, but there were no further shots.

"Didn't you get shot?" Dupé asked suddenly, remembering the shootout in the garage.

Justice opened up the vest pocket and pulled out the round. "Gonna have to do better than that to slow me down. I've had paintball hits that stung more. Unfortunately our friend here wasn't afforded such a luxury." Justice looked at the lifeless body and the massive head wound. "Right in the noodle," he murmured.

Chapter 28

Captain McMann shook both detectives' hands. "I'm glad to hear you're alright. What's this about you getting shot, though, Justice?"

"Got my vest. No biggie. Just an idiot with decent aim. Well, an idiot who got his head blown off, God rest his soul."

"He hurdled the second story railing to get the guy," Dupé said.

McMann smiled. "Always have to do it the hard way?"

Justice shrugged. "Dupé flushed him out and led him right to me."

At this, McMann showed visible surprise. "Working as a team, then?"

"Sure. Why not."

"I'm glad to hear it," McMann said heartily. He grew somber. "So tell me what the hell happened out there."

Dupé spoke up first. "Sniper. Waited until we were out in the open. He obviously knew where we were and where we would be heading. He was just waiting for us. It was a perfect shot, dead center of the forehead. Instant kill. He was professional."

"Justice? What are you thinking? I know that look."

"Whoever it was could have just as easily killed us too. He didn't fire another shot. He didn't take out any civilians and he didn't kill us. He was there for Noodles only."

"Noodles?" McMann asked with raised eyebrows.

"The suspect," clarified Dupé. "He wasn't even Asian." Justice shot Dupé a look. "What? It's worth noting."

"What did you arrest him for?"

"Well besides shooting an officer and running, he was in possession of coke that he supposedly got from this ghost crime lord," Justice said.

"This ghost guy again," McMann said, rubbing his fat chin. "And they kill the best lead before you could get him back here. Damn."

"We have the product. And we got a name. The same name Lenny threw out, more or less."

"What were you doing at Lenny's?"

"One of his guys was killed at Eagle Creek Reservoir."

"That was one of Lenny's guys?"

"Yeah," Dupé said. "He went by Nos. Real nice guy."

"One of my informants said he hadn't shown up in his usual spots in a couple of days," Justice added.

"They made it look like an accident, but he was killed. Pretty sloppy. We'll know more after the autopsy, but Justice figured we could at least pay Lenny a visit and see what he knew about it. Lenny told us about this supposed Protor or something."

"Protor?"

Dupé continued. "Well, that's what he told us. He couldn't remember what the name had been. Well, this Noodles told us the same thing. Protagoras. Freidrick Protagoras."

McMann shifted his position in his chair and immediately opened his drawer to pull out a cigar. Justice watched and pulled out a toothpick for himself. "Freidrick Protagoras," repeated McMann as he lit his cigar.

"That's what he said," said Justice. "Ever heard of him?"

McMann shook his head. "We'll check the databases and put out a notice. The last thing we're going to do is let some freakin' crime boss set up shop in our backyard. Let's keep Avon the beautiful town she is."

Chapter 29

"Listen, I know you didn't have to come over here. So, thank you." Elizabeth gave a weak smile that accented her black and yellow eye. The swelling had gone down a great deal.

"Blake told me what happened. I'm so sorry. Whatever I can do. How's Molly Grace doing?"

"My friend was with her." Elizabeth's response was sharper than she had intended. "She's fine," she continued. "This happens from time to time." She turned and went to the fridge, taking out two Sprites. She held one up and Tammy accepted. Elizabeth poured both the cans over ice and gave one glass to Tammy. Tammy watched as Elizabeth moved to the counter with her back to Tammy, and took out a small pill bottle. She washed a couple blue pills down with her drink. "Prescription," she said.

Tammy merely smiled and nodded. "If you ever need me to watch Molly Grace, I'd be more than happy to. I'm usually leaving school by 3:45, 4 at the latest."

Elizabeth took another drink. Her blond hair hung over her bruised eye. Tammy wasn't sure if this was intentional or not. Elizabeth looked Tammy directly in her eyes. Finally she spoke. "You know what I do, right?"

"Yes, I do."

"I don't need charity. I'm not ashamed of who I am." Elizabeth paused, waiting for a response—one that was expected? Tammy waited. Elizabeth started once more, a little less sure of herself. "Detective Justice has told me you go to church."

Tammy's voice was gentle. "I do. Christ's Chapel Christian Church, off of 10th street."

"Well, so, I don't need saving."

Tammy laughed. "You're worried I'm making judgments about you."

Elizabeth frowned and wiped at the condensation on her glass.

"But here I am coming over to your apartment because our mutual friend told me you had been hurt, and you assume I'm here to throw a Bible at you?"

"I, I'm sorry, it's just-"

"Listen, sweetheart. I don't know you. Only what Blake has told me. I know he cares for you. And a friend of Blake's is a friend of mine. What do I think of you? I think you are a mother trying to take care of her daughter, and someone hurt you. I know that the God who I worship made both of us and loves you very much. The Jesus I know would have been right here sipping Sprite with you. I'm here because I care that you were hurt." She paused and then added, "And I think Blake's idea of support is a tactical vest and backup."

The two women laughed and Elizabeth put her head down. When she raised it, there was a rim of moisture accumulating in her eyes. "Thank you," she whispered.

The sun was beginning to set when Elizabeth hugged Tammy at the front door. "I can't believe you didn't like *The Labyrinth*."

Tammy shrugged. "Just not a big David Bowie fan."

"But it wasn't just David Bowie," said an exasperated Elizabeth. "It was the music, the characters, the puppets. It was the whole atmosphere."

"We're going to have to drop this because you're not going to convince me to like it, and I'm not going to convince you that it was mediocre at best."

"Oh, so you went there, huh? Wow." Elizabeth grew more somber. "Thanks again. I'm glad Detective Justice called you. I, I enjoyed it."

"I did too," Tammy agreed. She opened the door and stepped into the hot night. The AC had seemed negligible in the apartment until she stepped back out into the elements. She began to walk down the sidewalk when she noticed a black SUV parked at the end of the parking lot, next to an older model Toyota Camry. She wasn't exactly sure what made her notice the vehicle. It was dark with tinted windows; she couldn't see anybody inside, but she felt like she was being watched. Then she realized what caught her attention. There were three antennas on it.

Tammy opened her purse and pretended to search through it. She made an exaggerated sighing gesture, and walked back inside the apartment.

"Did you forget something?" Elizabeth said in mild surprise at seeing Tammy walk in without knocking.

"There's an SUV out there that looks suspicious. I don't know. With what happened to you, I don't want to take any chances." She took out her cell-phone and parted the blinds. The SUV was gone.

Chapter 30

"Mom?"

"It's late, Blake."

"I know, I'm sorry. It's been a busy day."

"Well, I've been scared out of my mind."

Justice heard the tremors in her voice over the phone. She was truly shaken. "Do you want me to come over?" Honey was sitting in his lap licking her paws. She didn't weigh more than fifteen pounds, but he could feel his right leg beginning to fall sleep.

"I could have already been dead or kidnapped, Blake." Wanda was clearly hurt. More than usual.

"Mom, I wasn't ignoring you. I just got home."

"You were being shot at!"

"I'm OK, mom. Really."

"Of course you are. You're invincible. Just like your daddy."

Justice put his head in his hand. "Mom."

"You're going to be gone soon, and then it's just going to be me. How lucky. I'll get to attend my husband's and son's funerals. Not every woman gets to do that."

Justice poured a small amount of Old Scout into his mouth from his glass. He held it there momentarily and then swallowed. "That's not going to happen. You know why I do this. You know why dad did this. I want to stop the kind of people who killed dad. The people of Avon need someone to bring the criminals to justice. They need protection."

"Who's protecting you, baby? What about me? Who can look after me when I'm throwing dirt on your coffin?" Wanda's voice was a wavering mix of anger and sorrow. There was silence on both ends and then she spoke again. "There was a truck at the end of the street all day. Just sitting there. I'm being watched."

"Is it there right now?" asked Justice.

"No. It left a couple of hours ago."

"It was probably a neighbor's friend visiting. They can do that, mom. Remember Jenny's boyfriend waiting for her? I scared him half to death. Probably the same thing."

"Well, when I'm dead in the morning, look for a black truck."

"OK, mom. I will. I love you, goodnight."

There was a pause on the other end. "Goodnight."

Justice placed the empty scotch glass in the sink next to the other dirty glasses and plates. He began to place the bottle of scotch in the pantry, but unscrewed the top and took a swig. Dad had always despised the bottle, but he wasn't here, was he? Honey followed Justice back to the bedroom, tail still, as if she knew that her wagging would be inappropriate in the moment. Kimbers on the night stand and the vest on the chair. Honey under the covers. It was a good life, wasn't it? It was the one he wanted. It was what his dad would have wanted.

Was that true? Justice was what mattered most. Law and order. Black and white. It was simple. Grey didn't exist. Criminals are criminals. The innocent are innocent. You don't pardon the enemy. If a god existed, surely he would have a sense of right and wrong. Criminals should face the consequences for their actions. They had made their choices. That was where justice came in. As Justice turned out the light, he wondered what Tammy was doing.

Chapter 31

Officer Jane Grant's eyes scanned the dilapidated apartments and rotting houses like sonar seeking blips of illegal activity. Street lights created bright orange spotlights on the dark asphalt. Officer Mike Cruise hummed to himself, drumming his fingers on his knee as he gazed out his passenger side window. The apartment buildings appeared in rows, like dark silhouetted clones of one another. In them he knew loving families and ruthless scum lived side by side. He had grown up in an apartment complex similar to these, and he had joined the police academy because of what he had witnessed every day. And now things seemed to be getting worse than ever.

Jane slowed down as she came around a turn. Two young adult males were talking in very close proximity to one another. She saw the subtle exchange and they moved in separate directions. She hit the siren and accelerated, while the two men took off in all out sprints. Cruise called it in on the radio and prepared himself for a foot race. He wasn't the fastest, but he could not be outrun. He had too much heart to give up. He thought through how Detective Justice would handle the situation and visualized tackling the suspect. He might be armed. Jane nodded at Cruise who threw open the door as the cruiser skidded to a stop on crushed gravel and bedrock. The smaller man had run between the two apartment buildings. Grant accelerated away, siren still blaring, as Cruise took off after the suspect.

Cruise emerged from the alley, hand on his holster, looking for any movement on the dark street. He saw the man's legs as he ran through the glow of a street light. He was running down the sidewalk heading west. The perp didn't seem to be armed, and with the siren of his partner's car blaring somewhere down the road, Cruise took off once more.

The perp was breathing hard. Sweat dripping down his face, arms damp with perspiration. He slowed down to make a cut around the next apartment building when the siren in the back of his mind suddenly became deafening and a squad car veered onto the sidewalk directly in front of him, blinding him with the mounted spotlight. The door swung open and a blond officer emerged over the roof of the vehicle aiming a gun at his chest. "Freeze," she screamed. He froze, mind paralyzed with the flood of new input from the changing situation. He turned to stumble blindly back around the corner of the building. He desperately grabbed at the tiny bag in his pocket, trying to free it from his cargo shorts, when Cruise crashed into his shoulder from his right side. Both men went to the ground, but Cruise quickly righted himself and brought out his cuffs. Grant moved in, weapon drawn to assist her partner. With the perp's hands secured, Grant holstered her Smith and Wesson and Cruise fished out a small bag of white powder.

Jane let out a low whistle. "I hope that's not what I think it is."

Cruise held up the baggie. "Sir, this was in your pocket. Can you tell me what this is?"

"Man, I don't know what that is. It's not mine."

"It's not yours?" asked Grant. "It looks like coke. Is that coke? We have you on possession. Who was the other guy? Where is this coming from?" She knew they should be reading him his rights at this point, but the once fantastic rumor of a new player in town was suddenly becoming very real.

The man was sitting on the grass, hands cuffed behind his back, and he seemed to be thinking through his options.

"Why were you running if you don't have anything to hide?" asked Cruise. He opened up the baggie, licked the tip of his pinkie and dabbed the white powder. He touched it to his tongue and sealed the bag again. "That's not sugar, that's for sure. Who's dealing this, sir?"

"You're cops. You figure it out," the man finally said.

Grant spoke into her radio, while Cruise read him his rights. Cruise helped the man to his feet. Whoever was distributing the coke, the availability was greater each day, and it wasn't going away any time soon.

Dupé rubbed his eyes and looked over at his wife who was still asleep. The phone kept vibrating on the bedstand. 6:35am. He picked it up and took it into the bathroom before answering. "What's up, detective?"

Justice's voice came from the other line. "Grant and Cruise picked up a guy last night with some coke on him. They want us to ask him a few questions."

"Let me throw on some clothes and I'll meet you at the station in 10."

"Make it five," and Justice hung up. Dupé yawned and started the shower.

Chapter 32

"His name is Keshon Holt. 20 years old. A few priors: possession, minor theft. He claims he doesn't know anything." Officer Jane Grant handed a manila folder to Justice.

"Seems like a small fish. I doubt he'll know anything," Dupé said looking through the one way glass at the man sitting in the metal chair.

"He was running pretty hard for someone who doesn't know anything," Cruise added.

"You caught him, Mike?" Justice asked. Cruise nodded, trying unsuccessfully to mask his smile. "Good job. But they all run. Big fish, little fish."

"Fish don't run, Justice," Dupé said.

"Big bad Justice." Officer Emmitt Decker stepped into the small circle with a cup of coffee in his hand. "You going to make this guy squeal? Going to pound him 'till he talks?"

"Don't you have some place to be, Decker?" Grant asked with a scowl.

"This is where I am supposed to be. Isn't that lucky? So what about it, Justice? You got the knives and battery acid with you?"

Grant rolled her eyes. "Shut up, Decker."

"Got a woman doing your talking for you, Justice?" Decker laughed. He took a sip of coffee and quickly pulled it away, swearing.

"Need a woman to blow on your drink for you, Decker?" Grant asked.

Decker sneered. "No, but you can blow something else."

Justice stepped forward, towering over Decker. Decker stood his ground. Justice reached out and took the coffee out of Decker's hand. Decker stared up at him. His eyes were hard and cold. Justice's face was blank. He then took the cup and tossed its contents on Decker's groin. Decker began jumping, and shrieking, and blotting at his pants. "The hell?" he screamed as he stripped off his pants and held his boxers away from his waist. "You better believe I'm filing a complaint, and I'll sue you if I'm burnt down there!"

"Decker, do you want me to get you some more coffee? I spilled yours," Justice called down the hall as Decker hobbled down the hall in his boxers, swearing, and pants draped over his arm.

"That was awesome!" Cruise said as he pumped his fist.

"Calm down there, spaz," Justice said.

"Why couldn't you let me do that, Justice?" Grant asked, frowning. "It wasn't as satisfying as it could have been."

"I think most everyone here wanted to do that," added Dupé, "but we have a perp in there waiting for us."

The two detectives entered the bare, 12x12 room. The walls were cinder blocks covered in egg-shell paint. The door was green metal and in the center of the room stood a small table with four metal chairs, two on either side of the table. The two chairs on the far side of the table were bolted to the floor.

Dupé sat down across from the Keshon. Justice leaned against the wall with his arms crossed. Keshon glanced at him out of the corners of his eyes. Dupé casually thumbed through the folder and breathed in deeply. He set the folder down and leaned forward with his hands on the table. He sat that way for about 20 seconds. The perp was leaned back in his chair with a scowl, but he continued to glance at the massive figure against the wall in a full bullet-proof vest. The room was well lit, but the figure seemed to deflect the light, dressed in all black, deeply tanned skin. Only the silver outline of the black grips from the two Kimber 1911's registered the light. The perp swallowed involuntarily.

Dupé finally sat back and straightened his tie, never taking his eyes off the young man across the table. "My partner," Dupé motioned to Justice, "and I think you're a loser junkie." Keshon smirked at the comment. "We're supposed to ask you all kinds of questions about where you got the coke, who gave it to you, who's distributing it, but it's pretty obvious you're nobody." Dupé looked like he was attending an accounting lecture. He leaned his head back and looked up at the ceiling. "Why are we wasting our time with you? We'll send you to county. You'll make a lot of friends there. Do you have any friends? Do you get called names a lot?"

"Forget you, fool!"

Dupé made an exaggerated face and looked at Justice. Justice's face was empty of expression, but his eyes were piercing.

"Or do people even know who you are?"

"Forget you, pig. Civic drivin' punk ass." He uttered several more expletive laden insults that made Dupé wonder if Justice was going to come over and backhand him. Keshon laughed. "I got more honies and rolls than your broke ass could even dream of."

"What'd he have on him?" Dupé asked Justice.

Justice never took his eyes off Keshon. "Seventeen dollars."

Dupé nodded knowingly. He mouthed *wow* to Keshon. "High roller. Any baseball cards or bubble gum there, Keshon?"

"I just bought coke, man. That stuff ain't cheap. That's how I do. Broke ass."

"You used that one already." Dupé adjusted his tie. "How much did that run you? Let's see, 3 grams—60 bucks?"

"Man, I get the pure stuff. 300 hundred for that stuff."

Dupé didn't react to the statement. After a moment he said, "He's nobody; he doesn't know anything. How could he? Well, good talk."

"You don't know me," protested Keshon. "I know people you didn't even know existed. You wish you had the cred I do. Paper pushin', do whatever the man tell you to, broke pig. I've got the inside on everything."

Dupé looked at Justice. "Well?" Justice remained frozen, speechless. "OK. Fine." Dupé turned back to face Keshon. "We're looking for a top dog. But you wouldn't even be on the level to know about top dogs, would you, Keshon?"

Keshon leaned forward. "Man, I know everybody. I told you that."

"As much as I want to believe you, Keshon, I find that hard to believe. Have you ever heard of a man named-" Dupé paused, "Deeter? Matalar Deeter."

Keshon seemed to think for a moment. "Nah, never heard of him."

"I told you it was a waste. He doesn't know anything. He's just street trash."

"Your mom is trash," Keshon shot back.

"Waste of time. Waste of space."

Dupé picked up the folder and began to stand up. "Maybe I do know him," Keshon said.

"You don't." Dupé pushed in his chair and motioned to Justice.

"Man, if I give him up, you better give me something good." Keshon was pulling at his handcuffs.

Dupé opened the door; Justice remained against the wall. "Man, I can give you Deeder!"

The door closed behind Dupé. Justice walked swiftly over, slammed the metal chair down, and screamed at Keshon. "Who is he? Where is he distributing?"

Keshon slunk back in his chair, held his cuffed hands up, this time pleading. "Man, I can give him to you, but I need more time!"

"I don't believe you!"

"He's got a place off of, uh, uh, 38th street. He's running it out of there! See, I know him. I did my part!"

Keshon was sweating now, breathing hard. Justice was leaning over the chair with his hands on the back, triceps bulging under the black t-shirt. His face was hard with cruel lines. The hard lines faded into a sympathetic look. "It was Deeter." Justice stood up and walked out of the room.

Dupé was waiting for him on the other side of the glass. "Well that was kind of fun and pretty pointless."

"It was worth a shot. Obviously this Protagoras plays it close to the vest. Controls who knows him and who doesn't. Kind of seems like it's better for the people who don't know him."

"Have the ballistics reports come back for our friend Noodles?"

"Not yet. They claim it's precision over velocity."

Malatar? Maltar?" Justice tried to remember.

"Matalar Deeter."

Justice laughed. "Where did that come from?"

"Hey, that's an intimidating drug lord name. It's even got that exotic flair to it. Matalar."

"I think Malatar sounds better."

"Well, when you interrogate the perp you can come up with whatever fake drug lord name you want. You were too busy doing the whole, look I'm a badass brooding on the wall who could break every bone in your body, thing. Which you happen to do very well, by the way."

"Thank you, Detective Dupé. You were kind of threatening when you straightened your tie."

"Eh. Sometimes I can't hide my warrior nature."

"I'm gonna run by the school and tell Tammy about the name."

"You can't call her?"

"She has classes."

"So why would she be able to talk to you in person then? Wait- no."

"It's important that I share this information personally."

"One, that's bull. Two, we have reports to fill out on the shooting yesterday."

"That's right, I completely forgot about that. Good thing you're here to remind me. Well since I'll be at the elementary school, why don't you work on those reports for us? Thank you so much, Dupé."

"I'm not your servant," Dupé called out as Justice walked down the hall smiling.

"I agree," Justice called back. "You're the best partner I've ever had. Team work! Woooo!"

Chapter 33

"Detective, you don't need to sign in. I think we're safer with you here, than without you." Anne Lawson pushed her blond hair behind her ear and bit her lip slightly.

Justice picked up the pen with a smiley face attached to the top of the pen with masking tape. It read, "Make a Difference!" He signed his name and wrote "1:10" in the time slot. "I appreciate that, Anne, but remember, we have rules for a reason." He winked and she blushed.

"Are you here for Tammy?"

"Yes. Is she free?"

"I think any woman would be free for you, detective. I'm free tonight."

"It's tempting, but I have this case I'm working on. Kind of has me tied up."

"I could tie you-"

"Miss Lawson, it has been most pleasant chatting with you." Justice turned and walked briskly up the hall. Anne leaned over to watch him walk away, fanning herself with one hand.

Justice walked past the multiple posters plastered to the walls. "Attitudes are contagious. Is yours worth catching?"

"Reading makes the world come alive." "Math is the same in any language." The library door was open, but Justice heard the class inside before he ever entered. He poked his head in and spotted Tammy helping a little girl with a ponytail reaching for a book on the top shelf. Top shelves seemed cruel for elementary schools. Tammy looked up and saw him leaning in and motioned for him to come over. As he entered, each child stopped what they were doing and looked up at the giant man with a badge around his neck and guns holstered in his bulletproof vest. Some of the boys looked at each other with open mouths or smiles revealing missing teeth.

"Are you here to arrest Miss Shaw?" one little boy asked with wide eyes.

"No buddy I'm not. I'm just here to talk with her."

"Is that your boyfriend?" asked the girl who Tammy had been helping reach her book.

"No, Rachel. Detective Justice is one of my best friends. We grew up together."

"Are you in looove?" asked a boy who made his fingers kiss each other. All the kids started laughing.

"You need to grow up, son."

"Blake, he's in second grade. No, Eric, we are not in love."

"What?" Justice asked in defense. "That's immature and childish. We're two adults talking to each other. Everyone listen up." Justice held his hands up for silence; everyone closed their mouths and sat down. "Tammy, Miss Shaw, and I are friends. She is a woman, and I am a man. She does not have cooties. I do not have cooties. Boys and girls can be friends without being boyfriend and girlfriend."

"Nuh uh," said a girl in the corner.

"Yuh huh. Yes, they can. We are. Your librarian and I are friends. Now if you'll excuse us, we have some things to talk about." The kids began to snicker again.

Tammy walked over to Justice. "Blake, they're just kids."

"Yeah, but it's stupid to think that every guy and girl like each other or something."

"Blake, I have a class. What do you want?"

"I came here to talk about your assignment."

"Well, it's a dumb assignment. I searched every variation of "Proto" that you gave me." She took out a slip of paper. "Let's see, I got some hits for a beach in Cyprus, a recombinant virus, a song by a band called "The Lotanas". Do any of those sound like your guy?"

Justice shook his head. "I have his name now." He handed her a paper of his own. "Freidrick Protagoras. Let me know what you can get. Thanks."

"That's a little better. I'll do what I can."

Justice turned and headed for the door. He turned around, and addressing the room said in a loud voice, "We're just friends."

Dupé was staring at his computer screen like a zombie, typing slowly and steadily. Justice snuck up behind him and slapped the folder down on the desk causing a small spasm and an exclamation of, "Oh!"

"I didn't mean to make you soil your pocket protector there, Jeeves."

"Guess I was engrossed in typing up our reports. You know, reports, while you were going around living your glamorous life. What's this?" Dupé asked picking up the folder.

"Forensics came back as well as the autopsy results for Mr. Nos. Guess whose fingerprints are on the bottles."

"Starkman."

"Seems like Daryl has been part of a little extracurricular activity among Lenny's ranks. Killed from water in the lungs. The wound on the head was made before he died."

"So Daryl goes out with Nos, gets him drunk, knocks him out, and then he drowns?"

"That would be my guess," Justice said. "Let's go tell Lenny the good news."

"I'm kind of getting sick of that place, to be honest."

"Maybe this will be one step closer to getting them all off the streets for good."

Tammy called while the two detectives were on their way to Lenny's. "So I've got a little information on this Protagoras creep."

"OK, shoot."

"Well, for starters, the name is most definitely an alias."

"Well, we kind of figured that."

"Oh, my word. Let me finish. You're not paying me to tell you the obvious."

"We're *not* paying you, Tammy."

"I know. You're not, so you don't really get to tell me what information is pertinent to the investigation and which information is not. Also, I'm telling you some juvenile stuff to begin with because this is information you could have found with a simple Google search. If you're going to be so opposed to trivial research, then at the very least I get to patronize you with the trivial information I find when I'm doing your work for you."

"Point taken," Justice conceded. "I apologize. You tell me what I need to know."

"That's more like it. Apology accepted. Protagoras was a fifth century BC Greek philosopher. He was seen as very controversial by his peers for claiming that man is the measure of all things, or that something is true to the person who thinks it. Most Greeks saw the laws of the universe as constant and unchanging. He shook that up. Taken to its extreme, this view could lead to moral relativism; right or wrong depends on who you're talking to, that kind of stuff. Moral Relativism is also a philosophy contributing to Friedrich Nietzsche's worldview. I would bet that this is where the alias comes from, Friedrich Protagoras."

"Well, it gives us an idea of who we're dealing with at least."

"I'll let you know more as I do some more thorough research."

"Thanks, Tammy." They both hung up, and Justice told Dupé the news.

"So we're dealing with a criminal who doesn't care about wrong or right. This is some really insightful stuff, Justice."

"We do know that the guy thinks very highly of himself to put himself on the same pedestal as Nietzsche and this Protagoras guy. Also, he seems to think that what he does is right, however twisted it might be. It's a start."

Chapter 34

Lenny's street looked the same, the familiar houses. The familiar pot holes to avoid. But as Justice and Dupé neared the dead end where Lenny's house of drugs incorporated sat, they both noticed the suspiciously open entrance gate and empty yard.

"No guards?" Dupé asked in disbelief.

The Challenger crawled by the time they reached the driveway, both men scanning the grounds for any sign of activity. Justice parked halfway in the gate. Most situations that smelled bad were bad. This scenario smelled bad. "Get ready for a welcome party," Justice said while removing a Kimber and checking the slide. Dupé did the same with his gun, and the two detectives slid out of the car. "We are detectives with the Avon Police Department," Justice called out, holding up his badge. "We are armed. Place any weapons on the ground. We are considering this situation hostile." They paused, but there was no response.

"No vehicles," Dupé observed. Justice simply nodded, his eyes on the windows and roof. Then he saw the door slightly ajar. He pointed to his eyes and then the door. The two men approached on either side of the door, both hands on their pistols aimed at the ground at a 45 degree angle.

"The one time I could have kicked down a door, and it's open," Dupé whispered in frustration.

"Can it, detective," Justice hissed. He counted and the two men entered with guns raised, Justice first and Dupé covering. The scene was impossible to avoid; both men almost slipped while coming in. Dupé fought the bile in his throat, but he was able to recover. A quick search of the house revealed that its occupants had gone and probably weren't coming back. Food had been left mid-meal and drinks were still half full, but a quick search revealed nothing incriminating about the house save the sweet smell of marijuana.

After clearing the rest of the house, the two detectives met back in the front room. The door had been ajar when the two detectives walked in. Hundreds of shells littered the floor just beyond the door. A pool of blood had formed beneath a body. It lay face down in the middle of the room with a handgun on the floor beside it. The wall of the room farthest from the front door was aerated with bullet holes. The wall's studs were exposed where the wall had been torn apart like meet ripped off a ribcage. Justice guessed that was exactly what the body's ribcage would look like as well. He knelt down by the body. Dupé joined him in the kneeling position as he called in to the precinct for back up and forensics. Dupé had learned to let Justice work in silence when they first arrived on a scene. Justice's face wore a hard expression that Dupé recognizing more often whenever Justice was working through ideas and scenarios.

The room was mostly empty save some trash left on a coffee table, a couch, and a recliner. Justice stood up and walked around the body, careful not to step in the blood.

The body's back was soaked in blood as well with multiple wounds and a shirt torn to shreds.

"My god," Dupé murmured with a hand over his mouth.

"I think it's safe to rule out a gun accident in this situation," replied Justice. Carefully balancing on one foot outside the blood pool, he pushed the body onto its back with his boot.

"It's Lenny." Dupé shook his head in disbelief and swallowed bile once more. The eyes were open, face preserved in a permanent look of shock, but it was the torso of the victim that caused Dupé to glance away. The entire torso was completely eviscerated.

"Now we know where the blood came from," Justice said, studying the body. He stepped back and surveyed the entire room.

"Say hello to my little friend, huh?" Dupé murmured.

"What?" Justice asked, still studying the room.

"So Lenny gets it in his own house, huh? It's just like *Scarface*. Please tell me you've seen *Scarface*, Justice."

"I've seen *Scarface*, Dupé."

"Have you really, though, because it sounds like you're just saying it to appease me."

"Dupé, I deal with the law and justice in real life situations. I don't live in a movie. My life is not a story. So no, I haven't seen *Scarface*, but yes, I've seen the scene you're talking about. He gets blown away while he's firing an M16A1 with a grenade launcher attached to the rail. He dies in a pool. This is a pool of blood. It's symbolic, OK? I get it."

"Man, we're going to have a guys night soon and watch all these movies you've been missing."

"Can't, don't want to leave Honey alone at night."

"What? Who's Honey?"

"My Dachshund."

"*You* have a Dachshund named Honey?"

"Yeah, red long-haired. She's my girl."

"That's who you've been referring to? You just killed guy night, Justice. You killed it."

"You wear a tie and a button down every day, and *I'm* killing guy night?" Dupé rolled his eyes. Justice removed a knife from his vest, and bent down to pick up the handgun with the blade.

"There are a few things different in this scenario than the one in the movie, detective," Justice said, holding the gun up to his face.

"And they are?"

"One, our friend here, Lenny Phipps, AKA Blitz, was holding a gun, but never fired a shot. Why?"

"He was surprised? Never saw them coming."

"Possibly, except there's one minor problem." Dupé didn't take the bait this time. "How does a man who is prepared enough to be holding a gun, but surprised enough to not get off one shot, take what seems to be over a hundred rounds point blank in the chest?"

"They pump him full of rounds after he's already fallen."

""You saw his back. Those are exit wounds, not entry wounds. I don't think there was any shooting done post-mortem."

"OK, well, judging by the sheer amount of shells, there's gotta be more than one shooter."

"Good guess."

"Or maybe it was one man with six guns," Dupé said with a wink.

Justice returned the statement with a blank stare.

"Boondock Saints?"

Justice plowed on. "He wasn't moved. He died right here."

"OK, so," Dupé stood up and moved over to the door way, "so, we have all our shooters just standing here?"

"Most likely. Look at this wall. I'd bet money that every single one of these bullets passed through our friend before hitting this wall."

"So, it's point blank, but that wall is destroyed. Those would have to be some pretty high powered weapons to do that."

"Come here."

Dupé followed Justice into the next room. Dry wall and wood had been splintered on the next wall as well. "They did *that*?"

"You said they would have to be high-powered rifles, even from that distance. I'd say they were pretty high powered."

"You're saying that they passed through Lenny, then that wall, and then into this wall." Dupé swallowed. "That's some heavy crap all right. OK, so where are the other bodies?"

"That's difference number two from your Hollywood scenario. I think Lenny was the only person attacked here. He probably was alone. Unless they brought a bunch of body bags and extra drivers and hauled the other bodies away in their own cars."

"So his own guys turned on him?"

"I don't think so. The pattern of the shooting, the precision—I don't know that most guys in Lenny's outfit could even hit the wall with a high-powered weapon; they wouldn't know what to do with it."

"OK, hotshot. Then what happened?"

"I'm not sure exactly, but I think it *was* an inside job, just not executed by any of his men. Look, there's not one other body, one other area of shooting inside the house. The only shell casings we'll be able to find are in the front doorway. So someone literally walked in the front door, or several people walked in, and mowed Lenny down without firing another shot. I think Lenny's guys knew it was coming and they left. I think Lenny walks out, and he's facing several guys with machine guns just waiting for him."

"Hey, Scarface!" Dupé said excitedly. "No, Scarface. Tony. Daryl Starkman. What if he did this?"

"It's possible, but I don't know."

"Listen, he's committing robberies without Lenny knowing. He kills Nos for whatever reason, and we believe Lenny didn't want that either. What if it is like Scarface and you've got the underling gunning for the top dog's position. What if Starkman has created this ghost persona, this Protagoras, to get into the business? He buys off the rest of Lenny's men; they already respect him, and they see the new guy as up and coming. They want in, so they turn on their old boss. Or maybe he's got his own guys. What about that piece of paper we found on Nos? It had writing on it. Had some formations of crazy words, but I think one of them was *Protor*. So Nos figures out that Starkman is Protagoras, or he starts to put the pieces together. He gets too nosy, and Daryl offs him."

Justice mulled it over. "It's plausible. As good as anything we've got right now. I'm still not convinced Starkman could pull something like this off. But even if he's not Protagoras, he's definitely at the center of something, and I hope I'm there when it hits the fan."

"I mean, why would you put over a hundred rounds in someone? I've never seen anything like that."

"Neither have I," Justice admitted.

"You must really want someone dead to put that much lead in them."

The two detectives walked back out into the front room. Justice whipped out his gun in the direction of a figure, silhouetted in the doorway. The figure simply stood there. Justice quickly holstered his weapon as his eyes adjusted and dashed over to the Marla who stood with mouth half open, eyes wide, staring at the scene before her. Putting his arm around her, he moved her outside into the sunlight. Dupé followed. They heard the sirens of the coming squad cars and could see the flashing lights appear at the end of the street. Justice helped Marla sit down on the ground. Her eyes were far away.

"You know her?" Dupé asked quietly.

Justice nodded. "She was working when the gas station got robbed."

"So...much blood." A tear streaked down Marla's check, already moist with perspiration.

Justice pulled her in and held her head to his chest. "I want you to forget what you saw, OK? Close your eyes. Make it go away. There you go." Marla blinked and seemed to come out of the fog. "Why are you here, Marla?"

"I live on this street, detective." Marla spoke slowly, as if she didn't believe what she said.

"You do?"

"Yeah. I heard this yesterday. And then I saw your car. I wanted to find out what happened."

"You heard this?"

Yeah, right after you left. You left, and then they left, and then two black SUV's came. And then there were shots." Marla wiped her eyes. "I'm sorry I freaked out on you in there."

"Are you kidding me?" asked Dupé. "Who wouldn't be freaked out by that?"

"I think Detective Dupé almost threw up."

"Twice," Dupé said holding up his fingers.

"Nothing to be ashamed of, Marla," Justice said in a soothing voice. "Just breathe."

Yeah, right after you left yesterday, I can always hear your engine, all of Lenny's guys left too. I know all of their cars. They're goofy as hell looking, and they all left at the same time. Right after you left. And right after they left, two black SUV's, Expeditions or Suburbans or something, the big black SUV's you see, they came driving down the street really slowly. And then the gun shots came. I've never heard anything like it. You live down the street from a drug dealer, you hear gun shots. Everyone has."

"Why didn't anybody call it in?" Dupé asked.

"Because we were all scared, probably. I was. I am. Most of the time no one pays attention to them anyway because it's probably just Lenny's guys getting drunk and popping off some shots. But this sounded like thunder or something. I've never heard gun shots like that, detective. It scared the hell out of me."

"I bet it did. You're a brave young woman, Marla."

The police cars began pulling up behind Justice's Challenger. Dupé began giving them directives as they scurried out of their vehicles. His phone rang in the midst of the organized chaos. He looked over his shoulder, but Justice was still taking care of the girl. He walked to the outside of the fence and away from the officers. "I'm here chief."

"I heard what happened," McMann growled into the phone.

"It's a bloodbath. Lenny didn't stand a chance."

"I want you two to come in. It's time we bring Justice into the loop."

"I don't know."

"What do you mean, you don't know? Things are obviously getting out of control. He can see that. Now is as good a time as we're going to get. This is what we've been fearing. He's a good cop, and he'll understand what's at stake. He'll see our side. He has to."

"OK, I'll see what I can do."

"Just do it."

Dupé took his time walking back to Justice and the girl. Police had already sectioned off the fence with crime-scene tape as neighbors began filing out of their houses. Dupé knew it had to happen, but he still had no idea how Justice would react. The Captain was probably right, but it also felt off. But there wasn't any alternative was there? The crime scene in front of him was reason enough.

Chapter 35

The detectives made sure Marla made it home safely and then finished scouring the house, giving directions to the cops and the forensics team. When there was nothing left to do but wait for the findings from ballistics and forensic departments, they returned to the station.

Justice and Dupé walked through the symmetrical layout of grey desks. Phones rang intermittently. A few of the officers watched the two men, looking up momentarily from endless paperwork and reports to glimpse the larger than life detective and his seemingly ordinary partner. The two men contrasted in such a way that it was hard not to watch them. The 6'5" giant-of-a-man Justice with his dark hair and eyes, unshaven face, dressed as if he were going to battle with bulletproof vest, badge hanging like an oversized dog tag, and steel-toed boots. And then the barely 6 foot, slender Dupé with sandy hair swept to one side and the countenance of a young priest. Even their strides stood out from one another—Justice's an assured and heavy strut, as if each step was announcing impending doom, and Dupé's, easy and unassuming.

A young, dark-haired cadet with beautiful ebony skin smiled and quickly feigned interest in her paperwork as she met Justice's eyes. He returned the smile and gave her the slightest of nods. Dupé, however, noticed none of this. He seemed agitated, as if his mind was somewhere else. He pulled his tie loose as they neared Captain McMann's office.

Justice leaned over and whispered, "Relax, Dupé. You're acting like we're getting sent to the principal's office. It's a simple report." Dupé managed a half smile and nod.

Justice gave two quick knocks and opened the large oak door. McMann looked up from his desk and smiled as the two detectives came in. His head tilted as he looked at Dupé, eyebrows raised. Dupé returned the look with a blank expression, and immediately McMann's large eyebrows furrowed, wrinkling his forehead. He removed a cigar and stuck it in his mouth. He motioned to the seats in front of the desk. "Please," he garbled with mouth full of stogie. The two detectives sat, and Justice wondered if the Captain only smoked when someone was in his office. Perhaps it was a security blanket. Maybe it created a bond for those who appreciated smoking, and maybe it drove anyone unpleasant out of the office. He would ask the Captain about it sometime.

"The name Protagoras has tickled some big ears higher up. Apparently this ghost has a reputation."

"So what does that mean?" Dupé asked.

"Why don't you give me a second and I would tell you."

Dupé nodded and Justice smirked. "Everyone's always interrupting," Justice agreed.

"That goes for you too, Justice. I didn't call you two in here to talk about feelings. Now let me finish."

"Fair enough," replied Justice.

"Now before you two get your panties in a bunch and start interrupting me again, I want to say that this was not my idea. Now where was I? Right, this name Protagoras is stirring up some powerful people. And Avon, Indiana seems to be the hottest lead on getting some pertinent information on this guy. I don't know if he's real; I don't know if it's just some alias. But some guys in suits are sending some specialists out here just to make sure."

At this, Justice sat straight up and slammed his hands down on the desk. "They're wanting government goons to take over?" Justice's large hands were balled tightly into fists on McMann's desk, veins bulging out of his forearms.

"What did I say?" barked McMann, pointing his stogie with a heavy, outstretched hand. "This is not my idea, and it's out of my hands."

"I can't believe you're letting a bunch of spooks out here," Dupé said disgusted.

"They're coming, and that's that. Apparently this Protagoras nonsense is serious enough for their costly expenditures. The unit will be here in two days."

"You think we can't handle this, Captain?" Justice pleaded.

"I think nothing of the sort, detective. I have complete confidence that the two of you could mop up this mess. Your record is flawless, Justice, and I handpicked Dupé myself. The two of you make a formidable opponent I would hate to find myself up against, but we have no options. It's done, and we have to make the best of it. Listen, as far as I'm concerned, this is our case. And these are the hotshots. Why would they need our help? Short of withholding evidence, don't give them any help they don't need."

Both detectives sat glaring. McMann assumed the anger and hurt was directed in equal parts at him and equal parts at the unit coming in. He could handle that. He didn't get to where he was by questioning his decisions every time someone got their feelings hurt. Justice finally pushed himself and his chair back from the desk, jaw clenched shut. Dupé pulled his tie tight, and folded his hands neatly in his lap. He had never had someone highjack a case before, and he wasn't sure what the proper response should be as a detective.

McMann looked back and forth at the two detectives. After a few moments, when the tension seemed to begin dissipating, he began once more. "They're not here yet so stop pouting," McMann frowned between puffs on his cigar. "Give me some details on the Lenny Phipps murder". He leaned back in his chair with arms crossed.

Dupé looked at Justice. Justice began. "Lenny Phipps, AKA Blitz, was shot execution style in his home. Monday. I, or we," Justice corrected himself, nodding to Dupé, "know the act was pre-meditated and planned out by someone on the inside. Lenny's is the only blood and body found in the house. All action took place in the living room. The execution was done by several separate, high-powered, possibly military grade, weapons. Seems like professionals with professional weapons. The whole scenario is bizarre though. Our guess is that it was inside job. There are usually at least eight to ten guys at the main house at any given time. There's no sign of a firefight, no sign of struggle. There weren't any footprints or signs of entry except for the front door, and it was completely intact. This was no break in; this was no blitz, no pun intended." McMann nodded.

"Whoever it was simply walked right in and killed him. Now where any of Lenny's crew were when this happened, I haven't the foggiest." Justice put his hands up and leaned back in his chair. It would have hit him uncomfortably right beneath the shoulder blades, but his flak jacket gave him some additional support and padding.

Dupé spoke up, keeping his eyes on Captain McMann. "Tell the Cap about the kill." McMann looked at Dupé for a second and then returned his attention to Justice.

"This was a blood bath. For a non-torture scenario, this was about as overkill as you could get. The perps were standing at the door from the angle of the shots. Several high powered weapons, most likely all automatics, fired for an extended period of time." Justice paused. "To be honest, I've never seen anything like it. Lenny never got off a shot. There were no rounds fired from his gun. The floor was covered in casings. I would guess well over one hundred."

McMann simply shook his head. This was new for Justice, but McMann had probably seen it all in his many years of service.

"It gets better," Justice said grimly. "Every single one of them was a hit, and every single one of them passed right through ol' Lenny. I'm surprised he wasn't cut in half. I mean, it wasn't like they were firing from far away, but not one of the bullets was stray. Firepower like that means recoil and major kick. These guys knew what they were doing."

"And none of the shots were fired post-mortem," Dupé added quietly.

"Over one hundred rounds in the sternum and stomach," said Justice.

McMann sat up. "Any idea for why you would shoot one man over a hundred times?"

"We've been thinking about that," Justice said.

"It was personal; make him suffer," mused Dupé.

"You don't kill a man quickly with a gun if you want him to suffer," growled McMann, cigar in the side of his mouth. Justice remained quiet. "If there were that many guys and they wanted to make him suffer, they wouldn't be shooting him. Especially if they were professionals."

"This was in the middle of the afternoon," Dupé said incredulously. "They walked into a drug dealer's house they knew would be empty. They knew Lenny was there. And then they pumped a hundred rounds into him and walked out the same door. Broad daylight." Dupé talked through the specifics more to himself than the other two men.

"This is bad," McMann stated. "The news will want in on this one."

Justice took the toothpick out of his mouth and flicked it into the trash can. Dupé couldn't help but remember the first day he had met Justice and he had met the toothpick flying through the air. It seemed like an eternity ago. He watched the toothpick rotate through the air and then into the trashcan. Justice leaned back in his chair so that the front two legs were off the floor. He stretched his legs out until his boots touched the Captain's desk. "This isn't done," he said finally.

"What are you talking about?" McMann growled, his brows jutting out even further than before.

"These guys weren't stupid. They had professional hardware. They handled it in a professional manner. They didn't just throw this together. That was a message. The overkill wasn't because they were amateurs. It wasn't in broad daylight because they were careless. Day, night, it doesn't matter to them. They're letting everybody know there's a new player in town, and he's playing for keeps. They just walked into the doghouse and pumped a hundred rounds into the big dog himself and then walked away, easy as can be. They let everyone know, including us, that they don't want to just be a part of the city—they want to own it. It wasn't just about killing Lenny. Now that Lenny is gone, the coke is going to be on the street in full force."

"So you believe there really is this Protagoras guy?" mused McMann.

Justice paused for only a split second. "Protagoras, prophylactic, heck, I don't know. But I do know the weed kingpin is dead, coke is showing up on our streets now, and whoever executed that hit on Lenny is a bad dude. I think we better begin preparing ourselves for an all-out war."

Chapter 36

Dupé looked from Justice to McMann. The corners of McMann's mouth turned up ever so slightly. What looked like relief enveloped his face. His large frame settled back in his chair and he inhaled deeply from his cigar. He had needed Justice's approval for this to be effective, and Justice had just opened the door for him. Now he just needed to expertly pluck the strings of justice that were already deeply embedded in his top detective. The alliance was not sealed yet. He had to choose his words carefully. Justice had to realize that what was at stake was bigger than trifling details or squabbles over the letter of the law.

Dupé tried to control his breathing. He knew this was the moment he had been dreading since the end of that first day on the job with Justice. It had to be this moment. Justice's attitude was ideal, and McMann knew what he was doing. Justice had to see the bigger picture. It was more apparent now than ever. The threat was real; Protagoras was here. He hadn't been sure about the proposal initially when McMann had first approached him, but he could see the decision as the only option now. How else could they fight back? Still, he wondered how Justice would view him after it was all said and done.

McMann closed his eyes, hands folded on the desk, stogie hanging out the side of his mouth. He suddenly looked ten years older. Justice leaned forward. "You OK, cap?"

McMann opened his eyes and sighed. "Justice, we've worked together now for three years. You're one of the finest men I've ever had the privilege of working with. Though we may do things a little differently, we have the same goals, the same drive."

Justice nodded solemnly. He didn't like working with Lenny, but McMann had cleaned up the place; there was no denying that. He was a good captain.

"I'm tired, Justice. I'm tired of always being a step behind. You get one bad guy off the streets and another one takes his place. There's no sense of right and wrong any more. No decency in society. Everything is morally relative, and who gets the short end of the stick?"

"We do," Justice affirmed.

"*We* do. We're undermanned, underfunded, underequipped. Lenny's execution reaffirmed that quite emphatically I think. I'm not sure what's about to happen, but I don't want to lose this war. I don't want to lose our neighborhoods, and selfishly, I don't ever want to lose to scum."

"I wholeheartedly agree, sir," said Justice.

"But there's this Protagoras guy, this phantom, this bad taste in my mouth, and we have to have specialists come in with their fancy equipment and big toys-" McMann trailed off and looked out the window. The hook was there, the bait waiting to be devoured. If they didn't have Justice, it could be done, but with Justice...now there was a thought!

"We don't need their equipment. I've got my own," Justice said emphatically. "I can handle myself."

"I know you can, son. I know you can." McMann turned his attention to Dupé. "What about you, detective? Do you have a supercharged car?" Dupé smirked. "Do you have your Dessert Eagles or whatever?" Dupé shook his head. "Justice, we don't have the firepower to combat today's criminals, let alone this Protagoras character. And with budget cuts, well, forget about it. We're an island, fighting a sea of crime, with wave after wave of criminals gunning for us."

"I like that, Captain. Paints a good picture of our situation," Justice said, imagining the waves of criminals crashing against his beachhead. He was an impenetrable sea wall.

McMann floundered momentarily. "Huh? Right. Anyway, we're an island, and the waves are crashing over us. Those criminals don't have the red-tape we have. They don't have rules. They don't have federal regulations and asses to kiss. We- are- on- our- own." He was staring intently at Justice. "But not anymore. This is my town. I'm not going to stand by while low-life thugs take it over. Which is why we have been stockpiling our own weapons cache." McMann pushed on, not giving Justice time to digest the statement. "We have to bring the fight to them. We've had pacts and mutual relationships for far too long. Justice, I know you've been dying with a weed house sitting in the middle of your territory that was deemed untouchable. Our hands were tied. But they are no longer tied." Justice scrambled to make sense of what the captain was saying. "We'll be able to drive the streets and not have to look over our shoulders. We won't be afraid of leaving our wives and children, not knowing if we'll see them again. We won't fear those at the door, because we'll be at the door."

"Yeah, Walter White!" Dupé exclaimed. Sometimes he couldn't help himself. Both men stared at him.

"So if we don't have the budget, how are we paying for these weapons?" Justice asked.

"This is where it gets, uh, complicated," started McMann. "You might call it tax payers' dollars."

"What does that mean?" demanded Justice. Dupé swallowed and pulled his tie loose once more.

"Justice, when was the last time you took a vacation?" McMann asked, his brows furrowed, eyes intense.

"What does that have to do with anything?"

"Just answer the question, detective."

"I take a vacation when the bad guys take a vacation. I don't."

"I know you don't, Justice. Everyone here at the force knows you don't take vacations and we respect you for it. Hell, all of us are working our butts off. We put our lives on the line every time we go out on the streets. You work tirelessly; you sweat and bleed for these people, and what do you get? Disrespect? Complaints over procedure? Resistance. Lack of gratitude. We're putting our butts on the line every day, and all we want is a little respect. Is that too much to ask? Is that undeserved? I don't think so. So we worked out a deal with some, uh, undesirables to collect the funds from our wonderful citizens to fund our defense."

Justice's jaw ached with tension. His knuckles were pale. His mind was racing, trying to process the tidal wave of facts and implications being revealed. "You're telling me that these robberies we've been investigating, robberies in our own town, were perpetrated by the police department?" Justice felt his face flushing despite the AC in the room.

"No. Not by us. By some criminals who eventually will pay for what they've done. We take a little here, we take a little there, and in return the citizens of Avon receive a well-armed police department who can now fully protect its citizens."

"Protect the citizens?" Justice roared.

"Keep your voice down, detective! This is confidential information."

"Protecting them from who? Their own police department is robbing them!"

"You're not seeing the bigger picture, here, Justice," McMann reasoned. "A minor theft doesn't set them back any, and in return they don't have to worry about true evil coming in and destroying their future." McMann scowled and spoke through a cigar gripped between his teeth. "You think Lenny was some super criminal? Lenny was a moron. He's the tip of an iceberg, detective. Who cares about petty theft when we've got a guy mowing down crime bosses with military grade hardware? In our own freaking backyard!"

"We're the mafia, protection for payment," Justice murmured. Then he turned and looked McMann in the eyes. "But at least the mafia wasn't pretending to be someone else. They'd rob you to your face."

McMann let out a guttural sound and dismissed the statement with a wave of the hand. He turned toward the window again, hands clasped behind his back.

Dupé found he had been holding his breath for the last minute. He exhaled, not as softly as he had hoped. Justice turned his attention toward him. "And you," Justice started, pointing at Dupé. "You're nothing but a plant trying to butter me up to this, this, farce! I can't believe I thought you were a partner."

Dupé looked down. This was the moment he had been dreading since McMann had informed him of the situation his first day at the precinct. If he had hoped for enthusiastic support, or at the very least a reluctant tolerance of the chosen course of action, Justice's reaction quickly squelched any glimmer of that hope. "Justice, no one here *likes* what's happening," Dupé tried. "But we're doing it for their good."

"Oh shut up, both of you. There's a law, and we're supposed to uphold it. There are lines, and we don't cross them. There is justice, and I won't sleep until it prevails." Justice's tone softened. "Captain, when have we failed? And when have we had the equipment we needed? When has our budget ever been sufficient? But we make do with what we have, and we make the bad guys pay. That's what we do!" Justice pleaded.

"And we will, Justice," McMann said, turning toward the two detectives. "We will. Only now, we'll be able to make them pay much more effectively. We'll put the fear of God in them. We need you, Justice. If you're on board, everyone would be on board. Come on, Justice; imagine turning the tables on the criminals. Imagine fighting them with the latest weaponry. Imagine watching the criminals run because they're scared of us! Think about what that would do for our streets if the criminals were scared of the police. Think about how this community would respond to lower crime. It would be virtually non-existent!" McMann said, holding out his hand, stogie wedged between his fat fingers, as if he were offering this notion of peace to Justice in his large palm.

Justice stood up. "Captain, you know what my answer will be. I'm here to serve the people, not extort them. I'll always fight crime, but I'm not going to do it with weapons funded by blood money."

The Captain's round, doughy face hardened into a solemn determination. "Blood money is always problematic, Justice. If used in the wrong places, at the wrong times, it can make our lives very difficult." McMann's spoke each word as if it was part of a solemn phrase, carefully rehearsed. "The threat of exposure is always real. The implications could be dire. If one of us were to be found out…" He trailed off. McMann's eyes were fixed on those of Justice. He didn't blink. Dupé's eyes darted between the two men. The Captain stood a good 8 inches shorter than Detective Justice, but he seemed to draw up to a stature Dupé had never seen before. McMann continued, "For example, there was the money found at Lenny's."

"What money?" Justice said incredulously. "There wasn't any money. We searched the whole place."

"A sack of money. In a Marsh's bag," McMann said.

"What did you say?" Justice asked, eyes narrowed.

"Now listen, it was found in the evidence storage with everything else related to the case. And we received an anonymous tip. The caller mentioned your name."

"My name?"

McMann paused. He seemed reluctant to keep speaking. "They said, they said that they saw you give a Marsh bag to a hooker. And now this bag turned up at Lenny's after he was brutally murdered."

Blood rushed to Justice's face. His bullet-proof vest, usually unnoticed, constricted around his thick neck. His jaw and fists were clenched. "Someone planted that, Captain. You don't honestly mean to tell me you're buying it!" Justice looked at Dupé who stared at the desk.

"I may be just as incredulous as you are, but right now it's the only significant information we have. It's not a good look, Justice. But we take care of our own in the department. You *are* one of us, right, Justice?" McMann sat down and motioned to the chair behind Justice. Dupé thought he looked exhausted.

"I don't respond well to threats, Captain," Justice said quietly.

"No one's threatening anybody, detective," McMann sighed. "Think this through, Justice. No need to make a rash decision. Sleep on it. We need another good guy—hell, a great guy."

"There's nothing to think about," said Justice. He suddenly felt very tired.

McMann frowned. He glanced at Dupé. Dupé remained staring at the desk. "I'm sorry to hear that, detective. I really am. In light of the circumstances, and the unsettling testimony about evidence found at the scene of a murder, I'm afraid I'm going to have to suspend you, Justice, for appearance's sake."

Justice looked at both men and let out a laugh. "Don't bother. I'll save you the trouble." Justice ripped his chain from around his neck, pulling off his badge. He placed it on the desk. Then he unholstered his two Kimber 1911's and placed them on the desk. "I quit." McMann shook his head and sighed. Dupé didn't move.

"I'm sorry to hear that," McMann said, concern in his eyes. "Oh, detective," he said. Justice stopped. "Your flak jacket too."

Justice paused for a moment, then began unstrapping his vest. He removed his custom case of toothpicks, a can of pepper spray, 3 throat lozenges, and a pen. Then he placed the vest on the desk and walked out of the office.

Chapter 37

Outside Justice stretched, feeling an unnatural freedom extended by his loss of vest in the Captain's office. It unsettled him. He popped the trunk of his car. On the left side of his trunk were two pairs of combat boots, a number of neatly folded black t-shirts, and three bullet proof vests. A large, black metal case took up the other three quarters of the trunk. Justice removed one of the vests and began strapping it on.

Dupé appeared at his side. "Justice, I just wanted to say that I didn't know- whoa! How many spare vests do you have in your trunk?"

Justice continued strapping the vest on. "Three backups in my trunk. I have four in a closet in my apartment."

"How come you never offered me one?" Dupé said in a hurt tone.

"Because you made fun of me for wearing one around, so why would I think that you would want one?"

Dupé rolled his eyes. "I didn't make fun of you for wearing a bulletproof vest. I made fun of you for wearing it *everywhere*. It's like driving your car to the mailbox."

Justice undid the latches to the metal case. "Some people have long driveways." The lid opened, revealing a compartment with a pile of loaded magazines. In three inches of foam, four Kimber 1911's, two .50 caliber Desert Eagles, and two grenades sat nestled in their holders. Justice removed a detective's badge on a chain from the case and hung it around his neck. Dupé's mouth hung open.

"Are you serious? You have all this in the back of your car? This is unbelievable! Are those Dessert Eagles?"

"AE. .50 cal. It packs a mean punch."

"How come you never use those? Those are hardcore. Terrifying."

"My .45's work great. I'm not looking to go overkill. Those bad boys are only for only the most dire of situations. That one is Jack and that's David." Dupé looked puzzled. "My giant slayers. But I like to be a little more subtle in my approach."

Dupé nodded solemnly in understanding. "Why didn't you tell me about all this, Justice? This arsenal is amazing."

"Maybe I was afraid you might take it and add it to your stockpile," Justice answered flatly, while he removed two of the Kimbers and their respective magazines. He inspected the weapons, testing the slides, and holstered them in the vest.

"Listen, that's what I came out to tell you. I had no idea that was going to happen. Wait, are those grenades?"

Justice closed the trunk. He looked exactly like he did before he went to see the Captain. "So you didn't know about the weapon stockpiling using money stolen by criminals from local businesses?"

"Wait, you can't just change the subject! You have what I assume to be live grenades and your own personal weapons cache in the trunk of your car," said Dupé in wonder.

"Don't *you* change the subject," said Justice.

"Of course I'm not sure why any of this surprises me," Dupé said to himself. "This is actually pretty par for the course."

"Dupé!" growled Justice.

Dupé returned to reality, though the wonder of Justice's private weapons cache in the trunk of his custom Dodge Challenger sent his mind racing. He collected his thoughts. "I didn't know that's how you would be brought up to speed. Yes, yes I knew about the weapons. I was in Fort Wayne. I was told there was a special assignment and I would be promoted if I took it. We had a baby, and the thought of detective and a pay raise was a no-brainer. The way the Captain put it made the situation seem like a no-brainer too. It made sense at the time. Now I'm not so sure."

"Well isn't hindsight lovely. You're practically an innocent man."

"Listen, I was supposed to work with you and warm you up to the situation. Captain McMann knew—hell, everyone knows, that you do everything by the book. You're all about the law and there's even your name."

"What's wrong with Blake?" Justice asked indignantly.

"Not Blake! Anyway, he wanted you to see how necessary the whole thing was, and I was supposed to help the situation."

"Well, you sure botched your first job as detective, didn't you?"

Dupé swallowed. "Yeah, I guess I did. But now with this Protagoras spook out there, this is the best course of action, isn't it?"

Justice placed both of his large hands on the trunk and leaned all his weight against it. His triceps flexed, stretching the fabric of the t-shirt. "You brought Elizabeth into this," Justice growled, turning to face Dupé.

"You brought her into this! I didn't know what to do!" shouted Dupé. "How was I supposed to know you weren't banging some hooker when I saw what I saw? Yeah, handing a large amount of money to a hooker. Nothing suspicious looking about that! I'm sorry. I screwed up. I don't know that I've ever met a guy who was looking to help out a hooker without getting some action from it. I was wrong."

"Anonymous. You don't even have the courage to put your name to it."

"The bag of money I *saw* you hand to Elizabeth came up as evidence in a serious murder investigation. I felt like withholding information would have been wrong."

Justice let out a long laugh and faced Dupé. "Withholding information? Like from your partner? I'm glad that you felt so strongly about coming clean."

"What would you have done in my situation?"

"I would have made sure I had all my facts straight before I betrayed my partner," Justice shouted, jabbing a finger into Dupé's tie. "You don't know me, and it's obvious I didn't know you either. Even if I did believe what you guys are doing is right, there's no way I could join two people I couldn't trust. Have fun fighting Protagoras with McMann and his arsenal. It's obvious justice has no place here anymore."

"Wait, was that you referring to yourself again, or was-"

Justice slammed the door shut. The Challenger roared to life and peeled out of its parking space.

Justice looked at the picture. What would his dad have done? Honey began licking his elbow. Something *was* going on. The scene at Lenny's was still etched into his mind. Could he turn his back on the force when things were at their worst? He wasn't turning his back. He was standing up for something he knew to be right. It would be good for the king to be dead, wouldn't it? Even if the means brought you to a place you vowed you would never go? David knew that fighting one evil with another evil didn't right things. But the possibility of going out onto the streets with a powerful arsenal was tempting. But at what cost? Justice thought about what he would do to the man who killed his father if he ever found him. What would justice look like then? Justice closed his eyes, the war of arguments eventually bringing an overwhelming exhaustion.

Chapter 38

Justice couldn't remember the last time he had slept in. He didn't use vacation days, and most of his off days still involved some sort of detective work. A day of nothing to do or think about had actually been quite enjoyable. By midafternoon he had grown restless and decided to go see his mother. Check her house for terrorists and the like.

The street was almost completely empty. No black SUV's, no clandestine suspects lurking in the shadows. No Russian baddie with assault rifles. No aliens either, unless they were the shape-shifting, invisible type. His mother would be relieved. Daylight often assuaged the fears of the night time. Though Justice wondered if his mother's paranoia ever shut off. It could be frustrating, but could he blame her?

He could hear the TV through the door. *I Love Lucy.* He could hear Ricky screaming with a laugh track. Had his mom really become that old? Did she really need the TV on that loud? Justice opened the door and walked in.

"I'm being watched," Wanda Justice said, without looking up. Lucy and Ethel were stuffing chocolates in their face on the television.

"I know, mom," Justice said as he pulled a beer out of the fridge. Justice sat down on the couch next to his mother's recliner. He took a sip of the cold beverage and wiped his lip. "I quit my job yesterday."

His mom turned down the TV. "And why would you go and do a thing like that?"

Justice sat, watching the silent figures on the television scurrying about. "I'm not sure." Wanda watched as her son took another sip. "When dad was killed, all I wanted to do was find bad guys and make them pay for hurting people." He turned and looked at his mom. "They took my dad. I wanted them to suffer. But I realized that revenge wouldn't honor his memory. But our system of laws was set up to deliver justice. So I joined the academy."

"I was so proud of you."

"I know, mom. I wanted to honor dad's memory."

"And you have."

"But now the one thing I believed in, it's not what I thought it was. You don't uphold the law by going outside it. I'm not a vigilante. But my precinct, I can't be a part of that."

"Listen, I don't know what's going on," she held up her hands, "and I don't expect you to tell me. But handing over your badge? It feels like you're running away."

Justice took another sip. "I don't know, mom. I feel like if I stayed there, I'd be taking a big dump on dad's grave."

"That's one way of putting it."

"Seriously, if dad saw that his son was fighting for justice by breaking the law."

"Well there's man's law, and there's God's law."

"I only know one law. The law of justice."

"And who decides what justice is?"

"Now you're beginning to sound like that preacher."

"My son has been to church?"

Justice settled back in the couch and put his beer down. "Tammy wanted me to go."

"Well at least that young lady can talk some sense into you." The two sat in silence for some time before she spoke again. "Sometimes you may have to make a tough decision for the greater good."

"So I've been told. But this, it's just wrong. It is. I can feel it in my gut, and that's not what I signed up for."

Wanda stared at her son. "Just what did you sign up for, Blake?"

He shook his head. "I'm not sure anymore."

"I'll tell you what you signed up for. You wanted to help people. Your dad wanted to help people. He wasn't perfect. God knows he wasn't perfect, but he had it in his head and heart that God had put him on this earth to serve and help people."

"I thought you didn't believe in God."

"Your dad did."

"And that divine purpose ended up getting him killed."

"Yes, it did, Blake. You think I don't know that? Every single day." Her voice trembled. "But he died living how he thought he was meant to. And I see that fire in his son. A purpose and a passion. And I don't want to see that fire extinguished because of some delusional infatuation with the perfection of law enforcement. It's people trying to help people, and they're not perfect. If you're living for justice, how will you know when it's been accomplished? By whose standard? Yours? The law written in the books? If it lets you down, then what?"

Justice sat and thought. "So you're saying that there's no point, screw them all?"

"If that's what you've heard, then you're dumber than I thought, boy. If an imperfection in people or your system or whatever causes you to quit, maybe you're living for the wrong thing. I'm saying that you better find something other than your job or justice to live for, or you'll end up like your daddy."

"I'm not going to end up like him, mom. I promise."

"No, you're going to end up worse: a living person who's dead inside. So go ahead and quit, since things aren't perfect. See how that works for you. Now if you'll excuse me, I was watching my shows." Wanda turned the volume up louder than it had been before. Justice watched her as she laughed at Lucy's hi-jinks. He grabbed his beer, finished it in one drink, set it on the counter, and walked out the door.

Justice had just pulled into the parking lot for his apartment complex when Tammy called. She seemed excited. "I think I've got something. I don't know what exactly, but it seems important. I mean, it might not be anything, but I'll just tell you. OK, sorry. Here goes. Captain McMann knows Protagoras. Or not knows him. He was around him."

"Slow down, Tammy."

There was a pause on the other end. "McMann used to be an officer in Gary."

"Yeah, he's talked about it before."

"I was doing searches for Protagoras in, uh, certain databases-"

"I don't want to know."

"Which is why I'm not telling you. I got a hit. 1980. Gary, Indiana. McMann fought him, or at least ran him out of town. His partner was killed, and McMann ran one of the biggest drug busts ever recorded in the mid-west. I guess it hit Protagoras hard because things cooled down immediately. His name has been mentioned in other places too, here and there, but nothing like Gary. Saw one in Greece. But it might just be a common name. I don't know. What's going on, Blake?"

"I'm trying to figure that out. I don't know yet."

"Because if what these articles talked about is going to happen here, I'm terrified. This isn't some low-life drug dealer, Blake. The police and McMann had to go all out to stop him."

"I'm sure they did," Justice answered."

Chapter 39

The night was warm, but the heat had finally broken. Though the sky was clear, the moon was nowhere to be seen. The brick found its target with an explosion of glass that cascaded to the concrete below. The three friends stood in the darkness in front of the dilapidated two-story building.

"Nice shot," said Shane, obviously impressed.

"Why, thank you," replied Marla curtsying. The events of last week had shaken her badly. She found herself having reoccurring nightmares of a man in a chair facing away from her. She would call to him, and the chair would slowly turn around, only to reveal that the man's chest and stomach had burst open. Every window she smashed felt like the memories were being destroyed one by one. For the first time in a few days, she felt like it might be possible to return to normal.

Nicole picked up a small rock and hurled it at one of the second story windows. She missed two feet to the right, and the rock clanged off the corrugated metal siding.

The three college students instinctively winced at the blast of sound in the still night. The abandoned Archer building was one of the furthermost buildings on the Avon

Rail Yard, away from the majority of work traffic, but it was still trespassing. Though the Archer building (it had no formal name, but it was known for the faded red insignia of an archer on the side of the building) hadn't been in use by the rail yard for quite sometime, security guards and night watchmen knew to patrol there from time to time due to the building's allure to vandals. The three friends remained still, listening for any sign of patrol.

"Try hitting the window, next time," Shane teased.

"That's what I was trying to do," replied Nicole.

Marla laughed and picked up half of a brick that had broken off. She threw it as hard as she could at the window Nicole had been aiming at. It hit the top frame of the window, popping a small hole in the glass, while sending the brick clattering to the gravel road below. "Damn."

Shane picked up a large stone and sent it right through the middle of the window, creating a perfect hole in the center while the rest of the window cracked into a dark spider web. "And that's how it's done ladies.

The two girls were just about to fire back their retorts when they heard the whine of vehicle's engine coming down the road. They sprinted to the edge of the trees and took cover behind some thick bushes. The three friends watched as a beat up, white hatchback pulled around the corner of the Archer building and parked with its lights off. Marla frowned, trying to remember where she had seen the vehicle before. The pale glow of a streetlight mounted to one of the telephone poles illuminated the car. The light illuminated a figure in the driver's seat, but glare from the windshield obscured his face. He didn't move. They could see that he was staring straight ahead.

"What's he doing?" asked Shane.

"Is he security?" Nicole whispered back.

Marla hushed them both. "I've seen that car," she said in a low voice.

"This is freaking me out," Nicole said. "Why is he just sitting there?"

"He kind of looks like the Unabomber," Shane said thoughtfully.

"Shut up!" Nicole squeaked.

Soon they heard the approach of another vehicle with a throatier engine. A dark SUV pulled around the corner and parked next to the white hatchback. Marla felt a chill run down her spine. She suddenly began to feel clammy and nauseous. She didn't know what was going on, but she had seen enough movies and shows to feel that she was witnessing something she wasn't supposed to. The SUV windows were tinted. The students hardly breathed, as if there was a mutual understanding that the scene unfolding before them was sinister in nature. The man in the white hatch back got out of his car when the SUV pulled up.

"That's the guy who robbed me," she said in wonder.

"Are you sure?" Shane asked in disbelief. Marla motioned for him to be quiet.

Daryl Starkman wrung his hands and scratched the back of his head. He clearly wasn't in control of this meeting. Finally the SUV's door opened, and a bald, well-built man dressed all in black stepped out carrying a briefcase. The two men exchanged some words, and the bald man handed the Daryl the briefcase. As he took the briefcase to his car and opened it on the hood, the bald man walked back to his SUV. Marla noticed that the back window was rolled down, though she couldn't see who was inside. The bald man didn't speak when he approached the open window; he just stood by it as if listening, nodding occasionally.

When the bald man turned from the SUV he was holding a pistol in his hand. The three friends didn't move, didn't make a sound. Daryl looked up from the briefcase and flung his hands up. They heard him scream out, "Wait!" And then the metallic clicks from the gun's suppressor. The body of Daryl Starkman slumped to the ground. Two large men, wearing the same clothing as the bald man stepped out of the SUV and walked over to the body. If they hadn't just watched him get shot, it would have looked as if a drunk had passed out with one leg out, the other tucked underneath, and the torso slumped forward and to the side. The bald man took out a rag from a pocket and began unscrewing the suppressor.

To add to the horror, Marla and her friends' brains began to register that the two men were going to dispose of the body, and they were hiding in a prime spot. Marla tapped Nicole who broke out of paralysis, and the three friends began to move farther back into woods as quietly as they could. There was a fence that ran the perimeter of the rail yard, but if they could make it past that, they knew how to get back to the car. Shane always had parked in a convenient store parking lot, which meant that they had to walk to the Archer building, but it was easier to get away through the woods than outrun the cops in a car chase. Getting to that car was the only thought on anyone's mind right now. As soon as they felt like they were a safe distance away, they began sprinting as hard as they could. Blood roared in their eardrums, and their lungs cried out for oxygen. Marla felt a cramp in her side, but she barely acknowledged it as she willed her legs to move faster. No one looked back until they had scrambled over the eight foot chain link fence. Five minutes later they collapsed next to the car— dirty, bleeding, torn clothes. Nicole was wiping tears from her face.

When they were on the road, Marla dialed the number from the card she had in her purse.

The voice on the other line was groggy and hoarse. "Hello?"

"Detective Justice?" Marla managed, and she burst into tears.

Chapter 40

Justice eased the Challenger over the badly cracked entrance to the gas station and onto the street. The call last night had found him half asleep, half drunk, with Honey asleep on his lap. He had passed out on the green couch and had to fumble to find the phone. He too had been trying to forget the recent events, but for different reasons. He was no longer a detective. He was no longer part of the law enforcement of Avon, Indiana. But it wasn't just a job to him, and the alcohol helped to slow the wheels that were constantly turning in his head. He didn't' want to think about how black and white, right and wrong had been blurred. Thinking about the case only tore at fresh wounds.

Marla had told him everything last night, but he wanted to make sure she was OK. She had been through so much in the last month. He was shocked that she had gone into work, but she explained that she didn't want to be back on her street. Her mom was with her brothers. She wanted to work.

This visit was so much different than the first time he had met Marla and left the gas station. He looked in his rear view mirror. No fireballs; the gas station was still intact. But Marla was more battered than ever. The college girl had impressed him back then, and she impressed him more now. Not every girl in her situation could have handled, or would have handled, things the way Marla handled them. Perhaps things would turn around on her street with Lenny gone. And now Daryl Starkman was gone. Or perhaps this Freidrich Protagoras would make things even worse. At least there was another name they could cross of the list of possible suspects. Daryl Starkman was not Protagoras, but there was little doubt he had been working with him.

Justice picked up his phone and waited for the other line to pick up.

"Detective Dupé."

"Dupé," Justice repeated dryly.

"Justice!"

"I'm not calling as a friend. Professional courtesy. As the active detective on the Protagoras case, I wanted you to know that a source told me about a murder last night at the train yard."

"A murder?"

"Mr. Scarface himself, Daryl Starkman. I guess you can cross him off the list of suspects now that he's dead."

"Thanks for the heads up, Justice. I appreciate it. I'll get guys over there right now to look for him."

"The Archer building. It's some abandoned building on the edge of the rail yard. Hey, keep this quiet. There's a reason I told you and not those government a-holes."

"Of course. It turns out I haven't been as helpful as they would have liked me to be."

"Good. I would expect nothing less." Justice smiled, despite himself.

"Not sure why I'm telling you this, since you quit- not even sure I should tell you this. The forensics came back from sniper kill. Basic 7.62mm round."

"That's a NATO round used in military sniper rifles. Virtually untraceable, but at least it confirms what we already knew. These guys are professionals."

"Listen, Justice-"

"Alright, thanks for the info. Just wanted to give you a heads up. Good luck, Dupé," and Justice hung up. Justice pulled up to a red light and stopped behind a red pickup. He wasn't sure what he was feeling at the moment. Dupé had betrayed him, but it shouldn't have made him this upset. He had known him for such a short time. But for all of his quirks, Justice had actually liked working with a partner. Dupé had a lot to learn, but he also had some natural instincts that you couldn't teach. Justice hated to admit it, even to himself, but he wondered if quitting the force had been the right decision. His mom certainly seemed to think it had been the wrong decision.

Justice patted his bulletproof vest. It was almost as if it had become a part of him. Even after quitting, his first instinct had been to look like a cop. Was it really that deep inside him? But how could you work with someone you couldn't trust? How could you work to enforce law and justice when your commanding authority had willingly broken the law just to get an edge in the fight against crime? If the public couldn't trust their police and law enforcement to uphold the law, why should they be expected to live within the laws? It is the code. It is integrity. It holds the world together. Without the law, people would be animals, left to their own devices. Captain McMann had forsaken that oath in view of the bigger picture, but it was black or white, no grey. There couldn't be grey in law enforcement. If it was embezzlement today, what might it be in five years? For what? So that they could defeat some shadow crime lord? To get coke off the streets?

Justice had decided he couldn't be a part of that. He couldn't do it with a clear conscience. It was better to turn in the badge (officially) than to be a part of something he didn't believe in. He tried to convince himself of that sentiment as he sat at the red light, the engine purring in soothing idle. A car pulled up next to him, and he glanced over at the dark blue Impala. Thoughts and emotions flooded Justice's mind, but he willed them into submission. The driver was a young male with short, dark hair. It was gelled. The light turned green and Justice merged into the same lane as the Impala, keeping two cars in between the Impala and his Challenger. The Impala made a left at the next light then turned right down a side street. Justice looked around, but saw no other cars or pedestrians. He hit the light bar on his dashboard his siren screamed to life. He watched the familiar sight of the eyes in the rearview mirror, and then the Impala pulled over so that it's two right side tires were in the grass near a ditch.

Justice pulled out a fresh toothpick and straightened his Aviators. The blue and red lights flashed on his dashboard and his back window. His headlights and taillights held a strobe pattern. He approached the car, head cocked to one side, hands on his side. The man rolled his window down. "Was I doing something, officer?"

"License and registration, please. Keep your hands where I can see them." Justice was leaned over so that he could see inside the entire vehicle. It was empty, clean. The man handed Justice the papers from the glove box and driver's license from his wallet. "Daniel Mosley. Mmm."

"Yes, sir?"

"Do you go by Daniel? Or is it Dan? Maybe Danny to your friends?"

"I guess so." Daniel was looking at the dashboard, glancing up at Justice every once in a while.

"You guess so, what? That you are who you say you are, or that you go by different names?"

"No, I, uh, mean, yes. I mean, my name is Daniel."

"You seem nervous, son. Do I make you nervous?"

"Yes, sir. A little. I haven't done anything wrong."

"Then you have nothing to be worried about, Mr Mosley." Daniel was holding the steering wheel with both hands, knuckles white. "Why don't you turn the car off for me."

"Why? What is this? I didn't do anything!"

"You seem agitated and anxious, and I don't want you doing anything you would regret. So please take the keys out of the ignition." Daniel turned the car off and set the keys in the cup holder. "That's better. Mr. Mosley, you haven't done anything you regret, have you?"

"No, listen, I, I, don't know why you pulled me over, but I haven't done anything wrong."

Justice watched the man squirm and turned the pressure up. "Do you like hookers Mr. Mosley?"

The man's face went white. "What? No!"

"So you're saying you don't like to solicit women of the night for kicks?"

Daniel stared in disbelief. "No."

"You've never met a blond woman before? Picked her up? She had pizza and some money? Does that ring a bell?"

Daniel closed his eyes and shook his head back and forth. "No."

"Are your tail lights out?"

Daniel looked back up at Justice, clearly confused by the sudden change in questioning. "What, I, no."

Justice stood up and looked at the back of the car. He laughed. "You seem to have a strange idea of what has happened and what hasn't happened."

Daniel pleaded with his hands raised. "My tail lights are fine. I haven't done anything wrong!"

Justice walked to the back of the car. He took one of his Kimbers by the barrel and slammed the tail light with the butt of the gun, shattering it. He looked back at Daniel who had his head in his hands. "Yep, driver's side is out, son," Justice called out to Daniel. "Let's take a look at the passenger side." Justice walked over and smashed it with the butt of his gun. "Hmm, both out." He walked back to the window. His tone changed to a threatening growl. "Now that we have the tail light situation figured out, let's try and remember this woman again, shall we? My gun can break a lot more than tail lights."

"OK, OK!" Daniel was practically blubbering now. "It wasn't my idea. Martin told me about it."

"Martin, who?"

"Martin Leech. He said he got a job where we could make some fast money. All I had to do was pick him up. That's when we picked up the hooker. I never hit her, sir, I swear. I didn't know what we were doing! I told him to stop. I made him get back in the car! Please, I didn't know."

Justice reached through the window and grabbed Daniel, pulling him out of the car through the window. Justice held him by his shirt collar about three inches off the ground. "Where do I find Martin Leech?"

"He owns a storage unit, off of 10th street. More 2 Store. Across from the Shell station."

"Why her? What were you doing with her? What did you do with the money?"

"I don't know. It was all Leech. I've never met her before in my life. I don't know who she is. But I know that he's supposed to meet some guy this Sunday night. For another deal or payment or something."

"Where?"

"At the State Fair Grounds. At the Monster Bash."

"The monster truck show?"

"Yeah."

"Why would he be meeting him there?"

"I don't know. He just mentioned it to me. Said there might be another gig after Sunday night. I told him I didn't want anything to do with it, but he told me to wait until after Sunday night to decide. He's meeting someone there. That's all I know; I swear!"

"If you're lying to me, Mr. Mosley, I know your face, I know your address, I know your car. There won't be a place you can run." Daniel nodded as a tear leaked out. "And I'm going to let you off with a warning for those tail lights, but you need to get them fixed as soon as possible."

"Thank you, sir," Daniel managed to squeak.

Chapter 41

Dupé looked up from his paperwork to find Captain McMann standing over his desk, frowning. "What's up, Cap?"

"That FBI special unit just arrived. Come out and meet them." He paused. "You'll be working with 'em."

Dupé sat for a moment, then pushed back his chair and stood up to follow McMann. They headed to the back of the headquarters and out a side exit door. There, Dupé saw three Chevy Tahoe's with reinforced bumpers, presumably for pit maneuvers, and fully tinted windows. Several antennas stretched toward the sky on the back of each vehicle. There were men and a couple of women busy around each vehicle, clad in black tactical gear with yellow "FBI" lettering on the front of each squad member's tactical vest. They were certainly an impressive looking unit. McMann walked over to bulldog of a man in his 50's who stood about 6'2," made of all muscle and whose bald head gleamed in the sunlight. Stubble covered the square jaw. Dupé noted his intense eyes. He didn't need a profile on the guy to see he was the one in charge.

Dupé held out his hand, and the bald man shook it with one vigorous shake. "Bole Savage, Michael Dupé," McMann said for both men's benefit.

Dupé grimaced as Savage took hold of his hand in a vice-like grip. "Your name is Bole Savage?" Dupé asked in wonder, looking down at the hand that threatened to crush his own. Scar tissue from a deep burn covered the entire hand, climbing halfway up his forearm.

"I'm afraid it is," Savage replied with a smile that revealed a perfect row of gleaming white teeth.

"Savage comes highly recommended by some of my contacts in Washington. If we're going to cooperate with the feds, apparently this guy is the guy to do it with," McMann said with a half smile. "He's got multiple tours of duty, special forces, blah, blah, blah. Long story short, if this Protagoras guy is real, this is the man to take him down."

"Pretty impressive, Mr. Savage," Dupé said with his arms crossed, mainly to hide the pain in his hand. "That's some pretty expensive hardware."

Savage looked at his team and the vehicles. Several of the men were carrying MP5's, shotguns, assault rifles, light machine guns, the works. "We only work with the best because we are the best," he replied with a wink.

"I imagine," Dupé said with a yawn. "Well, I should really get back to the work at my desk. I'm sure I'll be seeing more of you guys later on."

"We'll be getting set up, and then we're on the trail. We'll be checking every snake hole we find to get this guy out of hiding. We'll let you know if we need any special forms or paper work to be filled out."

Dupé nodded solemnly. "Anything we can do for Uncle Sam." He gave a half salute and then turned around and walked back into the offices.

"Some group, huh?" McMann asked, nodding back toward the door they had just come in.

"They're something all right."

"It's not my idea of a good time either," McMann admitted. "But they could be useful. If this Protagoras is as dangerous as they say, we'll need every man and woman we can get." McMann motioned for Dupé to go into his office. He closed the door behind them. "The final shipment is coming in Tuesday night."

"The weapons?"

McMann nodded with a smile as if he had just announced that his child had made honor roll. "Business has been good recently. Or businesses." He laughed at his own joke, but then stiffened when he noticed Dupé's sour look. "I know, it's unpleasant. Believe me, detective. I don't do this lightly. If I thought there was another way, I would do it, but the bureaucracy makes it so that we can't even do our damn job."

Dupé paced. "Maybe Justice is right. Maybe there's another way. I mean these *are* the people we're supposed to be protecting."

"We are protecting them, Dupé. That's the whole point. If this Protagoras is as dangerous as the rumors, we can't mess around with the toys they give us here. We have to be on the offensive. The stakes are too high."

"So who's going to be in charge of the shipment?"

"I'll be there. I'd like for you to be there as well. A few others. Furman and Philips. I think you know them."

"Furman and Philips?" Dupé was in shock.

McMann quickly tempered Dupé's reaction. "Listen, they may be royal jackasses, but their heart's in the right place. They can be trusted. They're a few cards short of a deck, but they're loyal and they keep their mouths shut."

Dupé's expression remained hardened, but McMann continued. "11pm. The rail yard. We have two shipping containers coming in with some amazing hardware. I have to admit I feel much better knowing it's on the train. Combine that with the storage facility cache, and we'll be able to eradicate crime and keep it down."

Dupé couldn't hide his surprise. "You have another storehouse of weapons?"

McMann beamed once more. "In the storage unit off of 10th street."

"Who all knows about this?"

"Furman and Philips keep an eye on things. A little added security detail. Obviously the owner, but he's sympathetic to our cause, and we've got so much dirt on that scumbag that if he ever tried to blow the whistle on us, his ass would be grass. A few others."

"So now we're getting in bed with trash to store weapons to fight trash?"

"Leech is a means to an end," McMann said dismissively. "He's dumber than a box of rocks, and he happens to have a perfect storage facility for our purposes."

Dupé stopped his pacing. "What about that FBI unit? Does Savage know about the weapons?"

"Do you really think I'm an idiot, Dupé? You think I'm telling the Feds anything about this? I cooperate with them because I have to, but they get to use our parking lot and our urinals. That's it."

Dupé nodded approvingly. "OK, well, I guess I better take care of the deskwork so I can hit the streets some more."

McMann stopped him at the door. His mouth was grim. "Be careful, detective. Justice isn't with you anymore."

Chapter 42

It was only 6:30 in the morning, but heat waves were already dancing on the asphalt in front of Captain McMann's house. The sun was bright, and the sky was completely clear. McMann closed the front door of his house behind him and looked at his watch. He looked up to see the looming figure of Justice leaning against the hood of McMann's Jeep.

"Blake Justice, what can I do for you?" asked McMann beaming. "Have you come to your senses? We'd love to have you back on the force. I see you somehow have all the items you turned in last week."

"I have spares."

"Of course you do. I would expect nothing less from Blake Justice." McMann laughed. "That's why I've always liked you. So, ready to come back on, or are you enjoying your happy retirement, getting fat on donuts and free coffee?"

Justice stood up, and pointed a finger at McMann. "You lied to us."

"I did no such thing, Justice." Replied McMann with hands raised in supplication. "The men who know about the weapons are fully on board. Dupé knew from the very beginning. I was hoping bringing him in would soften you to the reality of the situation. We need you, Justice."

"That's not what I'm talking about, Captain. I'm talking about Protagoras."

McMann's face shifted into wrinkles of confusion. "I don't understand."

"You knew about him. You knew he was here before Dupé and I ever mentioned that name to you. That's why you've been stockpiling these weapons. You're getting ready for a war with some pyscho criminal, and you didn't tell anyone. I had a friend dig for information on Protagoras, and your name popped up in the same findings."

McMann's head dropped until his chin rested on his chest. He looked up. "You're right. I'm sorry. Come inside. Let's not discuss this out here."

Justice stood next to the doorway, arms folded across his chest. McMann was sitting on his couch. He had offered a chair to Justice. Justice refused. McMann began. "I do know Protagoras. We go way back. I've never met the man, but he simultaneously made my life a living hell and catapulted me up the ranks of local law enforcement. I assume you know about Gary?"

Justice remained silent, eyes boring into McMann.

"I'll take that as a yes. I was just on patrol back then. Been doing it a few years but still wet behind the ears, just happy to be serving the badge. There were the usual assaults, domestic disturbances, robberies, occasional murder. Honestly the worst part was the smell. Like rotten eggs, sulfur mills." McMann shuttered. "But that all changed one summer. Coke started showing up. Good stuff too. And then there were the brutal executions. Any of the bigger criminals were absolutely slaughtered. I had never seen anything like it. Nobody had. And then a name started floating around the streets. Protagoras. Friedrich Protagoras.

"That city would have been torn apart. But he started in on my sections of the city I patrolled. My partner and I, we vowed this thug wasn't going to take Gary. We knew that every night we went out could be our last. But I didn't care—just so long as we stopped this creep. I never saw him, only the wake of destruction he left. My partner was killed." McMann grew silent, and took a cigar out of the drawer of the coffee table. He cut the end off of the cigar and stuck it in his mouth and began speaking again. "We ran him out. It was one hell of a war. Lot of casualties. But he disappeared.

"No bodies. No identification. We never found him." McMann exhaled, smoke curling out of his nostrils. "I knew that one day he would show up again. Don't know why; just always felt it. He started my career; I ruined his. When the coke started up on the streets, I just felt it in my gut. A flood of memories came back. It seemed like the only option. I don't want to see the blood that I saw in Gary."

Justice was silent for a moment and then spoke up. "So you want to bring Avon into a war instead?"

"It's already in a war," McMann barked, "and the sooner you realize that, the better!"

"No thanks, Captain. Robbing our own citizens to protect them doesn't make a lot of sense to me."

McMann pleaded with arms outstretched, "A means to an end, Justice."

"I'm sorry. My idea of justice doesn't have that in the definition."

"Your idea of justice is an illusion."

"Then I'll be the one waiting with a rabbit and a wand." Justice turned and walked out the front door.

Chapter 43

It took all of Justice's discipline and will power not to kick down the door of Martin Leech's office and drag him out by his hair. Justice imagined throwing him across some tables, maybe through a window. He hoped that when the time came to confront Leech, he would throw a punch, giving Justice the excuse to crack his skull open. Justice had been in his car since late afternoon, waiting for Leech to come out of his office and go home. An almost empty bag of trail-mix sat in the passenger seat next to three Burger King wrappers and a bag of Twizzlers. Justice hated stakeouts more than anything in law enforcement. Well, he hated it almost as much as deskwork. He considered that since he was technically no longer an officer of the law, this would be considered stalking. The prospect of sitting, watching, sitting some more, and still more watching made Justice sick to his stomach. So he passed the time eating. He had become so adept at finding the perfect menu for every stakeout situation, he was beginning to almost tolerate the endeavor.

After confronting Chief McMann at his home in the morning, Justice stopped by his mother's house for some more lecturing and The Andy Griffith Show. Justice admired Barney's passion and dedication in arresting the jay-walkers. Mayberry had cross-walks for the protection of its citizens. His mother had gone on and on about the men watching her and scary trucks on her block. Justice had passed a man washing his pick-up a few houses down from his mom. Justice nodded politely as she spoke of epitaphs, regrets, eulogies, and what songs she would like played at her funeral when they eventually found her body. It was more than obvious to her that the covert men Justice was blatantly ignoring would kidnap her and take advantage of her. Justice assured her that no one would want to take advantage of her.

Justice used his straw to break up the ice in his cup and he desperately wished it was filled with scotch. The shadows had elongated when Justice finally spotted movement at one of the windows in the little office. The door opened, and Justice studied the man who had assaulted Elizabeth and would have possibly done more if his friend hadn't stopped him. He was a tall man, not as tall as Justice, with a mop of black hair. He was large but didn't look to be in shape. Justice watched as Leech pushed his hand through his hair while locking the door. Once more Justice imagined grabbing the hair and slamming Leech into the wall.

Justice weighed his options. His more primal side, the side he hoped would win out in the end, called for immediate violence directed at his friend's attacker. The more rational side, the side that Justice trusted but still found rather boring at times, called for him to be patient and wait until Sunday night. If what Danny said was true, Justice might be able to learn who was ultimately behind the attack of Elizabeth and the plant of the money he had given her at Lenny's. Of course, if Danny was lying about Sunday night's meeting, well, then Justice would be arranging a very special meeting of his own for both the men.

He was about to pull away, when a department squad car pulled into the entrance of the storage facility. Leech looked up at the vehicle and gave a less than confident nod in its direction. The window came down on the passenger side of the police cruiser and Justice strained to see the officer inside. A bright shock of red hair poked out the window as Leech walked up. "Officer Ed Furman," Justice muttered under his breath. "Seems like company you would keep." The two men exchanged words for a moment, Furman with an arm resting easily on the door and Leech gesturing toward the storage units in a way that seemed like someone trying to bolster confidence and command. Furman gave a few condescending nods, turned to say something to his partner, most likely Carl Philips, and then rolled up the window. Leech watched the cruiser pull farther into the storage facility before heading to his car. The gate rolled shut as Leech pulled onto the street, leaving Justice pondering the exchange before he, too, pulled out to head back to his apartment.

Honey greeted Justice as if he had been gone for a week with pitiful whimpers and indiscriminate licking. He fixed his usual nightcap, placed his vest and guns in their usual spots and for the first time in several months, passed out the moment his head hit the pillow.

Chapter 44

The Sunday morning sun illuminated Tammy's dress and created a semi-halo around her dark curls. "So back for round two?" asked Tammy as she got in the car.

"It wasn't so bad the first time," replied Justice. "You curled your hair. Nice. You have to get up 4 hours early to do that?"

"I see you're wearing your Sunday vest again."

"Yeah, it took me forever to get it just right."

Tammy looked disappointed. "Do you have to wear it everywhere?"

"I don't have to wear it anywhere, but I choose to wear it."

"No one does that. And to church?"

"Things happen, and you'll be thanking me that I have this when I do. You sound like the guy from a couple of weeks ago who wouldn't let me in the church."

"I don't blame him. You're scary looking." She threw her hands up in surrender. "Whatever. So did you talk to your Captain?" Justice nodded. "And? What did he say?"

"He admitted everything."

"Why? Why would he lie about not knowing Protagoras?"

"Maybe he was afraid. Maybe he felt like the more he talked about it, the more vulnerable he would be." Justice paused before adding, "He lost his partner to Protagoras."

"I'm sorry." She knew that Justice hadn't lost his partner, but it seemed like the right thing to say. "It must be a nightmare to know that he's following him. Do you think it's revenge?"

"Maybe."

"This is scary, Blake. We have a psychopath trying to turn Avon into his drug cartel."

"Well, McMann and his posse can fight him with their weapons paid for by the hard working citizens of Avon."

"Listen, I agree that it's really screwed up, I mean, really screwed up, but I for one would feel much safer knowing that you were out there trying to stop this guy."

"If I come across him, I'll stop him."

"This doesn't sound like you. What happened to law and justice man?"

"Maybe he's beginning to realize that it was all an illusion."

"Yet here you are with a bulletproof vest, two guns, and a detective badge hanging from a chain around your neck. Clearly you have no desire to be a part of law enforcement anymore. Or maybe you're going to be the lone gunman, the vigilante of Avon."

The church seemed much less daunting than the previous visit. And Justice noticed that though he drew just as much attention as his previous trip, it seemed to be more positive than anything. Tammy made small talk with several people as they came in the foyer. Justice was introduced to each bubbly couple, but he didn't pay attention to any of the names he heard. He made eye contact with the doughy, pale man wearing the plastic security tag he remembered so well. Justice smiled. "Ah, here comes Alan," Justice said, rubbing his hands together. Tammy looked up as Alan, sporting a blue blazer, made his way over to them.

"Hello, Tammy! And I believe your friend is Detective Justice, if my memory serves me correctly." Alan was beaming as he gave each of them a hearty handshake.

"How did you remember me, Alan?" Justice asked in a puzzled tone.

Alan's face lit up. "Hey, you remembered me as well. I have a steel trap of a mind," he said, tapping his head with his finger.

"I bet you do," said Justice. Tammy elbowed Justice in the side.

"Good to see you, Alan," Tammy said. "Say hi to Malory for me. We're going to go ahead and find a seat in there." Alan nodded and moved off to another couple who had come in. "Behave," Tammy said through gritted teeth.

"I was," Justice said in mock exasperation. "That was just Alan. We go way back."

Pastor Darren Henshaw arranged his sermon notes and then leaned against the podium with one arm. Tammy leaned over to Justice and whispered, "You're going to love this sermon. Exodus 4:1-17. Have fun ignoring Protagoras, Justice."

He turned and looked at her unknowingly. Pastor Henshaw cleared his throat and began. "What is it that you are running from? What mission have you been given, what purpose in your life, and you've thought of a thousand excuses for not doing what you were created to do? It's too hard; it's not fair; I don't know how; it's not what I was expecting. What are you running from?"

"You have got to be kidding me."

"You see, the plan was laid out for Moses, as he talked to that burning bush, God's presence. And Moses heard it. He knew it. But he didn't want to go through it. But God, what if they don't listen to me? What if they don't respect my authority? What if I'm not eloquent enough? What if I blow it? What if it's not what I expected it to be? What about this? What about that? And finally God says, 'Enough! My people are crying out, and I've heard their suffering. With you, or without you, I'm going to do something. But I want you there, Moses. I'll give you help, your brother Aaron. But I don't want excuses while my people, your people, are suffering at the hands of the Egyptians.'"

"This is not the same thing at all," Justice whispered. "This is a random passage."

"Shh," said Tammy. "I'm trying to listen to the sermon."

"Mr. Justice. It's good to see you again." Pastor Henshaw took Justice's hand in both of his and shook it vigorously. "And you didn't leave dear Tammy alone this time."

Justice smiled and looked away. "No, sir. She came with me."

"I'm glad to hear it. I didn't know if we had scared you off from last time."

"Oh, no. It's very nice here. Hard to ruffle me, pastor."

"Well, we'll see what we can do then," Henshaw said, winking at Tammy. "How's women's Bible study going?"

"It's good. We have a good core group, and we've had some really good discussions," Tammy replied.

"I'm glad to hear that. You've got some good material there. Tammy's a fantastic teacher, Detective."

"I bet she is, but I'm not sure I would fit in at a women's Bible study."

Henshaw leaned in and lowered his voice. "The bulletproof vest and weapons might make them nervous." He straightened up and clasped Justice on the shoulder. "Please come back. It was good to see you. I've got a wife around here somewhere that's going to kill me if I don't get our son out of the nursery."

The short man gave a final handshake and then walked out the doors into the foyer. Justice remained standing where he was.

"We going, Justice?"

"Are you sure you didn't tell your pastor what was going on?"

"Are you asking me if Darren wrote a sermon specifically to address you quitting your job? Yes, Justice. That's what pastors do. I heard a sermon the other day about why reading to young children benefits them in significant ways."

"Funny."

"Maybe," Tammy said smiling, "God's giving you some direction in where you need to go."

"So now God's talking to me?"

"I don't know. Why not?"

"I don't even go to church."

"Oh, so you think that God's waiting for you to tithe before he cares about someone he made?"

"That sermon could have been about anything, just a random verse."

"And yet, it happened to speak into exactly what you're struggling with right now."

Justice couldn't think of anything to say, so he held the door open for Tammy and they walked out the church doors into the sunshine.

"OK, so where to, then?" said Tammy, looking through her purse. She found the powder and flipped down the sun visor to look in the mirror.

"Do you have to powder your face in here?"

"Oh, are you afraid your car's going to turn into a Dodge Neon or something?"

"I'm afraid that all the testosterone in this environment is evaporating."

"Trust me," said Tammy looking away from the mirror toward Justice, "that will never happen."

"Speaking of testosterone, we haven't done anything in while."

"First, I have no idea where you could be going with that segue. Second, we're doing something right now: church and lunch."

"I meant going somewhere. I'm thinking you, me, tonight, at the state fair with some monster trucks at Monster Bash."

"OK, I'm listening. What time?"

"I'll pick you up at six. It starts at eight."

"Blake Justice and Monster Trucks. I do believe the testosterone is safe."

"We'll have to purchase extra tickets for all the other ladies who will want to sit by me."

"Good thinking. Planning ahead. Ladies love that. Now, will these ladies be chewing tobacco? Are we going for full rows of teeth, here?"

"Hey, come on. Don't penalize a beautiful woman because she happens to be missing a couple of teeth."

"I fan myself in your presence, Blake. It's too much. I can't take it." Tammy laughed. "I can't believe I used to have a crush on you."

"You used to have a crush on me?"

Tammy rolled her eyes. "No, you moron. See. You're so full of yourself, you're willing to believe anything. Now hurry up and get to Fazoli's. I'm dying for some authentic Italian cuisine."

"Endless breadsticks," Justice murmured back.

Chapter 45

"What are you wearing?" Justice stared at Tammy as if he had noticed a fly in his soup.

Tammy shut the car door behind her and put on her seatbelt. "Well it's nice to see you, too, Blake. What's wrong with this?" Tammy was wearing khaki capris, a short-sleeve turquoise top, and chic sandals. Justice wasn't necessarily concerned about the particulars of the outfit, but what he saw made a significant impression.

"You do know we're going to the Monster Bash at the State Fair, right?"

"Oh, look who's talking." Tammy spoke in a deep voice saying, "I wear black t-shirts, and black Wranglers, and a bullet proof vest, and combat boots, and Aviators, and a toothpick."

"You don't *wear* a toothpick, Tammy."

"Whatever. What is wrong with what I'm wearing? I think I look cute."

"You do! You look fantastic, Tammy."

"Well thank you, kind sir."

"But that's the problem. You look too good. They're not going to let us into the fair with you looking like that. You need rips in your pants. Your clothes are clean and you don't have any stains anywhere. You have too many teeth. You can't see your bra through a tank top." Justice pulled out of the apartment parking lot. "Great. We're not even going to get to see the monster trucks. Thanks a lot, Tammy."

"Oh come on. It's not bad to look classy. I'm not trying to look like one of the mechanics."

"Shhhh." Justice stared straight ahead at the road with a hard, determined look on his face.

"What?"

"I'm trying to grow a mullet." Tammy laughed and punched Justice in the arm.

Officer Ed Furman fumbled with the lid to his coffee. "These damn pop tabs, or whate'er they're called, are more hassle than help."

His partner, Carl Philips, grunted his agreement. He flipped through a thin stack of papers while punching the keys to the squad car computer. "Try using your key."

"I did that once and I ended up putting it through the side of the cup. Damn near emptied the entire cup in my lap."

Philips laughed. He looked out his window. "How much do you think that Leech guy is making on this place? Doesn't even need security, since we're doing it free of charge for him."

"Yeah, but we're definitely not paying him for the space we're using."

"What did he do, anyway?" Philips asked. "We have to have a lot on him to keep him from blabbing about a cache of secret police weapons."

Officer Furman had removed the lid from his coffee and sipped it. "Probably beat his wife or something like that. Other clandestine behavior. Not sure, but if he opens his mouth, I'll personally break his jaw."

"Man, there's that temper again. What did we talk about?"

"Do you believe this Protagoras bogey man stuff?" Furman asked, ignoring Philips' comment.

"Well, it doesn't really matter what I think," Philips said. "Cap does. So I guess I do. I mean, isn't that why we're here guarding a secret stockpile of weapons?"

"To be honest, we could probably leave this gate wide open, and nothing would happen here. At least not to our stuff."

"Oh, that would be a shame for our dear Saint Leech." They both laughed at Philip's joke.

The parking was horrendous in the designated public lots. It seemed like everyone was at the fairgrounds that night. It may have been the buzz around the Monster Bash (some of the top trucks would be there: Curbstomper, Pistoned Off, Gas Guzzler, Behomoth), or it could have been the fact that the temperature had dropped to 90 degrees and the humidity was finally reasonable. Justice by-passed the general public parking, and drove to one of the side entrances. Several police cars were parked alongside the road. Justice pulled into the grass behind a tan police cruiser. The sheer presence of the Challenger, coupled with its appropriate guttural rumble, had attracted the attention of all the officers on duty. A tall, well-built sheriff in his 50's, dressed in standard tan uniform, complete with hat, strolled over and stood by the driver side.

Justice rolled down his window. The sheriff's face betrayed a slight twitch as he realized the size of the man in the vehicle wearing a bullet proof vest with two pistols holstered, and Justice watched the man's right hand move instinctively to his holster. "Detective Justice, Avon Precinct," Justice said preemptively, holding up his badge.

The sheriff relaxed and smiled. "I was going to tell you that this was for authorized vehicles only son, and then I see an armed man in tactical gear sitting in the front seat." He exhaled, ending in a low whistle. "Have to tell you my heart started to stutter a sec." The sheriff had a distinct country drawl, and as if to complete the stereotype, he spit a stream of dark brown juice onto the grass. Tammy's nose crinkled. The sheriff dabbed at his head with a handkerchief. "You here on special business?"

"No, not tonight. Just here with a friend for the Monster Bash. Impressive vehicles."

The sheriff nodded. "This here's an impressive vehicle. What she got under the hood?" He stepped back to take in the entire vehicle.

"7.2 liter V8. Gets 600lbs of torque out of this girl."

The sheriff let out another low whistle. Tammy rolled her eyes. "You wanna give me the ticket and you guys can swap engine stories?"

"All right if we park here, Sheriff… Warren?"

"It's no problem. We can always use more police presence. We'll take good care of her for you. You sure you're not on assignment?"

Tammy leaned over, "He always dresses like this. It's a curse."

The sheriff smiled and nodded, stepping back so that Justice could open his door.

Once inside, Justice started walking towards the front entrance.

"So did you quit or not?" Tammy asked in low voice. This was a completely unnecessary precaution. The volume of people, rides, live music acts, animals, and announcements over the loudspeaker created a symphony of nostalgia that brought Justice back to when he and his father would visit the Coliseum for hockey matches and model train shows. It hadn't changed much since then, a few renovations here and there, but that was more than OK with Justice. Too many things had changed since he was a little boy. Tonight he would be spending time with two of the few constants in his life.

"Blake."

"Oh, what? Yeah, an elephant ear sounds good."

"Were you listening at all?"

"Sorry, I was just thinking, dad and I used to come here when I was little."

"Yeah, I know. Remember when we went ice skating for the first time here?"

"That was the other thing I was thinking about. This place reminds me of dad, and I miss him, but I'm glad that I've still got you. Mom's...different. She has been since dad was killed, but this place, you, it just feels good."

Tammy smiled and squeezed his arm. "I'm glad too. Geesh, Blake. Could you wear a tighter shirt?"

"It's double XL."

"Whatever. I think that chick over there with the fanny pack is checking you out." Tammy had made the joke, but the truth was she had always laughed at just how many women flirted or hit on Blake. She had already noticed several heads turning just in their short time in the fairgrounds.

"That dude with the mullet has been eyeing you since we got here," Justice said, nodding at a concession stand. "I think you're his type."

"Mmmm, mullets."

"Or wait, maybe it was *that* guy with the mullet. There's too many of them. I feel exposed, like I don't fit in somehow."

"You never fit in. Course, you actually might fit in dressed like that, here. Need more camo."

Tammy found herself being carried away by the smells of the fair—funnel cakes, corn on the cob, fried Twinkies, tender loins, turkey legs, corn dogs. Then a slight breeze stirred the air and the familiar smells from the stables squelched her salivary glands. She looked up and they were standing by the front gate.

"What are we doing here?"

Justice walked up to one of the workers, shook his hand, said something, and handed him a bill.

"What was that all about?"

"Listen, it's nice getting a free parking spot, but I'm going to pay for us to be here. Enforcing the law has its perks, but we still have to pay like everyone else. Come on, Tammy," Justice scolded, and then shook his head in mock disgust.

"I don't get it."

"Get what?"

"You don't want to be on the force anymore, but you like to play dress up and still act the part?"

Justice ignored her question. "Come on, I want to get in there and see these bad boys."

Chapter 46

The coliseum was surprisingly packed. The allure of the oversized trucks had brought in an eclectic crowd, and Justice scanned the crowd for an open place to sit. Tammy kept close to Justice as they edged past some spectators to get a seat. The strong, sweet smell of chewing tobacco mixed with the exhaust fumes from the trucks and the dollar beers that filled most of the hands in the arena. Roars from the 1500 horse power, supercharged, alcohol injected engines made Justice smile.

"These make the Challenger seem tame, don't they," he pointed out to Tammy.

"I don't know a single person who would call your car tame, Blake."

"See their structure? The tubing in the frame is geometrically designed to distribute the force from the impacts they take. It's pretty incredible stuff."

"I didn't know you liked them so much."

"Are you kidding? Listen to that. How could you not love that?" Justice pulled out a pair of small binoculars from his vest and began scanning the crowd.

"What else do you have in there?" Tammy asked.

"Just the essentials."

"Why do I get the feeling that we're not here just for monster trucks?"

"I don't know why you would say that," Justice said absently as he continued looking through his binoculars.

Tammy sighed as a stream of tobacco juice cascaded down the steps of the aisle next to her. She caught a whiff of beer as a man belched behind them. Justice stood up as the first monster truck roared out onto the course. The sound was almost deafening, like standing in a small tunnel as someone redlined their diesel engine over and over again. Tammy finally had something to distract her from her fellow spectators. The five-ton monster truck attacked the pile of cars and vaulted over them. She had to admit it was a marvel of vehicular engineering, even if it was engineering inspired by redneck pastimes. The five foot tall tires easily rolled over the cars in its path.

But Justice wasn't watching the spectacle in the center of the arena. His binoculars scanned the crowd row by row on the lower concourse and then down to the entrances of the arena. Part of Justice didn't believe that Leech would be here. He wondered who would be hiring a man like Leech for jobs. This thought reminded him of the job Leech had initially taken—a job that ended with Elizabeth bleeding in an empty parking lot and narrowly escaping rape. The primal side of Justice wished that he would encounter Leech in a deserted place at the fair so that he could pound Leech's face in without worrying about someone stopping him. Another part of Justice hated the fact that he was passionate about investigating a crime that was close to him, while he wanted nothing to do with a case that had possible implications that could destroy an entire community. He shook the thoughts from his mind. The Cap and Dupé had made their bed, and they would lie in it. And they were lying while making that bed too, Justice thought. And he didn't want to be in a liar bed. He continued scanning.

"So does this mean you're getting back on the force?" Tammy asked.

"I'm just here watching monster trucks with a friend."

"So I'm confused. Who are we looking for? I thought you were done."

Justice's binoculars moved back and forth. Finally they stopped. Through the frame, Justice watched the greasy Martin Leech standing in the entrance way about 10 sections over from him. He was eating peanuts. He shoved a handful into his mouth, staring blank faced at the spectacle in front of him. Justice felt the hair stand up on the back of his neck. Leech stood there without a care in the world. As he watched, a bald man, well built, walked up and stood side-by-side with Martin Leech. Tammy was saying something. Justice didn't hear her. The bald man looked older than Leech, but he didn't say anything; he simply stared straight ahead. Leech finally noticed him and turned to say something, but a quick word from the other man made Leech stop talking and turn back toward the action in the center of the arena.

"I'll be right back," Justice said to Tammy, already at the end of the row.

"Of course you will," she muttered.

Justice never took his eyes off the section entrance while he slowly made his way across another row of people. He didn't want to chance going into the hallway and not see them if they left, but he felt exposed as he made his way across aisles. The entrance was about 10 rows up from the bottom rail of the arena so Justice tried to remain as high as possible to stay out of their line of vision. Eventually though, he would have to go down. The two men were clearly talking to each other. The bald man was doing a better job of concealing it, while Leech couldn't help but turn his head slightly during the conversation.

Justice was beginning to think he might be able to successfully flank the two men when the bald one looked up and then slipped back into the tunnel. Justice cursed himself for not being able to hide his 6'5" frame better and began to clamber down the rows, jostling people and spilling numerous items in their hands from the concession stand. Leech saw Justice quickly working his way down the rows and panicked. He hadn't the slightest clue who the hulking figure in a tactical vest was bullying his way toward Leech in a hurry, but when his contact had left in a hurry, he wasn't going to stick around and ask questions. He sprinted towards the rail below him and hurtled it.

Tammy watched the man hurtle the railing, sprawling when he hit the dirt below, but he quickly scrambled to his feet and ran across the back of the arena at a surprising speed. Justice was still picking his way between people in the rows to try and get to the aisle the man had just run down. A monster truck was on the course as Leech ran, but it had just circled on the far end when Leech vaulted the railing. People noticed that a man had jumped onto the course, but few people reacted as he quickly moved toward one of the entrance tunnels and away from the truck. This was a spectacle after all; he could have been part of the show. As Leech reached the tunnel, the truck sped toward two ramps with seven cars in between. It vaulted into the air (which Tammy again found quite impressive, despite herself) and landed perfectly on the other side.

The crowd erupted as the truck skidded to a stop, the driver crawling halfway out his window, milking the crowd with fist pumps. Justice reached the railing, but Leech had already run down the tunnel. The bald man was nowhere to be found. Justice wasn't going to lose Leech.

Tammy watched Justice pause at the railing, looking at the tunnel the man had disappeared down and then at the monster truck sitting in front of him. Tammy put her head in her hands, her stomach rolling in nausea. She had known Justice too long, perhaps. She could follow his thought process almost as quickly as he could, and like a mother trying to stop the inevitable foolishness of her child, Tammy audibly groaned in anticipation of his next move.

Leech ran past several men dressed in yellow security t-shirts who yelled at him, but he didn't look back. Whatever he had gotten himself into, he was going to get himself out. Why had he never gotten the name of the man who hired him for the jobs? He knew the answer to that, and it was half of the reason he ran so hard now. Leech didn't know who the man chasing him was, and he didn't want to stop and find out. And deep in his gut, he had known better than to ask questions of his secretive employer. If someone was on to them, chances were Leech's services with the bald man would be terminated in one way or another. There were many unknowns in his entire business venture that were best left unknown. Leech ran because his life depended on it.

Chapter 47

Outside in the warm air, Leech allowed himself a second to gain his bearings. He was in a parking lot full of State Fair staff cars, trailers for animals, and everything the monster truck teams had brought for competition. His attention turned to a H2 Hummer pulling into the parking lot. Instinctively, he threw himself in front of the chest-high headlights, waving his arms frantically for the driver to stop. The driver blasted the horn as the vehicle lurched into a nosedive.

"Please help me!" Leech screamed; he even managed to twist his face into a look of pain/terror. He hadn't quite decided on what to go with in the situation, since he had never been that good at improvisation. The man in the Hummer had his window down, and Leech stumbled forward to the car door. "Please," he pleaded once more. The moment the man unbuckled his seat belt, Martin Leech reached through the open window, and with one clean motion, pulled the man kicking from his vehicle.

"The hell?" was all the man managed before Leech's shoe connected with his face, and he lay motionless on the pavement. Leech jumped in the passenger seat and slammed his foot down once more, this time on the gas. He sped to the end of the row and then, tires squealing, whipped the large vehicle to the right to come back down the next aisle toward the exit. His eyes were straight ahead, his heart pressing against his ribcage. Once he was out of the parking lot, he would be done with any further business proposals. But the man knew where his storage facility was. He would deal with that when the time came.

Martin Leech heard the vehicle before he saw it. The tunnel did nothing but amplify the unmistakable sound of the monster truck several times over.

Leech's silhouette turned toward the monster truck; a monster truck had no need for headlights, but the street lamps and neon signs from the fair illuminated what Justice saw as the dark shape of a monster in the Hummer's seat. Once his brain had registered that it was indeed Martin Leech in the vehicle, Justice downshifted causing the entire frame to torque under the power. The tires climbed over two sedans parked next to each other, reducing the vehicles to corpses of twisted metal and broken glass.

The Hummer's owner sat up abruptly, perhaps his subconscious mind reacting to the earsplitting roar. His eyes opened just in time to see the five-ton vehicle airborne and then drop down on top of a dark SUV.

Martin Leech let off of the gas, mesmerized by the spectacle unfolding to his right. Part of him was in awe, while the other part prepared himself for death.

The timing was perfect. Justice smiled as the passenger side tire ripped through the back half of the Hummer, essentially sheering it clean off. The monster truck handled much differently than the Challenger, but the feeling of literally sitting on a massive engine with massive wheels made Justice practically giddy with excitement. Flames ignited from the ruptured gas tank, and the owner who had just regained consciousness watched in horror as his prized possession sat engulfed in flames, half of what it used to be.

Justice ripped free from his harness, rushed to the hummer, and wrenched open the driver-side door. The airbag had deployed and Leech was slumped forward, completely dazed. Justice dragged Leech out by his hair and away from the burning vehicles. He knew he only had a small window before officials would reach the scene. Justice screamed, "Who was that man? He lifted Leech up by his shirt until their faces were inches apart. "Who told you to attack Elizabeth?" Leech's eyes opened and closed in an attempt to shake off whatever fog still remained, but he didn't answer the questions. Justice brought the back of his hand sharply across Leech's face. Leech was suddenly more alert.

"I, I don't know his name," he managed. He looked down wildly, trying to recall something, anything.

Justice punched him square in the nose, still holding Leech's shirt with the other hand. Immediately two streams of blood flowed down Leech's chin. He spluttered as Justice shouted once more. "You attacked a woman and stole her money! Why? Who was that man back there?" Justice could already hear the sounds of shouting and people running his way. He shook Leech and smacked him again, harder this time. Justice felt something rising up inside him, a rage that scared him. He pulled his fist back and looked into the eyes of a coward—a man who beat women and scavenged opportunity like a vulture around a carcass. *Don't kill God's anointed.* Anointed? The only thing that had ever anointed

Martin Leech was maybe an old bottle of Miller Lite, but something stayed Justice's hand. This man was defenseless. Justice held his life in his hands, and he could extinguish it if he wished. *My people are crying out.* He wasn't God's instrument or tool or whatever the sermon had said. He was just a man bringing justice to a hardened city. But this, this wasn't justice; it was vengeance. Something inside him ached. He had no qualms about breaking a man's nose, but taking his life while he was helpless—that would be murder.

The fair officials were close. They were shouting at Justice. He dropped Leech to the asphalt and stood up, flashing his badge, never taking his eyes off Leech.

Tears began to mix with the blood streaming from Leech's nose. One eye was already swelling. "I'm sorry," he whispered. "Just kill me."

Chapter 48

Officers Ed Furman and Carl Philips got out of their squad car, stiff from the 4 hours they had already spent sitting in the uncomfortable cloth seats. The heat was less oppressive than it was during the day light hours, but the humidity instantly created a moist bond between clothes and skin; it had not dissipated in the slightest. Furman brought a cigarette up to his large lips, lit it, and inhaled. He held up the pack to Philips; he declined. The squad car was parked in the middle of the aisle between the rows of storage units. It was a simple cover for their assignment: protect the weapons. You protect the storage unit, you protect the weapons. Some suspicious activity had been reported around the area—send a squad car to patrol. Easy.

Leech had left about 6pm. The two officers loathed the slimy grease ball, but it was his storage units they were using and so they put up with him.

"You know, I'm tempted to break into his office and see if he has any beer in that fridge by his desk," Philips said.

"Don't joke, man. I'd kill for some suds, but I think I would be out cold if I had one right now. I can't seem to wake up," Furman replied.

"Well you better. I'm not staying awake guarding this place by myself. It's a crap job to begin with. I'm not doing it alone."

"It's not a crap job."

"Well it sure is boring as hell," Philips said emphatically.

"Can't argue there."

The two officers snapped to attention as headlights flashed across the compound. Two vehicles stopped at the gate. From the height of the headlights, and the glow from the second vehicles lights, the officers saw that the two vehicles were SUV's or trucks. "What the hell is this?" Furman quietly voiced for both of them, as they shielded their eyes. "Is that the FBI guys? What are they doing here?"

The two SUV's, lights shining directly at the two officers, remained idling at the front gate.

Philips and Furman looked at one another. "What are they expecting, room service? Open your own damn gate," Furman said toward the vehicles.

He shifted his weight, apparently about to move toward the gate, when it suddenly creaked into motion. It slowly rolled across headlights of the front vehicle, creating rippled shadows on the asphalt. "Well look at that. They've got a garage door opener. Makes you feel real safe, doesn't it, knowing those Feds are looking out for your property." Furman spit in disgust.

The dark SUV's rolled to a stop in front of the officers. Though Furman would never admit it openly, the situation made him nervous. McMann hadn't told them about any visit from the special unit tonight. "Keep your eyes open, partner," Furman said as he began to walk toward the lead vehicle.

"I got your back," Philips replied, putting his hands on his hips as casually as he could manage in order to bring his hand closer to his weapon.

The window rolled down as Furman reached the driver. A woman with dark hair and darker eyes stared at him.

"Didn't realize you guys had a key to the place," Furman said in an icy tone.

The woman smiled. "There's a lot you don't know." She never broke eye contact.

Furman glanced away despite himself. "Can we help you with something?" he asked. It was a more polite tone, but it was an obvious formality.

"We need to check on our shipments," the agent said. It was not a request.

Philips watched his partner by the SUV shift his weight and then fold his arms. He wished he could hear what the agent in the vehicle was saying.

"I didn't realize-" Furman began and then caught himself. Did the agents know? The sudden realization that everyone going along with the weapons shipment was committing a felony rushed over Furman like a bucket of cold water. They had been the authorities in charge until this point, and the possibility of being arrested gave him heartburn. But he recovered. "What shipments do you have here?"

"I believe there's a large unit stocked with weapons recently acquired to fight Freidrick Protagoras. That shipment."

Furman cleared his throat. The initial threat of punishment was replaced by a new sensation. He hadn't been notified about any of this, and he took a great deal of pride about being on the inner circle with his Captain and his plans. The agent's words and mission were a direct assault to his ego. It was understood in all local law enforcement that Feds were to be treated as pampered pains in the ass, and all officers should offer the minimum requirement of cooperation. Furman knew this. And this was his and Philips' territory, their assignment. But it was still the friggin' FBI! He was caught between ego and awe.

"What guns?" was all he could manage.

The woman's face softened; her tone turned sympathetic. "Listen, you're doing your job. We sympathize with the cause. We get it. But call your captain if it makes you feel better. Who do you think sent us over? We're just trying to stop this guy, same as you. Same team."

Furman regained his composure. He gave a knowing nod and added, "It's nothing personal. But this is important, and we can't take any chances."

"You're right, and we appreciate everything both of you have done for the cause."

Furman turned to yell something important, something impressive to his partner, but when he looked back, no words came out. Philips lay on the ground, and one of the special unit agents was removing a knife from Philips' neck. Furman's mouth opened, his brain reeling, but nothing came out. He felt the sudden burning sensation of the metal cord around his neck pulling taut. He clawed desperately to escape, but his assailant was skilled. His head felt as if it were about to burst, and his attempts to inhale simply helped the cord pull tighter. The darkness came quickly.

Chapter 49

The phone rang three times before Dupé picked up on the other line. "Justice?"

"I found him, Dupé. Martin Leech—the dirt bag who assaulted Elizabeth."

"You didn't-?" Dupé trailed off.

"No," Justice said quietly. "I didn't. God knows I wanted to." He heard a soft exhale on the other end. "I did clear his sinuses for him, though."

"I would expect nothing less for the guy. That was thoughtful of you. What did you get from him?"

"Not much," Justice admitted. The traffic was surprisingly light on 38th street and he drove accordingly. "Technically I'm not a police officer, so I didn't have much time with him. He was just a pawn. But there was another man there. He was bald, a little older. Stubble."

"Did you say bald?" Dupé asked, suddenly animated.

"Yeah, like a cue ball. A lack of hair gets you going, huh?"

"Just a second," Justice heard Dupé say, his voice distant. "I'm sending you a picture."

"Did you draw it yourself?" Justice's phone buzzed, and he tapped the picture, enlarging it. He was staring at the man who approached Leech and disappeared when Justice gave chase. "That's him. Who is he?"

"Bole Savage. Head of the FBI special unit sent to back us up against Protagoras. Former special forces, decorated, you know the story. All around general badass."

"So, what, you just have their records stored on your phone?"

"It's a habit, I guess," Dupé said. "I got my hands on the papers sent over from Washington. Snapped pictures of the pictures in their files. But that's him?"

"Yeah," Justice replied, thinking about the face he watched through the binoculars. It hadn't been a close up, but the head, the face, were distinct. "Yes, that's him."

"OK, so what was the head of the FBI special task force doing with Martin Leech?"

"Your guess is as good as mine. I don't think Leech really knew what he was doing, why he was doing it, or who he was doing it for. He doesn't strike me as a man with a plan."

"Was Savage scoping him out, tailing him?"

"No, I don't think so. He was talking to him, but talking to him like he didn't want to draw attention to the fact that he was talking to him. It didn't seem to be the first time they had talked. And he disappeared when he saw me. He could have arrested him anytime."

"Why would Savage know Leech?" Dupé mused out loud.

Ideas and wild conjectures careened around inside Justice's skull, and he had to work to keep his attention on the road. He had thought he could walk away from the Protagoras case, but following Leech's thread had lead right back to a ball of yarn with Protagoras' name on it. The leader of the D.C. task force assigned to Protagoras. The same man meeting with the scumbag who had assaulted the acquaintance of Justice and then brought the stolen money to Lenny's before the execution. Perhaps he had planted it there later. Maybe he turned it into the cops. Maybe he knew Lenny. Maybe. There were too many maybe's. But however he did it, *why*-ever he did it, the task force leader was now holding covert meetings with the dirt bag in charge of the storage facility housing the secret armory of the Avon PD.

"Have you been to the storage unit recently?" Justice asked suddenly.

"No, why?" There was a short pause. "Wait, you don't think-." Dupé couldn't allow the thought to be voiced aloud. His brain tried to sift through the screaming implications of trail of thought he and Justice were now considering. Accusations against an FBI agent would not be dealt with lightly.

"Call McMann, and meet me at the warehouse."

"Furman and Philips should be over there," Dupé responded.

"Then they're working for Savage. Or they're not, and they have no idea how much danger they're in." The two men hung up, the big picture beginning to take shape before them, though the details remained elusive and ever shifting. Justice flipped on his dashboard lights (he had not turned those in to McMann), and the Challenger neared triple digits effortlessly. He left his siren off. There was no need to announce to Savage, or Protagoras or whatever his real name was, that they were closing in on him, but the lights warned off any naïve black and whites in the area. Justice wasn't sure who he could trust in the department anyway. If the FBI task force really was a front for Protagoras and his mercenaries, there was no telling how many police he owned through threats and intimidation.

The car downshifted, Justice whipping it sideways in the intersection to make the turn and then accelerating with a roar once again. Justice frowned. After driving the monster truck, the sound of the Challenger's engine seemed somewhat subdued in comparison. When this was all over, perhaps he would work on making the car a little louder, a little throatier; it deserved it. He put the thought out of his mind and focused on the looming questions:

Who was Savage?
Was he Protagoras?
Was his entire unit bad, or had he simply used his position within the Bureau to wage his war?
What was his endgame?
Why surface now?

Justice placed these questions in the background and instead concentrated on what he did know or thought he knew.

Nos died because he knew something about Protagoras, or he had been too curious. This wasn't conclusive, but Justice's gut told him it was right, and his gut was rarely wrong. Nos had been trying to remember Protagoras' name and had written variations of it on the piece of paper in his pocket before he was killed. Maybe he got too curious. Protagoras had most likely gotten to Daryl Starkman, or Daryl was scared of Nos' big mouth, so Daryl killed Nos to shut him up. Protagoras looked to move in on Lenny's whole operation, so he recruited the number two man, promising him more power, more wealth, and then Lenny's men abandoned him before he was gunned down by Protagoras and his crew. Protagoras starts to distribute the coke, but he's discreet, never in the spotlight. A coward? Or just smart? He and Dupé were followed when they talked to Maya and Noodles. Maybe Noodles had seen Protagoras. Maybe he just knew too much, so they killed him to shut him up.

Justice shuddered, as he neared Leech's storage facility. Whoever was deemed a threat was dead. They executed a drug lord in his own house in the middle of the freakin' day; it didn't matter to them. Dupé and Justice stood right next to Noodles when he was killed. Why not take the two detectives investigating the case out then? It would have been easy. It would have been a statement. McMann had known how ruthless and calculating this guy was. That's why he started creating an arsenal to fight him. Despite his own convictions, Justice hoped that McMann had the weapons to fight the war that was coming. Suddenly the fixed sides Justice had always known, always created, blurred and bent. He had always been so sure of what he stood for. For maybe the first time in his life, Justice felt the foreign sensation of doubting his own actions. There was no certainty in this outcome. He had lived for the law, for justice, since his father had been killed, and now it might not be enough. They had all been played.

Chapter 50

"Shut up, will you?" The officer driving glanced up in his rear view mirror at the figure of Leech, his stringy mop of hair pressed up against the window, crusted blood dried on his face under his nose. He looked like something off of an evolutionary chart of man, and he sounded like a zombie. He groaned again, softer this time.

"Damn, you sound like you're in labor," the other officer laughed, fully turning around to get a better look at the man in their custody.

"I'm gonna thoo," Martin Leech sputtered.

"You do that," the driving officer said. "So you met Justice, huh? That's one man I wouldn't want angry with me."

"What did he do?" asked the other officer.

"Hell if I know. Orders came from McMann. I'm supposed to bring him back to HQ. That's all I know. But if he's got Justice and McMann on his ass, he'll probably wish he was dead. Hey don't bleed on the seats!"

Leech's head throbbed. His face felt like it had been smacked by a sledge hammer. He was sweating. He was scared. The officers might have been right. At that moment, part of Martin Leech wished he were dead. The other part wanted a cold beer, but one part definitely hoped for death.

He grimaced as pain shot through his jaw. Even his eyes had been affected by the hit, as blue lights appeared first in his peripheral, and then throughout the squad car.

"Who is this?" the officer driving scoffed. He decelerated and eased the car to the shoulder. "This ass hat better not be playing around. We don't have time for this."

Leech gingerly eased his body into a position to get a better look at what was happening. Blinding, flashing blue lights illuminated the exterior of a dark SUV. He watched as the door of the SUV opened and Bole Savage stepped out. It was as if his mind short-circuited—individual thoughts scrambled into an unintelligible mess and he stared. The sharp sound of the squad door closing restarted his thought process as he watched the officer who had been driving walk past his backseat window. "It's a trap!" Leech screamed. He knew it was too late, but he had to do something. "Get back in the car!"

"Shut up," the remaining cop said, having to raise his voice to compete with Leech's yelling.

The officer outside walked toward Savage with an annoyed, arrogant stride. Savage pulled out his badge and held it up. Leech continued to scream and thrash in the back seat. Savage said something to the cop who had his hands on his hips. Leech's commotion caused the remaining officer to sigh and get out of the car. Leech pleaded with him, but to no avail. A thought popped into his head that maybe he shouldn't have begun his pleading with Admiral Ackbar's ill-fated line.

There were bright flicks of light and four loud pops in quick succession. Leech strained his neck and saw the first officer lying at the feet of Savage. He couldn't see the other cop. Savage poked at the cop on the ground with his foot; the officer didn't move. He bent down and removed the officer's gun with a dark cloth. Then he stepped over the body and began walking toward the car.

Leech looked about frantically like a large animal caught in a cage. It was more than a metaphor. A metal cage separated him from the front seat of the squad car, and there were no handles on the inside of the back seat. The only way to open the doors was an officer opening them from the outside to escort the criminal to wherever he or she would be spending their time. Savage walked steadily, unhurried. Leech slid to his back and squirmed so that his back was on the seat while his feet were resting on the passenger side window. He drew his legs back, coiled them, and lashed out, kicking the window with his boots. The glass remained, a smudge the only evidence of Leech's kick. He recoiled and kicked harder this time. The result was the same. He had pulled his legs back for a third kick when the upside down face of Bole Savage looked down at him through the window. Savage winked and fired two shots from cop's gun through the window, shattering it. Tiny shards littered Leech's hair and the back seat. His eyes were still closed when he felt the sharp pain of Savage grabbing him by his hair and dragging through the shattered window.

"Wait, wait, wait," Leech pleaded with no particular hope of Savage listening. Savage shot the driver's side rear panel of the squad car with the cop's gun. Leech looked at the car, puzzled. Then Savage shot Leech three times, once in the shoulder and twice in the stomach. He wiped down both guns, tossing his near Leech, and the other towards the cop. Finally, he found the keys for the handcuffs, removed them from Leech's wrists, wiped them down, and tossed them near the squad car. In all, only 7 minutes had passed when the black SUV drove off, leaving three bodies dead and a squad car still running.

Chapter 51

When Justice reached the storage facility, Dupé's tan Impala already sat idling outside the fence. The Challenger pulled alongside the Impala and Justice rolled down his window. "I hope we're not here for long; people might think we bought our cars together. What's up?"

"Well, we have a squad car in there, which I can only assume is Furman and Philips. Can't reach 'em by radio, though, and I have no visual affirmation either."

"Fantastic," Justice sighed. "Where's Cap?"

"He's on his way," replied Dupé. "I say we wait."

Justice surveyed the situation once more. Empty storage facility. No sign of movement or life. No sign of the two officers. The drive was a mix of streetlamp orange and black shadow. In the middle of the main row sat the dark squad car, obscured in shadow. "As much as I can't wait to charge into a potentially dangerous situation," Justice admitted, "I don't think waiting five minutes is going to kill us." Dupé shot a glance at Justice through the car windows. "OK, it *might* kill us. I'm with you. We wait for the Cap."

In all, the two men waited just over six minutes before McMann pulled up. Justice filled him in on the situation, and all three got out of their cars and drew their weapons.

McMann called loudly as he opened the gate, but there was no response.

"Keep your eyes open," he growled. "Keep in contact. Fan out and do a quick sweep. Meet at the car. I don't want to be surprised by any uninvited company."

Justice and Dupé nodded. Justice headed left and Dupé headed right, their guns pointed at the ground. Justice walked confidently, Kimber resting comfortably in his massive hands. Dupé wished he had a tactical vest. He wondered how many times Justice had been shot over the years. He wondered if the flak jacket came before or after the first time Justice was shot. Maybe it was why Justice seemed so confident all the time. He put that thought out of his mind as he rounded a corner. He didn't see anything. Justice and McMann were also coming up empty. Soon the three men converged on the vehicle.

As they approached the squad car, they could just make out two figures, obscured in the darkness, in the front seat. McMann held his hand out, and Justice and Dupé stopped and holstered their weapons. "Justice, give me a handkerchief," McMann said, motioning with his extended hand.

Justice scoffed. "What makes you think I have a handkerchief?"

McMann looked up at Justice. "Just give me the damn handkerchief. You have everything else."

Justice gritted his teeth and removed a white handkerchief, neatly folded, and handed it to the Captain.

Dupé whistled. "That is a nicely folded handkerchief right there."

"Can it, Dupé," the Captain growled. He eased forward toward the driver side door. The cicadas were eerily silent. Street traffic a block over was the only sound. McMann reached out and gingerly pulled at the door handle with the handkerchief. The door open, and McMann held the cloth up to his face. It was much darker than when Justice had handed it to him. "Blood," McMann grunted. He swore under his breath. The three men looked inside the quiet vehicle. Furman and Philips were inside. They sat upright in their seats, like test crash dummies dressed up as cops. Their eyes were open, grotesquely bulged as if in postmortem shock. McMann swore again.

Justice knew the men were dead before McMann opened the door, but seeing two fellow lawmen posed in their squad car after being killed made his insides knot up, even if they were complete dicks.

"Look at Philip's neck," Dupé noted, pointing. He shuddered. The dark blood stood out in stark contrast to his milky neck. "Did they do Furman the same way?

"I don't see any blood," McMann said slowly, stooping to get a better look.

Justice stood in silence, letting the other two men talk. It was obvious the men weren't killed in the car. The blood was on the handle outside of the door. There didn't seem to be blood anywhere else on the outside of the car. Why would there be blood just on the handle? He walked around to the other side of the car, moving the beam of his flashlight all over the exterior of the vehicle. Nothing. He bent down to examine the passenger side handle. No blood. As he moved back to the driver side with McMann and Dupé, he saw the large dark stain on the asphalt. Dupé was almost standing in it. They must have been so focused on the vehicle that they didn't notice the stain obscured by deep shadows.

"Dupé, I think I see where Philips was killed." Dupé and the Captain turned to where Justice's flashlight illuminated the asphalt. It was wet. Dupé closed his eyes and covered his mouth, while McMann stayed consistent in his curse words. "So they weren't working with Savage, which means that he somehow knew about this place, which means he knew about the weapons. How is that possible?" Justice questioned on behalf of all three men.

"We need to get to the railyard," McMann said absently, pulling out his cell phone.

Justice waited for the explanation.

Dupé frowned. "I thought the shipment was Tuesday."

"Another shipment of weapons?" Justice asked in surprise.

"There are still weapons we haven't transferred over here yet," McMann half coughed, half mumbled.

"You want a war," Justice said quietly.

"I want to win if there is one! Now quit your moral misgivings and get over there. I'll get us backup."

Justice remained where he was and glanced at Dupé. Dupé gave a small shrug. McMann dialed on his phone, noticed his detectives were still there and barked, "Damnit, move!"

Justice removed a toothpick from his vest, bit down hard, and began moving back to his car, sure of only one thing: if Savage was at the railyard, Justice was ending this tonight.

Chapter 52

The kettle murmured and then eased into a full-bodied whistle. Tammy poured herself a cup of the boiling water and walked over to the sofa where her cat, Audrey, waited for her. She sat down, Audrey curling up beside her, and took out a tea bag. Three sharp knocks at the door interrupted her before she could dip the tea bag into the cup. Justice would have just texted or called if he needed something. Maybe she had left something in his car; the odds of this happening were fairly high.

She was puzzled when she opened the door to see a slender woman with jet black hair, and a tall, dark skinned man with short hair in standard FBI wear, standing on her front porch. She flipped on the porch light and asked, "Can I help you?"

"Mrs. Shaw?" It was the woman who spoke. "I'm agent Marquez. This is agent Tannehill. We've been sent here by Detective Justice to keep an eye on you—to make sure you're OK." It seemed as if she was reciting a practiced greeting.

"Can I see some ID?" Justice's dad and Justice had always told Tammy to require ID from any person claiming to be an authority figure. They also always seemed to do it in movies and TV shows. It didn't hurt to be safe.

"Of course," the woman replied with a mirthless smile. Both pulled out wallets, revealed their badges, let Tammy stare long enough to feel as if she actually knew how to spot a counterfeit, and then returned the badges.

"Thanks," she said and stepped aside for them to enter.

The woman entered first, the man following. As he passed Tammy, his arm shot out, jamming into her side. Tammy gasped, eyes bulging. The man pulled the Taser back and caught Tammy as she fell forward. The agents placed her unconscious body between them and slowly carried her to the black SUV waiting around the corner.

Elizabeth's feet hurt. She felt like she was wearing funnels with her toes jammed into the narrow opening. It had only been two hours since she started working, and the tricks weren't showing. Everything was dead. There had been one guy in the first hour, but that wasn't going to cut it. She pulled at her dress with her clutch in one hand. It looked like she was going to have to try some of the strip malls. Or maybe the Walgreen's parking lot. She turned to one of the other girls to let her know she was trying different territory when headlights announced the arrival of a vehicle. All the girls stood straighter, making themselves appear more desirable in any way possible. Judging by the height of the headlights, Elizabeth reasoned it must be a truck.

The black SUV continued at the same velocity until it slammed on its brakes in front of Elizabeth. A side door opened and two men jumped out. There was a small burst of blue electric charge and Elizabeth slumped into their arms.

Elizabeth and the two men were already inside the SUV before the other women could react.

Blake's phone had gone straight to message again. Wanda had backed into the corner of her house, and tears were forming in the corners of her eyes. It seemed like the SUV had been there for the last few hours. As the sun had gone down, her anxiety had risen steadily. She had been sitting in her favorite recliner, peering out the blinds for the last half hour with her 1301 Tactical shotgun resting in her lap. Justice had stopped answering her phone calls, and in the moment, Wanda didn't think to dial 911.

The moment she noticed the vehicle begin to move, she navigated her way behind her television in the corner of the living room. She had a clear view to all entry points, and though she was literally backed into a corner, Wanda figured she wouldn't go down without a fight. The entire house was dark. She had never turned her lights on. The darkness seemed oppressive. She tried to calm her breathing, but she found it impossible to do so.

Wanda Justice had dealt with burglars and muggings before, and Al Justice and her son had taught her some self-defense, but waiting to be assaulted was much worse than a surprise attack. She closed her eyes to intensify her other senses. Outside, she heard the subtle change in tone as an engine turned off. She gripped the stock of the shotgun and pulled it tight to her armpit. She heard the metallic grind of someone trying the front door. It was never unlocked. She heard a different metallic sound and her door clicked open two or three inches. She positioned herself so that she could prop her arm up on the TV stand for a more steady aim.

She waited as a hand and arm, followed by a foot and leg appeared. Soon an entire person, dressed in black entered through the front door. What she couldn't make out was the apparatus around the person's head.

The night vision goggles painted the room in varying shades of green, white, and black. Anton stepped cautiously through the front door. The initial scan quickly revealed the woman in the corner of the living room. He had been expecting she would be hiding; he had not expected to see her with a tactical shotgun aimed right at him.

Wanda's finger waited patiently on the trigger finger, though her entire body seemed to be shaking. The entire figure stepped through; Wanda pulled the trigger.

The blast and muzzle flash momentarily blinded Anton, who was blinking furiously trying to shake the stars and retinal burn out of his vision. As soon as Anton had seen Justice's mother crouching with the shotgun, he hurled himself into a somersault to his left. The flash stunned him, but he recovered quickly firing a shot into the woman's sternum.

Wanda gasped as a sharp pain shot through her body. The violent impact knocked her back into the wall, her shotgun knocked free from her hands. She couldn't breath and the pain was almost unbearable. She placed a hand to her chest but she felt no liquid, no blood. She was just starting to wonder what had hit her when a second pain shot into her neck and then Wanda slumped to the floor unconscious.

Anton put his Taser away as three more men entered the house, two following Anton and one from the back of the house. The bean bag lay next to the unconscious woman. She would wake up sore and bruised.

Chapter 53

No security guard or night watchmen met Justice as he drove through the south gate of the railyard. The night was still. Though it wasn't a main vein of traffic, someone should have noticed a car driving through a closed property. Justice placed on of the Kimbers on his lap. The windows of the Challenger were down. The tires popped and cracked the gravel and bedrock in the parking lot as it inched along, Justice observing the numerous blind spots and possible points of ambush. He moved slowly through the maze of office buildings and warehouses. Up ahead he saw the web of tracks and giant train cars.

Headlights blinded him from his left, and he heard the roar of an engine. Instinctively his foot slammed the accelerator a second before the impact came. The dark Tahoe would have hit the Challenger squarely on the driver side door, but instead the impact came just behind the rear tire, sending the car into a violent spin. The gun flew out of Justice's lap and landed on the passenger side floor. With the lights no longer shining in his eyes, Justice was able to focus and corrected the spin. "So much for the element of surprise." The SUV had made a sharp left, skidding across the loose gravel and turning broadside toward Justice. The back windows lit up in a bright "x" of gunfire from an automatic weapon. Justice lowered his head as the Challenger was peppered with bullets. The Challenger launched forward, and the black SUV followed in pursuit.

The normal advantages of acceleration, speed, and handling were nullified by the gravel and rock roads mapping the majority of the rail yard. Most of the service roads were full of sharp curves which wouldn't allow a vehicle to near any sort of top speed. Justice hit the E-brake and skidded around the corner of a mechanic shed, the nose of the Challenger coming inches from the cinderblock walls. The Tahoe matched the Challenger as it tore around the same corner. A man hung out of either side of the vehicle, machine guns blazing. The back window of the Challenger burst into tiny crystals as bullets ripped through the glass. Justice whipped out his other pistol and fired over his shoulder. The chase wound back and forth through the buildings, the Tahoe whipping from the right to the left of the Challenger to stay out of Justice's line of fire. Meanwhile the men firing automatics began to eat away at the car's body until both men finally found their mark and the rear tires blew out with shreds of rubber flew off into the night.

Justice immediately dropped the gun and fought the tail of the car as it threatened to fishtail at any second. The Tahoe accelerated, ramming the back of the Challenger, knocking it sideways so that the driver's side wheels were off the ground. The Tahoe's reinforced bumper acted as a cowcatcher, enabling the vehicle to push the Justice's Challenger sideways. Justice let go of the steering wheel and dove to the back seat, crouching on broken glass. The gunfire was deafening. Both back windows disappeared in the midst of the barrage. Justice grimaced as he felt the searing pain of a bullet passing through his left shoulder. The SUV driver's face turned into a wicked grin. He pushed down on the accelerator. He would crush the car and the pathetic detective. The guns continued pumping out round after round. The car was more holes than it was metal at this point.

It only took a few seconds, but the driver of the Tahoe saw it in slow motion. The figure of Justice popping up at the steering wheel, the car lurching forward, rotating, the two vehicles side-by-side, drivers staring at one another, Justice waving. He reached out his window into the SUV and dropped the grenade as the Challenger spun off, slamming into the entrance of an office. He looked back through the missing rear window. The SUV had stopped, doors halfway open, two figures halfway out. The fireball blew the doors off, sending one figure flying lifeless through the air. Flames poured out of the open windows like burning eye sockets of a hollow skull.

Justice kicked his door open; it wrenched open and then fell to the ground, completely severed at its joints. The flames were dying away, leaving a charred corpse of a vehicle. Justice stooped to the ground and re-tied his boot. Replacing the cuff of his pants over his boot, he turned, aimed, and fired at the SUV. The bullet punctured the gas tank, and a steady stream began to pour from the vehicle. Ashes from burnt upholstery settled all around the SUV. After a few seconds, the ashes found the new stream in the gravel. The resulting explosion removed any semblance of a vehicle from the SUV. Justice shielded his face from the blast with his good arm. The flames illuminated the quiet train yard. He turned back toward his once beautiful Challenger, crumpled, battered. Justice extended a hand toward the decimated vehicle. The hand closed into a clenched fist. "They destroyed my car," Justice growled.

A wave of pain momentarily washed over his shoulder, overpowering the surge of adrenaline and reminding Justice that he had been shot. He quickly opened his trunk, removed a fresh shirt and an unopened bottle of Old Scout. He gulped down a quarter of the bottle and poured another half on the entry and exit wounds in his shoulder. Justice savored the complex flavors of the whiskey as the amber liquid disinfected the wound. Using his teeth and his free hand, Justice pulled the t-shirt into a tight knot to stop the bleeding. Grimacing, he pulled it tight until the blood flow had stopped.

The stakes had changed. Protagoras had brought all-out war. There would be no more slinking around. This ended tonight. The masks were off—Bole Savage had revealed his true nature, and Justice had just killed several of his men. It was probable that Savage would not take too kindly to that. Savage had the men, and they had the equipment. They were tough odds, but Justice wouldn't have it any other way. Of course, a few of the men were already dead. Not much of a fight. He looked down at the cache in his trunk. He had lost one of his Kimbers, and Justice was tempted to just replace the lost one. Then the two AE .50's caught his eye. The situation did dictate something a little subtle. If it was a war that Protagoras wanted, it was a war he would get. Justice grabbed several pre-loaded magazines and three grenades. The one grenade had proved quite useful against the first Tahoe. Justice knew of at least one other Tahoe as well. Better to take more than you need, than to regret what you didn't take later.

Justice raised his shoulder and rotated it. There was pain, but it focused him. He emptied the contents of the whiskey, soaking the t-shirt tied around his shoulder. It would have to do; there was no time for proper treatment under the circumstances. He raised both pistols, taking in the weight and balance. Satisfied, he holstered both weapons and locked his trunk. He shut the trunk as quietly as possible and began a slow jog toward the main tracks. He wasn't sure exactly what he was looking for, but it was apparent Savage and his crew were here, and that meant something important was here.

Justice moved quickly, leaning forward and head up. Both Eagles were drawn in case of an ambush. Justice came to the end of an alleyway that opened up to a wide gravel road between several large warehouses. Justice remained in a shadow, saw and heard nobody, and then stepped into the open. His head remained on a swivel, Eagles in loose grips in his hands. He had moved about twenty yards when the sharp impact knocked Justice forward, skidding along the gravel on his stomach. Both guns clattered onto the gravel road. He lay still. The 3A body armor had done the trick against the sniper shot, but Justice's *longissimus thoracis* throbbed. Had the shell penetrated the bullet-proof vest, it would have sliced through the back muscle, exiting through the heart and then rib cage. As it was, Justice felt like that was exactly what had happened. Pain surged through his shoulder like molten lava in the veins, and Justice's entire back was beginning to react negatively to the massive impact.

But he was alive. Justice hesitated, unsure of what to do next. He didn't dare move, knowing the sniper's sight would be trained on his body—most likely his head. However, the idea of waiting around until the shooter made sure he was dead didn't sound too appealing either. His body, already tense, waited for an inevitable second shot. He heard voices.

Without raising his head, Justice guessed the noise was coming from in front of him and around a corner of some object, most likely a storage building. He made out a female voice and two male voices. One was incredibly low, and Justice pictured Jabba the Hut sliding his hulking body over the terrain, machine gun in hand. Dupé would be proud of his Star Wars connection. Where was Dupé?

"Is that him?" It was Jabba.

"No, just another 6'5" guy taking out five of our guys." The female seemed to outrank the male agents. Justice smiled to himself. It *had* been a well-placed grenade. Five guys down. If they kept coming at him in vehicles it would make his job a lot easier.

"Protagoras said he's the best." Jabba again.

"*Was* the best," quipped the second male.

Despite the gravel cutting into his face, Justice managed to roll his eyes. He would kill that guy first.

The female spoke again. "Evans, check our six and make sure there's nobody else with him." She was almost on him. The crunching of boots on gravel stopped at his head. He felt a foot wedge underneath his shoulder to turn him over. Justice allowed the foot to easily roll him over, but he grabbed the leg that had pushed him, and using the momentum from the roll dragged the man to the ground. It was the agent who had used the cliché joke earlier.

Justice continued holding onto the man, rolling onto the agent's back. The female agent had already raised her MP5 into firing position and squeezed the trigger. When Justice saw the agent raise her weapon, he had continued rolling, pulling the jokester on top of him. The staccato pop from the MP5 left the jokester lifeless. At the sound of his partner's MP5 echoing off the buildings, Evans/Jabba turned to head back toward the fight.

Bracing himself against the ground, Justice grabbed the pants leg and vest of the dead man and hurled the body at the female agent. Dead weight. She sidestepped the body flying through the air, but the distraction did its job. Justice moved with surprising agility, drop-kicking the agent square in her chest as another shot rang out and the gravel next to Justice spit into the air. The female agent's body rag-dolled to the ground. One of Justice's .50 Cal Eagle's lay beside him. Jabba, the third agent, had reached the ruckus and paused to assess the situation. One of his partners was lying motionless, while the other was attempting to prop herself up on the gravel. Justice rolled to his right, grabbing the Eagle and fired twice at the surprised agent. The impact from the bullets dropped him instantly. Out of the corner of his eye, Justice noticed that the female agent was shaking the cobwebs free and reaching for a pistol from her leg holster.

Justice and the female agent fired simultaneously, two shots each. Justice reached toward his stomach. The female agent landed face down, and a dark pool began forming underneath her. Both of Justice's shots had found their mark; only one of the agent's shots had found its target, but the tactical vest again proved its worth. Justice popped the 9mm slug out of the vest and touched his skin underneath to make a quick assessment of the damage taken. The skin was tender to the touch, but unbroken.

"Stop shooting me!" Justice yelled, and immediately remembered the sniper. He dropped to the ground and scanned the building from right to left.

"Got any zip-ties?" The voice came from a large warehouse to his right. He whipped his gun to the right and spotted the dark figure of Dupé in a small window on the second story. "I thought we could ask him some questions later on. Unless you were going to just kill him like everyone else," Dupé shouted out. "He's sleeping."

Justice smiled. Despite prior years of working alone, the train yard somehow made his usual confidence seem smaller and underwhelming. He had taken out several of the agents/mercs already, but he had no idea how many more there truly were. For perhaps the first time in his life, Justice was glad to see his partner. "Took you long enough," Justice replied loud enough for Dupé to hear him.

"Are you going to need any zip ties down there?" Dupé yelled back.

Justice looked around him. Three agents; three dead agents. "I think we're good down here."

"That's what I figured. Now quit screwing around and help me with this guy up here."

Chapter 54

Justice and Dupé carried the unconscious sniper down a flight of cast metal stairs and placed him in a utility closet with his hands bound. Once outside, Dupé took a look at the man's weapon.

"M110 SASS sniper rifle. Not bad." Justice said, watching Dupé look through the scope and sight something down the road.

"Think it's our rifle that capped Noodles?" Dupé popped out the magazine. "7.62mm."

"Looks like we have ourselves a winner. You should try to get more of your fingerprints all over it so that someone will say you shot Noodles."

"Shut up, Justice. I'm using a Glock and they've got military grade weapons. Hell, you're carrying a fifty cal Eagle!"

Justice frowned. "You're not carrying your Glock. That's a .45. Kimber. Where did you get that?"

Dupé swallowed. "I saw your car. What happened?"

"Then you saw the SUV?" Dupé nodded. "That's what happened. So where did you get the Kimber, Dupé?"

"Listen, you've got an arsenal back there. I borrowed one from your trunk. You weren't using it." Dupé tried to sound nonchalant, but a tremor in his voice betrayed his anxiety.

Justice straightened up and took out a toothpick, never taking his eyes off Dupé. "We're going to talk about this when we're done here," he said quietly.

"And that's when I went out looking for you," hurried Dupé, "and I found you. I was about to call out to you, but I saw you drop and heard the shot. I looked for vantage point and circled around while you were busy screwing around with that crew over there. I got the drop on the guy. He was kind of preoccupied. And since we might need him, I didn't *kill* him. So you're welcome."

"Thank you," Justice conceded.

"So I'm taking the rifle now. It even has a night vision scope."

Justice took the rifle from Dupé and examined it. "AN/PVS-26 Universal Night Sight mounted in front of a Leupold scope. Not bad."

Dupé stared at Justice for a second and then took back the M110. "You probably just made that up."

"Some people collect stamps. I do cars and guns. You can Google it later."

"Nobody collects stamps, Justice. Nobody. You brought up stamps because you know you're a nerd for knowing this stuff."

The two men dragged the three bodies into the shadows of the alley Justice had come through. "Oh come on," Justice grunted as he laid the body of the female agent against the wall. "Everyone knows this stuff."

"The only things everyone would know are the guns found in COD games," Dupé countered.

"What's COD?"

"The first person shooter? Video game? You're telling me you don't know-" Dupé stopped. He knew he had been set up.

"Nerd."

The two men proceeded into the night, Dupé occasionally stopping to look through the rifle's night vision scope. After a seemingly fruitless search of the rail yard's grounds, the soft voices of two men could be heard on the other side of a building. Justice motioned for Dupé to stay behind him, and the two crept to the corner. With his back to the wall, Justice glanced around the corner. Dupé peeked as well. Two agent mercenaries stood in front of a red door lit up by an orange outdoor light.

"I'm guessing we want to go in that door," Dupé whispered.

Justice grunted his assent. "Think you can hit one of them?"

Dupé moved the light red crosshairs from one man's head to the other. "It's only like forty yards. I'm not that bad of a shot," Dupé hissed. "But shouldn't we try to take them out non-lethally? They haven't attacked us." He looked away from his sight and up at Justice who was tossing a large stone in his hand. "With that? You go from capping everyone in sight to throwing rocks at guys armed with MP5's?"

"Shh. Can you throw this or not?" Justice asked in a barely audible whisper. Justice knew it had been a while since even he had thrown a rock, but accuracy that earned several groundings and many raw backsides wasn't learned or forgotten. He wasn't so sure about Dupé, but Dupé held his hand out. "On three," Justice said. "I've got the far one. You take the closer one." Dupé nodded.

The countdown ensued, and the rocks flew silently through the air. The two detectives watched the mercenaries standing oblivious, bathed in the mounted light over the doorway. A split second later, the head of the Justice's target snapped backwards, he stumbled forward, and then dropped to his knees. Dupé's target clutched his side and dropped to one knee.

Dupé was about to offer up excuses about being rusty and Justice handing him the inferior stone, but Justice was already on the move. Dupé watched him moving like a cat on the prowl, staying near the building wall and out of the light. Dupé's man had caught his breath, checked on his partner, and then raised his machine gun, swinging the barrel back and forth. A loud rattle against the metal walls of the mercenary's building yanked his attention away from Justice's approach. Justice must have thrown some of the gravel. An old trick, but it was impossible not to devote attention to a significant noise like the one that had just taken place. By the time the man decided the noise was a diversion, Justice was blindsiding the man with his full 250 pound frame. The gun clattered away harmlessly, and Justice drove the man onto his back. Almost miraculously, the man staggered back up.

Though he knew how dangerous the situation was, Dupé had secretly longed to watch Justice in hand-to-hand combat. He raised the rifle and placed the two men fighting in the red crosshairs.

The agent pulled a knife from his boot with his right hand and held it poised beside his head. The two men circled each other, and then the agent lunged at Justice with the knife. He slapped it away with his left hand and threw a punch with his right that the man ducked under. The foot of the agent shot out, catching Justice in the side of the knee and causing him to stumble slightly. With lightning speed the knife arced down once more, but Justice grabbed the wrist with the knife. Immediately Dupé could see the expression of the man's face contort in pain. Justice stood up to his full height, the agent's wrist still in his massive hand. The knife fell harmlessly from the man's hand, and with a definitive motion, Justice snapped the man's arm by slamming his other hand into the back of the man's elbow. The man cried out and huddled over, holding his arm close to his body. Dupé watched, mesmerized, as Justice smashed the man's face into his knee, knocking him cold. Dupé exhaled and lowered the rifle.

The two agents' hands were quickly bound behind them, as with the sniper, and after kicking open the door and a quick sweep, Justice and Dupé dragged the bodies into the room they had been guarding.

Besides the two unconscious guards, no one could be found in the room. But the room was far from empty. Justice estimated it must have been about 40 feet wide and 20 feet deep. Concrete floor. Cinder block walls. A door along the back wall. And filled to the brim with weapon cases and crates of ammunition. "Is this all McMann's?" Dupé asked.

Justice murmured something inaudible, and Dupé turned to see him staring, mouth half open, and his hands lovingly running over the cases. "Have you ever seen anything so wonderful in your life, Dupé?" Justice asked in a trance.

"Um, many times and in many places."

"Look at that!" Justice practically bounded over to a large black case with G36 stenciled in white paint on the top. He opened it, revealing a sleek assault rifle. Justice took the weapon out of the foam mold and unfolded the stock. "HK G36K. A modern-day, urban assault rifle with a powerful punch—accurate too." He cradled it as if holding an infant for the first time.

Dupé had never seen Justice in such rapture before. It was almost vomit inducing, like middle school lovers smothering each other in the school cafeteria.

Justice almost forgot their mission. He had longed for the day he could aim the 318mm barrel down the range, shifting seamlessly between semi and fully automatic. The Germans knew their cars, and they knew their guns as well. In fact, he liked sausage too. He couldn't be sure, but he thought that Germans had invented sausage. Either way, he had the Germans to thank for the incredible craftsmanship he held in his hands. Though he didn't agree with what McMann was doing, he couldn't fault the hardware. This was sophisticated and lethal. Unfortunately it seemed Protagoras/Savage had helped himself to the cache. If Dupé, McMann, and he couldn't stop Savage tonight, he couldn't imagine what carnage might come. Where was McMann? He should have been there by now with the cavalry. Perhaps he was in his own firefight. Maybe he was slowly infiltrating the railyard. Maybe he was dead. Nothing seemed a stretch at this point.

A piece of hardware still in the case caught his eye. "Dupé, look! An AG36."

"Ah, 40mm grenade launcher. You can do some damage with that."

Justice looked at Dupé, a grin spreading across his angular jaw. "So you *do* know your guns."

"I'm telling you, Call of Duty, man. Video games have their worth."

Justice rolled his eyes and turned away, disgusted. "Every time you start to redeem yourself, you reveal yourself to be a bigger moron." He returned his attention to the G36. Beside the open case were three crates stacked on top of each other. Justice found an edge of the lid on the crate and punched the crate open with the stock of the assault rifle. "Beautiful."

"Is that ammo?"

"C-MAG drum. 100 round magazine. I might cry."

"Please don't. I'm uncomfortable enough as it is."

Justice finished attaching the grenade launcher on the rail. Dupé was about to say something when Justice held up a hand. Dupé waited. "Do you hear that?" Justice asked. Dupé listened intently. The low rumble of an engine could be heard through the cracked exterior door. Justice moved to the door, pushed it open, and stepped forward into the humid night air. Though the scope on the G36 didn't have night vision, it did enhance the low light, allowing Justice to clearly make out the landscape of buildings and structures. The rifle felt comfortable pressed tightly against his right shoulder. The sound of the vehicle grew louder; Justice aimed at the corner of the building he and Dupé had just come from. His finger rested on the guard, just barely touching the trigger.

All at once, a Tahoe skidded around the corner, the spray of tiny white dots kicking up from the wheels in Justice's scope. He squeezed down on the trigger and sent multiple rounds into the windshield, until it looked like it had been hit by dozens of tiny snowballs. The SUV closed to within 40 yards of the two detectives when Justice's finger slid down to the trigger on the mounted 40mm grenade launcher. There was the slightest of delays between the thunk of the launcher and the bright explosion underneath the speeding vehicle. Justice had aimed at the ground just in front of the Tahoe, and the resulting explosion launched the back of the SUV into the air, flipping it so it landed on the roof. One of the back tires spun slightly off its axis. Justice skillfully plugged another grenade into the launcher and snapped it shut. The second grenade reduced the Tahoe to a modern sculpture of twisted metal.

"That was incredible," Dupé said in awe.

Justice turned to Dupé who had been noticeably absent during the action. A phone sat in his hand, a bright light on in the corner. "Were you recording that with your phone?" Justice asked in disbelief.

"Yeah. I got all of it. The SUV flipping—all of it. Unbelievable. You always have to be ready," Dupé said, holding up his phone.

"You have got to be kidding me," Justice groaned.

"Oh come on. You might just watch this video with your grandchildren on YouTube someday.

Justice glared at Dupé. "Turn that thing off. We have work to do."

After skimming the rest of the small room and making mental notes of the inventory, the two detectives met each other at the door in the back between two columns of stacked crates. Dupé held his MP5 in standby, while Justice paused with his hand on the doorknob. He looked at Dupé, who gave a confident nod, and tried the doorknob. It was unlocked. He turned it, slowly at first, and then yanked the door open.

Chapter 55

Tammy touched her stomach and winced. She wasn't sure how long ago she had been kidnapped, but the spot where she had been Tasered still throbbed. She glanced over at Blake's mom, Wanda, and Elizabeth. Wanda's eyes were glazed over. Tammy had always wondered how much of her was really all there the last few years, and the events of the evening couldn't have helped. Elizabeth's face was wet with silent tears. Tammy began to reach out to reassure her, but she felt the cold steel barrel press harder into her neck. After the gunshots and explosions heard through the closed door, the relaxed guards had become militantly rigid and alert. She squeezed her eyes tight and prayed a simple prayer of petition. The closed door in front of the women and the guards swung open suddenly, startling them. Blake stepped through the doorway, machine gun raised, bleeding from his shoulder, clothes torn, dark hair grimy, face grim. Dupé followed, blond hair still in place, face clean, and looking slightly bigger than the scrawny frame she had last seen. Tammy couldn't imagine what they had gone through. Somehow she knew he would come, but to see his determined face come through the doorway brought a wave of relief and hope.

Justice's determination melted into a pool of confusion as he looked into the faces of the three women kneeling in front of three agents, guns aimed at the back of their heads. It felt as if all the vigor and adrenaline had been depleted in an instant. His mother, Tammy, and Elizabeth were all kneeling on the concrete floor with three men dressed as FBI agents standing behind them, MP5's aiming at him and Dupé. The moment they had burst through the door, all attention from the guards shifted to the two detectives. And there in the other corner knelt Captain McMann, hands bound behind him. Behind him stood Bole Savage, his own G36 aimed at the detectives. Justice shook the emotions out of his head and attempted to face the situation objectively. It didn't happen easily.

Savage smiled. "So good of you fellas to stop by," he said in a sweet southern drawl.

"I see you have an accent now, Savage," Dupé said in a cold tone. "Or should I say Protagoras?"

"My, my," Savage cooed. "What is someone as bright as you doing on the police force? You figured all this out on your own, did you?"

"So you infiltrated the FBI?"

"There is no FBI here. Stir up trouble, and when the call goes out, all you get is us—just me and my crew," Savage replied politely. He was calm, confident.

"What's left of it," Justice said softly, menace in his voice.

"And Detective Justice," exclaimed Savage. "Or is it just Blake? Last I heard you had quit the force, had a morality attack. You're going to church now I understand."

"You can go with us if you'd like sometime." It was Tammy. Her voice wavered, but her eyes flashed determination.

"Thank you, Tammy, but I think I'll pass. I have a town to take over and money to make. No time."

Wanda spoke up. "They shot me with a bean bag, Blake." Tears welled up in her eyes, and her lip quivered. "I tried so hard to be brave, to st-stop them. But there were too many. They had been watching me all day. I called and called, but you didn't answer!"

"Mom, this is not really the time or place."

"This is exactly the time and place, Blake Owen Justice!"

"Mom, I was busy with all of this," Justice said exasperated and motioning wildly.

"Too busy for your mother?" she practically screamed.

The gun shot was deafening in the non-insulated, tiny room. The bullet whizzed past Wanda's head and plunged into the concrete behind her. No one said anything as they turned to look at Savage and his raised weapon. "You think I don't know a distraction when I see one?" Savage asked condescendingly. "The VonJustice Family Singers? Stop with the fake arguments, or I'll smear your head on that wall behind you, Miss Justice." He flashed another wide smile.

Dupé exhaled. He had hoped for a second that the manufactured diversion might work, but Savage was good. The situation looked grim—even with Justice on their side. He noticed the burn on Savage's arm again. "How did you get that burn, Savage? It looks pretty bad."

"All in the line of duty, my dear Dupé. Keep working hard, and you might be so lucky as to wear one of these someday. That's how they repaid me." Savage's visage suddenly grew cold and, well, savage.

"You've got to be kidding me," Tammy whispered. Then she spoke up louder. "You're Captain McMann's partner, from Gary."

"Tommy Denton, at your service," Savage said, with a playful bow.

"I thought he was Protagoras," Elizabeth said softly, speaking for the first time.

Justice nodded as the pieces began to fall into place. "He is. That's his ghost name—the name with the reputation, to hide behind. That's what cowards do." Savage frowned at this. "Bole Savage is another alias. We won't find it if we make calls to Washington. It gave him an inside scoop to everything we were doing; heck, we placed the entire operation in his hands."

"I'm sorry, Justice," McMann said, eyes on the floor.

"Captain, it's not your fault. I understand what you did, even if I didn't agree with it. I've seen what this piece of trash coward is capable of."

"Coward? You keep saying that word. I took out your community's biggest threat and felon in broad daylight. We literally walked into his, his, well, it looked like his mom's house."

"It *was* his mom's house. Lenny kicked her out of it," explained McMann.

"Well, there you go. I did you a favor. No one wants some weed dealer who doesn't even care for his own momma hanging around, do you? And you wouldn't take care of him, so I did. Daryl Starkman was an easy pay-off. That and the threat of being killed if they were still there when we came. Everyone can be bought. Nobody's loyal. They'll betray you in a second."

"You're wrong, Savage," Justice said firmly. "You think the world is a destruction playground, and you've got your sandbox, and your plastic shovels, and your swing set, and your metal slide that heats up in the summer to scald your sweaty legs as you try to go down it." Savage tried to process the analogy. Justice continued. "But you've forgotten about the law and justice. What's right. What's wrong. There's loyalty and trust. My father taught me that." He looked at his mother. Wanda smiled reassuringly.

"There has to be order and truth," reasoned Tammy. "Even your own organization or whatever it is depends on it. That order and truth comes from a God who created this world."

Justice shifted. "Well I'm not sure about that. I just started with all of that."

Savage looked bewildered. "Do you hear yourselves? You're morons, all of you. And it's time you were dead."

"Yeah, you've been monologuing for a long time now," Dupé said through a yawn.

"Wait," pleaded Elizabeth. "Who's Tommy Denton?"

"Oh, sorry. I got sidetracked," apologized Justice.

"You're sidetracking me from killing you," Savage huffed.

Justice rolled his eyes. "You've been talking with us for, what, ten minutes now. Just let me explain to Elizabeth who is going to kill her."

Savage considered this. "Fair," he relinquished.

Justice took a breath. "Tommy Denton, Bole Savage," he began nodding in Savage's direction, "was Captain

McMann's partner a long time ago. They were ambushed on the street, and Tommy here was killed. But apparently he didn't die. What, did you go into hiding or something?" Savage shrugged. "And you were angry with the world, you felt betrayed by the police?"

Savage smiled. "I like money. Being a cop on the beat wasn't going to cut it."

"So McMann stops your efforts initially, not knowing who you were; he gets the promotions, shoots up the ranks; you plot your revenge; and you bide your time until you're ready to destroy him once and for all. So you come here, and as it turns out, we've practically handed you the arsenal that was being accumulated to fight you."

"Eh, close enough. Some details left out, but it won't matter because you'll be dead."

"Wait, I just have one more question." It was Dupé's turn to speak up.

"You have got to be kidding me," Savage exclaimed, throwing his head back.

"Why do you have the women here? What do they have to do with any of this?"

"Don't hurt your head thinking too much about it, Dupé. You'll be dead anyway." Savage turned toward his men. "Kill the ladies first."

Time froze as the men focused all their attention on the three women kneeling before them. Their eyes were closed as they waited for what they could only imagine. The three agents didn't get a shot off. Justice dropped to a knee and dropped the first agent before the other two agents knew what happened. The round from the AG36 struck the agent directly above his nose, and he fell sideways into the wall.

While the echoes from the first shot still tumbled around the enclosed room, Justice got off two more shots that found their mark and dropped the remaining agents.

Justice felt the impact from Savage's MP5 in his chest and dropped to the floor, but Dupé had not been sitting idly by. His MP5 ripped off several rounds, striking Savage across his torso and in his neck. He turned toward Dupé, staring wide eyed with a look of madness on his face.

"Hey, scumbag!" Justice was on one knee with his rifle raised. "Just die already." The G36 roared, and Savage stood no longer.

The women had huddled together, attempting to stay out of the growing pools of blood behind them. Dupé and Justice were almost synchronized in their deep inhalations; the adrenaline was still flowing.

"Hey, can I get some help here?" McMann barked, shattering the moment of relief and victory. Justice snapped to and quickly made his way over to McMann to cut the cords around his wrists.

"Justice, don't!" Dupé managed, but the knife had already freed McMann's hands from behind him. With startling speed, McMann drew his Glock and fired at Dupé, a double-tap to the chest. Dupé cried out and staggered to the ground. With a blur, the Glock smashed against the side of Justice's head. He saw stars for an instant, and then they faded into black.

Chapter 56

Justice didn't know how long he had been out. His head felt like it was in a vice. Then he remembered Dupé. He lay motionless next to Justice, face pushed into the gravel. Wanda was sobbing, and both Elizabeth and Tammy held hands over gaping mouths. Justice turned his head and looked up at McMann.

"Good morning, Detective. I didn't think I hit you that hard. Was wondering when you were going to finally come to so we could discuss business."

"Captain-," Justice began, but he didn't know what else to say, how to finish his thought. "You shot him," he finally managed. "You shot Detective Dupé." It came out as an observation.

"That's right. I did. Ah, stay right there. I can't have you moving just yet."

Justice propped himself up on one arm and took hold of Dupé's shoulder. He began to turn him over, but stopped. After a few seconds he asked, "But why? Why would you shoot Dupé?"

McMann lit up a cigar, took a drag, and positioned it in the corner of his mouth. "Justice, my boy, Dupé was a necessity who is, ah, no longer necessary. I don't take any pleasure in killing him, really I don't. He was a good man, but not good enough." McMann looked down solemnly at the body of Dupé. Then he turned to Justice with enthusiasm. "Not like you. You, my boy, are cut out of a rare cloth. Like the late Tommy Denton, here."

It was as if his mind had shut off, rebooted. Nothing seemed to fit, nothing made sense. Protagoras, Savage, had been killed. But now this. Dupé had known something.

Tammy was staring hard at the man who had just murdered a detective. She was holding hands with Wanda and Elizabeth. "*You* are Protagoras!"

"Tammy, what?" Justice held up a hand in protest.

"It's true, Justice," McMann said, exhaling smoke. "She's a smart woman, Tammy. Attractive too. Don't let her get away."

"We're not dating," Tammy assured him.

"Sure thing sweetheart."

"It's true."

"Why does everyone think it's impossible for a man and a woman to just be friends?" Justice asked, turning fully towards McMann.

"Because it just doesn't make sense."

"So you two aren't dating?" Elizabeth asked.

"Uh, oh, Justice. Your hooker is confused."

"Watch your mouth!" came the indignant response from Justice, Tammy, and Wanda.

"Trust me, dear, I don't know what's taking them so long either," Wanda assured Elizabeth.

"Wanda, please. This is not your decision. We grew up together. It would be weird."

"Well, not that weird," replied Justice.

"Oh, shut up Blake. Why are we talking about this? McMann is Protagoras. What happened?"

"It's actually not like this is some crazy twist, Justice. It would have been pretty apparent to anybody else. Dupé was just beginning to catch on. But you're too black and white. It was right under your nose, but the last person you would suspect, if you could suspect me, was your beloved police Captain. You had so much faith in right and wrong that it bit you in the ass.

"You're so naïve, Justice. I admire you, but you're naïve. I don't know if you truly believe that this world is black and white, good and bad, or if you just try and convince yourself of that every night. Look around you; look at your whole life. Your dad died defending, what? The law? Good?"

"You killed my dad?"

McMann was caught off guard by the accusation but recovered. "No, I didn't kill your dad, Justice. I didn't even know your dad. I'm trying to point out that these rules, these laws, these ideals, you live by—why? What does it serve? You're alone."

"I have Honey."

"Honey?"

"My dog."

"And me," said Tammy.

"And her."

"You live alone, Justice," McMann continued. "Your mom has never recovered from losing your dad. No offense, Wanda. Every day you come to work, you think about how much you hate that there are criminals out there—criminals that you know about, that you can't touch! The criminals hate us, the common citizen despises us—where is the justice in that?"

Justice tried to clear his head. It throbbed. The Captain, his boss—he was a bad man. "But why? Our laws are good! We protect the innocent. We stop the bad guys."

McMann waved his hand in disgust. "Innocent? Who's innocent? By what standard do you judge innocence?"

"You're robbing hard working people, selling crack on our streets, and starting an arms war," Tammy cried out. "How can you question what's good or bad?"

McMann took a deep breath. Justice half expected a cigar to materialize in the fat fingers. "That day Tommy was attacked, something changed. Up until that point I had thought just like you, Justice. That this, what we do, makes a difference—that I was making a difference. I believed in right and wrong. I believed in the law. I watched a man who had fought for his country in Vietnam come back home an outcast, not a hero. And when he decided to protect us here, he was forgotten. My wife left me when I was protecting the community. When Tommy was in the hospital, do you know that all they did for him was give him a pathetic pension package and thank him for his service. They kicked him to the damn curb, Justice! For upholding the damn law! I was the only freakin' person who sat with him in the room at night.

"Tommy was discharged, but we kept in contact. I made a decision that I wasn't going to be on the receiving end of the shaft anymore. Look at what being McMann got me."

"You're a Captain," Justice frowned.

McMann laughed and broke into a coughing fit. "You still don't get it. Protagoras made me a Captain. It wasn't until I stopped this fictional madman that I received any honor, any accolades. When I saw Tommy dying, the lie came unraveled and I knew what I had to do. So Tommy became my muscle. Protagoras was created, and we defeated him. We moved in on the crime lords. We took out whoever opposed us, and we weren't hindered by any department bull crap. We finally had money, control, respect. We could come in, wipe out existing crime in a city or community; I would step in and run Protagoras off; and I got my promotions. Nothing too extensive; I didn't want a lot of attention into my personal life, but it helped provide some spending money.

"So I came here. Tommy was taking care of business elsewhere. I played Captain. Watched Lenny squirm around like the worm he was. I watched how this beloved little Avon didn't give a rat's ass about you or me or anybody watching out for them. Daryl Starkman became useful. Rumors of a new player in town started circulating. A guy named Protagoras. Scary guy. Money and fear are great motivators, Justice. Remember that.

"We begin taking money from the low-life citizens and creating a cache of weapons to fight, well, myself. You find the right cops, those who are corrupt, those who simply need a little pep talk from their fearless leader, and they'll bend the rules for you. Simple means to an end. Greater good, all that crap. Take a little from some ungrateful citizens so you can defend their lives from a true threat. Wasn't that hard." McMann's face was calm, serene almost. He slowly scanned the room from the women to Dupé's body.

Justice swallowed. "And Michael Dupé? How did he figure into all of this?" he demanded. "Why him?"

McMann's brows furrowed and he shook his head mournfully. "Not everything in the business is rainbows and kittycats."

"Isn't it sunshine?"

"I don't think it really matters, Justice. It could be roses for all I know. Hell. Dupé was a plan for the future. Two functions, really. He's bright—was bright. I wanted to see if I could get him on board, see how good he was." He looked back at Dupé. "Didn't pan out. Anyways, the second function of our dear deceased detective was to get you on board."

"Me?"

"Of course. You're the best of the best. That's pretty obvious now that Tommy finally found his end."

"Wait a second. What I can only assume was your closest friend is dead, and you don't care?"

"Of course I care, damnit. Just cuz you don't see no tears doesn't mean I ain't got a heart. But he lost. I mean, he had a pretty impossible handicap and you beat him."

"This, this was a tryout?"

"Of sorts. I put you in an impossible situation, and for that I must beg your forgiveness. I stacked the odds against you. Gave you a ghost assignment, tested your loyalty. I knew you wouldn't be easy with that law and order mumbo jumbo."

"I never watched the show."

"I'm talking justice, Justice. Plus there are far too many seasons for my taste. Even the petty stuff like stealing to buy guns to beat a crime boss would be difficult for you to accept, so I brought Dupé in to help soften you up. I appealed to his, family, and the almighty dollar. He was reluctant to join in on the weapons scheme, but he saw the logic in it—something you just wouldn't accept. So I raised the stakes. I had to keep you in the game."

Justice watched McMann turn and wink at Elizabeth. He almost launched himself in a rage at McMann, but another well-placed shot that passed between the ladies stopped him. "Ah, ah. You stay *right* there. Don't make me hurt them."

"You sent Dan Mosely and Martin Leech to attack Elizabeth?"

"Not necessarily that, but something, yes. That Martin Leech is a lecherous creature, isn't he?"

"You bastard!" Elizabeth shrieked.

"You slut," laughed McMann.

"I swear I will kill you." Justice said softly, clenching both fists, a look of hatred in his dark eyes.

"Now hold on. Don't get riled up quite yet. We're getting to the good part. You connected the pieces, and we all ended up here, at the train yard—the ultimate test site. You were the warrior, the odds stacked against you. Your women had been kidnapped, no back up was coming, you had skilled killers patrolling the playing field, and you were fighting for your very survival. Kind of like Katniss, huh?"

Justice stared in incomprehension.

"Really? Dupé was right. Go see a movie sometime, Justice. Anyway, you conquered. You even beat my best man, God rest his soul."

"Dupé and I beat your best man."

"You and anybody could have done it. You are the man, Justice. Your father would have been blown away by who his son has grown up to be. You're a physical specimen, you're brilliant, you're a skilled killer, and maybe just a little naïve. Come with me. We can own this town, then Indianapolis. No one would be able to stop us."

"You're crazy, you know that," Tammy said.

"Well technically if I knew it, I probably wouldn't be crazy. They say insane people don't know they're insane. Kind of a paradox. Also, they say that anyone who claims they're not a hero must be one. Kind of a cheap way to become a hero, I think."

"I'd never join you in this," Justice said in disbelief. "I trusted you as my Captain. You were my leader. What makes you think I would join in this madness? There's nothing you could do to me to make me turn my back on law and justice and become a killer like you."

McMann winced. "Ooh, don't make ultimatums, Justice. You know that there's *always* something else. I was hoping that you would want to join me, but I don't take no for an answer and I always have a contingency plan." McMann moved his Glock back and forth between the kneeling women.

"You can't do that, McMann! You think you would get away with killing three women?"

"No, Justice. You killed them."

"Why would I kill them?"

"I tried to stop you, but you gunned them down. They had found out your secret." He paused for effect. "You were Protagoras. Let it sink in. Tammy over here will probably pick it up faster than you will though, judging by her track record. We found money at Lenny's that eyewitnesses say you gave hooker Elizabeth here, right before Lenny was killed. That's a little fishy, but doesn't mean you killed him.

But you *were* head of the investigation and had been over there multiple times. You had been so frustrated that there was nothing legal that could be done to stop him. So it seems you took justice into your own hands. You had been working with Daryl Starkman to amass a cache of weapons. Can't find Starkman now. I guess it seems you disposed of him. You were storing weapons at Leech's warehouse. You must have had some way to blackmail him. Leech tried to sell you out so you hunted him down and killed him and the cops who were escorting him back to the precinct to spill on you. Meanwhile, Furman and Philips had been leading their own little investigation."

"You scumbag," Justice interjected.

"Oh come on. This is good. You got a hold of them snooping around the warehouse where you were storing your weapons, and you killed them. They had called me so I drove over there to back them up, but I found them dead in their car, but I did find something interesting—a handkerchief with their blood on it." McMann withdrew a plastic bag from his pocket with a bloody handkerchief. "Wait a second, Justice. This looks familiar. Is that *your* handkerchief? My god. It is!

"You must have known your plan was unraveling because you turned on your own hit squad and killed them, and finally you came here to kill the only people close enough to you to start to suspect you weren't the man you claimed to be. Your mother, the hooker you were obsessed with-"

"He helps me and my daughter!" Elizabeth cried out.

"-and his childhood sweetheart," McMann finished.

Tammy threw up her hands. "Oh my word, we're friends!"

"I want you to join me, Justice. I want to turn you loose against the true criminals. You could be completely unhampered by bureaucratic red-tape."

Justice stared in disbelief at the man he trusted and had looked up to. "You threaten the people I love and slander my name and then expect me to be buddy-buddy with you afterwards?" he asked incredulously.

McMann sighed. "You don't have to like me, detective, to realize that this is what's best for everyone. "Justice, all you have to do is say yes, and this entire unfortunate set of events is over. All in the past. We can eradicate crime and live the life we deserve."

"And if I don't say yes?"

"Then I'll make you watch as I execute these precious women, then I'll kill you, and everything I've ever done will be pinned on your name." McMann's spoke as if he would regret what he had to do. Then he smiled, displaying a set of teeth that even in the dim light shone bright white.

"I just can't believe this," Justice said again. McMann rolled his eyes. "Captain McMann, you're Protagoras?"

"I'm beginning to think you're a tad slow, boy. Yes, I'm Protagoras."

"And you robbed all those innocent people, killed Lenny and Daryl, and all those cops just to blackmail me to you to join you in your criminal activities?"

"It finally sounds like you've grasped all of it, Justice. That would be an accurate depiction of the events that have taken place here recently, yes."

"OK, I just wanted to make sure it was all clear," Justice said, a twinkle in his eye.

"Of course," agreed McMann.

"Well, Captain, it turns out there will be a happy ending after all."

McMann beamed. "Good! I'm glad to hear it."

"Oh, not for you, sir," Justice clarified. McMann's eyebrows raised. "This was all a pretty convoluted situation, but you've clarified it quite well for all of us. And now if you don't mind, I'm tired and I've been shot and I need food in a bad way."

McMann's mouth hung halfway open. "Son, now I'm not sure *I* understand."

Dupé sat up, a .45 Kimber II resting in a two-handed grip, McMann's chest in the sights. "Understand this!" Dupé's finger remained moving even after the seven rounds were discharged into McMann, and the chamber finally clicked empty.

Chapter 57

Justice helped Dupé to his feet who rose gingerly, stretching and twisting the ache out of his body. "That is not a comfortable floor," Dupé complained.

Justice laughed. "You can take a hot bubble bath tonight. I think you've earned it. Did you get it?"

"Every word, right here," Dupé said, pulling out his phone. "Have you learned nothing here tonight, Justice? I told you, you have to always be ready."

"You were dead," Wanda protested.

"No, ma'am. I assure you I was not. I learned a thing or two from your son."

"You mean you stole a thing or two from me," Justice said with insincere anger. "First my guns, and now this." Justice ripped at Dupé's shirt, tearing it and revealing Justice's tactical body armor.

Tammy remembered Dupé entering the room. "I thought you looked less scrawny than usual."

"Uh, thanks."

"You didn't tell me you grabbed this from my car too," Justice protested.

"You were stressed. You were already mad about the guns. Combat is a lot easier when you can get shot and keep going. Speaking of, how are you doing?"

Justice raised his shoulder and winced. "I'll live."

"If it bleeds, we can kill it," Dupé mimicked.

"Was that supposed to be Russian?"

"Arnold, man! I'm done with you. You're hopeless. Predator?"

"Girls." It was Wanda who spoke up. "You two can banter all night, but I'm tired and sore, and I need to throw my clothes in the wash before this blood sets."

"Sorry, mom. Ladies, are you OK?"

"I think I'm going to puke." Elizabeth's face was pale. "I just want to go home and see my baby."

"OK," Justice said. "Let's call in the cavalry and get out of here."

The once quiet train yard which had been enshrouded in the shadow of night became a chaotic scene of lights and sounds. Squad cars littered the scenery—blue and red lights flashing off of the many buildings. Ambulances and medical teams, along with forensic units and a bomb squad combed the carnage. Wanda and Elizabeth had both been cleared by EMT's before being escorted home by no less than four squad cars each. Wanda had scoffed at the parade, but Justice insisted on it.

Justice, Dupé, and Tammy answered general questions before he called off the dogs, and the three made their way to Justice's Challenger. Tammy and Dupé stood a few paces behind Justice, allowing him time alone with the slain beast. Two of the wheels were bent at a 45 degree angle on the axles. No windows were left and the exterior looked like a screen door from the hundreds of rounds pumped into it.

"It's amazing he made it out alive," Dupé said quietly.

"It's not as bad as I thought it would be," replied Tammy.

Just then a police cruiser pulled up, the headlights illuminating the three figures. The front lamps shut off, and Officer Cruise and Officer Grant stepped out of the car. "Justice, Dupé," Grant called. "My god, are you guys OK?" She and Cruise jogged up to where Justice was performing last rites for the Challenger. "You're bleeding, Detective," Jane Grant gasped when she saw the extent of wear and tear on Justice.

"Eh, this? Just a scratch," he smiled.

"Are you kidding?" Cruise scoffed to his partner. "This is Detective Justice we're talking about. He's invincible."

"I wouldn't go that far, Officer Cruise, but thank you for the vote of confidence. Listen, I need a favor of you."

"Anything," Cruise said enthusiastically.

"My baby," Justice motioned to the car. "She's hurt badly. I need you to make sure she gets taken out of here to the address I'm texting you now. They'll know what to do for her. Nowhere else. You understand?"

"Only to that specific address. Got it."

"Thanks. Now officers, Grant, Cruise, I'm sure you have your hands full, and we're starving."

"Shouldn't you get to a hospital?" Grant asked, unable to mask the worry in her voice.

"The wound isn't going anywhere, and if I don't get some food soon, I'm going to die of starvation."

"Hey, um, Detective, if you'd ever like to talk about all of this, you know, what you're allowed to share, just to vent, or therapy, or, or- whatever," Grant swallowed, "you can talk to me."

Justice looked into Jane Grant's eyes and then back to Dupé and finally Tammy. "Listen, like I said earlier-"

"He'd love to. Hi, I'm Tammy. I grew up with Blake, and he needs to get his feelings out more. So he would love to talk to you, uh, Officer Grant. Are you free tomorrow night, Blake?"

"Well, I don't know."

"He's free tomorrow night. 7pm. You're cops. You'll get all the particulars straightened out. So 7pm, Blake. You'll pick up Officer Grant, and you'll go on a date. I'll make sure he picks out a good restaurant, which is where we need to be going to right now. It was so good to meet you, officers, and good luck with, well, whatever you have to do right now."

Officer Grant smiled, while Cruise made an exaggerated look of approval, and the two officers headed back to their car.

Justice turned to Dupé. "Don't look at me! This is between you two," Dupé protested.

"Don't start, Blake Owen Justice. She seemed like a nice girl, smart. Not a bimbo, and I'd hate to think of you sitting in that little apartment of yours, cleaning your gun and watching *Cobra*, saying the lines before Stallone does."

"Well when you put it that way."

Chapter 58

It was 3am when Justice, Dupé, and Tammy stood at the IHOP hostess station. The mocha skinned girl who walked up was half asleep, ready to go into her automatic routine, when she saw the appearance of the new patrons. Her eyes grew wide. Justice fumbled out his badge. She started to say something and then thought better of it. "Right this way please."

Justice remained standing where he was. "Could we please be seated in the far corner area?"

"Uh, sure. Yeah, no problem."

"Thank you."

The three survivors followed the hostess to the booth and took their seats. After handing them their menus she concluded with, "Your server will be right with you for your drinks."

They all thanked her and sank into their seat cushions.

"Oh my gosh, this feels so good. I might just sleep here tonight," Tammy murmured, eyes half closed.

Dupé was reading his menu intently when Justice interrupted him. "You tried to get me to stop before I cut McMann free. How did you know?"

Dupé put the menu down and looked up at Justice. "LA Confidential." Justice looked questioningly at him. "Movies, man. LA Confidential. It was all the same. They say there's nothing new under the sun."

"Ecclesiastes," murmured Tammy, eyes still closed.

"It wasn't your fault. You idealize honor and truth. The idea of the leader of law and order corrupting the office didn't compute with you, but the Captain of police has almost unlimited power and force at his disposal. All of it felt too personal, too much of an inside scenario. Create an armory to fight a ghost enemy. Create a problem to solve a problem and gain all the accolades. Operate in the grey for the greater good? McMann brought me in to get you, so what else was he willing to do? So I kept my eyes and ears open. I mean, Savage knew *everything*. It didn't add up. And then McMann was just captured and the three most important women in your life. I mean it wasn't exactly LA Confidential, but pretty close."

"Huh. Think your wife would mind if I came over and watched a movie sometime?"

"Hell no, man. I mean, heck no. You're welcome anytime."

"Aw, you two are cute," Tammy said almost unintelligibly.

"Detective Justice?" It was practically a squeal.

Justice smiled and turned toward the voice. "Marla, it's good to see you again."

Marla threw her arms around Justice's neck and then caught herself. "Can I get any drinks for you guys oh my gosh, what happened to you? You look terrible. Well, I mean, not terrible. You look gorgeous. I said that out loud. Are you bleeding? I mean, you look- what happened?"

"So this is Marla?" Tammy asked, sitting up and rubbing her eyes.

"In the flesh," replied Justice. "We wouldn't have been able to crack the case if it wasn't for Marla's help throughout, and the night just didn't seem complete without her as part of the celebration."

"Hi, everyone," she said, giving a sweeping wave of the hand. "I'm Marla. I didn't really help that much. I just lived down the street from Drugs R' Us, and I witnessed a murder. Should I say that out loud?"

"It's OK," assured Dupé. "The bad guys are gone. We got 'em all. Thank you for your help."

"Oh, anytime. Maybe I could be like a consultant or something for the police force. I'm thinking of changing my major this fall to criminal psychology."

"We'll keep that in mind," said Justice.

"Weren't you working at a gas station last time I heard?" Dupé asked.

"I was, but I decided gas stations just weren't for me. So I decided to be a waitress. Thought I'd at least give it a shot. Oh, crap. I haven't even taken your orders yet, and you must be starving. I'll bring out some coffee right away." And she hurried to the back.

Justice laughed. "She's sure got spunk, huh?" Dupé and Tammy nodded in agreement. The three drank their coffee silently, savoring the aroma and heat in their throats. Marla took their orders and continued to fill up their saucers, trying not to appear like she was hovering. The weight of the evening was beginning to dissipate and exhaustion was quickly taking its place. Marla was dying to talk to them, but she could see the weariness in their faces. Finally, their food was ready, and Marla was relieved to be able to take them their food. Whatever hell they had been through, the least she could do was serve up some hot stacks fresh from the griddle and keep the coffee coming.

The plates were passed around: hash browns, eggs, pancakes, biscuits—it seemed like they had ordered the entire menu. Finally, Marla set a plate containing bacon, eggs, and five pancakes in front of Justice. He breathed in the delicious scent and put his arm around Tammy who immediately accepted the hug and rested her head on his shoulder. Dupé smiled back, nodded slightly, and began to cut up his pancakes. Justice looked down at his plate. "It seems justice has finally been served."

About the Author

Mark Anthony Taylor's first story came to fruition in first grade. It was also the first time he learned about plagiarism, as many parts of the story came straight from "The Hobbit," which his mother had read to him many times. He's been writing short stories ever since. Though he has many different passions, such as sports and animals, reading and writing have always occupied his time. Watching and enjoying cliché-riddled action movies is another hobby. This is Mark's first novel, taking the saturated detective genre and injecting unique characters, action, humor, and themes into the familiar territory. Mark lives with his wife in a full house of dogs, snakes, and whoever else needs a place to call home for a while. When he's not writing, he's working with the youth at his church.

Printed in the United States
By Bookmasters